"Quilts and mysteries from Civil War days, with at least one family member demanding that one mystery never be revealed. [*The Legacy*],Cherie Dargan's dual-time story is rich with details about both whites and slaves escaping from the South during the 1860s. It's also the love story of Iowa descendants of those folks, and their quest to learn who made the Rustic Rose quilt and whose blood stains were on it? A very satisfying novel."

Joy Neal Kidney, author of *Leora's Stories*
Leora's Letters: The Story of Love and Loss for an Iowa Family
Leora's Early Years: Guthrie County Roots
Leora's Dexter Stories: The Scarcity Years of the Great Depression

"As with Cherie's debut novel, this story [*The Legacy*] intermingles Civil War history and modern-day events, a strong combination."

~Gail Kittleson, author of:
Until Then
A Mystery on Church Street

"Cherie Dargan delivers a second charming historical cozy in *Grandmother's Treasures Book 2: The Legacy*. In this dual timeline book, a bloodstained Civil War Era family quilt stirs a search for answers rooted in mystery and history. War, injustice, danger, romance, and reconciliation—How could a reader ask for more?"

~Shelly Beach, Christy Award winning co-author of:
Love Letters from the Edge

"A blood-stained rose quilt holds the secret to a lost Civil War family crossing—a story of romance and danger and of women and men joining forces and rescuing each other from hate and intolerance in two separate eras. In this novel [*The Legacy*], as in the last, Gracie and David *are on the case*."

~Barbara Lounsberry, Author of:
Virginia Woolf Diaries trilogy

"I love this story! Cherie Dargan can sure paint a beautiful word picture! She spins a gorgeous adventure in the first installment of her *Grandmother's Treasures* series where she treats us to an up-close look at one of her personal family stories in *The Gift*. I, for one, am grateful. It's a colorful, lush and adventurous story, infused with grit, determination, and gutsy, likable characters (especially the females!). Her descriptive style had me craving corn muffins and chili as well as traveling and travailing with her on her journey of discovery. I would highly recommend this book and I can't wait for the next in the series!"

~Wanda Sanchez, Executive Producer, Salem Radio Network
Christy Award winning co-author of:
Love Letters from the Edge

"*The Gift* is a peek into an Iowa farm family. It pieces the present day and past into a quilt filled with details about World War 2. Through the eyes of Gracie, the main character, readers see how past trauma and life choices impact family relationships for generations to come. Those who enjoy books about family, quilting, and the 1940s will find this one to be a comfortable read."

~Jolene Philo, Author of:
Does My Child Have PTSD?

"Cherie Dargan captured my imagination with the first heartwarming book in her five-part *Grandmother's Treasures* series, *The Gift*. It was inspired by her marvelous collection of antique quilts and other heirlooms and the strong women in her family, especially her mom and aunts, who have been Dargans' lodestars."

~Melody Parker
"Five Memorable Stories"—*Waterloo Courier*

the legacy

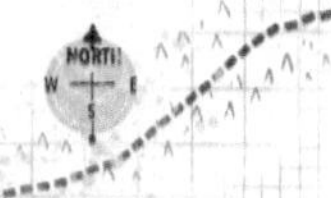

MAP LEGEND

1. Jubilee Junction Depot
2. Retirement Home
3. Community College
4. Jubilee Junction Café
5. Courthouse
6. Museum
7. Newspaper
8. Ruby's Restaurant
9. Vern's Farm
10. Violet's Farm
11. Rich's Farm
12. Cemetary
13. Vera's Farm
14. Library
15. Quilt Shop
16. School

GRANDMOTHER'S TREASURES
BOOK 2

the legacy

a dual time-line novel

CHERIE DARGAN

WordCrafts Press

The Legacy
Copyright © 2023
Cherie Dargan

ISBN: 978-1-957344-95-9

Cover concept and design by Mike Parker

Map & Family Tree designed by Patricia Tiffany Morris for Tiffany Inks Studio LLC

Published by WordCrafts Press
Cody, Wyoming 82414
www.wordcrafts.net

For Hope, Barbara, Beth, Shelly, Mike, and Gail.
You encouraged me to find the stories in my family quilts
and to think bigger and bolder.

MAP LEGEND

1. Jubilee Junction Depot
2. Carlson General Store
3. Teacher's School
4. Town Café
5. County Seat & Jailhouse
6. Carlson Lumber Yard
7. Jubilee Times
8. Hotel & Saloon
9. Nelson Family Farm
10. Carlson Family Farm
11. O'Connor Farm
12. Cemetary
13. Telegraph Office
14. Livery Stable
15. Blacksmith
16. Town School
17. Butcher Shop
18. Bakery

I made two decisions as I wrote the dialogue in Sarah's story, set during the American Civil War (aka ACW). First, I wanted to avoid the *Gone with the Wind*-style vocabulary, which is offensive, and second, to use the word Black to denote race.

*M*y name is Gracie O'Connor. I live in a house with my cat Agatha in Jubilee Junction, Iowa. Jubilee Junction is an old railroad town near the Jubilee River, founded by three big families in the early 1850s.

My parents own the town weekly newspaper *The Jubilee Times*. I write articles for the paper and teach English classes at the local community college. You'll find me at the county museum arranging exhibits most afternoons.

My boyfriend, David MacNeill, teaches history. We met at our community college and became friends last year. He and I enjoy discovering family stories, exploring American history, and solving puzzles.

I'm named after my grandma, Grace Nelson Walters. She died two years ago, not long after Grandpa Richard passed. I'm thankful to have her brother, Great-Uncle Vern, his wife Great-Aunt Maggie, and sister, Great-Aunt Violet in my life. Last fall, Aunt Violet moved out of her big farmhouse to a small apartment in a retirement community. She gave me a gift from Grandma Grace—a wicker basket containing a quilt, aprons, and two shoeboxes.

One shoebox held 24 cassette tapes with a tape recorder tucked underneath. I visited Aunt Violet each week, and we listened to the tapes together as grandma told her story about three sisters going to California during WWII. Grace and Vera got jobs at an aircraft factory producing B-17 bombers, while Violet, a nurse, snagged a position at the naval base hospital.

The girls lived in a boarding house, where they made friends. They attended a Methodist church filled with military families and other migrants here to work on the home front. Then something terrible happened between the twins that shattered the family. A California patchwork quilt hidden away for sixty years in my Great-Grandma Ginny's bedroom held the answer to the dispute.

Grandma Grace revealed the family secret and asked me to do what the family failed to do six decades earlier: talk about what happened in California. I was nervous, but David offered to be there to support me, which helped. We brought together my mother's family and listened to several cassette tapes. Violet and Vera finally reconciled, solving the mystery of the *California quilt*.

David and I grew closer, and our friendship turned romantic. So now, it's the holiday break. It's also my first Christmas with David. I can't wait!

One

A Plan Goes Awry
Sarah

"Men say that women's lives are without danger
They stay at home while their husbands go to war
False! I'd rather stand ten times behind the shield-wall
In battle than but once carry a child."

~Medea

A village ten miles from Winchester, Virginia, during the Third Battle of Winchester
Sunday, September 18, 1864

*B*oom! *Boom!* The cannon fire seemed a long way off, but still shook the house. I walked around my parlor impatiently, worrying about Emily, my big sister, about to give birth. *Why didn't I stay at the Plantation House last night?*

The dogs barked just as someone knocked on the door. I opened it to find Thomas, Emily's driver, standing there.

"Thomas, it's time?"

The slave nodded. "Yes, Miss Sarah. Your mama said things aren't going well. Miss Emily needs you."

The morning air seemed chilly, so I grabbed my shawl and big bag and shut the door. My house—a large white two-story home on a corner lot with ten acres—was one of only a handful still occupied in my village, about ten miles from Winchester.

My hounds barked again, and I called out to them.

"Good boys, Scout and Duke. Watch over things. I'll be back."

Then I turned to Thomas, Emily's driver. He was perspiring and not his normal cheerful self.

"Is Emily alright?" I asked.

"Your mama sent for old Doc Winter, but he never came," Thomas said flatly. "Emily asking for you."

Thomas took my hand and helped me into the small buggy, and as soon as I'd settled in the seat, he cracked the whip, sending the horses galloping down the road. My heart raced as I gathered my flapping skirts, and gripped the bag to my body, as I grasped the seat with the other hand.

I pondered this bit of news. Why had Mother sent for the doctor? Devastated when both his sons died during a battle several months ago, Dr. Winter had taken to drink and was useless most days. The midwife was more than competent, wasn't she? *Why didn't I stay at Evaline last night? Why am so stubborn, hanging onto to my empty house?*

As we raced toward Evaline, I tried to breathe in and out slowly, the way Abigail taught me. I could almost hear her telling me I couldn't help Emily unless I calmed down. My dear friend had taught me so many things when we were roommates at college in Boston seven years ago.

Grief did strange things to people. I knew that all too well. Four years ago, I married my childhood sweetheart, Simon. Simon gave me his grandmother's ring before I left for college. I loved him, but the girl he married was not the same girl who'd accepted his ring. We argued over my new beliefs, made up in bed, and then argued more.

"Sarah, you're the most stubborn woman I know. If I didn't love you so much, you would drive me completely mad." More than once, Simon expressed his frustration.

He left three years ago when a group of local men joined the Confederate Army, including my father. Simon died in the middle of fierce fighting at the Battle of First Manassas on July 21, 1861. I still grieved three years later and refused to leave our lovely home. Mother argued that I'd be better off living with her or at Evaline with Emily, but I clung to my lonely independence. *After all*, I told her, *I had the hounds and my shotgun. I was safe.*

At twenty-four, I stood five feet four inches tall, with thick black braids down to my waist complementing my bright blue eyes. I styled my hair up in a bun and wore all black, customary for a well-bred young widow. When I'd returned to Virginia from Boston with my education certificate five years ago, I'd looked much the same on the outside. I still had my soft Virginian accent, my ladylike demeanor, and fine fashion, thanks to Mother. But I felt like a different woman on the inside because I was now opposed to slavery. I taught school for a year and then married Simon. Within a year, he'd gone to war and died, leaving me a widow at twenty-one.

There were too many widows and too many dead soldiers these past three years. My brother-in-law, George Phillips, left with Simon, along with most of the white men in the area, including my father. About nine months ago, during a lull in the fighting, George received a furlough to spend a week with Emily before returning to his regiment.

Six weeks after George left, Emily began having morning sickness. She'd only received one letter in March and nothing since then. She'd written to George to let him know of her condition but never heard from him again. Whenever Confederate troops passed through town, Emily sent Thomas or Peter, another house servant, to enquire for news about George. However, no one knew his whereabouts or if he was dead or alive.

The first half dozen times Peter had come back without news, Emily had been inconsolable, taking to her bed and sobbing for hours. George had two brothers who had already died in the war. She hoped to present him with another son, since she acknowledged Bobby was his son. Emily grew sadder and more resolved to leave Virginia as Peter came back with no news of his master.

George's lawyer sold Evaline's field slaves, leaving crops in the field. Half a dozen loyal house servants remained to help the young mistress through the birth of her first child after a miscarriage. They loved Emily and the kind way she treated them, especially Rebecca and Bobby. But Emily needed me for emotional support. I regretted not staying at Evaline last night.

Emily, I'm sorry. I'm coming.

Other families in the neighborhood had left or were leaving, seeking safety. They had already endured two battles and the awful aftermath that turned their large plantation homes into hospitals for wounded soldiers.

We had suffered Union occupation several times, but the town had changed hands a number of times. And people lost their houses to house soldiers or have them turned into hospitals. Other homes were burned or destroyed. Several people who spoke out against the occupying force were forced to leave town.

Now, war had returned to our part of Virginia. General Phil Sheridan's Yankee cavalry fought Jubal Early's barefoot Southerners only ten miles away. The thunder of the artillery and cannons echoed through the valley.

I pondered all of this on the ride to Evaline.

Thomas guided the buggy up to the hitching post by the front veranda of Evaline and lashed the reins to a post. He helped me down from the buggy and into the arms of Mother. Her wrinkled dress, bloodshot eyes and disheveled hair made her look much older than her forty-six years.

"Sarah, thank God you're here. Things aren't going well. I sent Peter to fetch the doctor yesterday, but he hasn't come yet. Emily is in excruciating pain—Mama Cee tried to help her last night, but the midwife made her leave. Oh, what shall we do?"

"Is the midwife still here?" I asked as we climbed the steps to the front door. We walked inside the beautiful home, past the once elaborately furnished front rooms to the ornate formal dining room, no longer as lovely as it once had been. We'd removed much of the furniture two summers ago to accommodate the cots for wounded soldiers from both sides. No matter how we scrubbed, I still sometimes smelled blood.

"Yes, she's still here," Mother confirmed as she slumped in fatigue at the dining room table.

Next to her, Bobby, the son of Emily's maid, sat with his head down on his arms, his legs dangling below the chair.

Bobby lifted his head when he heard my voice. "Is Miss Emily all right? I heard her screaming last night."

"She's having a baby, and it can be painful, but I'm here to help now." I tried to sound reassuring. But my stomach turned as I began walking quickly towards the stairs, pausing before I placed my foot on the first step and glancing back. *Was that Emily crying upstairs?*

"It's going to be alright." I straightened my shoulders, gathered my skirts, and rushed up the steps to my sister's bedroom and stopped outside the opened doorway.

Emily was sitting up in her canopy bed, supported by pillows, with Susanna and Rebecca, her two young slaves, standing on either side of the head of the bed. Emily's nightgown, soaked in sweat, bunched around her distended belly. Perspiration drenched her face and hair as she trembled from exhaustion and cried.

Rebecca held a half-filled glass of water to Emily's lips and encouraged her to take a sip before greeting me. But there was something wrong with Rebecca's facial expression. She was young but had assisted Mama Cee at many slave births.

Why wasn't I told it was this bad? Why did I leave yesterday?

Mrs. Brown, the midwife, reached under the sheet and positioned Emily for the next contraction as she spoke soothingly. But Emily wasn't listening. She saw me, cried out, and fell back against her pillows.

"I'm here now, Emily," I whispered as I took her hand. The scent of blood mixed with sweat and urine filled my nostrils, and I struggled not to gag as I set my bag down.

The midwife walked around the bed and guided me a few steps away. Her eyebrows were drawn together in concern above hazel eyes. "Your sister's pelvis is too small for the baby," she whispered. "She's been in labor since last night, but she begged us not to call you too soon. We sent her manservant to fetch the doctor yesterday, but he hasn't come. Your mother hoped Doctor Winter would respond, since he and your father were such good friends. Now she's too exhausted to continue."

I felt my fists clench, and I willed myself to push back the grief flooding my soul. Instead, I took on the demeanor of a stern schoolteacher.

"I brought tea from a Boston midwife that eases childbirth pain.

Quickly, bring me a teapot full of hot water," I commanded Susanna. She rushed out the bedroom door while I dug into my big bag for the tea.

A tea pot and cups were on a tray on a table near the fireplace. I moved to the table and carefully measured the loose tea into the tea ball, hoping Emily couldn't see my hands shaking. *Where is Susanna?*

Emily tried to clear her throat, and I turned toward her as she beckoned me. Her eyes were wide with pain. "Sarah, something's wrong. The baby isn't moving anymore. I'm so tired—I can't go on." She closed her eyes, panting.

I reached out and clasped her hand in mine. "We will do this together, Emily. I promise." I gently massaged her back, feeling her tremble.

Rebecca's eyes met mine over my sister's head, and I understood at once her fear for her mistress' life. She, too, massaged Emily's back while we waited, murmuring encouragement.

Within minutes, Susanna returned, and I poured the tea into one of Emily's delicate porcelain cups. "Drink as much as you can," I whispered.

With help from Rebecca, Emily slowly sipped until the cup was empty, then fell back on her pillows. "Get the papers, please, Rebecca," she panted.

Rebecca picked up a brown document folder on the side table and handed it to me.

I shoved the folder into my oversized bag. I knew what it held and hurriedly put my bag by the door and rushed back to Emily's side. Her eyes were closed.

I motioned to the midwife to step away. "How far along is she?"

"Almost ready to push, but the baby's too big. It's gonna to tear her something fierce. I got out my forceps last evening, but they frightened her, so I put them back in my bag and gave her whiskey to ease the pain. The doctor would have given her ether or chloroform and cut her, but he never came."

I couldn't take my eyes off Emily's contorted face and twisting body. *If she can't push the baby out, someone must take it out. Or they both could die.*

My heart raced, and a wave of dizziness washed over me as contractions seized Emily's body. Rebecca and Suzanna supported her. I rushed to help.

A few contractions later, the midwife told us, "It's time."

The two young women and I supported Emily as Mrs. Brown positioned herself in front, checking Emily's progress.

The midwife and I urged her, "Push. You can do this. Push."

I couldn't believe my sister's endurance. Finally, Emily screamed in agony and then lay back and panted. The two young women comforted her.

"I have him," Mrs. Brown cried. She freed the child's neck from the umbilical cord, wiped the blood and matter from his limp body, swaddled him in a towel, and tied and cut the cord. She gently laid three fingers on the baby's upper chest, opened his mouth, and felt for anything blocking the airway. But the baby boy's skin was pale blue and his chest still.

Mrs. Brown called out, "It's a boy."

I stared in awe at his tiny features, blinking away tears, willing him to breathe. *Lord, we need a miracle. Please!*

Emily finally opened her eyes, expecting a cry.

After several more agonizing minutes, the midwife shook her head.

Rebecca's frightened voice grabbed my attention. "Miss Sarah, we have a problem." She held a blood-soaked towel between Emily's legs, and Emily's face had paled.

Susanna ran for more towels. I grabbed a cloth from the dresser and Rebecca pressed it tightly to Emily's body.

Mrs. Brown stared in alarm at Emily. She lay the baby down on the bed and looked at the reddened towel. She shook her head at me as I watched my beautiful sister bleed out.

No, no, please Lord. Let Emily live. I can't lose her too!

Mother walked in and saw the quiet baby, then the scene at the bedside. She cried out, "Emily! Why is she bleeding so much?"

I shook my head. "She tore, mother. Rebecca, do you have anything to stop the bleeding?"

Rebecca shook her head. "I have my bag of herbs here, but they wouldn't have time to help, ma'am. She's losing too much blood too quickly."

The midwife agreed. "I'm sorry."

Emily's hand was limp in mine. "Is the baby dead?" she whispered. She was growing weaker by the minute. "I want to see him."

Mother picked up the baby and placed him in Emily's arms. Mother then kneeled by the bed, tears coursing down her cheeks as she supported the baby.

Standing beside Emily, I grappled with what was happening.

Emily gazed down. "Such a sweet little face. Last night, I dreamed . . . we both died. Promise me . . . to carry out the plan, Sarah. Take Rebecca . . . and Bobby . . . to freedom."

"Yes, Emily, I promise." I knelt then, wiping tears with one hand, tasting salt, while helping Mother support the baby in Emily's arms. *I can't do this without you, Emily. Don't die.*

Susanna cried as she handed more towels to Rebecca.

Rebecca continued to apply pressure on the towel. "I love you, Miss Emily. I'm sorry about the baby. Please don't die. Don't leave us."

"I love you, Rebecca . . . and Bobby. Mother . . . and Sarah. Name the baby George, Junior and . . . bury us together." Emily gasped. Her struggle ended as she fell back.

Weeping, I kissed her forehead. She was still beautiful in death. Only twenty-eight, she'd married George Phillips, a charming, wealthy man almost seven years ago. George was selfish and impulsive, having raped Rebecca only months before his wedding to Emily. I was relieved when he left for war. Father thought he'd be the perfect match for my beautiful older sister, but George hadn't made her happy.

Rebecca was her maid but also became her confidant. Emily adored Bobby, born seven months after her big wedding to George. Since then, Rebecca and I had spent hours with my sister, helping her through a miscarriage right after George left, three years ago, and now this pregnancy in George's absence.

Rebecca stood, sorrow on her youthful face, tears streaming down her cheeks. She left the room and returned with a pitcher of water. Then she poured the water into the large bowl on the dresser.

At last, Mother let go of Emily's limp hand. She sat in a bedside chair with baby George cradled tenderly in her arms.

I slumped in Emily's wingback chair, unable to believe my beloved sister and nephew were both dead. Rebecca washed my bloody hands with a sponge, but blood had splattered on my skirt and the floor. She turned to clean up her young mistress, tears dripping down her face.

Our eyes met, and she whispered, "I'm sorry, Miss Sarah. Mama Cee tried to help last night—she had a knife and wanted to cut Emily, but the midwife stopped her from coming in."

Mother hadn't told me that detail downstairs. "Could Emily and the baby be alive if Mama Cee had helped?"

She shrugged and continued working. "Maybe. I don't know. Mrs. Brown told your mother she didn't need that old slave woman's help, but Mama Cee delivered lots of babies. Sometimes she needed to cut a woman to keep her from tearing and bleeding more."

I stood to talk to the midwife, my face hot with anger.

Rebecca wiped tears from her face wearily as she continued to clean Emily. "We can't bring her back, Miss Sarah."

The midwife glanced at Mother, shook her head, offered her sympathy, and left before I could confront her about why she hadn't allowed Mama Cee into the room.

I sat, tears streaming down my face. I'd dreamed of the day when Emily and I would both have children. Now, that dream was dead, too.

Susanna picked up the bloody towels and left. When she returned, she approached Mother. "Oh, Miss Harriet. I'm sorry about Miss Emily and the baby."

Mother nodded through her tears. "Thank you, Susanna."

Then she turned to me. "What did you promise her, Sarah?"

"To free the slaves and give them money so they could start new lives. Emily and I planned to take Rebecca, the baby, and Bobby to a free state as soon as the baby could travel," I answered, thinking, *You know full well our plans, Mother. You heard me talking to Emily a hundred times. We were going to leave the plantation and take Bobby and Rebecca to freedom once the baby could travel.*

"To free the slaves? Sarah Elizabeth McDonald, what can you mean? The nation is at war. It's returned to Winchester with a battle taking place a few miles away! You can't travel anywhere with Rebecca and Bobby. It isn't safe, and I forbid it—I've lost one daughter, and I don't want to lose you, too."

I sat up a little straighter. "Mother, my husband, sister, and nephew are all dead. I'm keeping my promise to Emily. My house is going to Peter's parents, and we're leaving soon. The papers are in my bag."

"What about me?" she asked.

"You're welcome to come with us, Mother."

"I can't leave. My life is here. Your father might come home." She stood up, laid the baby on the bed near Emily, and paced in agitation.

Touching Emily's cool hand, I whispered, "Emily, I hope you find peace. I'll miss you and baby George."

Mother stopped pacing. "Alright, I'll bury my daughter and grandson without you. But you must take Thomas with you because he can protect you."

Then she inspected me. "Sarah, take off your bloody skirt."

Mother turned to Rebecca. "Rebecca, please find something for Sarah to wear."

"Yes, Miss Harriet. I'm sorry, ma'am."

Mother shut her eyes. "I should have insisted that Mrs. Brown allow Mama Cee to help. I'll regret that mistake until my dying day."

Mother sobbed. "I'm sorry, Sarah. Forgive me."

What could I say? I didn't understand why the midwife had failed Emily so badly. *Yes, why didn't you insist she allow Mama Cee's help last night?*

Rebecca helped me remove the bloody skirt and brought me a clean one. The familiar routine released the tension on my shoulders. My anger toward the midwife and Mother dissipated, replaced by sorrow at our loss.

Mother sat down to hold baby George.

Rebecca picked up the dirty skirt and left us.

I stood by Emily's bed. "This was your plan, Emily. We were leaving once the baby was a few months old. I can't do it alone.

But with the battle raging in Winchester, we can't wait. I promised you, didn't I? I must try."

Two

Grandma's ACW Quilt
Gracie

"Secrets are dark things. They don't exist in the light. They glow faintly in forgotten corners, in mysterious mind nooks, in lost memory maps. Secrets are the shadows of the soul."
~Sukanya Venkatraghavan

Jubilee Junction—Grandma Molly's house
Saturday, December 15, 2012

David glanced at me as he parked in front of my grandparents' farmhouse. "Are you excited, Gracie?" he asked.

I nodded. "Yeah. It's the first day of our Christmas break, and I'm about to introduce you to my grandparents. And we're finally going to see Grandma Molly's mystery quilt, possibly dating to the Civil War. What gave it away?"

He grinned. "You had your hand on my leg, and the closer we got to your grandparents' house, the faster your fingers were moving like my leg was a keyboard."

"Sorry," I said.

"Don't apologize. It's kind of cute," he replied.

"Grandma Molly can be a handful," I warned David as we walked up the steps.

We knocked, and I watched David's face as Grandma greeted us. Molly Walsh O'Connor was a tall woman, five foot ten inches tall, with lovely blue eyes and strawberry-blonde hair, streaked with gray, up in a simple twist. Her glasses dangled on a gold chain around her neck.

David stood straighter and poured on the charm.

Grandma opened her arms to me, and I smiled and hugged her, avoiding her glasses. "Hi, Grandma Molly."

Before I could introduce her to David, she turned to him and smiled, extending her hand. "Hello. You must be David. Welcome."

He shook her hand. "Hello, Mrs. O'Connor. Yes, I'm David MacNeill."

Grandma Molly turned briskly. "Let's go see the mystery Civil War quilt, shall we?" As we walked towards the dining room, I admired her attire. She dressed more like a retired librarian than a farm wife in her gray and pink checked wool skirt, soft pink turtleneck, and matching cardigan.

I whispered, "See what I mean?"

We followed her to the large dining room, where two quilts lay side-by-side on the dining room table, a white sheet underneath. Folded to show the pattern, at first glance, they appeared to be identical—red and green flowers on a cream background. I couldn't remember the pattern's name, but I knew it'd been popular during the American Civil War.

Grandma Molly looked at us. "Where are my manners? Would you care for some tea or coffee? I made some cranberry bread. It's all in the kitchen."

"We just had breakfast, Grandma, but thanks," I told her. "Tell us about the quilt—or quilts, I guess."

Grandma exhaled. "Forty years ago, your Grandpa Patrick's Grandma Mary died. His sisters asked me to help sort things out. We found this quilt in Grandma Mary's closet in one of those plastic zippered bags. Inside, there was an old safety pin fastening a large, yellow envelope to it. Once I got it home, I took it out of the bag to admire the pattern and found a note wrapped up inside the quilt folds. I recognized his Grandma Mary's writing. I copied the note a few years ago. The original note is fragile now."

She held out a sheet of paper, and we read the photocopy.

"Dearest daughters, your ancestor, Great-Grandma Beth, saved this quilt and thought it saved her son's life. He came home from the war wrapped in it. You should reward the kindness of strangers. Find the woman who made it, please. It is my dying wish."

I glanced up. "Grandma Mary didn't know who made the quilt? I don't understand."

Grandma Molly shrugged. "We don't know."

"Do you have the original?" I asked.

"Yes." She produced a large zip-lock bag, the original note visible inside.

"And you never thought to open the envelope pinned to the quilt?"

My fearless Grandma Molly hesitated, clearly uncomfortable. "No. The envelope seemed, well, sacred. It was a large lawyer's envelope tied up with string."

David examined the two quilts before donning a pair of latex gloves and handing me the other pair. We took several minutes to examine the two quilts, turning the fabric from front to back.

"This quilt has initials on the border. R and S, I think. See, Gracie? Do they fit anyone you know? Also, I see another word here, but I can't quite read it. Ev—something."

Grandma shook her head. "RS doesn't match anyone in the family."

"This is the one you found, right?" I pointed to a rust stain on the fabric of one quilt. "Here's where the envelope was safety-pinned." I turned the corner over. "What's this brown stain—is that a bloodstain?"

David peered at it closely and got out his iPhone, snapping several pictures.

"We think so." Grandma shrugged. "We aren't sure why it's there."

"What is this pattern? I recognize it but can't recall the name," I asked.

"It's called rustic rose. The red and green dyes are distinctive here. Notice the curved stems, the red flowers and green leaves and the large round shapes with an orangish star-like shape inside. It's a challenging pattern and the mark of an experienced quilter. At least, that's what my quilting friends tell me."

"So, you have two quilts done in the rustic rose pattern. One has initials and a bloodstain," David remarked. "The other quilt appears better cared for."

"Yes, you're observant, David. Please verify if the quilt with the bloodstain goes back to the Civil War era, and if possible, find out who made it." Grandma Molly said, "I've waited a long time for answers."

I nodded. "Sure, Grandma. But why did you wait so long?"

We peeled off the gloves and stared at my grandmother. She hesitated.

The back door opened. Grandpa Patrick O'Connor came into the room dressed in a pair of old jeans, denim work shirt, heavy sweater, and boots.

His green eyes twinkled when he saw me. "Gracie, is this the young professor you keep talking about?"

I was just about to greet him with a hug when I saw his expression change. I stopped. *What's up with Grandpa?*

Grandpa walked closer and saw the quilts on the table. He stopped smiling. *Was he glaring at Grandma?*

David held out his hand. "Hello, Mr. O'Connor. My name is David."

The older man shook David's hand absently and stared at his wife. "Ah, Molly, what are you doing with this old quilt again? Can't you let it go after all this time?" He was angry.

Grandpa Patrick shook his head, and I thought his hair looked grayer. Once, he'd had dark blondish hair the same color as Mark's.

He turned and left the room, saying nothing to me or giving me his usual hug. We heard the basement door creak open and shut loudly, and then footsteps thumped as he retreated to his office downstairs. *Talk about drama. What was that about?*

Grandma had lost her sparkle and was on the verge of tears. She sat down. I couldn't remember seeing her so distraught or Grandpa Patrick so grumpy. *What's going on with my grandparents?*

"Grandma Molly, are you alright?"

David and I sat back down. I found a box of Kleenex and brought it to her.

"It's all right, Gracie. I'm sorry, David. What an awkward introduction. Patrick's been after me to get rid of this old quilt. He says I'm obsessed with it. Maybe I am. But, forty years ago, my life revolved around our children and volunteer work with the League of Women Voters and other community organizations. Patrick was the editor at *The Jubilee Times,* and I'd help him in the office. I was busy, so I put the quilt in my closet and promised myself I'd investigate it later. Every few years, I'd get it out and try to find out more information. But I never did. So, I'd put the quilt back up in the closet."

"It gets worse," she confessed. "The family had a big argument about the quilt years ago. His older sister Catharine mentioned the quilt—and the mysterious envelope—to an aunt who called me up. She called and urged me to burn the quilt and forget I'd ever found it. She'd overheard her mother and grandmother arguing about it when she was a teenager. Her grandmother asked her mother, 'Do you want *those* people in your family tree? Get rid of it.' About then, the envelope disappeared after a big family gathering here, and I always thought his aunt snuck upstairs and took it." She wiped her eyes and blew her nose.

I'd never heard this story before. "Grandma, that's an entire season's worth of family drama." *Reality TV has nothing on my family.*

Grandma Molly stood up, folded up the mystery quilt inside the sheet, and put it all in a plastic zippered case. Then she folded up the other quilt and placed it in its zippered case. She walked to the staircase. "I'll take it upstairs later. It goes in the big hope chest. And yes, my rustic rose quilt goes back to the 1860s from my Great-Grandma."

"Let me take it up for you, Grandma." I picked up the quilt. *This is crazy.*

I paused on the stairs to listen when Grandma Molly said to David, "You must think insanity runs in the family."

"No, I don't. Gracie and I understand every family has its secrets. You have a long-standing mystery here, and you need to solve it. This quilt has already created conflict in your family. I'm sure your husband means well. We'll find your answers."

"Thank you. I see why Gracie is so fond of you. You're a kind man and a diplomatic one, too. We'll have you two over for supper and give you a chance for a proper introduction to Patrick."

"I'd like a do-over."

I returned from my errand. "All set." Grandma Molly smiled, having a plan in place. *David, you know just what to say! Grandma's okay again.*

David ran one hand through his thick brown hair.

"Grandma, what did you say happened to the yellow envelope?" I asked.

Grandma Molly stared down at her hands, fiddling with her wedding ring. "It disappeared."

"Is the aunt still alive?" I asked.

"No. It was Patrick's Great-Aunt-Hattie, and she died a few years later." Her voice trembled.

"Don't worry. We're on the case." I hurriedly assured her. We put our coats back on and prepared to leave.

David picked up the quilt, and I grabbed my purse.

I hugged Grandma. "We'll be in touch. Love you."

David clasped her hand. "Yes, we'll investigate this matter, ma'am."

Grandma Molly smiled. "Oh, David, please call me Molly."

It's about time. David's charmed every woman in my family, especially those over sixty-five.

I hesitated. "Should we say goodbye to Grandpa?"

"Not with that quilt."

I compromised. Opening the basement door, I called, "Goodbye, Grandpa! Love you!" and heard a muffled response.

Grandma Molly said, "Wait a minute." She came back with a loaf of cranberry bread wrapped in foil and handed it to me. Then she walked us to the door, and I gave her another hug. "Thanks, Grandma!"

She stood, watching us walk down the porch steps, and waved.

We inhaled the frosty December air. We'd gotten a light dusting of snow overnight, looking festive on the fields, trees, and roofs.

David placed the quilt and bread in the back seat. "Now what?"

"Let's head for the Jubilee Library and the new librarian, Charlotte Lewis-Garcia. Have you met her yet? She's wonderful. Then, we should go see Carl, because he'll have resources for ACW research. First, though, I need to call Mom."

David started the car while I called home. Mom answered right away. I told her about seeing Grandma Molly's two rustic rose quilts and my grandfather's strange response.

Mom sighed. "Gracie, the business with the old red and green quilt is a mess. Don't get involved. Your father tried to get his parents to sit down and talk about it years ago, but all they do is fuss. They need a marriage counselor."

"Well, we promised to figure out this business with the old quilt. Have you ever seen it, Mom? It's beautiful. But I've never seen Grandpa so grumpy, and Grandma was on the verge of tears. David tried to introduce himself, and it was a mess."

"Oh, dear. No, I've never seen it. Let me call Dorrie, your grandpa's middle sister. She usually knows the gossip. I'm sorry David had such a strange introduction to your grandparents."

Next, I called the library. "I have something to show you, Charlotte. I need your help. Are you busy?"

"It's quiet, so come on in. I'm shelving books and could use some excitement."

"Thanks. We're on our way."

I settled back in my seat, trying to understand what I'd just seen between my grandparents. *How could an old quilt cause so much trouble?*

Three

Keeping Promises
Sarah

*"Every great dream begins with a dreamer. Always remember,
you have within you the strength, the patience, and the passion
to reach for the stars to change the world."*

~Harriet Tubman

*Evaline Plantation—Winchester, Virginia
Sunday, September 18th, 1864*

*R*ebecca returned to the bedroom. She'd changed clothing from the bloody dress she had on earlier. Susanna had changed as well and brought in several small satchels.

Rebecca stood by me and glanced down at Emily. "She always treated us kindly. She didn't hate me for what Mr. George did. But we need to go downstairs, Miss Sarah."

"Yes, you're right. Let's go downstairs." I touched my sister's cool cheek. The stench of death and blood filled my nostrils. *I must be strong. It's up to me now.*

I turned to Mother. "We're leaving for my house soon."

Mother held the baby and cried. "Be careful."

"Thank you, Mother. Please come downstairs and make the arrangements for Emily and her baby."

Then I told the two young women, "Please ask the house servants to meet us in the dining room," and followed them down the stairs with my big bag. They carried the other bags and satchels downstairs.

Rebecca whispered something to Thomas, who left the room.

Bobby gazed at me, but I shook my head. He burst into tears and ran to his mother, who tried to comfort him.

I sank down into a chair at the dining room table. Susanna and Rebecca put the satchels next to me. I opened the first bag, found the documents we needed, and laid them on the table.

Then, I found envelopes of coins for each person, as well as soft linen drawstring bags to hold their "freedom papers." The bags fit around a person's neck, hanging down onto their chest, under their clothing. We made one for each of us. This way, the freed slaves always carried their freedom papers on them, and Emily and I had copies.

Emily and I'd been teaching them all to read, write, and count money for almost three years, ever since our husbands left to fight for the Confederacy. We told them they'd be free soon, and they needed to read and write to buy and sell things.

The house servants entered the dining room. Mama Cee, the cook, was the matriarch and a skilled natural healer and midwife. Her husband, Papa Joe, helped serve dinners, managed the kitchen garden, and helped with other household matters. Thomas, the young man who drove Emily in the buggy, helped serve dinner, had been George's manservant, and loved helping with the horses. Susanna was a maid and assisted in the kitchen and helped with laundry. Her husband, Peter, managed the stable and was Papa Joe and Mama Cee's son.

Then there was Rebecca, twenty-one, and Bobby's mother. She had light brown skin, delicate features, and big brown eyes. Her son shared her eyes but was more light-skinned and could pass as white. Rebecca worked as Emily's maid and seamstress and had experience nursing and using herbs after working with Mama Cee as an apprentice.

"Miss Emily has died, and so has her baby boy. I promised her to free all of you. I'm giving you envelopes with your manumission papers. Keep these papers close to you because they're precious. I suggest you fold them up and put them in the bags we made. They go around your neck, so you always have them with you. I'm also giving you some money in silver and gold coins."

Rebecca listened as Bobby sobbed into her skirt, clinging to her. I gave her the document. She folded it up, and put it into the bag, slipping it around her neck. The rest followed her lead.

Mama Cee held her manumission paper longer and sobbed. "I knowed you were different when you come back from the college up north. But I never thought we be free in my lifetime," she marveled. She read the document again, her mouth forming each word with satisfaction.

Anthony Edward Smith, Attorney at Law

I, Emily Ann McDonald Phillips, of Winchester, Virginia, grant freedom to the slave once known as Mama Cee Phillips from the bonds of slavery that George Phillips had placed upon them.

All former claims to Mama Cee Phillips are now severed. Mama Cee Phillips is now considered a free person. In witness whereof, I have hereunto set my hand to seal this on the 10th day of September 1864.

Sealed and delivered in the presence of these witnesses.

John E. George

Roger J. Smith

Emily Ann McDonald Phillips

Then Mama Cee folded up the paper, placed it in the bag, and slipped it around her neck before wiping her tears.

Mother walked downstairs to see me handing each person their papers and an envelope with some money. She sat down at the table.

Rebecca asked, "Miss Sarah, can I take my quilts?"

"Yes, certainly. Please gather half a dozen blankets for the trip."

Rebecca left. Bobby stood beside Mother, watching all the activity.

"Thomas?" The young man walked up to me. "What do you want to do? Do you want to go with us? Mother thinks you can protect us. We're headed for Boston to take the train west. You're free now, understand?"

Thomas stood up to his full five foot eight inches. "Yes, I want to go with you. Your mother's right. I can defend you. Besides, I cannot leave Bobby and Rebecca."

"Thank you. Do you have a carpet bag? Pack what you need.

We're taking the big wagon and the four best horses." He nodded and left, taking Bobby with him.

Mama Cee embraced me. "Child, I'm sorry about Miss Emily and that poor baby."

"Thank you for trying to help Emily last night. I'm sorry the midwife wouldn't let you in the room."

"It broke my heart to hear her in so much pain. She's done with her suffering now, poor child."

Papa Joe shook my hand. "The good Lord be watching over you and these young ones. Thank you for the money."

I shook his hand. "No need to thank me, Papa Joe. This is a pittance. Miss Emily thought the world of you and Mama Cee." My voice broke, and I struggled to regain control.

They gave their condolences to mother, which she accepted.

Susanna and Peter were next. "Thank you, Miss Sarah, and Miss Harriett. We're so sorry about the baby and Miss Emily."

"Peter, would you notify the lawyer and undertaker?"

He nodded. "I best leave now," and left the room.

I turned to Mama Cee and Susanna. "Take any animals here to my barn. The grove of trees hides it. Confederate or Union, hungry soldiers will search for food. Pack up any food and take it to my house. We don't have much time."

The freed slaves left the room.

"Mother, once you've made the arrangements for Emily and her baby, come to my house. The armies are fighting outside of Winchester. When we leave, you'll be safer with these folks at my house. Tell anyone who comes along, Yankees or Confederates, that Emily and I went to the lawyer and got their freedom papers."

She nodded.

"Mother, could you please go to Emily's closet and find the bag we packed with a set of clothing for Rebecca and Bobby?"

Mother agreed. "Yes, I'll go get them." She hurried upstairs.

Rebecca returned and placed half a dozen quilts on the table. "Miss Sarah, your sister told me to pack up any valuables—her jewelry, silverware, and such. She got into the safe once Mr. George left. Here's a small bag of gold and silver coins for the trip. There's also a folder with papers about the plantation and Mr. George's will. Miss Emily figured he'd died since she hadn't heard from him in so many months. The estate goes into your name since she has no heirs. Here's the information about her lawyer."

"Thank you, Rebecca. What would Emily and I have done without you? She trusted you, and so do I. The plantation should go to your son with George. Let's worry about those matters later, once we're safe, all right?"

"My son—a slave? Owner of Evaline?"

"Your son, a free child. I asked Mother to look for the bag we packed with your traveling clothes, but you're welcome to take several of Emily's dresses if you can fit them into our trunks. Tell Susanna to take a few as well."

"Thank you, Miss Sarah." She left.

Alone, I grieved. But I sensed the urgency in Emily's dying words. "Promise me!" We both knew that slave catchers and stray rebels roamed the countryside, and most in Virginia supported the Confederate Army. Even with the documents showing their status, it would be dangerous to travel with freed slaves.

I thought again of my friend Abigail and her parents. When I'd gone to Boston to train as a teacher, Abigail and I met and instantly bonded. She became my best friend. Then I met her parents, abolitionists and suffragists, and my *real education* began as I learned about the inequities of women and Blacks. I had determined then, if given a chance, I would help take a slave to freedom. Now, I was about to embark on a journey to do just that—and take three slaves to freedom. I pushed down my grief at Emily's death and the death of my nephew, and anger at the doctor and midwife who'd failed my sister. I would think of such matters later.

Four

The Rest of Grandma's Story
Gracie

*"I may sometimes be willing to teach for nothing, but if paid
at all, I shall never do a man's work for less than a man's pay."*
~*Clara Barton*

As we walked into the Jubilee Junction
Public Library, Charlotte greeted us. I introduced her to David,
and she smiled.

I laid the bag with the quilt on one of the study tables and slipped
on a pair of gloves from Grandma. Then I unzipped the plastic bag,
lifted out the quilt, and laid it on a table, using the sheet wrapped
around it as a protective drop cloth.

Charlotte watched with interest. She was an attractive woman,
half Meskawkie, half white, in her late 30s, with dark brown hair
hanging to her shoulder blades, soft brown eyes, and an expressive
face. She peered at the folded quilt.

"What a beautiful old quilt. What do you need from me?"

"We need to magnify the writing on the quilt's border," I explained
as I laid it out to show the edge. *We need to figure this out for my
grandmother.*

I told her Grandma Molly's story about a wounded Union soldier coming home on the train, wrapped in a red and green quilt.

"We have several options," Charlotte replied as she looked around.
"I have a machine for magnifying print for vision-impaired readers.
Let's try that first."

We walked over to the machine.

She put on some cotton gloves, placed the quilt under the machine, and carefully rotated it until she saw the hem. We could see the initials much better. "R. S. Evaline."

I took several pictures with my iPhone. "Do you think R. S. Evaline is a person's name?" I asked.

David, already seated at one of the library's public computers, typed away. "No, I don't get any hits for an R. S. Evaline." He had his pocket notebook out and scribbled in it.

"What could it mean, then?" I asked, frustrated.

"Have you thought about tracing its origin from the other end?" Charlotte asked. "Did your grandmother tell you who arrived home with the quilt wrapped around him?"

"Unfortunately, no. Grandpa sort of freaked us out. I should have asked Grandma."

She nodded. "I'm intrigued. It's a beautiful old quilt."

David closed his notebook and slid it into his back pocket, along with a pen. "We need more information."

I thanked Charlotte while I refolded the quilt and place it back in the case. After witnessing the drama between Grandma Molly and my grandfather, I hadn't thought to ask her that most crucial question.

I was quiet as we walked outside. *I feel foolish calling Grandma, but what else can we do?*

David opened my door, and I handed him the quilt as I settled into the front passenger seat and called Grandma, putting her on speakerphone. David put the quilt on the back seat and waited to start the car.

"Grandma, who was the soldier who came home from the war with the red and green quilt wrapped around him?"

"Oh dear, I didn't tell you that? Patrick startled me when he came in and made such a fuss. As I recall, it was either Michael or Daniel O'Connor, your third great-grandfather and uncle, or one of their two best friends, the Nelson brothers. What were their names? James and Richard—no, no, James and Joseph. The four boys joined the 24th Iowa regiment together."

Great. We have four candidates. At least we have their names.

"Thanks, Grandma." I grabbed my notebook and wrote down

the names. Curious, I asked, "So, is Grandpa still mad at you? I've never seen him behave like that before."

Grandma Molly laughed. "He got over it. He's glad to have the quilt out of his house, and there's a lovely brisket in the oven for supper."

"I need to remember your strategy, Grandma," I chuckled. "Thanks. Love you." Relief flooded me. *Oh, good. I didn't like seeing Grandma so upset and Grandpa so grumpy.*

"Love you too, Gracie, and hello again to David. Hope this information helps."

I assured her it would before we hung up.

"So should I expect brisket if you pull shenanigans some day?" David looked at me as I hung up, his brown eyes amused.

"Only if Grandma teaches me how she does her brisket. It's the best," I told him truthfully. What I didn't say is that while I like to bake brownies, I don't really cook much. Cooking for one isn't much fun. So, I eat takeout from Aunt Shirley's café or Mom's leftovers. Most nights, I microwave Lean Cuisine frozen meals or make grilled cheese sandwiches or even toast with peanut butter. I've eaten a bowl of instant oatmeal with bananas and yogurt for supper or a bowl of popcorn and peanut M&Ms. I also drink a lot of hot and cold tea, and Diet Dr Pepper.

David pulled out of the parking lot. "Speaking of food, how about lunch?"

"Yes, please! I think I need some chocolate," I told him.

He laughed. "Hopefully, Aunt Shirley has some brownies or chocolate chip cookies."

After a quick lunch, we walked into the Jubilee County Museum and headed for Carl's office. I was pleased to see his intrigued reaction to our project. Not only is Carl my boss, but he's also an American Civil War history buff, just like David.

We showed him the quilt, the pictures of the hem on my iPhone, and the names of the four young men.

Carl sat down at his computer, pulled up a Civil War database, and typed in the names of our four Jubilee Junction soldiers. Then he emailed me the results and printed the report.

"Here you go." Carl handed the printout to David, and I peered over his right arm to read it. "Those four young men were with the 24th Iowa Infantry Regiment. At least forty men from Jubilee Junction and surrounding farms signed up. On April 16, 1861, President Lincoln called for 75,000 volunteers. The response was mixed, since it caused more states to secede, but over 75,000 volunteered and over two million served in the Union Army. The Iowa Temperance Regiment gathered at Camp Strong, near Muscatine, Iowa, in the summer of 1862 under Captain Leander Clark from Tama, Iowa."

David examined the printout, nodding in excitement. "This is helpful, Carl. It lists each battle the soldiers in the 24th engaged in and the places they traveled to along the way."

I stared at the paper in David's hands. "Why is it written all in capital letters?"

David scanned the printout. "The military uses all caps for military orders," He answered. "Here's the listing for Michael O'Connor, your distant grandfather."

I stared at the printout.

MICHAEL O'CONNOR ENLISTED INTO THE UNION ARMY ON 21 AUG 1862.

HE JOINED THE IOWA 24TH INFANTRY REGIMENT.

THE REGIMENT WAS ORGANIZED AT CAMP STRONG, NEAR MUSCATINE, IOWA, IN LATE SUMMER 1862 UNDER A CALL FOR THE IOWA TEMPERANCE REGIMENT. THE REGIMENT PASSED THE WINTER IN HELENA, ARKANSAS.

THE REGIMENT WAS INVOLVED IN SOME MINOR BATTLES. THEN THEY WERE ATTACHED TO THE 2ND BRIGADE, 12TH DIVISION, 13TH ARMY CORPS, DEPT.

"IN FEBRUARY 1863, THE 2ND BRIGADE WAS INVOLVED IN THE BATTLE OF PORT GIBSON, MISSISSIPPI. THEN THE BATTLE OF CHAMPION'S HILL, MISSISSIPPI. FOLLOWED

BY THE BATTLE OF VICKSBURG, MISSISSIPPI. MOVED TO NEW ORLEANS, LOUISIANA. THEN TO MADISONVILLE, LOUISIANA, IN JANUARY 1864.

JULY, MOVED TO FORT MONROE, VA AND THEN TO WASHINGTON, D. C.

AUGUST, ATTACHED TO 4TH BRIGADE, 2ND DIVISION, 19TH ARMY CORPS, ARMY SHENANDOAH.

SEPTEMBER 19 THIRD BATTLE OF WINCHESTER AND THEN BACK TO SAVANNAH, GEORGIA, WHERE IT WAS MUSTERED OUT IN JULY 1865.

THE REGIMENT LOST 9 OFFICERS KILLED OR MORTALLY WOUNDED. 3 OFFICERS DIED OF DISEASE, 119 ENLISTED MEN KILLED OR MORTALLY WOUNDED AND 212 ENLISTED MEN DIED OF DISEASE OR ACCIDENT.

MICHAEL O'CONNOR WAS PROMOTED TO CORPORAL IN DEC 1863 AND WAS MUSTERED OUT 17 JULY 1865 IN SAVANNAH, GEORGIA.

"So, Michael got promoted to full corporal. That's good, right?" I asked, staring at the printout. The all caps still bothered me.

Both men nodded and Carl turned to his computer to show us a website explaining the organization of the military during the ACW. "The basic unit in the ACW army was a company with one hundred men, commanded by a captain," Carl explained. "Ten companies made a regiment. So, the privates stayed together while they were fighting. The corporals would have been responsible for directing them," he concluded.

"Is it significant that the other three stayed at the rank of private?" I asked.

"It shows Michael had leadership potential, but it doesn't reflect on the other three. Most men were privates." Carl looked up from the computer.

David agreed.

I read the dates on the printout again. 21 AUG 1862 to JULY 1865. This can't be right. Did more soldiers die from illness or accidents than from combat injuries in three years?" The numbers astounded me.

David did the math on his iPhone's calculator. "My total is 343 dead. The Civil War was brutal, and conditions at the camps were far from hygienic."

Carl's phone rang, and he answered it quietly as David gestured toward the computer.

Carl mouthed back, "Yes," so David took a seat at the computer and brought up the National Park Service database.

"I've used this site before. Let's see if the database has any additional information about your soldiers." He searched for the first soldier, Michael O'Connor, from Jubilee County, Iowa. However, it only told which side he fought for (Union), his place of origin (Iowa), the Battle Unit (24th Regiment, Iowa Infantry), and Function (Infantry). Still, I felt impressed that the National Park Service knew about my grandfather's service!

David chuckled at my expression and then searched and found the Wikipedia article about the Iowa 24th Regiment. "This article has good information about the Regiment's individual battles. I'm going to send the link to these websites to both of us."

I scanned the printout about the 24th Iowa Regiment as questions flooded my brain. *Four boys from Jubilee Junction left to go to war—two sets of brothers who were best friends. Which one of them came home with a quilt wrapped around him? Why did he need it? Was he simply cold or bleeding from an injury?*

My memory of the bloodstain brought an icy stab of fear. *What happened?*

Saturday evening, my brother Mark and sister-in-law Kathy invited us for a family meal at their farmhouse. We ordered takeout from the Jubilee Cafe, and Mom and Dad offered to pick it up on their way to the house. David and I arrived first, set the table, then sat and chatted with them. Something wasn't right between Kathy and

Mark. I couldn't figure out what was going on, but they weren't acting normally.

Kathy wiped a section of the kitchen counter for the third time as she stared out the window. Mark was wearing a goofy grin and checking his watch every five minutes as he tried to carry on a conversation.

What was going on with these two? My grandparents apparently aren't the only ones with a secret.

Mom and Dad eventually walked in with two large bags of take-out food, and Mark grabbed the bags and set them on the dining room table. He quickly pulled out the food and distributed it on the table, as my parents shrugged off their coats and hung them on hooks by the back door.

"Thanks for coming over," Kathy said, finally pulling herself away from the window and putting down her dishcloth.

Mark was grinning. "Uh, before we eat, we have a gift for you, Mom and Dad," Mark announced as he glanced at Kathy.

She walked over to the living room, picked up a gift box with a big, bright red bow, and handed it to my parents.

"Go on, open it," Mark urged. Kathy was excited, too, fiddling with the bottom of her t-shirt.

Mom unwrapped it while the rest of us observed. A look of shock swept over her face as she paused, then pulled out a white baby onesie with "I Love Grandma and Grandpa" written on it.

Mom held it up to let us see. Mark and Kathy laughed.

"You're having a baby?" Dad asked, his eyes glistening.

"How wonderful! We're going to be grandparents," Mom exclaimed, looking around the room. Her eyes were shining with tears and soon, so were mine.

Family hugs followed.

I'm going to be an aunt, I marveled. *What would cradling a niece or nephew in my arms feel like?*

"Congratulations," I whispered into my sister-in-law's neck as I hugged her. "I'm so happy for you and Mark."

Thank goodness, Mom found the Kleenex box and passed it around.

David wrapped an arm around me and gave me a shoulder

squeeze. "We'd better start checking out the baby section of Target."

"This is wonderful, so wonderful," Mom blew her nose. "Can I ask, how far along are you?"

"A little over nine weeks." Kathy's voice faltered, and she looked at Mark. "We wanted to wait to tell until after the first trimester, but I couldn't stand it!"

Mark added, "You're the first to know. Keep it a secret for a few more days, please. We're going to tell her parents, too."

We calmed down and ate our taco salads and roast beef sandwiches, still preoccupied with the baby announcement. Kathy was glowing with happiness, and Mark could not stop grinning. My parents were both excited as well.

Silently, I asked God to help her with her pregnancy and delivery. Memories of two years ago flooded my mind as I watched Kathy eat her taco salad, smiling and laughing. Occasionally, her hand rested on her still-flat belly. *Please God, I don't think I can bear to see her like that again. Sobbing in her bed, asking me what she did wrong to lose her baby? Boxing up the baby shower gifts to donate to a needy family.*

After dinner, Mom grabbed her purse, calendar, and phone. She'd recorded all the family activities for the next two weeks, and I wondered when David and I would find time to do more investigating.

"We're eating supper at your Grandma Molly's and then attending church together on Christmas Eve. On Christmas Day, we'll be here and have a big holiday meal with Vern, Maggie, and Violet." Mom circled the events on the calendar with a purple gel pen.

She looked up, seeing David holding my hand, and added, "David, you're welcome to join us at all these events."

"Thanks, Becky. I'd like that," he replied, squeezing my hand.

Mark and Kathy stood up, and we helped clear the table. Mark brought in the kitchen trash can for the takeout containers and bags. After we stuffed them in, Mark grabbed the container and returned it to the kitchen. Then we wandered to the living room to get comfortable, Mom still dragging her pen and calendar and checking her phone.

David and I chose the love seat and sat down. I took a deep

breath and dove in. "David and I are visiting his family the day after Christmas."

Kathy and Mom beamed as I slowly expelled a sigh of relief. *Yeah, I'm meeting his family for the first time. We're a couple. Will they like me?*

David grinned as Mom wrote it on her calendar. "How exciting." Mom smiled at David.

Mark gave a thumbs up. "You've arrived, David—you're on Mom's calendar!"

Kathy chimed in. "Meeting his family over the holidays—that should be fun."

"I'm a little nervous—but excited," I confessed. Meeting Mark's parents was a big deal. The butterflies started tap dancing in my stomach. *I haven't met someone's parents for what? Eight years. That was Steve's parents. I should have told them years ago, your son is a control freak with anger issues, and I'm afraid he's going to hurt me.* I rubbed my wrist, remembering when he'd grabbed it so hard that he left a bruise and a red ring around my wrist. *That was the night he'd stopped me from leaving the restaurant after his fake proposal.*

Dad looked at David. "I'm sure things will go well when you introduce Gracie to your family." His tone was reassuring, and my anxiety backed off. David was nothing like Steve, and he knew all about our breakup.

David nodded and took my hand. "My folks will love Gracie. How could they not? She's wonderful." I had to will myself not to cry in relief. The contrast could not be more apparent. David had been there at my lowest, and we'd become friends before we began dating.

Mark stood up. "Another five minutes and we'll be planning the baby shower games and doing our nails. You need to see my cool man cave, David. We got a new TV for an early Christmas present, and we decided it fit downstairs."

David gave me a quick smooch and nodded at Mom and Kathy. Then, he and Dad walked downstairs to tour Mark's new digs, which Kathy had shown me on a previous visit. Markd had taken over a large room with a fireplace and built-in bookshelves on the lower level. They'd furnished it with a comfortable sofa and masculine recliner. He also had a desk in a corner for his laptop, where he paid the bills. The new TV made the room the perfect spot to watch the Hawkeyes, Cyclones, or Panthers, depending on the guests' preferences.

Soon we heard a holiday movie and laughter coming from downstairs. Upstairs, Kathy, Mom, and I were discussing the raging hormones of pregnancy, exotic food cravings, the holidays, and, of course, our men. I tried to laugh at my earlier emotional response to meeting David's family. Of course, I wanted it to go well.

After so much family heartbreak earlier in the fall, I was ready to celebrate Kathy's pregnancy and my new relationship. David and I had literally run into each other in the hallway at college early last semester. We'd become friends, and he stood with me through the breakup with my longtime, abusive boyfriend. We'd become a couple, and he'd helped me bring my great-aunts together, twin sisters Violet and Vera.

Later, when David drove me home, I told him about Kathy's miscarriage two years before and the heartbreak it caused for our family.

"I'm thrilled about the news, but this is a high-risk pregnancy. So, I want to help her rest and take care of herself. I can't imagine what a second miscarriage would do to her." Just the thought shot my anxiety to the moon. *How would Mark deal with another miscarriage? It devastated him, too.*

David parked the car in my driveway, then cupped my face in his hands. "You have an incredible family, Gracie. We'll do whatever we can to help. Together." He kissed me.

I realized he'd said *we* and *us* tonight. I liked it almost as much as I enjoyed kissing him back.

Five

Preparations for the Journey
Sarah

"If you haven't already, you will lose someone you can't live without, and your heart will be badly broken, and you never completely get over the loss of a deeply beloved person. But this is also good news. The person lives forever, in your broken heart that doesn't seal back up. And you come through, and you learn to dance with the banged-up heart."

~Anne Lamott

Evaline Plantation—Winchester, Virginia
Sunday, September 18th, 1864

$\mathcal{I}$ stood in the large dining room of my sister's once lovely home, surveying the pile of things on the dining room table. It was up to me to make some decisions. *Emily, you trusted me. I want to do the right thing.*

Mama Cee, my mother, Susanna, and Rebecca looked at me expectantly.

We'd asked Papa Joe and Thomas to go up to the attic and bring down several trunks. They found four large trunks and brought them into the dining room where Rebecca and Susanna dusted them out.

"Evaline is too valuable for the Union Army—or the Confederates—to ignore. It's likely to become a hospital for wounded troops, and so might your large house, Mother. Pack up the essentials as quickly as possible and take them to my house, where I hope you'll all be safe, but we need to hurry," I told them, looking around the room and remembering the row of cots from last summer.

My village lay ten miles from Winchester and Evaline, and I hoped the battle would spare us.

Mother agreed. "Yes, I think you're right." She straightened wearily, no doubt remembering the previous summer when we had cared for wounded troops.

Rebecca placed several satchels inside the first trunk, including the ones with the valuables. She added the quilts on top and a stack of blankets and several pillows. In the other trunk, she placed the small carpet bags for herself and Bobby.

"I want to keep my bag of herbs with me," she said. Rebecca kept them in a canvas bag, and the contents included a variety of medicinal herbs, including chamomile tea flavored with peppermint, used to ease Emily's upset stomach.

Thomas handed her his carpet bag, my bag, and the one Emily had filled. Rebecca shut the lid.

Peter entered the dining room, nodding at his mother, Mama Cee, and then turning to me. "I told the undertaker about Miss Emily and the baby. He's coming here. I got to the lawyer's office, and he says for you to be careful, Miss Sarah. You can hear the battle something fierce, and he's going home after he sees you. Miss Sarah, you all best skedaddle now. I saw that wicked Mr. Hayes out riding, looking for runaway slaves."

Papa Joe stood up. "I'm gettin' the gun and the dogs. There's going to be just four of us, plus your mama once you folks leave. But that slave catcher don't care about our freedom papers. He'd grab us, anyway."

"Where was he?" I asked. Mr. Hays personified the word *dis-reputable*—he was greedy, careless in his appearance, and prone to violence. I'd only seen him from afar, but I'd heard plenty about him from my father. He was the sort of man I wanted to avoid. Just hearing his name made me feel uneasy, since I'd taken on a crucial mission alone—delivering three former slaves to safety. *Please, God, don't let that man come anywhere near us.*

"He was riding his horse near the big house across the way. He must know the Gaylord family left last week," Peter replied. "I'm sure he's got some lootin' in mind."

The war changed our community over the past three years. Winchester once had half a dozen large white plantation houses with pillars, ornate gardens, outbuildings, and verandas. Each plantation then had its fields, barns, outbuildings, and slave quarters. Now, Evaline was one of two plantations still occupied. All the young white males left to join the Confederate Army. Their women tried to hold on to their family property, but with each new battle, more women left, trying to flee to safety.

Without realizing it, I'd turned my sister into an abolitionist in my letters home. Mother was another story, however. She had a gentle nature, and I'd never witnessed her acting unkind to a slave. Now her safety might well rest with Mama Cee, Papa Joe, their son Peter, and his wife Susanna.

Peter and Thomas carried the trunks outside to the carriage house, then loaded the big wagon with larger items to take to my house. Thomas hitched up the four horses to the sturdy Studebaker wagon while Peter put saddles on the other two horses. Thomas gathered a few essential grooming tools and stowed them.

Papa Joe's two hounds ran in circles around the wagon, barking and jumping.

Thomas and Peter walked around the wagon, checked it over, then examined each horse. They ran their hands down each leg and lifted each foot to check their shoes, checking for missing or loose nails. Peter adjusted a few straps but nodded at his friend. "You 'bout as good as me at taking care of these horses. The wagon looks good."

Thomas grabbed a tin bucket for water and another for oats. "We best take feed for the horses," he commented as he secured the buckets on the side of the wagon. Then he found a canvas bag filled with oats in the barn and added it to the load.

After we'd loaded our supplies, I inventoried the carriage house. We were leaving a large buggy, another wagon, and six horses for Mother and the others. She assured me it would be enough with her buggy and horses.

The freed slaves bid each other goodbye with kisses and sorrowful embraces. Susanna and Rebecca wept. Mama Cee gripped Rebecca as she whispered something in her ear, then wiped a tear from the face of the child who'd so quickly blossomed into a woman. Then Mama Cee hugged Thomas and whispered in his ear.

My mother stood with the former slaves near the wagon.

Did I make the right decision? I don't even have a route planned. What was I thinking? For a moment, panic seized my heart.

Out of the corner of my eye, Papa Joe earnestly shook Thomas's hand and told him to take care of the womenfolk. Thomas nodded soberly. Then they all hugged Bobby, who seemed both excited, yet reluctant to leave behind the only extended family he'd known.

I turned to Susanna and Peter. "Go to Emily and George's closets and take whatever clothes you want. You'll find shoes, hats, coats, all kinds of things." My voice tightened as I thought about my dead sister upstairs with her child. *How could any of us go on without her?* Yet even as the thought passed through my mind, I knew we had to press on—if only to honor Emily and baby George.

Susanna placed her hand on my arm and squeezed. "We promise to watch over your sister. And we'll help Miss Harriet lay Miss Emily and her poor child to rest. Don't worry."

Mother gently rearranged the tendrils around my face. "Be safe, my darling girl. Let me know where you are. If your father doesn't return, I promise I'll join you."

"We'll take good care of Miss Harriet," Mama Cee consoled as Mother dried her tears on her handkerchief.

"Yes, Mama, I'm glad to have you folks."

Mama Cee took charge. "Miss Sarah, you take the back roads home, and let's put Bobby up with you. He so white he can pass. Rebecca, you sit behind with the trunks. Thomas can ride one horse and watch out for slave catchers. You be fine."

Unfortunately, her voice didn't sound convincing.

Peter grinned. "I got a better idea, Mama Cee. Let's give the man a show to distract him. First, I ride around in front while you folks leave in the back. Then I ride right up to the front door of Evaline. So, he be watching me, not you folks in the wagon."

Mama Cee's eyes followed her son, who was heading into the carriage house. "Don't get yourself shot, Peter."

He waved as he proudly trotted out of the carriage house after saddling a horse.

Susanna followed, her eyes on Peter. "I'm watching him, Mama."

Papa Joe raised his hand. "God bless this trip and good luck to you all. Remember to look for quilt squares placed on big barns. Ask for help, and friends will appear."

"Quilt squares?" I asked, puzzled, as I approached the crowded buggy.

"I'll explain later," Rebecca whispered.

I quickly inventoried our supplies—four trunks, with Rebecca's quilts, blankets, clothing for Rebecca, Thomas, and Bobby. Valuables from the safe. The plan was to empty one trunk at home and refill it with supplies from my house. We'd hide two trunks. We'd done all we could to prepare.

I climbed up onto the driver's seat, with Bobby sitting beside me. Rebecca sat behind us in the wagon with the trunks. Thomas rode one horse and tied the other to the wagon.

Bobby grinned.

I told him, "You hang on tight to the seat, all right? I won't drive fast. If we run into trouble, crawl further back in the wagon with your mother." He nodded.

Papa Joe suddenly spoke. "Miss Sarah, you got yourself a gun? Have you ever handled it?" I could hear a tremble in his voice.

"Take it. Thomas is an excellent shot. And bring them hounds of yours."

"Yes, I have a shotgun. Simon made me practice, and I'm quite good at hitting the target." I said.

But even as I assured Papa Joe of my marksmanship, I wondered —*could I shoot a person? Take a human life?*

I silently prayed I'd never find out.

Six

The Holidays
Gracie

"I sustain myself with the love of family."

~Maya Angelou

Christmas Eve, David joined my family for dinner at the O'Connor grandparents' house. We admired the decorations and made introductions. Then we devoured Grandma's pineapple ham dinner served on her holiday tableware.

We carpooled to church for a brief candlelight service and returned for pumpkin pie a la mode, Christmas cookies, and the stocking gifts.

Dad had two brothers and a sister. A third brother had been killed in action in Vietnam—Patrick Junior, the photojournalist who died only weeks before his expected return home. We'd taken flowers to his grave in the family cemetery. One day, I intended to find his name on the Vietnam Memorial's wall.

Dad's sister Elizabeth married a doctor and moved to Kansas City, Missouri, where she worked as a nurse. This year, Elizabeth sent regrets because their twins were performing in a Christmas program.

Dad's two younger brothers, Joseph, whom everyone called Joey, and Sean, were there. Sean worked the family farm, married his college sweetheart, and had three children. Joey went to Drake University, became a lawyer, and worked with the family law firm in Jubilee Junction. He and his wife had several children in elementary school and a toddler.

Tonight, Grandma Molly was having fun, holding the toddler, and talking to the other grandchildren.

Then, Mark and Kathy gave our grandparents a gift box like they gave my parents. Only this onesie proclaimed, "I love Great-Grandma and Great-Grandpa." Grandma Molly was ecstatic, and so was my grandfather. He shook Mark's hand and hugged Kathy. Our O'Connor uncles and aunts expressed excitement for them as well, and David and I acted surprised as we had promised.

Grandma Molly declared, "It's about time we got busy with the next generation." She smiled at Kathy and Mark, "Congratulations, my dears. We'll have to start a quilt. When will you know the gender?"

Kathy replied, "I don't know. I've scheduled a sonogram for right after Christmas. I'll let you know how it turns out."

We passed around slices of pie, nibbled on Christmas cookies, drank cocoa or tea, and chatted as the younger children opened a few gifts. Several of the older children helped Grandma pass out the Christmas stockings. Grandma surprised David with a stocking like the rest of us. They had the same contents each year, with candy, nuts, and a $25 gift certificate to Aunt Shirley's restaurant.

It was as if our earlier visit hadn't happened. I introduced David to my grandpa, and he was very cordial. "So, you teach history at Jubilee Community College?" he asked David.

"Yes, sir," David replied. "Your granddaughter and I literally ran into each other on our way to class. Then Carl introduced us at the museum and gave us the chance to talk and discover we had a lot in common."

"And you helped Gracie figure out the situation with her Grandma Grace and the California quilt? Your father told me about it, Gracie."

"We both enjoy solving problems and doing research, but Gracie deserves all the credit for figuring out the California quilt mystery." David gestured to me and put his arm around me.

"Well, I hope you two can help Molly with her Civil War quilt. It's driven her to distraction for the past forty years, and I've had to fight the temptation to burn it or hide it," Grandpa Patrick confessed.

"We'll do our best, sir." David and Grandpa shook hands like it was a business deal.

Later, I told David he'd made an excellent impression on my grandfather, and he grinned.

"You did all the work solving the California quilt puzzle with your Aunt Violet. We hadn't been friends for long, and I hoped I could provide some support. The way the secret affected your mother's family fascinates me. I wonder what we'll learn about your father's side of the family."

I also wondered.

On Christmas Day, the extended Nelson family gathered at Violet's farmhouse for dinner. Others brought side dishes and desserts. My parents fixed a ham in the oven and a turkey sizzled in the countertop turkey roaster. We set up the food buffet-style on the dining room table.

David and I came early to help set it up. David and Mark carried the tables and chairs and put them in place, joking about the *food hangover* from my O'Connor grandparents' house the night before. The women organized the food, then got out the paper plates and plastic silverware. Many of us hummed to the holiday tunes on the radio.

Uncle Rich sliced up the ham, and Dad carved up the turkey with Uncle Vern offering advice. We arranged the feast on Grandma Ginny's sideboard and dining room table. Dad recruited David and Mark to pass out glasses of juice, pop, or iced tea.

We filled our plates, sat at two long church tables, and chatted as we ate. David had met my great-aunts and uncle several times, and they liked him. Now we sat opposite Aunt Maggie and Uncle Vern with Aunt Violet sitting beside me. He and Uncle Vern talked about Jubilee Junction and our family's history. I noted how well David fit in with our family and smiled at him.

I chatted with my aunts, both excited by David's presence at our holiday meal.

"He's a good man, Gracie love. Hang onto this one!" Aunt Maggie whispered, and Aunt Violet squeezed my hand.

Aunt Violet turned to me. "Gracie, I've been going through a box of old papers and found some poetry I wrote in high school. You might find them amusing. Stop by and see me sometime, won't you?"

I assured her I would.

We'd decorated the house with a scotch pine tree in the living room corner, surrounded by a small pile of gifts. The family had established a rule about gifts long ago. The adults drew names at Thanksgiving, and the limit was always twenty-five dollars. Children got two toys and a stocking full of candy and small gifts.

This year, the gifts for the adults were Christmas sweaters or Iowa State University sweatshirts. Dad gave us all DVDs with family pictures he'd scanned.

Aunt Violet and Aunt Maggie crocheted colorful dishrags each year and wrapped them around a jar of homemade blueberry or strawberry jam. They ignored the drawing. All the adults got a crocheted dish rag and a jar of jam. We loved both.

Mom had re-wrapped the box with the white onesie and asked Mark and Kathy to give it to her and Dad again. So, Mom, Dad, David, and I all acted surprised. It was hilarious but worth it, seeing the happy looks on people's faces.

R. J. and Ally, Uncle Rich's oldest son and his wife, got up and hugged Kathy and Mark.

Aunt Delores promised to work with Mom on the baby shower and my cousin James, the only single guy in the room, offered to babysit with a grin.

David and I enjoyed a night out with Mark and Kathy over the holidays. We started with dinner at Ruby's Steakhouse on the edge of town. We ate our salads and breadsticks while telling them about our investigation into the ACW quilt.

Just as our meals arrived, I tried to describe how Grandpa had behaved when he saw the quilts laid out on the table.

"I've never seen him act like that. He barely said hello. He fussed at Grandma, shook David's hand like a robot, left the room, and walked downstairs to his man cave in the basement."

Mark stopped cutting his steak and stared at us. "Seriously? I can't imagine."

Kathy looked up, concerned. "Your poor grandma. Patrick's a wonderful man. I'm sorry you had such an unpleasant introduction."

David nodded. "She's a resilient woman. Once we solve the mystery, the tension will go away between them."

"Imagine having that quilt for forty years and not being able to get answers. No wonder she's frustrated," I added.

Mark cut into his steak again. "So, David, what did you think of Grandma Molly?" He glanced over at Kathy and me.

David thought for a moment. "She made an impression. Was she in the military? She has a straightforward, businesslike approach and commands authority. She was kind to me, but I thought she could walk into a college classroom, law office—or courtroom—and fit in."

Mark and Kathy laughed.

I reprimanded my brother with an annoyed look. "Grandma Molly's been a full-time volunteer since I can remember. She's President of her local League of Women Voters, active at church, in at least two book clubs, and when anyone needs something organized, they call her. Grandma taught high school before she married Grandpa and she helped at *The Jubilee Times*. I'm surprised she didn't ask if you'd updated your voter registration when you moved."

David nodded. "Yes, I did it right away. Would I have scored points if I mentioned that?"

Mark leaned forward. "Mention it next time," he suggested. "She'll love it. Wait until the next election."

Kathy stole one of Mark's French fries. "Yes, she's wonderful. Molly will ask if you voted yet and give you a list of websites where you can check out the candidates and issues. She comes to the high school to do voter registration each year."

"She's civic-minded." David looked up.

Mark grinned, "Yes, just imagine my high school graduation party. She passed out voter registration forms and pens and gave us that famous Grandma Molly stare that meant, "You better do this now!" Maybe two or three dozen of us sat down and filled them out. How many grandmothers would crash a party to register voters?" He laughed.

David glanced at me, and I confessed, "Yes, same thing at my 18th birthday and high school graduation party. And bonus—Dad took pictures for *The Jubilee Times*."

Everyone laughed.

After finishing our meal, we caught the early showing of *The Hobbit: An Unexpected Journey*.

Afterwards, we enjoyed coffee and tea with desserts at Aunt Shirley's café as we compared reactions to the movie. We'd all loved it, but Gollum frightened me. "He's so creepy. I know it's all Hollywood movie CGI magic, but every time he was on screen, I felt anxious."

David spoke up. "Of course, I did my best to comfort Gracie. I put my arm around her, but movie theatre seats aren't really made for romance."

Mark laughed. "Yeah. I hear some theaters are going for better seating. Wouldn't it be nice to have a reclining chair?"

Kathy sighed as she finished her brownie sundae. "I've only gained four pounds, but it feels like ten, and I'm only ten weeks along."

"You look great. I'm so excited for you both," I told her.

Mark put his hand on hers. "I bet I gain some weight, too! We'll burn it off later, running around after our little one."

David agreed. "Yes, get set. I have a niece and nephew, and I love hanging out with them. We'll be happy to babysit. In fact, I can teach you a few tricks about changing diapers and getting kids to sleep."

"I didn't know about your babysitting skills," I spoke up. I realized he'd used "we" again and liked it. But changing diapers? I would have never guessed.

Mark confessed, "I've never changed a diaper. I hope YouTube's got a video."

David offered, "I'd be happy to show you some techniques if you borrow a baby doll and buy the newborn diapers. Remember, wipe from front to back, regardless of sex. You're going to need to stock up on diapers soon, anyway."

Mark got out his phone and started doing a Google search. "Here we go. I found a dozen videos on YouTube, several of them too graphic from the description."

I peeked over his shoulder. "How to change a dirty diaper? Too graphic?"

Kathy, David, and I laughed at Mark's obvious discomfort as he watched a video.

I suggested, "You better let David give you lessons."

We watched as Mark's facial expression changed while he viewed the diaper changing video. My battle-hardened brother's facial features registered disgust.

David held up a hand to illustrate his main points. "After a few dozen times, it gets easier. You learn to keep the baby wipes handy and a can of Lysol spray. Plus, with baby boys, there are obvious dangers. Never remove the diaper until you see what you're dealing with. The babies learn the drill. You can do it."

I stared at Mark's face as he viewed the next video. He glanced at Kathy, sympathetic, who reached over and grabbed his free hand.

David asked, "Too much information?"

Seven

A Startling Discovery
Sarah

"As I would not be a slave, so I would not be a master. This expresses my idea of democracy."

~Abraham Lincoln

Sarah's house, a small village ten miles from Winchester
Sunday, September 18th, 1864

We drove the back roads to my war-ravaged village, which was no longer a lovely place. Many of my neighbors had left, so their gardens and fields lay abandoned, with corn ready for harvest and potatoes rotting in the ground. People had dismantled the fences for firewood. Virginia was not a cotton state, so the plantations grew crops like tobacco and raised cattle, and smaller farms grew vegetables. Now stray soldiers looted, seeking food or valuables—even a horse.

Our village was at the northern end of the lower Shenandoah Valley and close to several railroads. Winchester was the gateway between the North and South, and control of the city had changed many times during the war.

Some residents had welcomed the conflict three years ago, but now were tired of it. It'd taken away our men, left us to be occupied multiple times, and made life miserable. Our valley had seen two terrible battles already, and the third was underway. Those of us left behind—the women, older men, and slaves—cared for the wounded and buried the dead when the battles were over.

Last year, Mother, Mama Cee, and I cooked all day at the plantation's big stove, baking bread and making soup, porridge, or pudding for the poor boys left behind.

Peter and Thomas scoured the abandoned houses searching for flour, sugar, salt, coffee, beans for cooking, and bed sheets to tear up for bandaging wounds. It didn't matter if the injured man was Confederate or Union. He became our responsibility.

We set up a tent on the veranda for surgery. We packed as many cots as we could find inside the large dining room and front rooms, stripped of their normal furniture. And then the house was full of injured soldiers, gray and blue alike, moaning, screaming, praying, begging for a cup of water, a slice of bread, relief from the pain.

Their injuries were horrific. I soon discovered I couldn't stomach helping our doctor with amputations, but I could change bandages and feed the wounded a warm meal. Rebecca was the strongest of us. She stood by the doctor's side, helping to comfort the patient, giving him a swig of whiskey, or administering ether or chloroform. Peter hauled off the limbs and buried or burned them. The sickening smell of incinerated flesh hung in the air for day, but we had no time for our own discomforts. We were needed to care for the wounded men who filled the rooms of the plantation house.

Once we arrived at my house, we unloaded the wagon and stowed it inside my barn. Thomas and I cared for the horses while Bobby and Rebecca made several trips with smaller bags to my back door. Thomas brushed each horse down, and I got them food and water.

The hounds came running to me, so I stooped down to pet them, rubbing their tummies. They were affectionate, as always. I told them to settle down and introduced them to our guests. "Meet Duke and Scout. Duke and Scout, meet Bobby, Rebecca, and Thomas."

Rebecca was comfortable with Papa Joe's hounds, but Bobby was nervous.

Thomas kneeled as the dogs came to him, licking his face and nuzzling his neck, and Bobby relaxed.

After sniffing and getting acquainted, the dogs took turns lying on their backs, waiting their turns for a belly rub. They were black and tan coonhounds bred in Virginia, excellent hunters, and they'd been my companions for the past three years. They were puppies when Simon left, and he'd looked forward to returning home and training them to go hunting.

We carried the two larger trunks with valuables to store into the house and debated where to hide them. Finally, we put them up in my attic. Next, I showed my guests to the bedrooms, where they'd stay for a few days until we were ready for our journey. As we walked around the house together, I prayed, *Lord, guide me. Help us find the safest route.*

Once, I'd hoped to fill the six bedrooms with children, but that dream had died with Simon. So, I had plenty of room. I walked into the room next to mine with two single beds. Bobby and Rebecca followed me with their carpet bags.

"It's wonderful." Rebecca glanced around, smiling. Bobby saw a set of children's books in a bookcase and looked up at me for permission to look at them. I nodded. He walked over to the bookcase, selected a book, and sat down in the rocking chair to read.

I led Thomas to the room across the hall. "This is nice," he told me. He had a large window with a view of the flower garden.

Each bedroom had a large bowl and pitcher we used to wash up. We had a privy in the backyard and chamber pots in each bedroom.

I walked into my bedroom and gazed in the mirror. My face was pale and my hair disheveled, but I had no energy to fix it. Instead, I walked back downstairs to find Rebecca admiring my kitchen.

"Your home is lovely, Miss Sarah." She lightly touched the top of the large wooden table in my kitchen. It had been a wedding gift from my grandparents and made from fine oak.

"Thank you, Rebecca." I tried to smile.

We worked together to fix a simple supper of beans and molasses, cornbread, and canned peaches.

Thomas and Bobby came in from outside, where they'd fed and watered the animals.

Bobby asked, "Can the dogs come in?" I nodded, so we had two extra guests sitting patiently under the table.

We sat down, filled our plates, said a blessing, and ate.

Bobby chatted about my yard, barn, dogs, and the set of children's books upstairs as he asked for extra food and fed it to the dogs under the table.

The three of us adults did our best to carry on a conversation.

After supper, Rebecca and I checked my pantry for several large empty Mason jars to fill with water to take along. We looked at what else might be useful for our journey.

She washed the supper dishes as I sorted out a few things. *Do I need to take some tea along? Molasses? Canned peaches?* I walked around, feeling a little overwhelmed by so many small decisions.

Bobby and Thomas brought in the other two trunks.

I'd packed a few clothes already and gathered my valuables, putting them into a small bag, which I placed in the smaller trunk. I'd packed a few books, my sewing kit, and quilts to take along but would leave behind the rest of my possessions.

Rebecca looked at me, standing in the middle of the dining room. "Can I help you, Miss Sarah?"

I explained, "I hadn't expected to leave here so suddenly. I thought I had months to prepare while the baby was growing stronger."

She nodded sympathetically.

On the one hand, I hated to leave it and my memories of living here with Simon. But I'd promised Emily, hadn't I? And we needed to leave before the armies started taking over Winchester. *Simon, I loved this house when you were here. I thought we'd fill it with children. I still miss you.*

Rebecca asked, "What else did you want to take?"

"I trained to be a teacher, and I'll need to support myself, so I should take my books." She nodded and helped me fill a canvas bag with my notebook of lesson plans, dictionary, Bible, McGuffey's Readers, *Moby Dick, Uncle Tom's Cabin,* several Almanacs, and one of my prize possessions, *Narrative of the Life of Frederick Douglass,* a gift from Abigail's parents at graduation. I put the bag into the trunk.

Next, I opened one of the large trunks and found the clothing

Mother retrieved from Emily's closet and gave it to Rebecca. "Change into these clothes tomorrow. Wash up. We want you three to look like the freed Blacks you are."

"Let's go upstairs," I suggested, and they followed me.

I gave Rebecca several dresses from my closet.

"Please take these. No reason to leave them here." I told Rebecca. "I'm packing my hoops and big skirts because I can't wear them while traveling." For almost the past three years, I'd been wearing all-black mourning dresses with fitted bodices and full skirts, but I didn't wear hoops every day.

"Yes, I think you need to dress however you want. You're a grown woman," Rebecca replied.

Then I handed Thomas two pairs of pants, shirts, nightshirts, socks, and undergarments from my husband's closet and dresser. I hadn't been able to touch his things before now, but our circumstances eased the sting. I added a pair of shoes.

Thomas stood patiently in the hallway. He thanked me for the clothing. "Where we headed?" he asked excitedly.

I responded. "It's 90 miles to Baltimore where we can catch a ship to Boston, then the train west. Otherwise, it's twice the distance to Pennsylvania across rough territory." I didn't need to add that we hoped to avoid the Confederate Army and slave catchers either way.

Thomas headed off to pack, but Rebecca lingered.

Bobby walked down the hallway, peeking into rooms. He peeked into my bedroom, where his mother and I were standing.

"I like your house, Miss Sarah."

"Thank you. I'm giving it to Mama Cee and Papa Joe," I told him.

He looked around and then back at me, smiling. "They'll like it here."

Rebecca glanced at my closet. "It's a shame to leave these pretty dresses behind. How long do you plan to wear black? It's been nearly three years." She picked out three dresses and put them in my arms. "You shouldn't waste them."

I protested, but after thinking about her gentle rebuff, I relented. Why let them go unused? "Maybe you're right. I'll pack two or three. Mother always said proper women wore black for two years. It's been closer to three."

"You need to let him go, Miss Sarah," Rebecca spoke gently before she left the room to pack.

I looked at my open bag beside me on the bed, trying to remember Simon's face and voice. *Was it time to put the black dresses aside?* I rose and examined my closet. *Had I gotten so used to wearing black that it was the easiest choice?*

Simon had been an only child, and his parents died shortly after he left for war. All his other relatives lived out of state. I could hear Mother's voice in my head, scolding me when I broke protocol.

I tearfully packed undergarments, a nightgown, shoes, two plain skirts and blouses, belts, jackets, a sunbonnet, and a shawl, then closed the lid.

Am I really leaving my beautiful home?

I'd packed two black dresses earlier, but I'd leave the last one in the closet. My new attire might scandalize mother, but Rebecca was right. I needed to let Simon go.

I turned and walked to the room Bobby and Rebecca shared. Rebecca was adding dresses to her carpet bag while he ran his hands over the children's books that filled the cherry bookcase. I handed Bobby a small canvas bag he could use and held it open so he could place the books inside. I fought tears for the memories I would never make with Simon's and my children.

Bobby sat down in the rocking chair and paged through a book, sounding out each word. He was such a sweet boy, and my sister loved him dearly. I realized suddenly that I cared about this child as well.

My expectations for the house—a wedding gift from Simon's parents—and my dreams for my marriage had come to nothing. No children, no husband, just my empty heart and an empty house. Better the books go to Bobby.

I willed myself not to cry as I put Bobby in one of Simon's nightshirts, held him close to me on the edge of the bed, and read him a story. Rebecca sat beside him on the other side. After we finished the first book, Bobby held up a second book while fighting sleepiness. I glanced at Rebecca, and she nodded yes, knowing he wouldn't make it past the first three pages. We tucked him in and started reading the second book. Within three pages, he fell asleep, clutching a small rag doll he'd found on top of the bookcase.

Rebecca began gently removing the doll from his arms, but I stopped her. "He can have it. It's fine."

Of course, I'd hoped my child would clutch the toy someday, but Simon and I were married for more than a year before the war started, and I hadn't conceived.

Rebecca glanced at me. "You should go to bed, too, Miss Sarah." She put her hand on my arm. "It's been a hard day. I'm so sorry about Emily and Baby George."

I heaved a sigh. "Thank you, Rebecca. Yes, it's been an exhausting day."

At that moment, I fought the urge to drop my head on her shoulder. Rebecca had become my friend over the past three years as we worked together to help Emily through two difficult pregnancies. Seeing my beloved sister die like that had been shocking. I couldn't remember *ever* feeling this exhausted before.

Can I really get everyone to a free state safely? Simon would say I'm foolhardy to be attempting this trip. It's too dangerous.

I refused to let the thoughts settle.

I stood up. "Let's check on Thomas and lock the doors."

We slowly walked downstairs and found Thomas sitting with folded hands on the parlor sofa. "I'm packed," he announced proudly. "I'm mighty grateful for the clothing. This is a fine house you be giving to Mama Cee and Papa Joe, Miss Sarah." He paused. "Bobby asleep?"

Rebecca answered. "He found a rag doll and fell asleep while we were reading him stories. Miss Sarah says he can keep it." She smiled, and I dropped my eyes.

"He's a sweet little boy," I replied. "He's welcome to the books and rag doll. I hope they help comfort him." I tugged the front door to assure myself it was closed, bolted it, then moved through the first floor, pulling the heavy curtains closed.

Thomas rose and joined me as I walked to the kitchen to close the curtains and lock the back door. Suddenly, he froze.

"What's that?" He motioned to me, and he and I moved toward the noise.

I opened the thick pine door a crack and peered out. Before he left, Simon built the doghouse near the kitchen door. The hounds were standing, barking at the barn. *Someone's on our property!* I fought the urge to panic.

Thomas and I stepped outside as Rebecca entered the kitchen.

"We closed the barn doors, didn't we?" I asked softly.

"Yes, ma'am," Thomas whispered.

"The barn doors are open, and I can see light from the kerosene lamp. Someone's inside."

We stared at the flickering light inside the barn.

"I best go check things," Thomas straightened up.

"I'm going, too. But let me grab my shotgun." I hurried back inside and to the closet, where I kept the gun and shells. "Rebecca, stay in the house and keep the doors locked."

"Be careful!" Rebecca choked out as she wrung her hands.

We crept outside and tried to calm the dogs. I debated letting them loose but decided my shotgun was better protection. Thomas and I patted their heads to quiet them.

"Stay, Scout. Stay, Duke," I whispered.

Thomas and I crept toward the barn. The closer we got, the more my alarm heightened. Someone *was* inside! I could hear them.

Men's voices drifted in the night air. Yankees' voices. Suddenly, the barn door opened, and a tall soldier in a Union uniform ambled out, holding a canteen.

I froze, remembered the shotgun, but did nothing. He froze, too.

From behind the barn door, a voice spoke. "Daniel's in pain, and we need to find water." The man broke off as he stepped outside. He, too, wore a dirty, worn Union uniform.

The first soldier spoke. "Ma'am, we apologize for frightening you. We didn't know what to do. We got separated from our regiment after the battle today, and two of our friends are hurt. Will you help us?"

Sincerity and desperation shone in his green eyes. *What was I to do? They were technically enemy soldiers whose ranks would soon invade my beloved village. What would Simon do? But what had we done for the past two summers but cared for wounded soldiers on either side?*

I found my voice. "You'd better bring them inside the house."

The second soldier went back inside the barn. Several minutes later, three men emerged, one supporting a man whose arm and shoulder they wrapped in a bloody uniform shirt.

The second soldier who'd spoken to us through the barn door shut it and staggered toward the house.

"Thomas, help him. Please."

"Miss Sarah, you reckon these soldiers are trustworthy?"

"I have no idea," I whispered, "but two men are injured, one seriously. No one is dying on my property tonight if I can help it."

The dogs perked up again and barked to greet us all.

"I'm going to enjoy working for you, ma'am." Thomas hurried his pace and placed the good arm of the wounded soldier around his neck.

Before I could point out to Thomas that we were working together, I changed my mind. There would be time for lectures later.

Rebecca was waiting, the door open.

I led the men through the kitchen door and into my immaculate kitchen. Moments later, all of us were inside, the back door locked behind us.

What an absurdity, I thought. *I've just locked myself into my home with four Union soldiers? Have I lost my mind?* But after my time in Boston with Abigail's parents, who were abolitionists, it was difficult to see these four young men as enemies.

A quick assessment told me all four men were exhausted, hungry, and thirsty, and two were wounded. And I was responsible for all of them.

I imagined Simon's reproachful voice. *Sarah, what foolish thing have you done now?*

Eight

Meeting David's Family
Gracie

"The sun looks down on nothing half so good as a household laughing together over a meal."

~*C. S. Lewis*

David and I drove to Prairie Falls to meet his family the day after Christmas.

I wanted to make a good first impression by taking some kind of hostess gift. We debated what to get.

"My family doesn't drink wine. Mom might have a glass of champagne on New Year's Eve, and my dad would prefer a beer, but he doesn't drink very often," David explained.

"What about flowers?" I asked.

"Mom will already have a pretty centerpiece and a few poinsettias." David pointed out.

"Well, what do you suggest?"

"Mom hates making pie crust, so we usually have cheesecake from Sara Lee or cookies. My grandma made pies, but she's been gone for five years."

Finally, we decided the best gift for his family was two of Aunt Shirley's homemade pies. We agreed on pumpkin and French Silk.

We turned into the driveway, and the butterflies in my tummy did a wild dance. However, as soon as we parked, his parents walked down the steps of their big ranch house.

David opened my door and then retrieved the pies from the back seat. "Hi, Mom and Dad."

His parents came to greet us with friendly smiles, and the butterflies settled down.

Before David could utter a word, his mother greeted me. "Hello, you must be Gracie. I'm Ruth, and it's good to meet you." She hugged me, and I relaxed. Ruth had David's striking brown eyes and dark brown hair streaked with gray.

"Hello, yes. Thanks for inviting me."

David's father stepped up and took the pumpkin pie from him. "I'd hug you, too, Gracie, but I'm safeguarding a pie right now," he joked. "By the way, I'm Harry."

Harry was about six feet tall with dark wavy hair streaked with gray, dark brown eyes, and wore gold-rimmed glasses.

We walked up to the house, festive with its Christmas lights that lined the roof and front porch. A large nativity set on the lawn, also lit up, and a big sign shaped like a greeting card, wishing everyone A Merry Christmas.

Ruth warned us, "I hope you like chaos. The grandchildren are here. My son-in-law Jared is down in the basement watching football with David's younger brother, Alex, and they all want to meet you. David's told us all about you and the adventures you've had with these quilts."

I grinned, "I can handle a little chaos, no problem. It's wonderful to meet you both. Yes, David and I have a new quilt mystery and I'm happy to have his help."

As soon as we walked into the house, we saw two small children running around, and their mother chasing them. David laughed.

Their mother called out, "Don't hit your sister. Give me the spoon!"

They all stopped when they saw David.

"Uncle David's here!" yelled the little boy, maybe five or six years old. He dropped a large wooden spoon and ran for David. A sturdy boy with dark hair and brown eyes, he wore a red and green holiday dinosaur shirt and red sweat pants.

David handed his pie to his father, took off his jacket, and got down on the floor to hug his nephew. "Hey, big guy." They fake-wrestled and came up smiling.

"Uncle David's got a girlfriend." The little girl might have been 4.

Her brown hair was long and wavy. She danced around the room in her Disney princess Christmas top and skirt, red tights, and Mary Jane shoes.

David picked her up and hugged her. "Hi, sweetie. Yes, I have a girlfriend, Gracie."

I followed David's example, taking off my jacket, putting down my purse, and kneeling to say hello to the children. His nephew walked over and put out his hand. "Hi, Gracie, I'm Jack."

I shook his hand. "Nice to meet you, Jack. You have such nice manners!"

He grinned. "My mama and I practiced. Did I do it good, Mama?"

David's sister caught her breath. "Jack, you did it *well*."

She wore a Christmas sweatshirt and a red and green apron. She was beautiful, with green eyes and delicate features.

Jack's little sister danced towards me. "My turn, my turn! Gracie, I'm Daisy."

I resisted the urge to giggle. "Daisy, what a pretty name. It's nice to meet you."

Daisy ran over and hugged me, smelling of baby shampoo. Then she danced away. "Come see all our toys!" Her brother ran after her.

"Later, guys. We need to help grandma first." David called.

David and I stood up.

Joanna smiled. "They've been driving us crazy all morning, waiting for you to get here." She had the family's dark hair, which she'd pulled into a long ponytail.

David grinned. "Sis, meet Gracie. Gracie, this is my big sister Joanna."

"Hello, Gracie. Welcome. Yes, we need to get lunch ready, folks. Thanks for the pies. I think we should eat them first."

I relaxed, and the butterflies behaved. David and I helped set the table with his grandmother's lovely blue and white china.

The pies found their place on a beautiful antique oak sideboard next to a plate heaped with cookies.

We peeked in the kitchen to help. Then Ruth slipped a holiday apron over my sweater and jeans, and I began cutting up a crusty corn casserole on top of the stove. It smelled heavenly, and I resisted the urge for a sample.

David helped his father transfer the honey-glazed spiral ham from the turkey roaster onto a serving platter. The caramelized pineapple slices added to the banquet's aroma. His sister and mother got the casserole dishes out of the oven and refrigerator and put the still-warm dinner rolls into a basket as they hummed holiday tunes.

His father yelled down the steps to the basement. "Lunch is ready, gentlemen!"

Two men came up the stairs. "We'll help clean up, Mom and Dad," said one.

"It smells amazing!" said the other.

The first man I recognized as David's younger brother, Alex, because he resembled his brother. He walked forward to introduce himself. "Hey, Gracie, I'm Alex, David's much more handsome younger brother. How are you?"

I tried not to giggle and kept cutting up the large casserole. He and David back slapped their hellos.

The second man smiled. "Hi, Gracie. I'm Jared. The two kiddos belong to me, and so does Joanna." Jared had curly brown hair and eyes and wore glasses.

Joanna glanced up. "I'm yours? That sounds so 1860, dear. Women are voting now, you know."

I grinned at their bantering, and David caught my eye. I could imagine him saying, "Gracie, what did I tell you?"

We enjoyed a wonderful meal—plates heaped with slices of ham, corn casserole, cranberry jello, green beans, mashed sweet potatoes, and rolls. We cut the pies into skinny slices because some of us wanted a little piece of both. Next time, David and I would bring three pies and add pecan pie.

After lunch, we helped with cleanup. Then David and I followed the children to the playroom, sat on the floor for a tea party, and built something with magnetic blocks. The children showed off their dolls, games, puppets, and stuffed animals and handed a book to David to read aloud.

Ruth walked into the room. "The boys finished their football game. Do you want to open a couple of stockings?"

The kids jumped up. "Open stockings!" they chanted.

Ruth looked at them. "Settle down, you little heathens. You two opened yours this morning, remember?"

"Watch Uncle David open his." Jack and Daisy danced around.

So, all the heathens gathered in the spacious family room, arranged with several couches, two recliners, and two small chairs for the children.

A large fir tree dominated the corner, decorated with tinsel and hundreds of flickering LEDs. His mother handed the children two stockings, and Jack brought David a stocking, and then Daisy surprised me by giving me one, too.

David whispered, "Smile," so I did.

Daisy whispered, "Open it up, Gracie. I helped."

Jack declared, "Me too." They jumped up and down, so we hammed it up with our stockings.

"Thank you, but I wasn't expecting anything." I opened the stocking, as David did the same with his. He got Burberry cologne, a yellow/Black/red plaid winter scarf, a can of roasted and salted almonds, and a bag of Swedish fish.

I got a purple and pink winter scarf, a bag of Dove chocolates, a mini clipboard and purple pen, and homemade cards from the children.

I opened the cards, and the kids crowded in to point out the features in their scribbles. Jack had drawn a hill with trees and sleds and signed it with his name. Daisy drew a couple of stick people and a Christmas tree.

We tried on the scarves to their delight, switched scarves, sniffed the cologne, and pretended to sample the Swedish Fish and Dove chocolates. I made a list on my mini-clip board with Daisy's help and slipped it in my purse.

We sat and talked. The kids entertained us by showing us their stockings and what was inside.

Three hours later, we pulled out a few leftovers, made sandwiches and polished off the jello and most of the platter of cookies.

Then we watched *Rudolph the Red-Nosed Reindeer* while the boys watched a grown-up movie downstairs. Ruth and Joanna stayed upstairs with us. Joanna glanced over at us and nodded her head.

David whispered, "I think we can count on babysitting for both sides of the family. The children love you already. I've never seen them so welcoming."

Jack and Daisy snuggled between us with their little blankets, and David had his arm around us. I felt a flash of maternal protectiveness and imagined holding Mark and Kathy's baby, with David beside me.

When we left, I got hugs and handshakes from his parents, siblings, and the children, who were getting sleepy but determined to stay awake.

Ruth slipped a Ziplock bag of cookies in my hands in case we got hungry on the way home. "It was so nice to meet you, Gracie. Please come back soon." Harry stood behind her, his arm around her, and smiled and waved. "Safe travels home," he called.

We stepped outside to a chilly evening with the stars and moon shining brightly against the sky. The snow seemed to sparkle.

Driving home, David smiled at me. "Not so scary, are they?"

I grinned. "You have a wonderful family, David." *I was silly to worry*, I told the butterflies.

Nine

Four Yankees and A Proposition
Sarah

"No one is useless in this world who lightens the burdens of another."

~Charles Dickens

Sarah's house, a small village ten miles from Winchester
Sunday, September 18th, 1864

*R*ebecca pumped a pitcher of water and poured water into glasses for the four men. Then Thomas pumped more water and poured it into the big basin on the table, next to soap and rags.

All four men sat down and guzzled the water as the dogs lay down and watched.

Rebecca placed the arm of the injured man on a towel on the table and gently held him steady. I tore his uniform's sleeve, glanced at the wound, and winced because they had shot him straight through his upper arm. The bullet exited near the shoulder. We cleaned the wound as best we could, daubing it with water and pouring apple cider vinegar over it and into a basin, warning the young man it might sting. Rebecca gave him a wooden spoon and suggested he bite down on it.

Rebecca found what she needed in her bag of herbs—something for pain and something to help the wound heal. She packed yarrow herbs next to the wound, bound up his arm with clean bandages, and wrapped the bandages around his chest, securing his arm.

Rebecca then put shredded white willow in a teapot, let it steep, and told him to drink it down because it would help with the pain and swelling. He grimaced at the taste, but swallowed obediently and thanked her.

She turned to the young soldier who'd limped from the barn with Thomas's help. Rebecca lifted his foot onto a kitchen chair and examined his swollen ankle. With great difficulty, we removed his boot, but Rebecca had to cut the sock to get it off. She examined his ankle and foot as I looked on.

Rebecca announced, "I don't think it's broken. Did you trip and fall?"

He nodded. "We chased a mob of Confederate soldiers heading for Winchester, and I tripped on some rocks."

Rebecca told him, "I need to get a better look at your knee." She cut a slit in his pant leg and pushed the ragged material away from his knee. She frowned at the sight. "Looks like you wrenched your knee when you fell. You may have torn something."

I fetched some kitchen rags and dipped them in cool water. We washed his foot and leg, then wrapped cool rags around his ankle and knee, leaving the limb elevated on the chair. "We'll wrap it tighter later," Rebecca promised. "Right now, you need to eat something."

Thomas pumped more water and gave them a second glass while Rebecca and I set to work putting together a quick meal—the rest of my bread and jam and the leftover beans from supper. I got out more canned peaches and found some cheese and hardtack. The soldiers wolfed it all down.

"Where are you all from?" I asked.

"Iowa. A small town named Jubilee Junction," one of them told us between bites.

"We're with the 24th Iowa," another mentioned. "This is delicious. Thank you. We know you're taking a risk helping us. Thank you."

The tall soldier extended his hand toward me. "Michael O'Connor, ma'am. That's my younger brother, Daniel, with the hole in his arm. This is James Nelson, my best friend, and his younger brother Joseph, who tore up his ankle and knee. We're grateful for your help."

"I'm Sarah Elizabeth McDonald. Pleased to meet you all." I shook his hand, adding, "These are my friends, Rebecca and Thomas," as if introducing two former slaves as my friends was an ordinary thing.

"Thank you, Miss Sarah, Thomas, and Miss Rebecca, for supper and caring for our friends. Do you mind if we sleep in your barn?" Michael asked.

Rebecca grimaced at Joseph's swollen ankle and knee. She glanced at me and shook her head.

I agreed. "We shouldn't move these two men. Thomas and Rebecca, let's get blankets and pillows and get them comfortable downstairs."

My house had a parlor with two sofas right off the kitchen. We laid blankets down and got the injured men settled on the sofas, laying a quilt on top. Rebecca fussed around with pillows to make them more comfortable.

I turned to the other two soldiers. "Follow us, please."

Thomas and I led the way to the second floor.

I stopped at the doorway of a room with two single beds in it. "This will work."

Michael looked at the room and turned to me. "We're filthy, ma'am. I don't want to sleep in your beds. The floor will be fine."

James nodded. "I haven't slept in a bed since we joined the army."

I sighed. "Thank you for your concern, Michael, but we can fetch water so you can wash up. Or we can launder the sheets later. Either way, I'm exhausted, so I'll say goodnight."

Thomas nodded, and left to fetch water for the basin, soap, washcloths, and towels for the men.

Weariness took over as I turned to go to my room, and I staggered. Michael caught me, and I flushed.

"Thank you," I murmured, then straightened myself and walked down the hallway toward my bedroom, calling over my shoulder, "Goodnight, all."

When Rebecca came upstairs, I told her we should offer soap, water, and washcloths to the men downstairs tomorrow after they'd had an opportunity to rest.

She nodded,. "Yes, good idea, Miss Sarah. That young man sure is modest. Can I take him a nightshirt?"

"Yes," I replied. "Follow me."

I gathered four pairs of men's pants and shirts, socks, underwear, and nightshirts from Simon's closet and bureau, piling them on a chair.

She picked up the stack of clothing.

"Those clothes are for the soldiers. Thank you for all your help, Rebecca."

"Yes, ma'am. It's been a long day. You get some rest," she said, gently shutting my bedroom door.

I couldn't speak for the tears suddenly flooding my eyes. If only this day were a bad dream. If only Emily and the baby had lived. If only I wasn't about to leave our home and risk everything to fulfill my promise.

I undressed, put on my nightgown, and crawled into bed. Even after three years, I hated sleeping alone and missed Simon's warmth and comfort.

I lay back on the pillows and sobbed for Emily and her baby. I prayed for my mother, the other freed slaves, and my village—so close to the battle again. Then I prayed for the four soldiers we'd taken in. I prayed for strength, but my thoughts seemed jumbled, and I kept repeating, "Lord, help me—help us."

What have I done? Can I get our group to safety in a free state?

Then I thought about fixing and eating dinner together, gathered around the kitchen table with Thomas, Rebecca, and Bobby. We talked about our plans, and we mourned for Emily and her baby. It had been a welcome change from eating another lonely dinner by myself with the dogs at my feet, hoping for a dropped biscuit.

Who was I to trust four strangers—Yankees, at that—sleeping down the hall and downstairs? However, as I drifted off to sleep, I realized I felt safer with all of them here.

Monday, September 19, 1864

I woke up smelling fried sow belly, eggs, grits, toast, and coffee. I dressed quickly and went downstairs to the kitchen. Thomas and

Rebecca had fixed breakfast while Bobby handed forks and knives to the four soldiers now dressed in my dead husband's clothing.

The men glanced up when I entered the kitchen. They certainly didn't appear dangerous in the daylight. I couldn't help but notice that the O'Connor brothers were handsome men with light brown hair and green eyes. Their friends, the Nelsons, were also handsome, with light brown hair and hazel eyes.

"Thank you, young man," Joseph told Bobby. Someone had helped him clean up and don clothes, but they had cut the pants above the knees.

"Are all of you soldiers?" Bobby asked.

Daniel answered. "Yes. Our uniforms are all muddy, so your mama let us wear clothes from your daddy."

Bobby seemed confused, but Rebecca nodded at him.

"Thanks for the clothes, ma'am. It's good to be clean." Michael stood up and took my hand, and I fought not to pull it away. No proper Southern woman would allow such familiar behavior. However, his tone was one of kindness and consolation. "Rebecca told me your husband died several years ago, and that your sister and her baby passed yesterday. I'm so sorry. We all are." He gestured to the other men as he released my hand.

I dropped my head as I struggled to keep my composure. I couldn't believe Emily was gone. The pain of her loss was too raw, but I had to be strong if I hoped to keep my promise to her.

"Thank you, Michael. Yes, it's been difficult." I accepted a cup of tea from Rebecca, hoping my hands weren't shaking. Her understanding nod steadied me. I sat down at the head of the table and watched the men eat.

I gestured to Bobby, and he came to me. I hugged him, and he sat down beside me.

Rebecca served the food, and the men ate, then washed it all down with the coffee Thomas served.

"Thank you so much for handling breakfast, Rebecca and Thomas. I didn't mean to sleep so late." I tried to sound normal.

Rebecca glanced up from the stove. "We was going to let you sleep as long as you needed, ma'am."

"We're glad to help with breakfast," Thomas replied. "I slept in the best bed and the nicest room last night. I feel fit as a fiddle."

Rebecca served more food, and Thomas got the soldiers another glass of water and helped to fill plates. There was a sweet affection between the two that I didn't recall seeing at the big plantation house.

I listened to the chatter as I ate my breakfast. I'd taken on carrying out our plan by myself, and we were entertaining four soldiers who were technically the enemy. Mother would question my sanity, no doubt. But as someone whose sympathy belonged with the North because I opposed slavery, it didn't seem as strange to me. However, I needed to understand the situation.

I turned to Michael. "So, can you tell us what happened? Did you get lost or run away? Should we burn your uniforms or wash them?"

Michael explained. "We followed a group of Rebels who ran towards Winchester." He glanced at Bobby and faltered. "We chased them for a long time, but after a while we realized we couldn't see any of our soldiers. I climbed a tree to look for the battlefield. We didn't realize we had run so far. A Confederate soldier shot Daniel as we ran after them, and then Joseph got into a fight with a reb and fell. We wrapped up Daniel's arm, and James helped his brother as best he could. We walked down a side road until we saw your barn and got Daniel and Joseph comfortable inside. I was searching for water when you saw us. I'm sorry for scaring you and your dogs. We didn't think we could come up to the door."

James added, "We want to find our unit, but we need to take care of Daniel. He's not able to march or fight. And neither is Joseph."

Rebecca was washing dishes as Thomas cleared the plates. "Please sit down and eat your breakfast, Rebecca and Thomas. We can wash the dishes later." *They aren't my slaves. We can share the work.*

They sat down and ate breakfast, but Bobby listened to the men with wide eyes, ignoring his food.

"Eat your breakfast, Bobby. These men needed our help." He began eating.

Michael glanced at Bobby. "Your son must be seven or eight years old?"

Bobby giggled, "I'm six."

Rebecca glanced at me, and I hesitated. I didn't correct him.

"Ma'am, I'm going to work on those uniforms, if you gentlemen could bring them down," Thomas offered. "Then Miss Rebecca can wash the dishes."

I gazed at them. "We aren't in a rush. Enjoy your food."

They sat down and finished eating as we talked.

James stood up. "Thank you, folks, for the meal. You don't need to wait on us. I'll get the uniforms. You just show me the washtub and soap, and I'll get them clean."

"We're rather isolated here, so we don't need to worry about neighbors seeing the color of your uniforms."

Thomas got up. "I best go take care of the horses." He left.

Rebecca glanced at Daniel. Blood seeped through the bandage. "Let's check your wound, Mr. Daniel."

Daniel seemed more alert this morning, but he'd lost a lot of blood yesterday and looked exhausted. He flinched when Rebecca touched his arm and grimaced as she redid the bandaging.

"You're lucky the ball didn't shatter the bone," she said. She gave him some more willow bark to chew on for the pain.

Michael and I helped him stand and move back to the sofa. Daniel sat down with a groan. We propped him up with a few pillows and covered him with a light blanket.

Rebecca turned toward Joseph. "Let's take a look at your ankle and knee. Might be good for you to elevate it again today."

I explained, "Evaline became a field hospital two years ago, and again last summer, so Rebecca and I learned a great deal about caring for wounded soldiers."

Rebecca gave Joseph some white willow tea to drink to help ease his pain, then Michael and I got him settled on the other sofa and positioned pillows on a chair to elevate his leg. I covered him with a green and gold eight-point star quilt Emily, Rebecca, and I had stitched together.

A few minutes later, James left with an armful of laundry. Rebecca and Bobby followed to show him the rainwater cistern, tub, and clothesline. Bobby carried the soap flakes.

Suddenly, I was alone with the three men, the two patients talking quietly in the parlor around the corner while Michael and I were in the kitchen. He sat at the table with a cup of coffee. I busied myself with filling a second teapot with Rebecca's shredded willow bark. I sat down to let the tea steep and refilled my teacup.

Michael gazed at me. "We're mighty grateful for your skills in caring for Daniel and Joseph. You and Miss Rebecca are capable nurses."

I nodded, but my stomach felt full of butterflies. I wasn't comfortable being alone with this man. *Does he sense my discomfort?*

Then he leaned forward with a look of deep concern. "So, how soon do you folks plan to leave?"

"What? How do you know..." I clutched my cup of tea and then put it back down. I didn't trust myself to take a sip.

"Ma'am, we saw your big wagon in the barn loaded with a few things you might need on a trip. Your friends appear to be slaves, and if I were in your position, I'd be taking them to freedom, too."

I sighed and stood up. "My sister Emily freed her slaves and made me promise to take them away from Virginia. It was her dying wish."

"Where do you plan to go?" Michael's tone was earnest.

"It's 200 miles north to Philadelphia, Pennsylvania, but that route means going through mountains and forests. It's not quite 100 miles to Baltimore, Maryland, where we can sell the wagon and board a ship for Boston. We can catch the train from there. I think it's the better choice."

Michael nodded. "I agree. It's closer. So, it's just the four of you?"

"Yes, I can't persuade my mother to go with us. She's holding out hope that my father is still alive. I've signed my house away to a couple I've known all my life–Mama Cee and Papa Joe and their son and his wife Susanna. They're the last of the house servants from Evaline. None of them want to go west."

"And they understand the danger of staying here?" he asked.

I sighed. "Yes, as much as anyone can. We've been through a terrible time these past three years. Emily's big plantation house was full of wounded soldiers, some of them so horribly injured that all you could do was offer a cup of water and a prayer. Seeing the town change between Union and Confederate control more times than I can count. Helping slaves dig huge pits to bury the dead. I promised Emily to take these folks to a free state. I'm a schoolteacher and I figure they could use a few out west."

We sat for a few moments in silence, while I fought for composure. "It's dangerous to stay and dangerous to go on the road. I have a shotgun, but I'm no match for stray soldiers or slave catchers." My voice caught in my throat, and I had a sudden thought. "But if I had a couple of soldiers escorting me, that would be a totally different matter."

I looked up at Michael who stared at me.

"What if I promised to care for your brother and your friend, and take them home to your mother on our way out west, and in return, you and James came with us to Baltimore to protect us? Then you could go find your unit."

"That's called desertion, Sarah. We could be court-martialed and shot." Michael shook his head. "I'd have to talk to the others."

I sighed. "You're right. It's a crazy idea. What would my mother say?"

He looked at me. "You would promise to take care of Daniel and Joseph? You just met us."

I exhaled. "It's the right thing to do. If my husband Simon had been wounded and ended up in a northern state, I'd hope someone would care for him. But he died at Manassas, and there was nothing anyone could do to help."

I got up from the table and walked around the kitchen, wiping a few tears from my eyes. I walked in to check on our patients and both were napping, so I picked up their teacups and brought them back to the sink.

When I turned around, Michael was standing by the table. "I can't make this decision lightly. I need to go talk to James." He went outside to find his friend.

I tried to imagine Mother and Simon's objections. Traveling with Yankees? How could I consider such a thing? Yet we shared the same view of the dignity of Blacks and their right to freedom.

Michael returned to the kitchen. An odd mixture of excitement over trepidation tinged his voice. "Your wagon has plenty of room for our two injured men, along with your boy," he said. "The rest of us would need to walk at times to give the horses a rest. All we have are our weapons and small packs. You have six horses, so one of us could ride lookout, and one could drive the wagon. We'd have an extra horse so we could switch horses on the wagon if needed."

Hope stirred in my heart. "Does this mean…"

"We'll see you to Baltimore," he said, the set of his mouth grim. It was obviously he had weighed the risks. "When we get there you can sell the wagon and four of the horses. The Army needs horses. They will fetch a high price, more than enough to buy tickets to Boston. Then you'll let us take two horses, so we can return to our unit. We're not deserters. We want to make sure our brothers are alright, but we can't ask you to take them to Iowa without helping you get to the train."

Tears glistened in my eyes as I gazed at him in surprise. "Michael, you already have it all planned."

"I'm afraid it is a character flaw of mine," he grinned. "My father always encouraged me to plan two moves ahead when we played chess. It seems to have bled over into other areas of my life."

Intrigued, I asked him, "What did you do before the war?"

"I worked with my uncle in his business, selling and repairing wagons and buggies," he replied. "But I plan to study law and practice with my father once the conflict is over."

"You have a good grasp for planning. How long do you figure it will take us to get to Baltimore?" I asked, going to my drawer for paper and a pencil. I began making a list of what I needed to do.

"Four or five days—it depends. With the loaded wagon, we might make eighteen to twenty miles a day. I don't know the territory here." He shrugged. "However, I think we should leave soon. Whoever wins this battle is bound to show up."

"I agree." I sat up straighter. By taking these men into my home, I'd already taken the first steps to align myself with them, to trust them with my life—and the lives of Rebecca, Bobby, and Thomas. They had shown themselves to be honorable. And they could provide protection. I could keep my promise to Emily.

Michael held out his hand with a solemn smile. We shook hands, and if he noticed my hand trembling, he gave no sign.

Then his face became serious. "I would ask for permission if I knew where my regiment was, but we went down the sideroad to your village to avoid a large group of Confederate soldiers heading for us. There was no way for us to double back. James and I talked about this situation—if we run into Union troops, we will surrender ourselves and ask that our brothers be given medical discharges so they can go with you. But I think it's more likely we'll run into Confederate troops."

We shared our plan with the others. Each member of our party nodded their agreement. I didn't need to tell them the journey would be dangerous, or that I needed their help as much as they needed mine. It was equally clear that my friends faced even more danger from men like Mr. Hays. I shuddered, just thinking of his name. Yes, four brave soldiers might balance the odds. I hoped so.

Ten

Quilts and Questions
Gracie

"The world is not in your books and maps, it's out there."
~Gandalf (JRR Tolkien)

Once the holidays were over, we headed back to work. David taught a variety of history courses full-time, and I taught English part-time at Jubilee Community College. Most semesters, I had one or two composition classes and a section of literature three mornings a week.

The night before the semester began, we had dinner at my house. We'd picked up taco salads and lingered at my dining room table polishing off chips and salsa as we chatted. Agatha played with a toy mouse nearby.

David teased me. "How do you juggle it all, Gracie? The newspaper, the museum, the college—and me?"

I held up my trusty planner and clipboard. He'd watched me plan my days. I spent the mornings at the college or newspaper and the afternoons at the museum. "I always find time for you, David, but I've had this routine for several years. It keeps me busy and pays the bills."

David held up his own planner. "So, tomorrow is faculty in-service, Tuesday, we have departmental meetings and faculty committees, and Wednesday is our so-called prep day. I hope to work in my office on Thursday. How about we plan to work on the ACW quilt investigations on Friday afternoons? Once classes start, I'm out at noon on Friday."

I nodded, and we both scribbled notes in our planners.

I looked up. "Isn't this romantic? Planning our weeks together?"

David snorted and reached for the paper bag with our dessert—brownies.

My friends and fellow teachers—Shelly and Tiara—and I compared our holiday breaks in the adjunct office the next day. Shelly and her husband had gone to Des Moines with their two children. "His folks always spoil the kids, but it's okay." Shelly grinned. "They spoil us, too."

Shelly was my lifelong best friend. We'd grown up together and gone to school together from kindergarten through high school. She also taught composition and some other writing courses. We lost touch when she went off to a private college while I stayed in Jubilee Junction. She met and married her husband, got her master's degree, and then they moved back to Jubilee Junction, where she landed a job at the college. Then, when I moved back four years ago, we reconnected.

Tiara was perhaps fifteen years older than us but had become our mentor and friend. She taught Oral Communication, had her own talk show on the college radio station, and had helped incorporate oral history into my quilt exhibits. Her students got credit for helping us capture audio clips describing quilts and family stories about quilts. Tiara was a remarkable teacher, mother to twin girls—both living and working in Iowa City—and widow of a soldier killed in Iraq.

Tiara had a large family with several sisters and brothers and spent the holidays with her siblings and parents in Prairie Falls.

"Samantha brought home her new boyfriend, and he's a nice young man, but he acted like he was terrified of me. I hugged him and said hello, and I could see him stiffen up. I found out my big brother told him I'd scared off three boyfriends. So untrue. I only scared off two," she told us, laughing. "Savannah came alone because her boyfriend had to work—he's a resident. She had lots of stories about him. I've met him, and he's a smart young man who's going to be a surgeon, so he passed the mama test."

Shelly and I laughed.

"Gracie, how about you? Did you have a good holiday break? Did you spend time with David?" Shelly asked.

"We had a wonderful break. David enjoys playing board games, loves the same kinds of movies I do, and likes cats. My family likes him. We saw a movie with Mark and Kathy. We spent a lot of time together over break," I confessed. "I met his parents and family. So far, things are going well."

"Your smile says it all," Tiara told me. "You're in love, girl, and it's wonderful to see you happy."

I couldn't deny that I was falling in love with David.

I conducted more research on the Underground Railroad in Iowa. I told Tiara that Carl, David, and I wanted to show her something at the museum. I arrived first and headed downstairs to my workroom where we'd arranged eight quilts on two long tables. We had identified their patterns as belonging to the era of the Underground Railroad, including the rustic rose quilt from Grandma Molly. I laid out some gloves for her, Carl, and David and put on mine.

David walked in with Tiara. He took her coat and placed it on a chair back.

She asked, "Have you found any clues?"

I grinned. "Yes, and we need your help."

Carl walked in. "Hello all. Thank you for coming, Tiara."

The three of them each donned cotton gloves laid out on the table, standard protocol for handling old quilts.

I gently picked up the red and green quilt. "Let's start by examining this quilt—the one Grandma O'Connor gave us. It's a classic red and green quilt in the rustic rose pattern, made around 1860. See the initials on the border—R. S. and Evaline."

Tiara reached out to touch the quilt with a gloved hand. "Interesting. It's lovely." She picked up one of the other quilts, stared at the borders, and pointed out, "Here it is again—R. S."

Carl and David looked over her shoulder. "Where is it? Oh, I see it."

Tiara's voice rose in excitement. "So, who is this R. S.?"

"We don't know yet," I confessed. "But we think it's someone my third great-grandfather met when he was serving in the Army during the ACW."

I told her about our research.

"You know much more about this era of quilts than I do, Tiara. Or, you know more about the symbols for the Underground Railroad and where we think it came into Iowa. I hoped you could make sense of the fact that we have eight quilts that appear to date back to the 1860s. I didn't think the Underground Railroad made it up into Jubilee County, but we don't really have records," I concluded with more frustration than I meant to convey.

Carl cleared his throat. "Gracie told us you did a major research project in graduate school about the Underground Railroad in Iowa and quilt patterns. Do these all fit?"

Tiara walked beside both tables, looking at each quilt before she answered. "Yes, they do." She picked up each quilt and identified its pattern. But Tiara and I were both struck with the initials on two of the quilts. "I've heard of a few people stitching their name and the date, but not so much their initials." She paused, thoughtfully.

She gazed at the three of us. "Did I ever tell you what prompted my research project in graduate school? It's the story my great-grandma told me when I was just a little girl. She said that one of our relatives was a freed slave who made it to Jubilee Junction with the help of the Underground Railroad. Quilt patterns marked safe houses along the way. This is important work you're doing, so keep it up."

The next week, David and I made a quick jaunt to see Robin, the quilt expert at the Grout Museum in Waterloo. She took us into her workroom where we laid the rustic rose quilt on her workbench. She donned gloves and inspected it. "Yes, this quilt dates to the ACW. I would say early 1860s. The dyes used for the green and red are distinctive, starting with the green. It's called poison green because it's made with copper arsenate, or arsenic, which is toxic.

The red is turkey red, using the root of the Rubia plant as the colorant. This quilt is expert work, and it's in remarkable condition."

"Do you mind?" She picked up her camera and took pictures of the quilt, front and back. "This is exquisite stitching." The colors had faded, and some of the material was fraying, but the quilt was intact.

Robin discussed the rustic rose pattern, the fabric, and the techniques used to construct the quilt. David patiently jotted notes in his notebook.

She paused, flipped the quilt over, and re-examined the bloodstain. "Fascinating. I've never had a quilt with a bloodstain here. It's probably too old to analyze for DNA."

I thanked her, wrapped the quilt in the sheet, and put it back in its protective bag.

"Let me know when you get your answers," she told me.

We promised to keep her updated.

We stopped for coffee and pastries at a nearby coffee shop. David stared at his notebook in deep concentration as he sipped his coffee.

I chuckled. "So, do you plan on taking up quilting? You were taking a lot of notes back there."

David glanced up. "Robin impressed me with her in-depth knowledge about the construction of the quilt, the fabric, and dyes, and that helped pin down the date to the 1860s. I wondered how many hours of work go into making a quilt, how many stitches, and how many hours of cutting out fabric and piecing things together. My grandma had some lovely quilts, but I never thought about who made them or how they were made before I met you."

"Yes, it's a lot of work. My grandma and great-aunts used to babysit me when I was a little girl. They took me to the church quilting club every week. I watched the women work and chat around the big quilt frame, and they gave me little scraps to play with. I loved the pretty fabric and patterns, but I'd get bored. So, I'd make up stories in my head. Grandma started taking along a book for me. I don't think I have the quilting gene or the patience for quilting. I'd rather read a good book, take a walk with a friend, or write something."

David thought about it. "Well, they didn't have modern

conveniences like washers and dryers, refrigerators, television, radio, and the world wide web back then, so I imagine women enjoyed quilting because it was a social thing. Didn't you just say your aunts and grandma gathered with friends to quilt and socialize?"

I regarded this smart man I loved and grinned. "I suppose so. You're saying quilting gave women a chance to sit and chat while working on something of beauty and utility?"

The revelation struck me as I studied his face. *I just admitted I love David, and yes, I do.*

I can't explain why a statement about the social aspects of quilting sounded romantic, but my heart raced as I watched David sip his coffee. I hadn't felt like this since—I tried to remember my feelings for Steve when we first met. Had I ever felt this way before?

David gazed at me. "Yes, I suppose so. What's going on in your brain, Gracie? You have a sweet expression on your face right now. But it's a lovely old quilt."

I tried not to smile like a fifteen-year-old with a crush. "Yes, it is, indeed, but there is so much more I want to know about it. We've established the quilt's age, but we still didn't know who made it. Who is R. S.? What does Evaline mean? What's the story behind the bloodstain?"

David nodded. "We don't have the answers to all of those questions, but we aren't giving up, Gracie."

I shook my head in frustration. "How do we proceed? I feel stuck." David reached over and put his hand on mine. "We keep asking questions and reaching out to your family. We're going to figure this out together."

Apparently, I'm a sucker for a handsome man with gorgeous brown eyes who knows how much I love the word, *together.* Yes, David made me believe we could solve this puzzle together. And as much as that mattered, I realized suddenly that I trusted him.

Eleven

Fried Chicken and A Plan
Sarah

"It's a dangerous business, Frodo, going out your door. You step onto the road, and if you don't keep your feet, there's no knowing where you might be swept off to."

~JRR Tolkien

Sarah's house, a small village ten miles from Winchester
Monday, September 19th, 1864

*O*nce Michael and I shook hands, I felt relief. Surely, I could keep my promise to Emily now.

Michael stood. "Let's take a closer look at your wagon, Miss Sarah."

James returned, listened to our plan, and nodded in agreement. Rebecca and Bobby were in the kitchen, where he read a book while she continued packing.

We walked outside and I introduced them to the dogs while Daniel and Joseph napped. The soldiers knelt, patted the dogs' heads, scratched their ears, and rubbed their bellies.

Michael glanced at me. "Are the dogs coming with us?"

I reached down and patted Duke. "They've been my companions since Simon left for war. I can't leave them behind."

He nodded. "Yes, I understand. They could be valuable in scaring off slave catchers and bushwhackers."

We entered the barn to evaluate the wagon.

"Joseph and Daniel can sit back here with blankets and pillows. There's plenty of room." Michael said, gesturing.

James checked the horses and examined their shoes. "They're up for the trip. Beautiful animals." He walked around the big wagon. "The wagon seems sturdy enough. Can the two women and Bobby fit in here, too, if we need to cross a stream?"

Michael looked at the interior. "Yes, we can fit everyone in the wagon or on the horses."

After more discussion, we returned to the house. I sent Thomas to check on my mother. He rode a horse to her house, five miles away, and when he returned, he reported the rest of the freed slaves were there. She'd made the funeral arrangements for my sister. They were packing up to come to my house later tonight.

Rebecca and I caught two chickens and killed them for supper. I found enough flour and lard to make biscuits. We opened two Mason jars of the green beans I'd canned and two more of preserved peaches. Rebecca fried the chicken while I made the biscuits.

When dinner was ready, we sat down like family to eat and passed dishes back and forth. James and Michael served their brothers. The simple gesture touched my heart.

Bobby squeezed in between me and Michael.

"This is a feast," declared James, and Michael agreed. "Yes!"

"Thank you, ma'am," Joseph and Daniel chimed in, too.

After the meal, James and Thomas helped clear and wash the dishes.

I announced, "Let's sit back down. Michael and I want to talk to you. Thomas, please take this box of Mason Jars filled with water out to the wagon, and Bobby, can you help?" Thomas and Rebecca made eye contact and nodded.

They walked out the back door.

"Before they come back, I need to explain a few things. When my sister died two days ago, she freed her slaves—including Rebecca, Thomas—and Bobby."

The men looked surprised.

"For the journey, we will act as though Bobby is my son to protect him. He's the child of my brother-in-law, George, and Rebecca. She was only fourteen when he raped her. Rebecca's been a wonderful mother, and my sister Emily loved them both and wanted to take them to safety. Mother wisely told me to bring Thomas along to protect us. Rebecca and I will talk to Bobby when he comes back and explain the situation."

Rebecca sat across from me and whispered, "Thank you, Miss Sarah."

The four men glanced at us.

"You're a brave woman, Miss Rebecca—and you, too, Miss Sarah," James spoke up.

"We'll do whatever we can to help," declared Daniel.

I put my hands in my lap so they couldn't see them tremble. "Thank you all. One more thing. Mother is coming later today with four more freed slaves, and they're going to stay here. Mother's large house and the big plantation house will probably get used for hospitals again, as they were last year. We hope they'll be safe here. Now, Michael wants to speak."

Michael glanced around at all of us before speaking. "Eventually, soldiers will move into Winchester—and possibly the village. While we want to rejoin our unit, we can't abandon our brothers or new friends. We may encounter slave catchers or deserters from both sides on our journey, and it will be easier to protect ourselves with five men—including Thomas—when two of those men are injured."

"We'll escort our new friends folks to Baltimore, which is about ninety miles away. Miss Sarah will sell the wagon and four of the horses and book travel by sailing vessel to Boston. From there her party, including Joseph and Daniel, will travel by rail to Iowa. James and I will send a telegram to our folks to expect you all, the we will take the remaining horses and use them to find and rejoin the 24th Iowa, where we will explain our absence and seek a medical discharge for our injured comrades. We leave early in the morning. Does anyone have any questions?"

No one did. I stood and said, "We have work to do. We'd best get to it."

Rebecca checked her bag of herbs then scoured my garden to gather more herbs. James checked on the uniforms he had scrubbed clean and found them almost dry on the clothesline. The four brothers debated whether they should wear their uniforms or civilian clothing on the first leg of our journey, where we'd likely see Confederate soldiers. This is, after all, Virginia. Of course, being caught in civilian clothing in a war zone would make the men vulnerable to espionage charges—punishable by death.

I didn't want the soldiers being accused of being spies by the Confederate Army, but neither did I want Union officers to think they had deserted. I suggested what appeared to be the lesser of two evils, that they start the journey in civilian clothing, then change into their uniforms once we were past Confederate lines. The four men discussed it in low tones in the kitchen, while Rebecca and I talked with Bobby in the parlor.

Rebecca knelt next to Bobby. "You know how you like to play pretend? We're going to pretend Miss Sarah is your mama for this trip. Will you pretend with us?" Rebecca asked him.

His eyes lit up. "Sure. I like to play pretend. But why?"

Rebecca replied, "Honey, hold out your arm."

He did.

"Now, Miss Sarah and I are going to hold out our arms. Which arms look alike?"

Bobby compared arms. "My arm looks like Miss Sarah's arm!"

Rebecca told him, "Yes, you're right. So, we know you're my boy, but we are going to pretend you're Miss Sarah's son for the trip, okay?"

"We're going on a trip with these soldiers. You can call your mama Auntie Rebecca," I suggested.

Bobby nodded, and I thought he'd been dealing with so much his whole life. His white father had acknowledged him a handful of times, giving him a gift on some of his birthdays, but ignoring him the rest of the time. Thomas, Peter, and Papa Joe did their best to help raise Bobby, but they had to be careful to do it when George was not around, or he would get angry.

I walked around upstairs, planning. My mother could sleep with me tonight and then take my room. That left two rooms: one for Peter and Susanna, and one for Papa Joe and Mama Cee. I placed folded clean sheets on top of the beds, deciding to let Susanna and

Mama Cee take care of them. I sorted our linens and found two older sheets to cut up for bandages.

The dogs barked, then stopped. I hurried down the steps to the kitchen as Rebecca opened the back door. It was mother, and the four freed slaves. Rebecca let them in and smiled. "You not gonna believe what Miss Sarah's done now."

I handed the worn sheets to Rebecca. "I don't know how wide to cut these for bandages. Can you please do it? Hello Mother! You folks made it."

They came in, sat down around the big kitchen table, and I explained our plan. James was sitting in the kitchen and stood up to greet the guests.

Michael walked in from the barn, stopped, and greeted the new folks as I introduced everyone.

"This is my mother, Harriett Douglas. Our friends Mama Cee and Papa Joe, Peter, and Susanna. Private James Nelson and Corporal Michael O'Connor. Their brothers Daniel and Joseph are resting in the sitting room, both injured."

Mother turned to Michael. "I take it you're the leader of this expedition?"

Michael nodded and gestured at me. "Sarah's helping me navigate, of course, but she's in charge."

Susanna and Rebecca began cutting and rolling the bandages on the kitchen counter behind us. They looked up in surprise.

"Simon drew a map, and I've been to a few towns, but I don't know the route to Baltimore, so we'll find our way one step at a time," I explained, trying to hurry past the awkward moment when he announced I was in charge.

Mama Cee reminded us, "You all gonna need some help, a safe place to rest, water for them horses, and such. If nighttime, watch for a candle in the window and a quilt square."

Papa Joe nodded at James. "If it was me, I'd take the road to Berryville and keep watch for the Underground Railroad quilt squares. It's about seventeen miles."

Rebecca glanced up from cutting up the sheets. "I'll tell her all about them."

Papa Joe put a can of coffee beans on my counter. I knew it was from his stash at the plantation. "I'll make some coffee in the morning."

Next, I took mother and Papa Joe up to the attic and showed them the trunks I'd brought from the plantation and the things I wanted to safeguard, and they approved. Mother told me she'd done something similar at her house and gazed at Papa Joe.

"Papa Joe's been a big help," she told me. "So has Mama Cee, Susanna, and Peter. Who knows what will happen, but we did our best."

I showed Susanna and Mama Cee their bedrooms and told Mother she could sleep with me.

I told Mama Cee and Susanna I'd left sheets and blankets on their beds, and they headed to their rooms to make their beds. Then I said goodnight and headed for my room, where I quickly donned my nightgown. Mother came in afterward and embraced me.

"Sarah, you've taken on quite a task. I'm so happy you won't be alone."

As we climbed into bed, I listened to the quiet chatter reverberating through the walls. My house was full, at last. Mother gently pulled the blankets over us.

My thoughts turned to Simon. I was leaving the house we'd shared, but I dared not think about it. Images of Emily writhing in anguish and baby George in her arms surged through my mind. I fought not to cry as a guttural moan slipped from my throat.

My mother's hand slipped into mine. "I'm proud of you, Sarah. And I'll be praying for you every day."

"Good night, mother," I squeezed her hand and swallowed. *Will I ever see you again? And what about the Union soldiers? Did I place us all in harm's way by bringing them with us? What made me think a white woman with a Southern drawl, two freed slaves, and a little white boy can elude slave catchers?*

I stared into the darkness as questions raced through my mind, listening to mother's soft, steady breathing comforted by her presence. Then, I prayed, mourning for Simon—and Emily and her son—praying for safety through the night from soldiers on either side, as well as merciless slave catchers. *Lord, help us. Lord, help me.* I listened to mother's soft, regular breathing until I fell asleep.

Tuesday, September 20, 1864

The morning brought a whirlwind of last-minute tasks. We ate a quick breakfast of porridge and coffee. Susanna and Mama Cee made two pans of cornbread for our trip. Once cooled, they wrapped them in tea towels and put them into a canvas bag. Rebecca and I carried down our carpet bags which Thomas and Michael grabbed. Bobby carried his little canvas bag of books with his doll tucked in on top. I had a smaller trunk of clothing and personal effects.

Bobby and my mother fed the dogs and put their bowls in the wagon afterward. Papa Joe's hounds had arrived the night before.

Peter, Thomas, and the soldiers walked out to the barn to check the harnesses, horses, and wagon for any potential problems. They found a small water barrel, filled it, and tied it to the wagon.

Michael and James helped straighten the barn, gathered their packs and rifles, filled their canteens, and stowed everything in the wagon. They helped their brothers climb into the wagon and got them comfortable with pillows and blankets. Michael and James loaded the two bigger trunks, filled with quilts, carpet bags and packs. Peter and Thomas added the third, smaller trunk with my personal possessions. Michael climbed into the driver's seat while James tied one horse to the back of the wagon and climbed on the second horse.

Thomas stood beside the wagon with Bobby and Rebecca, the hounds by his side.

I bid an emotional farewell to Mother, and the four freed slaves, fighting tears. After embracing my mother again, I asked, "Sure you don't want to caravan and come with us? I'm worried about you all. This village may not be as safe as I hoped."

"We gonna be fine," Mama Cee replied serenely, looking at Papa Joe, standing beside her on one side and my mother on the other. "Papa Joe and I don't want to be pioneer people. We look after your mama and enjoy this fine house. Thank you for all you did, child. We gonna help your mama bury Miss Emily and her baby in the family cemetery."

"You'll send a letter or telegram when you're safe?" Mother asked. She examined the piece of paper where I'd written "Michael O'Connor, Senior. Law office, Jubilee Junction, Iowa." It was the closest thing I had to a new address, or destination.

I blinked back tears. *Would I ever see my mother again?*

Mama Cee put an arm around Mother, and I told myself she would be fine. Emily and I had tried to talk our mother into coming with us. She wasn't interested. Now, with Emily gone, it was up to me to take the freed slaves to freedom, far away from Virginia. But I wasn't going to have to do it alone. I was thankful to have my companions.

Papa Joe, Susanna, Mama Cee, and Peter gazed at Thomas and Rebecca, and little Bobby. They shook hands or embraced, exchanged heartfelt words, and then Thomas helped Bobby climb up into the wagon. The soldiers beckoned him to sit with them, between them.

We'd arranged the trunks on either side towards the front. Rebecca had her bag of herbs, and I had my big satchel as well, with my Bible, diary, and reticule tucked down inside. We had blankets and pillows to make the ride more comfortable for the patients.

Papa Joe peered at all of us. "God bless you. You be in our prayers. Take care of each other." He raised one hand in farewell.

Peter added, "And keep them horses watered." Thomas nodded.

Susanna ran over to give Rebecca one more hug. They had been friends ever since either could remember. This parting would be difficult.

Tears threatened my composure. "Thank you all for your help these past few days. Take care of each other and stay safe, too." I found my handkerchief and dabbed my eyes.

Then I looked up at Michael, who slapped the reins, and the horses began pulling the wagon, walking slowly at first.

I called out to the dogs, "Duke and Scout, come!"

Rebecca, Thomas, and I began walking alongside the wagon, the dogs following.

And then we were on our way to Berryville. Whatever lay ahead, we would face it together.

Twelve

Fiction, Frustration and Family Stories
Gracie

"Don't adventures ever have an end? I suppose not. Someone else always has to carry on the story."

~JRR Tolkien

As I slipped into the rhythm of my spring teaching schedule, my M/W/F literature class became a highlight of my week. A group of diligent students consistently read the assignment, spoke up, and discussed the short stories in small groups.

We started the semester with the "Story of an Hour," a short story about a woman who gets bad news from a family friend—her husband has died in a train derailment. She goes upstairs to process the news in her bedroom and suddenly realizes she's now free to live for herself. So, she walks downstairs, head held high, with her sister, when her husband walks in the door, very much alive. She collapses and dies.

The story's conclusion always shocks my students. "Story of an Hour" takes place on just two pages and appeared in *Vogue* in 1894. My students picked up on the feminist themes but seemed surprised when I pointed out how the author incorporates the classic stages of grief in the story—denial, anger, bargaining, depression, and acceptance—eighty years before Elizabeth Kubler-Ross developed the theory.

"We just studied that in our psychology class," Stacie spoke up.

"Yes, I went through all of that when my football team lost homecoming my senior year," Clay commented. Several of his friends laughed.

"What are the first and last things the author tells us about the main character?" I ask.

There was a pause.

"She had a heart condition." Stacie offered.

Joe spoke up. "She died of heart disease—the doctor said, of joy that kills. Man, that's twisted."

"Does it grab your attention?" I asked. "It's important information."

Heads nodded.

"Think about the options for a woman in the 1890s," I told them. "Housewife, maid, shop girl, nurse, or schoolteacher, as long as she stays single. Think about the concept of living for yourself and what that means to you. Then write your response to the story for our next class. Three to five paragraphs."

After class, I reflected on how much life had changed for me since I'd discussed the story last fall. I'd been in a long-distance, unhealthy relationship with my college boyfriend, Steve, creating stress that I'd tried to ignore. I was grieving the end of the relationship for months before we broke up. Then, I met a wonderful man, the new history teacher at the college, and we'd become friends. David and I shared common interests, and he made me happy. More importantly, he treated me like an equal.

Another day, we read a story by Alice Walker, "Everyday Use," written in the early 1970s. It's about a Black family living down south—a single mother with two daughters, Maggie and Dee. Dee moved away to go to college while Maggie stayed home with her mother.

Dee brings her boyfriend home for a visit. She acts like she's superior to her younger sister and mother. However, when she mentions a grandma by name, Maggie can recite the history of the person. Maggie also learned to quilt. Dee wants two quilts, but the mother promised them to Maggie. Dee protests, saying Maggie would be foolish enough to put them on the bed for everyday use. Mama says, what else would you do? Dee says, hang it up, and we see how she has changed.

Dee pouts, but the mother remembers she offered to send a quilt to college, and Dee turned her down. She gives them to Maggie instead, surprising both daughters. Dee talks about knowing your heritage and making something of yourself as if her mother and sister are wasting their lives. She leaves, angry. However, the mother and younger daughter sit and enjoy the sunset as the story ends.

I reminded my students of the mini-series *Roots* in the 1970s and show them a video clip. My Black students often commented on the natural hairstyles and custom of giving children African names that started about the same time.

Darnell snickered. "My grandma had one of those big Afro hairstyles when she was in high school. My dad showed me pictures of her wearing an African dress."

We discussed the idea of understanding one's heritage or knowing your family's history. Dee attended college and learned about her African culture, but Maggie knew their family lineage. Mama knew her family's history and preserved things like the butter churn and old family quilts.

I shared a few highlights about what I'd discovered about my family's heritage. I told them about the California quilt and listening to the cassette tapes with Aunt Violet. Grandma Grace talked about going to California with her twin sisters during World War 2, where they worked at an aircraft factory and a nearby Navy hospital.

The students listened intently.

"Your grandma helped build bombers? Cool!" Rachel said.

"Jubilee Junction didn't have electricity until 1942? I should ask Grandpa about his stories," Joe added.

I chatted with Shelly one day while we both ate quick lunches in the adjunct office. "We're making such slow progress of finding information about the red and green ACW quilt, but don't know who made the quilt. We need to find that missing envelope."

"Keep asking around, Gracie. Someone must know something. Have you talked to your dad? Doesn't he have old newspapers?"

"Yes, but it's hard to search for information without knowing their last names. Did Sarah stay here? Did she leave? R. S. doesn't work for Sarah," I complained. "David says we must be patient, but I'm frustrated. I wanted to create an exhibit, but I can't do it with eight quilts!"

"So, write a column for *The Jubilee Times,* and see if anyone else has an old quilt or family stories about quilts and the Underground Railroad," Shelly suggested. "Tell them you're searching for diaries, letters, quilts, etc."

Tiara walked into the adjunct office. "I thought I heard you two." She put her messenger bag by her desk, sat down, and swiveled to face us.

Shelly explained her idea.

Tiara endorsed it. "What a good idea. I'll mention your article to some of the older folks at the Christian Methodist Episcopal Church. We have several families who go way back in terms of Jubilee Junction history. Why didn't I think of it myself?"

Tiara sat back in her chair and then leaned forward. "Here's another idea. Let me interview you on my radio program this week and explain what you need."

I grabbed a notepad. "Shelly and Tiara, I can always count on you two for ideas. Thanks."

I jotted down some notes and talked to Tiara about going on her radio program. Then I left for the museum.

There, I checked in with Carl. He shared my frustration and liked the idea of the newspaper column and going on Tiara's radio show.

"It can't hurt to ask people to dig around for ACW quilts, letters, and diaries. The Nelson, Carlson, and O'Connor families have been here for generations. Who knows what some of them have in the attic?" he urged. "And Tiara's right about interviewing you on her radio program. You can make a personal appeal for help to find quilts and information."

I headed for my basement workroom to draft the column and send Tiara a text. Meanwhile, upstairs, the Jubilee quilt exhibit was still drawing crowds to town while getting the younger generation more interested in hearing family stories.

Tiara had a radio show every Thursday afternoon. I joined her in the broadcast room. The control room was next door, with a technician and several students. She and I sat at a table with microphones. We rehearsed the questions until it was time to go live.

"Our guest today is Gracie O'Connor. She's an instructor here at Jubilee Junction Community College, so some of you know her. She also works at the Jubilee County Museum, where she designs the exhibits, including one right now with quilts made in Jubilee County. Gracie's here today to ask for your help with her next exhibit. Let's find out more."

Then she interviewed me about my quest for more quilts made during the ACW, Jubilee Junction's role in the ACW, and the mystery of our red and green quilt.

"Please ask your family if they have any old quilts, diaries, letters, or other treasures dating back to the American Civil War in an old trunk in the attic. We need them! Thank you all for your help," I added.

At the end, Tiara told listeners my email address and phone number and signed off.

Tiara nodded. "You did a good job, girl. You'll get more old quilts donated if there are any left to find."

There are several ways to get the word out in a town like Jubilee Junction. We have *The Jubilee Times,* and then there's Aunt Shirley's Cafe, officially known as the Jubilee Junction Café. After work, I stopped by and David met me there. We enjoyed some of her hot soup and fresh muffins for supper. Aunt Shirley stopped at our table to fill David's coffee cup and check in with me.

"Aunt Shirley, have you heard we're working on a new quilt mystery?" I asked.

"Yes, your mother told me about it—Molly's old red and green quilt from the Civil War, right?"

"We need old letters or diaries talking about newcomers to Jubilee during the Civil War. They came back on the train with the Nelson and O'Connor boys, who were both wounded out in Virginia."

David interjected, "Gracie's also collecting more quilts for an exhibit of Civil War quilts."

"I got it. You need Civil War quilts and information. We'll get the word out to other community clubs." She glanced up and added, "See you later," before moving on to another table.

David grinned. "Aunt Shirley's on the case, too."

David had previously talked with Uncle Vern and Aunt Maggie about his research on German prisoners who worked on Iowa farms during WW2. He often mentioned wanting to interview Uncle Vern, and we finally found time for a meal together. Aunt Maggie made her shepherd's pie, a concoction of sauteed vegetables, meat, spices, and cheesy mashed potatoes. David brought along his big notebook, a digital recorder, and extra batteries.

First, we ate, savoring the shepherd's pie, but saved dessert for after the interview. We cleared the dining room table and then sat back down, and David asked all his standard interview questions. I enjoyed seeing him work, professional and yet so warm, putting my Uncle Vern at ease.

Uncle Vern talked about a couple of friends who farmed in Algona and Clarinda, where some of the prisoner of war branch camps were located. Vern deployed to England during the war, but when he returned, he talked to several families who used prisoners on their farms. The prisoners built or improved existing fences, repaired equipment, harvested crops, and detasseled corn. They helped process hemp for rope-making and canned green beans and carrots.

Uncle Vern told David, "I'll give you their names, but they've both been gone for twenty years or more. Chuck and Jim told me the German prisoners were glad to be done with the war, but worried about their families back in Germany. They liked Iowa and being on the farm. They were hard workers, too."

Aunt Maggie and I walked into her kitchen to chat, and to cut big slices of pie for the boys. We figured pie would motivate them to stop talking.

She put the kettle on the stove while I selected a teapot from her collection and put two Constant Comment tea bags inside to brew. She already had a tray on the table, with teacups, plates, forks, and napkins.

Then we sat to chat while the water boiled.

"Your mother mentioned you're working on a new quilt mystery, something about a quilt from the Civil War. How's it going?" she asked.

"We found some information, but I have more questions than answers. I asked Aunt Shirley to help, since so many people go to the cafe."

Aunt Maggie was a wonderful listener. "Asking for help is a smart thing to do, Gracie love. Every family needs to go through a few boxes or trunks from their grandparents. It was also a fine idea to go on the radio. We'll go through our things, but Violet has most of it. I'm sure you'll get more information. Try to be patient."

The kettle whistled. She poured the water into the teapot. I sliced up the pie and put pieces on each plate.

Aunt Maggie got the lemon slices, sugar, and cream ready. She asked, "Have you talked to your Aunt Violet yet?"

"She's on my list. I'll call her tomorrow. This pie looks amazing with that lattice work. Give me another lesson in pie crust, please." Then, my mouth watering, I added, "Let's take the pie out before I grab a fork."

We carried out the trays of tea and pie and placed them on the dining room table.

I made eye contact with David, who chuckled. "We see the apple pie. We're wrapping up. Thanks, Vern. You and I need to chat again."

Uncle Vern nodded. "I'd like that, too."

We ate our pie, and I smiled at my aunt. I always felt better after enjoying a cuppa tea with her.

Thirteen

The Journey Begins
Sarah

"Don't ever stop. Keep going. If you want a taste of freedom, keep going."

~Harriet Tubman

On a road toward Berryville, Virginia
Tuesday, September 20, 1864

Michael drove the wagon slowly down the road while James rode ahead. Scout and Duke scampered alongside Thomas, who said he'd walk for a while. Rebecca and I joined him.

We had the rough map Simon had made for me, but it wasn't really detailed. We took the road to Berryville, as Papa Joe suggested. He estimated it would take us about four hours and warned us to evade either army, slave catchers, or stray soldiers.

As we took off, Rebecca called, "Remember, I'll be watching for candles and quilt squares."

"Yes, and what quilt squares are those?" I asked. Emily and my mother had been the quilters in our family.

"For the Underground Railroad. Slaves escaping the south use the patterns to guide them to safety," she replied.

"What kinds of patterns?"

"There are at least twelve kinds. It's a code. Sometimes you'll see a quilt through the front window, or maybe over the railing on a front porch. At night, some people add a candle. We hear there are several barns around with a quilt square painted on it." Rebecca listed the quilt squares and explained what each symbol meant.

Michael joined the conversation, handling the reins. "I've heard of quilt squares, and I've seen a few, but didn't know what they meant."

I glanced behind. "Rebecca, how are our patients?"

She replied, "Daniel's dozing, and Joseph's awake and watching behind us. I'll check Daniel's dressing at our next stop."

An hour later, we stopped for a brief break. We ate a piece of cornbread and drank some water. The women walked one direction to do our business. The men waited for us to return and then walked another direction. Thomas took Bobby with him.

Papa Joe sent a couple of Mason jars filled with coffee, and Michael took a drink from one. "What excellent coffee!"

We got back on the road and started moving. I sat by Michael, and we chatted for another hour. Thomas and Rebecca walked beside us.

When the dogs started barking, James rode ahead to see what agitated them. He returned to us and said, "Something going on ahead. Two men are riding around in a wooded area. They're shouting, and they have a couple of dogs."

We stopped. Faint shouts, barking dogs, and horses' neighing came from farther down the road. Scout and Duke barked and looked at Thomas for permission to run towards the sound. He held them back with a gesture.

Rebecca got my attention. "Miss Sarah, Mr. Michael, that sounds like slave catchers. Some poor soul's getting hunted like an animal."

Thomas spoke up. "Yes, sir, I agree."

Michael asked, "Sarah, get your gun." He glanced at James. "Let's see what's going on."

He got down from the wagon, untied the spare horse, and climbed up.

"I hate slavery. If I can save a slave, I will." Then he told Thomas. "You're in charge."

Thomas climbed up to the driver's seat. He told the dogs to lie down. He glanced around, alert, as he held the reins.

I grabbed my shotgun and stood by the wagon, my heart

pounding. *Who or what was ahead? Were we in danger? Were slaves being hunted?*

Michael and James rode off.

Thomas glanced around us, alert. "I wonder who it is? It couldn't be old man Hays, could it?"

Rebecca drew a quick breath. "I hope not."

A few minutes later, we heard more shouting—and a shot, and we all lurched upward, including Bobby, who woke up. Rebecca climbed back into the wagon and comforted him. I climbed up, too, and sat beside Thomas, my heart pounding.

The injured soldiers grabbed their guns. The dogs stood up and barked and ran ahead of us and then back.

I passed the shotgun to Thomas. He stood up, staring off into the distance, glancing to his right and left. We heard horses coming toward us, and Michael galloped to us with a small body in his arms, clinging to him for dear life. Michael lifted down a small Black girl, maybe four years old. She wore a dirty dress, was barefoot, and sobbed for her mother. Thomas handed me the gun and lifted the child onto the wagon.

Rebecca opened her arms, and the girl crawled to her, whimpering. Thomas got a rag and wet it from a jar of water and Rebecca cleaned her up, making soothing noises. She had deep scratches on her arms and legs.

Michael glared into the distance, his eyes watchful and full of fire and fury. "We saw two men were chasing the girl and her mother like they were animals. James fired a warning shot in the air, and it spooked their horses. One horse galloped off, and his rider ran after him with the dogs. The other man swore and ran after his partner, his horse racing around aimlessly. The mother lifted the girl up to me and begged us to take her. James waited with the mother to make sure those men didn't double back."

I shifted in my seat and suggested Rebecca find the hardtack biscuits and a cup of water. Thomas poured some water from a Mason jar into the tin cup.

How could anyone chase down a little girl? I seethed. *What would they do once they caught her?*

Bobby patted the girl's leg as Rebecca talked to her. Rebecca gave the child a piece of hardtack, and she gobbled it down as if she hadn't eaten for some time. Thomas got her some more water, and the little girl drank it down rather quickly. She ate several more pieces and sighed.

The dogs barked, alerting us to an approaching rider. We all looked down the road. I clung to the reins and and raised my shotgun. Thomas stood beside the wagon, his hands balled into fists.

It was James. He returned with a young woman not much older than Rebecca behind him, clasping his waist. She wore a torn dress and was barefoot. Michael helped her down from the horse and lifted her onto the wagon.

Rebecca offered her some water and food. She accepted, sinking down to the wagon bed, breathing hard. Tears streaked down her thin face, but she didn't make a sound until she saw her daughter. Michael and James wheeled around and headed off at a fast pace. The dogs got excited, but Thomas called them back.

The little girl saw her mama and reached for her. Her mama glanced at her, "Oh, child, you all nice and clean and your mama all dirty." Rebecca handed her a wet washcloth, and she wiped off her arms and legs as best she could. She, too, had deep scratches on her arms and legs.

When she got her breath, she told us, "Thank y'all. You saved us from a nasty man who does bad things to the slaves he catches. Everybody was leaving my plantation. I took my baby, packed a bag, and snuck off two days ago. Somehow, those wicked men found us. They been chasing us ever since. We fell once or twice, and I lost my bag, but I not gonna lose my child. My name is Lucy, and this is my daughter, Chloe."

We introduced ourselves. Rebecca opened a nearby trunk, glanced at Lucy, and announced, "Gentlemen, close your eyes. Lucy is putting on a new dress."

The men obeyed, and Lucy protested, "Oh, miss, I can't take your dress. It's right pretty."

Rebecca gazed at her. "Your dress is torn and dirty. This is Miss

Sarah's old dress, and we have more, so let's put it on." Her voice took on an air of authority rivaling my best school-marm voice.

Lucy slipped off the old dress, and Rebecca and I saw her back, scarred with lashes. I winced. *Those weren't fresh lashes. This woman has been beaten repeatedly.* Rebecca slipped the new dress over Lucy's head and helped her adjust it. When Lucy was decent, Rebecca spoke again. "All right, you can open those eyes. Thank you, gentlemen." She handed a comb to Lucy and a few minutes later, Lucy was cleaning up to be a beautiful young lady as she combed her daughter's curls.

Before long Michael and James returned. "We need to get moving. The slave catchers ran off after their horses, but they'll be back." I climbed out with help from Thomas. The wagon started moving. James' horse trotted alongside the front of the wagon, the dogs following him. Thomas and I walked beside the wagon.

Lucy asked, "Where you folks going? I didn't know where to go. I saw others leaving and knew we had to leave, too."

Rebecca glanced at Daniel and Joseph, who nodded. I told her, "Yes." Already, Bobby and Chloe were talking away like best friends. Rebecca opened the trunk next to her and found Bobby's nightshirt and her sewing kit. She hemmed up the nightshirt.

She showed it to Lucy. "What do you think?"

Lucy replied, "It's clean, and I dropped my bag. So, yes, please."

Lucy called her daughter over and took off her dress. Chloe was painfully thin. Rebecca handed her mama the washrag, and Lucy finished cleaning her up and slipped on the nightdress. *We'll find her more clothing later.* Rebecca folded up the dirty clothes and put them in the trunk. Then she grabbed her bag of herbs, found a little jar, and offered it to Lucy.

"It's a special cream for scratches and scars," she explained. Lucy thanked her and dabbed a few places on Chloe's arms and legs before applying it to herself.

Rebecca opened the trunk and found a blanket. She handed it to Lucy, who wrapped it around herself and her daughter.

"Back to your question. These soldiers are escorting us to Baltimore, where we'll board a boat to Boston. Then we get on a train and travel west to Iowa. That's where the soldiers are from. Want to come with us?"

Lucy lowered her eyes. "I don't have no money for a ticket."

I told her, "We've some money, and we're going to sell the wagon and four of the horses. We can get your tickets."

Lucy said, "Thank you, ma'am. I'm a hard worker, and I can clean and cook real good. I sew and make quilts. Chloe's a good girl and she don't cry much. I appreciate everything you all done for us."

Rebecca asked her, "You like to quilt? So do I." They chatted softly.

An hour later, we stopped for a rest. I broke chunks of cornbread off for each person, and they got a drink of water from the Mason jars filled with water. Thomas climbed into the wagon and rested in the corner by the soldiers.

He'd given me back the shotgun and held out his arms to the children. They crawled on his lap, snuggled down, and fell asleep, Chloe with a thumb in her mouth and the other hand hanging onto Bobby. Rebecca covered them with a blanket and told him, "Thank you," with the sweetest expression on her face.

I realized then what had been in front of me all along. Thomas and Rebecca loved each other. Back at Evaline, he'd told me he couldn't leave them. He loved children, and they loved him. Chloe and Bobby had fallen asleep in his arms, and I couldn't help but wonder if either child had ever experienced much kindness from a man, Black or white.

I hope he and Rebecca will have a long life together, unlike my experience with Simon. Bitter tears spilled down my cheeks, and I turned away so the others wouldn't see them.

A few minutes later, Thomas laid the sleeping children near the soldiers, almost snoozing. He climbed down and helped me and Rebecca down from the wagon, and the three of us walked.

Later, Michael called back, "Daniel, check your pocket watch. How long have we been moving?"

Daniel replied, "About four hours. It's almost noon now. I think Berryville was four hours away."

We passed through the outskirts of a small village.

Then Rebecca spoke up, "Mr. Michael? I see something over there and it's good news—a log cabin patch. Someone will help."

We approached a farmhouse with an unlit candle in the window and a quilt draped over a chair on the front porch. Michael pulled over to investigate.

The front door opened, and a large man stepped outside. "Do you friends need help?" he asked, studying us. He had a kind face and a full beard.

Michael replied. "Yes, please. We could use a place to rest and water our horses."

The man walked down the steps. "I'm Reverend Williams. Follow me, please. I have a big barn back here—it's our church." He led us back to the barn, a welcome sight, with a cross at the top and a small quilt square painted underneath.

We followed him, and he opened the double doors. Once inside, Rev. Williams lit a lantern and shut the doors. The barn smelled of sweet hay. James got down from his horse.

"This is lovely. We have blankets. We'll rest and then get back on the road," I told him. "Thank you, Reverend Williams."

Michael climbed down from the wagon and James dismounted from his horse.

Rev. Williams surveyed our group and smiled. Then he saw the young slave woman and her little girl—barefoot and frightened. He told them, "You're safe here, I promise."

He glanced at Michael. "Run into some slave catchers? A couple of them roam these parts."

Michael was still angry. "Yes, this woman and her child needed help. Two men chased this mother and her little one like they were animals." He shook his head. "So, we created a distraction and rescued them."

Rev. Williams put a hand on his shoulder. "You did the right thing." Then he gestured to me. "Do you see the two chests marked *for missions*? You'll find clothing inside. There are shoes in the barrel. Our congregation keeps it stocked. You folks rest. We'll come back with food."

He pointed. "Go out this side door, and there's a privy for the ladies and another one for the men. You'll find a water supply in both corners—one for the horses, and one for the humans, along with a pitcher and glasses on the table. Hide in the loft or use the emergency exit in the back corner if there's trouble. The exit takes you to a trapdoor leading to a tunnel, going out into the woods. Most of our folks enter from the tunnel and trapdoor."

Rev. Williams lit a lantern and put it on the table. A dozen chairs arranged around the large table invited me to sit down and rest. That is when I realized he hosted slaves regularly—and this was my first stop on the Underground Railroad.

Fourteen

Aunt Violet's Discovery
Gracie

"We dance round in a ring and suppose, but the secret sits in the middle and knows."

~Joseph Frost

Late January 2013—Friday

$\mathcal{O}$ne morning as I was filling Agatha's water dish, I got a call from Aunt Violet. I'd chatted with her the previous week, after my talk with Aunt Maggie.

"I have some boxes of things I need to sort," she'd told me then. "This is good timing. During the winter I can't work in the garden. I have several boxes of family papers in the guest room and will start working on them."

She'd promised to watch for any information about the two Nelson brothers, who had gone to war with their friends, the O'Connor brothers.

Now Aunt Violet sounded excited. "Gracie, how are you? I found something you might want. It's a telegram from my great-grandfather, Michael, to his mother that said two soldiers were injured and they were taking the train home with Sarah."

"Wonderful. I can stop by today after I leave the museum. Let me see if David can come along, okay?"

"Yes, I'd love to see you both. Let me know if he can join us," she replied. "Take care, Gracie!"

I checked my planner where I had scribbled down David's class schedule. His last class ended at 3:30, and I'd finish at the museum by 4:00. I sent him a text.

He responded,

`"Yes! Meet you there."`

I found it hard to focus until I could see the telegram. I taught my classes but wanted to talk to someone about this development. Tiara was at a workshop, and Shelly had students in her office, so I couldn't chat with either friend.

I stopped at Aunt Shirley's and picked up a club salad and headed for the museum where I told Carl about the telegram.

He replied, "I can't wait to see it. Wait. Here's a folder with a plastic sheet to protect the document if your aunt lets you take it. Otherwise, take pictures."

David and I met at Aunt Violet's apartment around 4:20. As she opened the door, Beatrix peeked out behind her—a gray tabby kitten, a gift from Uncle Vern and Aunt Maggie from last fall.

We sat down in Aunt Violet's living room where she had an opened banker's box with a scattering of documents on the coffee table. Aunt Violet handed me a large mailing envelope. Inside was the telegram.

"Be careful, Gracie. It's old and fragile." Aunt Violet watched me. "Thank goodness you have the protective sheet."

I slipped on a pair of gloves, placed the telegram inside the protective sleeve, and then squinted to read it. "Daniel & Joseph injured. Coming home on the train w Sarah & friends. Michael & James." The paper was brittle.

David glanced over my shoulder, trying to read with me.

"Sarah? How do you fit into this puzzle?" I pondered aloud.

David told me, "It's a clue. Now we know someone helped the two wounded soldiers get back home. What's the date?"

I checked it. "It's sort of smeared. Looks like September something 1864." I replied. "Aunt Violet, do you know anything about Joseph and James Nelson, who left for the Civil War with Michael and Daniel O'Connor?"

Aunt Violet thought for a minute. "I have four boxes of old family papers. They should all go to the museum, but first, I want to sort them out. So far, I haven't found letters or diaries, but I'll ask Vern and Maggie."

I hugged her. "It's one more puzzle piece, Aunt Violet. Thanks."

David hugged her, too. "Keep digging. I bet you find more treasures in those boxes!"

We got into the car, where I held the plastic sheet. Something hit me. I turned to David. "We checked Michael's military records, but not anyone else's. If the boys were injured, the Army would have discharged them early, wouldn't they? What about James?"

David nodded. "We need to talk to Carl, but we'll have to wait until tomorrow, Gracie. The museum is closing in half an hour."

I replied, "Carl wanted to see this telegram. I'm going to send him a text and a photo."

A moment later my phone *pinged*. I checked the text, grinned, and showed the screen to David.

David sighed. "Okay. To the museum."

Carl waited at the back door. As soon as we walked in, he extended his hand toward me. "Hand it over, Gracie." He took the fragile document and ran with it to the photocopier/scanner.

David and I glanced at him. "You'd think he'd never seen a telegram from 1864," I joked.

We sat at a table in Carl's office. He handed me a plastic folder with two copies of the telegram, along with the original. I took it. He stared down at his copy. I gave David the other copy, and we all read the document.

"This is a significant find." Carl's voice was incredulous. "It makes you wonder what else your aunt's got in those boxes."

"Yes, I know. I wanted to sit down and grab a box."

David reminded me, "She's going to give the museum the contents of her boxes. She wants to sort through it all first."

We discussed the telegram's simple message and its ambiguities.

"Daniel & Joseph injured. Coming home on the train w Sarah & friends. Michael & James." David read out loud, then mused, "Why doesn't he name each person? Of course, back then you paid for each word in telegrams."

I sighed. "Who is Sarah? I want to know more about her."

David agreed, "I know, Gracie. But we're getting closer to our answers."

Then Carl checked the other three men's records.

Private Joseph Nelson—medical discharge, Nov. 1864.

Private Daniel O'Connor—medical discharge, Nov. 1864.

Private James Nelson—Discharged 1865.

David thought out loud, "Okay, Joseph and Daniel sustained injuries in combat. Sarah is escorting them home—with friends. Where was the telegram sent from? Any ideas?"

We stared at the telegram again. "I don't see." I squinted.

Carl stared at his copy. "Well, keep digging, Gracie. I think the original should stay here. Ask both sides of your family to check for diaries, letters, or anything else to help us untangle the puzzle here."

I handed the original to Carl for safekeeping. *Someone knows something more, but who?*

The days ticked by into February, with no fresh breaks with the ACW quilt. I kept busy with my routine of teaching, grading, and prepping for my college classes, while working at the museum and writing articles for the newspaper. David spent his days with classes, committees, prepping, and grading.

My column asking for help with locating more ACW-era quilts ran in the next edition. We gathered an additional ACW-era quilt from a relative and another quilt from a friend's family, so now we had ten, not counting the red and green mystery quilt. People also donated quilts from the turn of the century, letters and diaries, and several old photo albums.

In the meantime, we'd discovered another mystery. One quilt had the name "Lucy" embroidered on the border, and one had "Rebecca." *Who was Lucy—and Rebecca?*

I checked the newspaper archives at *The Jubilee Times*, but a fire had destroyed some of the oldest papers around the turn of the 20th century. I'd gone on several databases searching for census data. However, without last names for Sarah, Rebecca, or Lucy, I had little luck.

I talked to my parents one evening after supper, filling them in on our progress so far. I showed them my copy of the telegram, and they listened intently.

Dad got out his reporter pad and jotted down the names of the four soldiers and the women—Sarah, Rebecca, and Lucy. "I'll do some more digging at the office. We've some of those older papers on microfilm. We can contact the Iowa Historical Museum in Des Moines, because they have the older newspaper archives."

Mom asked, "I wonder if I should offer to help Aunt Violet with those boxes?"

"Thanks." I hugged them goodbye.

David and I met for coffee and brainstorming at Aunt Shirley's the next day.

Aunt Shirley stopped to take our orders herself and greet us. "How's your Civil War quilt search?"

"We're sort of stuck. We've some information, but not enough."

She took our order and came back with it. Then she made eye contact with one of her daughters and joined us at our table.

"Don't give up. I believe we need to preserve our past. I wish I had something juicy to give you besides my food." She smiled. "Keep asking. Remember, the Civil War came along not even a decade after our Nelson, O'Connor, and Carlson ancestors settled here." Aunt Shirley was a member of the Carlson family, one of the original three founders of the town.

"Thank you," David said.

"Yes, thanks. I have ten quilts now, but I need at least twice as many for an exhibit. Three women came back with the injured soldiers: Sarah, Lucy, and Rebecca, but we don't have their last names," I told her.

She scribbled it down on her order pad.

Aunt Shirley stood up, smiling at both of us, and told me, "Be patient, Gracie."

David began eating his cranberry orange muffin. "Aunt Shirley could be a motivational speaker, you know? I feel better already."

He glanced at me, stirring my iced tea. "Gracie—are you okay?"

"I'm an idiot." I sighed. "Aunt Shirley is from the Carlson family. I've talked to the O'Connor's and the Nelsons, but I haven't checked in with the Carlson family. They might have some information."

I explained my mother was a Walters, and my father an O'Connor, of course. But my Grandma Grace's mother, Virginia Grace, had been a Carlson, and her father, Patrick, was a Nelson, so I had some distant Carlson cousins, like Aunt Shirley.

"I need to talk to Aunt Violet." I got out my phone and walked to the entryway and stepped outside before I called her. "Aunt Violet, who do you know at the Prairie Fields Apartments from the Carlson family? Could you ask them to look for old quilts, photos, and letters?"

"Well, let me think. Ruth Carlson lives out here," Aunt Violet responded. "Ruth's rather deaf, so I'll go see her and check back with you tomorrow, Gracie."

"Thanks, Aunt Violet. Love you." I walked back to the table and sat down.

"Okay, Aunt Violet's going to talk to a woman tomorrow. She said the lady is deaf, so she's going to go visit her in person."

David finished his muffin and was checking out my scone.

I pushed the plate over to him. "I don't deserve a scone."

David broke the scone in half and gazed at me while he put on a wild, over-the-top Shakespearean accent, earning him a smile. "Milady, wilt thou split a scone with your unworthy suitor?" I grabbed half of the scone he was offering and ate it.

Aunt Shirley walked by. "Young love is so sweet." She delivered another scone to our table. "This one's on me, Gracie."

David broke it in half, and I ate my half.

"Now what?" I asked.

"Let's sort through all the correspondence that has piled up since your article came out," David suggested. "Then I need to grade papers and get ready for classes."

We returned to my workroom, divided up the stack of papers between us, and sat down at opposite ends of one of my long tables. I got out some sticky notes and pens. We sorted everything with dates and put them into piles from the newest to the oldest. We found things from the 1870s, 1880s, and 1890s, but only a handful from the 1860s. Later, I would assign each artifact a control number and create a spreadsheet record.

After an hour, I reached the bottom of my pile, finding nothing exciting. Then I noticed one more piece of paper, stuck to another document. I picked it up—a clipping torn in half; the print had faded, so it should get tossed into the pile of unimportant documents, but I hesitated. I stared again, squinted, and grabbed my full sheet magnifying glass.

Was I seeing right? *Michael O'Connor marries*—but the article was ripped in half, so information was missing. The headline identified the groom—but not the bride. I couldn't decide if I should show it to David, who was plowing through his own pile. I set it aside, more frustrated than ever. Was it my great-great-grandfather's wedding announcement? If so, who did he marry?

Fifteen

The Kindness of Strangers
Sarah

"… there ain't no journey what don't change you some."
~David Mitchell

The Williams' barn near Berryville, Virginia
Tuesday, September 20, 1864

Michael and James talked with the minister and shook hands, thanking him. Thomas took the dogs out for a short walk and got them watered. I dug in my bag, found my warm shawl, and wrapped it around me.

Rebecca led Lucy and her daughter across the way to the chests. Lucy was shy, but Rebecca found two dresses, a nightgown, underwear, and shoes for Chloe, who danced around with a dress in her arms. Rebecca found clothes for Lucy and a canvas bag to put the clothes in.

Joseph and Daniel called Bobby over and entertained him until Thomas returned with the dogs. Then Bobby climbed down to explore the barn with his four-legged friends.

I filled the pitcher with water from the pump and took our patients a glass of water. Daniel seemed warm again, so I found Rebecca's bag and gave him some white willow bark to chew. He thanked me with a smile.

"Rebecca will check your bandage in a few minutes," I told him.

"She's an excellent nurse," Daniel exhaled and then got to work chewing the bark.

Joseph was squirming with discomfort, so I handed him some white willow bark as well. Both settled back, chewing the bark, trying to relax.

Rebecca, Lucy, and Chloe came back to the wagon, climbed up, and showed us their finds. Lucy was in tears. "I never met such wonderful people." She put her bag of clothing down and embraced Rebecca.

I told Rebecca I'd given both patients some white willow bark, and she thanked me. "You did the right thing. I'll ask for hot water and a teapot, and make tea from the bark, because that works well."

I gestured to the chests. "Find anything for Bobby or you?"

Rebecca glanced at me and replied. "We have plenty, thanks to Emily. Other people need those things more."

I regarded her bare feet. "What about shoes? When you're done here, go back and find yourself shoes. I would, but I don't know your shoe size." That was the one thing we forgot about—shoes. Fortunately, Thomas could wear my late husband's.

She relented. "Let me check our men first."

Daniel was tired from the ride. Rebecca checked his wound, which was reddish, so she repacked it with the yarrow herbs to promote healing. Then she wrapped his arm and shoulder with new bandages. Afterward, she checked Joseph's foot and knee—still swollen. We found some rags, got them wet, and laid them across his foot and knee.

"I'm so glad you're here and know what to do, Rebecca. You've been a big help. "

She smiled. "I'm glad to help, Miss Sarah. If I was white, I might go to school to become a nurse."

"I wish you could, Rebecca, but you're already a wonderful nurse," I told her. "You've picked up on everything the doctors talked about the last three summers. Your knowledge of herbs will fascinate Joseph's father, an herbal doctor. Michael told me that Dr. Nelson learned from the local Meskwaki healers."

Michael and James helped Thomas take care of the horses, grateful for water and hay. Rebecca took Bobby to the barrel and found pairs of shoes for both. They walked back to the wagon, wearing their new shoes.

Scout and Duke padded around the barn and got their share of pats, then came seeking their mistress. I bundled my shawl around me and sat on a chair set away from the table. The dogs lay down at my feet, and I dozed.

I woke to knocking on the barn door. Then I heard voices and chairs sliding. Rev. Williams and several other people arrived, with food.

"You awake, Miss Sarah? I mean Mama?" Bobby asked. "The preacher man brought food."

Standing up, I yawned. "I didn't mean to doze off."

I walked to the table. Daniel and Joseph joined us with their brothers' help.

Michael told me, "We're lucky to find this place. The pastor's coming back later to talk about the best route, but he's seen several Confederates skulking nearby earlier."

Rebecca poured some concoction into teacups and passed it to the two patients. "Drink up. It won't taste good, but it's a form of the white willow bark tea."

Our host family brought out thick slabs of cheese on wheat bread. Beans and molasses. Coffee. Apples and oatcakes.

After lunch, the women cleaned up the table, gathered the dishes, and washed them in the tub by the well, while Thomas, Michael, and James groomed the horses.

We heard a commotion outside—and the sound of horses approaching. Inside, Scout and Duke barked several times, sounding urgent, and moved to the doors.

Michael climbed the ladder to the hayloft to look out the window. He jumped down. "Two men are arguing with the minister. Thomas, Rebecca, Lucy, and Chloe, please hide in the haymow and be quiet. Everyone else, carry on down here."

Thomas grabbed Chloe as the three adults scampered up the ladder to the hayloft and hid.

James and Michael brought two horses up front and got the box of grooming tools. They began combing them, removing burrs from their manes, and cleaning their tails. Daniel and Joseph produced a deck of cards and sat at the table, playing cards.

The dogs stood alert by the doors, looking at me.

Bobby and I stared at each other. I led him over to the pump, grabbed a washcloth, had him take off his shirt, and gave him a good scrubbing.

Duke and Scout barked as someone knocked on the door.

"Anybody inside?" A man snarled just outside the barn.

Then we could hear Rev. Williams say, "It's just a few travelers. We don't need to bother them."

The first man disagreed. "We need to check. There's escaped slaves in the area."

The barn door opened, and we went into action.

Michael came over and patted my shoulder. "Bobby, you let your mama wash you up good, son," he drawled in a southern accent.

He winked.

Bobby replied, "All right, Daddy. But I don't like her washing my ears."

Michael recognized the visitors in the doorway. "Good morning, Rev. Williams. Got visitors?" in the same southern accent.

Rev. Williams replied. "Yes, brother, I was just telling these fine gentlemen they're wasting their time. No escaped slaves here."

A man stepped into view in the barn's entrance, and Michael's eyes narrowed.

Michael walked over to block the man's view of the barn's interior.

Dressed like a gentleman, the man's long, dark hair hung down over his shoulders, and his beard concealed his mouth. He carried a short coil of rope in his left hand. I recognized him as Mr. Hays. He might have been handsome as a younger man, but time and cruelty had done their work.

The man stared at Michael. "How many people are in this group? Have you seen any runaway slaves on your travels?"

Michael told him, "There's me, my wife and our boy, my brother and his two friends, and our dogs, of course. We ain't seen no slaves, mister." The dogs were alert, waiting for a command.

I realized the two men playing cards now held their rifles upright.

The man stiffened and turned to leave. "If you see any runaway slaves, you tell the good reverend here. He knows how to reach me."

Rev. Williams replied, "I'm certain they will."

A second man's voice outside said, "We musta missed them, Rufus." The door closed.

We all breathed easier.

I gazed at Michael, shaken. "That was the man who chased Lucy and Choe? I've never seen him up close, but that's Rufus Hays."

He nodded. "Yes. Both of you did a good job."

Bobby stared at me, his eyes big. I helped him dress and embraced him. "We won't let anything happen to your mama, Thomas, Lucy, and Chloe, don't worry."

Michael peeked out the door. "They're leaving."

Thomas peered out the window from the hayloft. "I saw them men before. They hunt runaway slaves. That's crazy Mr. Hays."

He carried Chloe down the ladder, and Rebecca and Lucy followed. The little girl clung to Thomas while he talked to her, reassuring her she was safe.

He sat down, still holding Chloe, and called the dogs over. They licked his fingers and Chloe's hands. Thomas talked and encouraged Chloe and Bobby to pat the dogs, and the children calmed down.

I spoke up. "I don't think we're going back on the road today."

Michael sighed. "I'm afraid you're right."

A few minutes later, Rev. Williams came in. "I'm so sorry."

Michael asked him, "Does he come here often?"

The minister sighed, "No, he travels around the state. Mr. Hays comes here about every two months. He hasn't found any of my visitors. Most of them come through the tunnel in the woods."

"Do you think it's safe for us to travel further today?" Michael asked.

The minister replied, "No. Wait for tomorrow. I think they'll get tired and leave."

We occupied ourselves. The patients played euchre. The children played with the dogs, with Thomas keeping a careful watch.

Rebecca asked for some hot water. When Rev. Williams' teenage son brought it, she made more tea with the willow bark, letting it steep. She poured cups for Joseph and Daniel, who sipped it gratefully.

Rebecca checked her bag of herbs and found several in short

supply. She talked to our hosts about whether several plants were in the woods nearby. She and the Williams boy left the barn, and when they returned two hours later, they had three baskets full of plants.

"We found everything on the list," she said. "We also discovered some chamomile."

She put the baskets down on the table, and I peered inside, trying to identify them. She pointed out each one, identifying yarrow, lavender, and white willow bark.

The William's boy grinned and told her he was glad to help. "I've seen all those plants and trees before, but didn't know I could use them for healing. I wish you were staying longer, because I'd like to learn how to help people with those herbs." He seemed wistful.

Rebecca told him, "I learned about herbs from Mama Cee, a woman back at Evaline, my plantation. She took me herb picking with her when I was a little girl and showed me how to find and use them. Mama Cee learned how to use herbs to heal as a young woman captured by the Cherokee. But she told me all native people used plants for pain, stomachaches, and to heal wounds."

I gazed at her. "I've never heard the story of Mama Cee being held by the Indians."

"She doesn't talk about it much. Mama Cee was a young teenager and held captive for three years. Fortunately, they were kind to her. Papa Joe found her and came with the master and traded bales of cotton for her. I arrived at Evaline as an infant, an orphan, and she and Papa Joe took care of me and became my folks. I don't remember being anywhere else," Rebecca said.

A shadow crossed her face that I wasn't sure I'd seen, but I thought I knew what she was thinking. Her skin was a lighter brown, and she had fine features. Rebecca's father had almost certainly been white, and her mother was a slave.

Rebecca asked for some paper and a pencil, which I fetched out of my big bag. She wrote instructions for how to use two herbs: chew white willow bark for pain or make tea, and pack yarrow in wounds to help stop the bleeding. "You can also use yarrow to make a poultice," she told the boy, and gave him generous samples of both.

"Go to the nearest bookseller and ask for a book on natural herbs and healing," Rebecca told him. Then she dug in the trunk and showed him the book Emily had purchased for her. It was her prized possession.

As they chatted, Daniel and Joseph spoke up about how her methods helped.

"I wasn't sure about chewing on bark, but it helped with the pain," Daniel admitted. "I thought the tea helped, too."

Joseph added, "We sleep better after we chew the white willow bark. She's a smart young lady."

We read a few books with the children.

Rebecca and I checked Daniel's bandages, changed them, and made him comfortable. We examined Joseph's injured ankle and knee. We put more wet rags on his leg to relieve the swelling. She poured the rest of the white willow bark tea into a Mason jar to take with us the next day.

When it was time for supper, I noticed how Lucy and her daughter savored every bite of food and thanked Rebecca for her alertness.

After our meal, we cleaned up, thanking our host, his wife, and their two children. Then we settled down for the night.

Thomas and Lucy took care of the children, getting them bedded down, and Bobby and Chloe fell asleep holding hands. Rebecca and I checked on the patients and got them settled. Then we found places to rest. She slept near Lucy and the children. Thomas slept a respectful distance away. Michael and James slept near the wagon to watch the door, and I slept between the two groups.

Wrapping my shawl around me and then the blanket, I lay down and wept for my sister and her poor baby, for Simon, and for fear and worry of what lay ahead. Then I heard whimpering, and Scout's muzzle was nuzzling my hand. The two dogs lay near me, comforting me.

Wednesday, September 21, 1864

As the sun rose, our hosts brought a hearty breakfast. We thanked them, ate the food, and helped clean up.

We repacked the wagon, refilled our Mason jars with water, and hitched up the horses.

Rev. Williams urged us to be careful. "Any wandering soldier is likely to be on foot and watching for horses. Keep an eye out, and Godspeed."

His wife gave us a small basket tied up in a towel with cornbread and another one of apples.

Then he opened the barn doors. Their son walked inside to say goodbye. He assured us the slave catchers had moved on because there was no sign of them.

Just the same, we headed down the road with Michael at the reins, Thomas riding a horse ahead, and James riding the other, with Joseph alert, guarding the rear. Rebecca, Lucy, and I walked. The hounds kept pace with the wagon, and the children gazed around, excited for another day on the road.

Sixteen

Looking for Answers
Gracie

"The world is indeed full of peril and in it there are many dark places. But still there is much that is fair. And though in all lands, love is now mingled with grief, it still grows, perhaps, the greater."
~JRR Tolkien

My days were full between classes, the museum, and *The Jubilee Times*. I'd taken to carrying a small notebook documenting what we knew, and it was precious little. Aunt Shirley found two more quilts, but no information. Tiara found three more quilts. Our Carlson Great-Aunt Ruth was getting out her old family papers, as was Aunt Violet.

I'd stopped by her apartment after class, and she showed me poetry from her high school days. She had a single banker's box open on the bed of her guest room and was sorting the contents with documents scattered across the quilt. She picked up an old composition notebook and handed it to me with a smile.

"I've been meaning to look at these things for some time," she confessed. "I thought you'd agree that I make a better nurse than a poet."

Snowfall

by Violet Nelson

White flakes of snow are drifting down
Upon this little village town;

Covering up the once green grass
   Over which we used to pass.
Sounds of shovels echo near,
   Through the air so cold and clear;
Children, voices high with glee,
   Wave their mitten'd hands at me;
Windows piled high with snow,
   Roads in front an icy glow;
Night is slowly creeping on,
   Snow will fall until the dawn,
Then the world will all awake
   To find the ground a frosted cake.

After reading the poem, I looked up. "I like it, Aunt Violet. The metaphor of the snow being a frosted cake works, especially in Iowa, with our enormous fields, farmyards, and parks in town."

She looked pleased. "Thanks, Gracie. How are you getting on? Your mama said you're looking for information about Molly's red and green quilt. Let's make tea, if you have time."

I slipped my notebook out of my purse. "I've taken to writing everything down. The red and green quilt is an example of the rustic rose pattern. It has bloodstains and initials on the hem–R. S. I thought about sending it off to a genetics service for testing and talked to our science teacher at the college. He was dubious, saying it would be difficult to do much with such an old bloodstain, but he'd love to show it to his students."

Aunt Violet pondered. "I'd never seen the quilt before Molly gave it to you. The bloodstain is certainly troubling. What else?"

I looked at my list. "The telegram you found that mentions Sarah, Daniel, and Joseph, the men being injured and coming home with her on the train."

I continued, "We have a group of quilts made by Rebecca and Lucy. The O'Connor brothers and Nelson brothers were friends and left for the war together. Thanks to Carl, we know where their regiment traveled and the battles they fought. Michael made the rank of corporal during the war."

I stopped, frustrated. "That's about all. I found a list of the dozen quilt squares used by the Underground Railroad, and their meaning, online. Two seemed especially useful. Log cabin—friends here will help, so safe houses. Drunkard's path—beware of slave catchers, and don't move in a straight line."

Aunt Violet nodded. "Yes, I think they also used the Drunkard's path pattern in quilts for the temperance movement."

I flipped a page in my notebook. "I checked Wikipedia for the facts. The slave population in the South reached four million people by the time the Civil War began, and it isn't clear how many southerners owned slaves. But there's no doubt that the labor of Black slaves enriched their white owners."

Aunt Violet looked sad. "To think of the slave auctions—buying and selling human beings, mothers, children, and babies. It's unthinkable today, especially for those of us living in the north. Of course, our great-grandfather, Michael O'Connor, and other relatives fought the war to end slavery, and saw the nation torn apart by that conflict. Thank goodness the Underground Railroad helped people escape slavery. What have you learned about them?"

I checked my notebook. "The Underground Railroad was a network of safe houses run by conductors who helped slaves escape to the north. Sources suggest anywhere from 60,000 to 100,000 people escaped via the Railroad by 1850. Some ventured to Mexico, others traveled north, to a free state, and others ended up in Canada, where slavery hadn't been legal since the 1830s."

I looked up. "The Underground Railroad was secretive, so they didn't leave many details about it except for a few journals and letters."

Aunt Violet had fixed tea while we chatted in her little kitchen. We sat and sipped our favorite Constant Comment tea.

As if she were the teacher, Aunt Violet prompted me, "So why did they call it the Underground Railroad?"

"The invention of the railroad changed transportation in the 1800s, just as it changed the landscape of cities and towns. The people who created the Underground Railroad worked to move escaped slaves to freedom," I told her, looking at my notes.

She nodded. "I remember reading that people hid in cellars, barns, and caves until it was safe to move on to the next place. I think they came up into southern and central Iowa to go to Canada."

"They used the terminology of the railroad, with conductors, stations, agents, and cargo. Agents helped slaves find the Underground Railroad. Guides, or conductors, accompanied people to the next place. Hiding places became known as stations. Station masters hid enslaved people in their homes or barns, and escaping slaves became passengers or cargo. Stockholders gave money to help finance the Railroad." I glanced up from my notes.

"Most slaves traveled alone, but sometimes groups escaped together, traveling by foot or wagon, boat, or train. Many of the station masters held religious convictions against slavery, such as the Methodists or the Friends or Quakers as they were called. And then there was Harriet Tubman, a freed slave who made thirteen trips south to rescue seventy people. Later, on June 2, 1863, she led one hundred and fifty Black Union soldiers in the Combahee River Raid, which freed seven hundred slaves. Of course, the Underground Railroad violated the Fugitive Slave Act of 1850, but supporters saw the act as immoral."

Aunt Violet smiled. "I'm proud to be a Methodist! I remember learning about Harriet Tubman in school. We memorized her quote, 'Every great dream begins with a dreamer.' What a strong woman!"

I flipped a page. "Yes, she was an amazing woman. Here's my problem. I found a half dozen websites that claimed quilts laid over a chair had patches that signaled a safe place to rest—a station on the Underground Railroad. But another half dozen websites expressed outright skepticism about the role of quilts. So, which is it—did quilt squares signal safe places or not?"

Aunt Violet was an exceptional listener. She told me, "You'll get all your answers, Gracie. Personally, yes, I think they used quilt squares, but I have no proof."

As we drank tea and chatted, her cat Beatrix played with a toy nearby. She was a wonderful companion for my aunt and a source of constant amusement.

Half an hour later, I hugged my aunt, petted Beatrix, and headed home. As I drove, I reflected on what I'd learned about slavery. Many people in the South had amassed enormous wealth by buying and selling slaves and using their labor. The Underground Railroad was an informal network of people helping slaves escape, and they did an amazing job. But we were still dealing with widespread racism, fear, and inequities 150 years later.

Tiara, Shelly, and I discussed racism during the ACW-era and since then as we sat in the adjuncts' office. Tiara, a proud daughter of African roots, educated us about the struggle for equality a century beyond the ACW. Of course, I'd studied the events of the Civil Rights movement with Rosa Parks refusing to give up her seat on the bus, the peaceful protests, college students going south to register Black voters and the assassination of Martin Luther King, Junior, and other leaders.

My mother told me about watching race riots on television when she was growing up, and Dad told me about the newspaper headlines he remembered. But it happened a long time ago. As a white girl growing up in Iowa, it was difficult for me to understand how hard life was for people who were not white during those days. Then Tiara described what her relatives experienced growing up in the 1960s.

"Aunt Sandra lived out east, in New York City, during the race riots of the late 1960s. One night, her parents bundled the kids in the backseat of their car, covered them with a blanket, and drove the back roads to grandma's house. At one intersection, several white men with baseball bats yelled at them, but her dad sped away."

Tiara's mother grew up in Jubilee Junction, attended college at Iowa State University, and then moved to River City after marrying a man she met at college. Her mother worked for the state as a social worker, while her father was a lawyer, specializing in civil rights cases. They'd since moved to New York. Her grandma stayed in Jubilee Junction, and Tiara spent time here during the summers.

Tiara grew up in River City, where she attended college. "I experienced little racism. It was a college town, and I was hardly the only Black person. I met Benjamin, my husband, in River City before he joined the National Guard. We got married and moved to married student housing, and I got my master's degree. He completed his

MBA and found a job with a company at one of their branch offices in a medium-sized town in Indiana. I taught for a year and then got pregnant with the twins. But I noticed the suspicious glances I got in the grocery store and at our apartment building. This was during the late '90s, and it wasn't a very diverse town."

Shelly told us a story her mother had told her. Her mother was trying to get a full-time teaching job and signed up to work as a substitute teacher in two different school districts, one rural and one suburban, back in the 1990s. Someone told her they needed subs for the Sac and Fox Reservation School, so she applied. She worked there half a dozen times, and it was a remarkable experience.

"Mom walked into the cafeteria the first day and realized she was one of six white people in the room. Meanwhile, about one hundred and twenty Meskwaki children, teachers, and aides stared at her before glancing down. She said later she'd never felt so white or so different. The children were curious but were taught to show respect by glancing down. It was a profound, uncomfortable experience," Shelly told us. "It gave her compassion and empathy for her minority students.

"Midday, two adults came into her classroom to teach a class about Native American culture and the Meskwaki language. So, Mom sat in the teacher's lounge for an hour, thinking that this must be what it was like to be the only Black student in the class. She subbed again for them five or six times before getting the interview landing her a full-time job. But she never forgot the experience," Shelly concluded.

Tiara agreed. "Been there, done that. For most of my career, I've been the only person of color in a room full of white people. But it's worth it when I walk into a classroom with Black, Hispanic, or Native American students and see them smile back."

David and I talked about it over supper. Since he'd lived in the Chicago area, he had more experience with diverse students and faculty.

"Our history department included courses developed by my Black and Latino colleagues, interpreting American History from the perspective of minorities. Native Americans, African Americans,

Latino Americans, and Asian Americans—America hasn't treated any of these people fairly." He added, "We also had a Women's History course and a course on LGBTQ history."

I glanced at him. "So, are you cheering me up? This is depressing."

"I have ways of making you feel better, but not in public. Aunt Shirley might toss us out on the street." David's brown eyes danced, and then he took a more sober tone. "Race and gender still determine how successful people are much of the time, and it's not right or fair."

I nodded. "I know, and it makes me angry."

David reached over for my hand. "I understand. Me, too. Isn't that why your Grandma Molly is so involved with the League of Women Voters? The League has done good work, registering voters of all races, educating them on key issues, and holding candidate forums."

"You've been studying up for Grandma Molly?" I asked. "Grandma brags it took a woman from Iowa to get the 19th Amendment passed. Carrie Chapman Catt then founded the League to educate new voters."

He nodded. "I've admired the League of Women Voters for a long time. Several faculty members in my department belonged to the League back in Chicago."

We finished our meal, making small talk. But later, I wondered what Jubilee Junction was like as a frontier town, what life was like for my ancestors, and what role race and gender played in their stories?

Seventeen

The Slave Catcher Returns
Sarah

"Those who deny freedom to others deserve it not for themselves, and, under a just God, cannot long retain it."

~Abraham Lincoln

On a road toward Charles Town, West Virginia
Wednesday, September 21, 1864

We took the back roads northeast towards Charles Town, using Rev. William's directions. As we walked along, the children asked for stories, and we took turns entertaining them with a story or song. Daniel dozed off and on, in pain with his shoulder wound.

The rest of us remained vigilant. Joseph stayed alert and watched the rear. Michael, Thomas, and James took turns riding the horses and driving the wagon. At least one soldier had his rifle ready at all times. The women took turns walking and riding with the children.

Thomas walked with the dogs as we started out. Rebecca and I walked with him until we grew weary.

Several hours passed. We stopped to rest and eat, and then got back on the road with James riding ahead of us and Thomas riding behind. The dogs trotted along behind him. Michael had the reins. I'd climbed into the wagon and curled up with Rebecca and Lucy and the children, chilled by the autumn air.

Suddenly, the dogs began barking, and we heard a rifle shot. It spooked the horses. The children woke up crying. I woke up to feel the wagon careening down the road, with Michael straining at the reins to calm down the agitated horses.

I glanced around, my heart beating. *Where did the shot come from?* The wagon came to a shuddering halt as Michael regained control of the frightened horses. The three of us women wrapped our arms around the children to calm their crying.

Then Thomas galloped from the rear. Breathing hard he announced, "We been followed."

Scout and Duke bayed loudly, their hackles up. "Hush, you dogs!" Thomas commanded, and they slunk under the wagon, the hair on their backs still high.

"Where is he? Is it the slave catcher?" asked Lucy, frightened. Her daughter whimpered and clung to her mother's body, trembling.

Thomas peered through the trees while gripping the reins. "I don't know. I don't see him now, but I caught sight of someone following us a few minutes ago."

Michael assumed the command. "Thomas and James, get off the horses. You're a target up there."

Thomas and James obeyed, dismounting their horses and then tying the reins to the wagon.

"Sarah, have the women and children lay down in the wagon right now." Michael's voice was calm. "Thomas, take Sarah's shotgun."

All four soldiers grabbed their rifles and gazed around. I peeked from my position in the wagon bed to see what was happening. Thomas crouched beside the wagon, shielding us with the shotgun in his arms. James sat next to Michael in the front seat and scanned the terrain in a half-circle, his rifle at the ready. There was an unearthly quiet, as if nature herself was holding her breath.

At last Michael said, "Keep alert, and let's keep moving."

Daniel cradled his rifle with both arms, as did Joseph, watching behind us.

We hadn't started moving more than a minute when the dogs started barking again. Thomas pointed at the trees across the road. "Someone is moving over there—it's a man on horseback, and he's coming right at us. Do you see him?"

The road wound through a heavy cover of pine trees on both sides making it hard to distinguish anything more than a few yard away. Another shot rang out from the forest, passing over our heads and splintering a pine tree beyond the wagon. Thomas fired back in the direction of the man he saw, then Daniel and Joseph followed.

We heard a man's horrible scream, and though he was our enemy, I prayed for his soul. Lucy trembled against me, Bobby stiffened, and Chloe whimpered in fear. Rebecca and I threw back the quilt and risked a glance over the side of the wagon.

"I think we got him." Daniel put his rifle down. Rebecca stared at him in concern because his wound was seeping blood again.

Michael focused on soothing the horses while James turned to check behind us.

A horse broke through the trees galloping down the road straight at us. A man slumped over in the saddle, a rifle still grasped in one hand, but swinging slowly back and forth, like a pendulum of a clock that had wound down. The horse stopped, panting, fifteen feet away. We recognized the long hair and clothing of the slave catcher at Rev. Williams' barn. He rolled to the side, and dropped unceremoniously to the ground, his rifle still clutched in his hand.

Thomas walked stealthily to the man, his eyes shifting through the trees to see if the man's partner might be around. The dogs followed him and sniffed the man on the ground. After a brief examination, Thomas shook his head and declared, "He's dead."

Michael took charge. "Drag his body off the trail and cover it with leaves. There's nothing to be gained from taking a dead slave catcher with us. But bring the horse."

Thomas approached the animal slowing, speaking to it in a low and soothing voice. He took the reins and led the now compliant horse to the wagon and losely tied the reins to it. Then he and James dragged the body into the underbrush and hid it beneath a veil of leaves and branches. Their grizzly task completed, Thomas returned to the dead man's horse, rummaged through the saddlebags, and removed a bundle, then handed it to me.

"Ma'am, Mr. Hays would like to present you with a little something for your trouble." Thomas handed me a small drawstring leather purse filled with gold coins. "We can use this for tickets on the ship, and the train later on."

Now I don't approve of stealing, but I don't approve of slavery, torture, rape, or chasing mamas and babies with rope. This man chased Lucy and Chloe for two days. I don't know where his partner went, but Mr. Hays was following us and chasing us down with a loaded weapon. What's more, he had no fear of the four soldiers escorting us and tried to ambush us with two children and three women in the wagon. No, I would shed no tears for a dead slave catcher, and what better use of his ill-gotten money than to help take five slaves to freedom?

So, I accepted it. "Thank you, Thomas," and I put the purse in my bag.

He turned to the slave catcher's horse and gave it water and did a more thorough examination of its saddle bags. Lucy and Rebecca took the children for a potty break, while James rode off in the direction the slave catcher had approached from to see if his partner might still be in the area.

The rest of the men and women walked off in opposite directions to take care of business. When we all returned, we lifted the children into the wagon and got them settled. Thomas smiled at Lucy and passed over a bundle of fabric he had discovered in the saddlebag.

Her face lit up. "My bag. Thank you."

On further examination I realized it was an old sheet rolled up and knotted to sling around her shoulders. She undid the knot, and inside was one of the prettiest little quilts I'd ever seen, along with a faded old dress, a comb, and a tattered dress for her daughter.

Lucy regarded the quilt. "This ain't my best work, but I couldn't leave it behind. I did it with my mama, and it has bits and pieces of clothes from Grandma." She and Rebecca inspected the small quilt, done with vibrant colors in an intricate pattern.

James returned in time to witness the scene. "Good job, Thomas," he declared.

Thomas shrugged. "Well, I figured someone should do it."

"I didn't see any sign of any other folks around," James told Michael. "It appears that fellow was alone."

Michael nodded, but his eyes never ceased to roam the horizon.

I located my satchel and found the extra linen bag we'd made for Emily. I took out a few dollar bills and placed them inside, and then called Lucy over.

"Lucy, when we get to Iowa, we'll get your manumission papers to declare you and your daughter free. Rebecca, Thomas, and Bobby have these bags with their freedom papers. This bag is for you, and it goes around your neck. Go west with us." Then, I showed her my bag, with copies of the papers for Rebecca, Bobby, and Thomas.

Rebecca pulled out her linen bag from under the neckline of her dress, and so did Thomas and Bobby, reaching under the neckline of their shirts.

Then Rebecca stared at me, and her eyes filled with tears. "Miss Emily's bag?" she asked, and I held back the tears, unable to speak.

Bobby rejoiced, "We all free!" He raised his hands, like a good little Sunday school boy.

Chloe echoed, "We free!" and clapped her hands.

Lucy slipped her bag around her neck and touched it under her dress. Then she wrapped up the small quilt in the sheet, rolled it up, and held it to her chest. "Thank you, Mister Thomas," she said. "Thank you, Miss Sarah."

Michael walked around, checking the wagon for any breaks or cracks in the harnesses. He looked handsome in my dead husband's shirt. I pushed the thought from my mind. James kept guard.

Rebecca and I checked Daniel's wound, which was bleeding again. He shouldn't have fired his rifle, but he was protecting his new *family* from harm. His forehead felt warm, but he complained about being cold, and seemed shaky. Rebecca dressed his wound, then opened a trunk, grabbed her red and green quilt, and put it around him.

He protested, "No, no—this quilt is too pretty."

"Don't argue. It's warmer than a blanket." She handed him some white willow bark, which he gratefully chewed.

He thanked her and settled down against a pillow. He pulled the quilt tighter. The children snuggled near him and Joseph as they chatted. Daniel's color improved as he warmed up.

Joseph was in better shape. We elevated his leg on a couple of folded-up blankets with a pillow on top. In the commotion with the slave catcher, he sat up straight and knocked his leg off the pillow. But we didn't see any increased swelling.

Michael announced, "Let's get moving. We need to find a stream the horses can cross. We should be in West Virginia soon."

As we walked alongside the wagon, I asked Rebecca, "What's the pattern called? It's a lovely quilt."

"Mama Cee called it Rustic Rose," she answered. "Miss Emily bought the fabric. It turned out real nice."

I pulled my shawl around me as I scanned the road ahead and then the people in the wagon. We'd become a family on this journey, taking care of each other.

The children fell asleep and then Daniel, but Joseph kept his vigil.

Thomas walked alongside the wagon, and the dogs sniffed the ground, poked around, and returned to Thomas.

After a few miles, Rebecca glanced at me. "You should rest awhile Miss Sarah. Lucy and I can walk." So, I climbed back into the wagon.

James told Michael, "I'll check for a stream," and rode on ahead.

The familiar sensation of the wheels rocking and squeaking, and the warmth of my shawl, lulled me to sleep beside the trunk. When I woke up, it was to chaos—water rushed around the wagon wheels and threatened to tip the wagon over. Michael held the reins and strained to guide the horses through the stream to the other side and right the wagon. He turned his head to check on us. "Everybody alright? I'm sorry. The water's deeper than we thought it would be."

Water didn't get inside the wagon, but everything shifted to one side, including our patients. Rebecca crawled over to check on them while Lucy tried to hold on to the children. Fortunately, none of our trunks tumbled out and Rebecca held onto her herb bag. My reticule was on my wrist, and I'd tucked my big bag underneath me. But several of our mason jars fell over, spilling water.

Then I saw the children leaning over the higher side of the wagon to see what was going on below. Lucy lunged for them, but Chloe slipped out of her reach. Bobby grabbed for Chloe, and both children tumbled into the chilly autumn water, clutching onto each other as the strong current carried them downstream.

Rebecca cried out, "Thomas! James! The children!" while Lucy cried, "My baby! Chloe!"

James and Thomas were leading the two spare horses across the stream, which was chest high. Thomas ordered the hounds to go after the children. Duke and Scout grabbed each child by their clothing and dog-paddled back towards the far shore. Then Thomas and James reached shore, mounted and galloped to where the dogs were struggling to drag the children to safety. James grabbed Chloe while Thomas grabbed Bobby.

The whole thing took only moments, but felt like a lifetime. Michael guided the wagon to a secure stop on the dry land, while James and Thomas returned the children to their mothers who wrapped them in the blanket and held them close, sobbing all the while.

"Thank you, James and Thomas." I forced my voice to sound steady. "That was quick thinking."

The hounds shook themselves dry, then barked as if it were a fine game, and they were rewarded with ear scratches and praise.

The children observed the adults, unsure if they were more excited or frightened. It had been an adventure. They were thoroughly soaked and shivering, but did not appear to be much worse for the wear.

We were all shaken, especially the three women. We needed a safe place to stop and rest, make a fire, and get everyone dry and warm. Michael pointed to an opening in the trees a bit farther down, and James and Thomas rode ahead to gathered wood and start a fire.

Before long we were settled into a make-shift campsite with a small but welcome fire warming our hands and feet. We found dry clothing for the children, Rebecca checked the patients, and I distributed cold coffee and cornbread then wrapping my shawl around me against the afternoon chill and sat close to the crackling fire.

The fire's warmth drew us all in, and we gratefully gathered around it while the horses grazed. The dogs lay down by the children and received plenty of pats.

Suddenly Duke and Scout rose and bayed.

Michael and Thomas motioned for us to remain quiet, then got up to investigate. When they returned they brought a teenage boy who carried a fishing pole and stringer of fish.

"My name is Peter," he stammered. "I wasn't spyin' or nuthin'. Honest. I was fishing downstream and saw the children fall into the water. That was a brave thing you did, catching them before they got washed away. The water gets choppier as it flows toward the river. They's been a number of folks that got drowned there."

The boy's eyes flitted from Michael to me to Rebecca, then settled back on Michael, as if he had descerned who was the leader of our band.

"I know y'all don't know me, but if you are doing what I suspect you're doing, it ain't safe for you to camp here." He licked his lips as if nervous. "Slave catchers travel these roads, and so do deserters and bushwhackers who would just as soon kill you as look at you. My father's farm is just over the hill. He helps folks who are...uh... in your situation."

Michael gazed deeply into the boy's eyes, then he turned to me and nodded. It appeared he trusted this boy. And if he trusted him, then I would trust him too.

James scooped dirt and rocks on top of the fire. We broke camp, climbed back into the wagon and onto the horses, then followed Peter down a faint wagon trail. But whether we were heading toward his father's farm or into a trap, we would know soon enough.

Eighteen

Tiara Finds the Journey Quilt
Gracie

"Families are the compass that guides us. They are the inspiration to reach great heights, and our comfort when we occasionally falter."

~Brad Henry

February 2013

Monday morning, I got a text from Mark with an image of Kathy's first sonogram. He wrote, "We think it's a girl, and both baby and mama are doing well." I sent it on to David, Shelly, and Tiara.

I was thrilled. Mom sent a text with a prayer of gratitude. Kathy's pregnancy was going well, even though it was high-risk. She was almost four months along and due in early August. When her doctor put Kathy on semi-bed rest, she asked for a long-term sub for her high school classes to finish out the spring semester.

I tried to call her several times a week and sent a couple of texts a day. I'd also taken Agatha over for several playdates with Kathy's cat, Felix, who was a littermate, and another frisky calico. It was fun to watch them play together and see how they enjoyed seeing each other.

Kathy asked me, "You ever wonder what Agatha's thinking?"

I laughed. "Agatha's not so deep," and I listed them off. "Food & water, pet me, treats, play with me, don't bother me."

Just then, Agatha came up to me and meowed. I sighed, picked her up to cuddle, and laughed. "Okay, add one more. Cuddle me."

Kathy laughed. She took a couple of pictures of us and sent them in a text. "Thanks for cheering me up. Felix says to come again."

I gazed at those pictures now on my phone, remembering our visit to Kathy and Mark over the previous weekend.

A few minutes later, I walked into my literature class. We'd left the fiction unit behind and started the poetry unit.

Today, our assigned poem was "The Wound Dresser," by Walt Whitman, about his real-life experience nursing wounded soldiers during the ACW. Published in his collection of poetry, *Leaves of Grass*, the poem examines the suffering of wounded soldiers.

I brought the poem up on the projector from the poetry foundation website. "The Wound Dresser" is a long poem. I read a portion out loud and then asked them to focus on several stanzas.

> *"Bearing the bandages, water and sponge,*
> *Straight and swift to my wounded I go,*
> *Where they lie on the ground after the battle brought in,*
> *Where their priceless blood reddens the grass, the ground,*
> *Or to the rows of the hospital tent, or under the roof'd hospital,*
> *To the long rows of cots up and down each side I return,*
> *To each and all one after another I draw near, not one do I miss,*
> *An attendant follows holding a tray, he carries a refuse pail,*
> *Soon to be fill'd with clotted rags and blood, emptied, and fill'd again.*

Students discussed the poem in small groups.

Jenna spoke up. "This is really sad."

"Yeah, and gross—thinking about a bucket full of bloody rags makes me feel sick to my stomach," one of her partners commented.

Across the room, someone else asked, "So they took care of patients in a tent outside?"

"Yes, they're called field hospitals because they aren't far from the battle itself. When my brother served in Iraq, Mark tripped and fell during a rocket attack on his base, and a doctor at their field hospital wrapped up his ankle. Fortunately, he was okay," I told them.

"The conditions during the ACW were terrible. Soldiers were crowded together in the camps, where they didn't have good sanitation, clean water, adequate food, or the ability to wash their hands, leading to outbreaks of pneumonia, typhoid, diarrhea/dysentery, and malaria."

Class ended, but students left chattering about the poem, the ACW, and the impact of war on society. As I packed up my messenger bag, I savored the satisfaction I got each semester from teaching literature. So many students related better to short stories and poetry when they understood a little more about their historical context. I also enjoyed watching my students' attitudes to literature change over the course of the semester as they read short stories, poetry, and drama.

I returned to the office.

Tiara was excited. "I found two more quilts for your exhibit, and guess what? They both have Lucy's name stitched on them. I got permission from the owner—a sweet older lady in my church—to exhibit them at the museum. Want to see them?"

"Yes, but I wish we knew who Lucy was."

She picked up a large bundle on top of the file cabinet—two quilts wrapped up in an old sheet. We laid the bundle out across several desks and admired the quilts. I found a pair of gloves in my messenger bag and put them on.

The first quilt was bright purples, pinks, greens, browns, blacks, and reds in the wagon wheel pattern. The artist had added patches, too—a wagon with small people and trunks, a horse, a train, a bridge, a large barn, cornfields, and a quilt in the window of a house.

I sniffed, detecting the odor of mothballs. I inspected it, amazed. "This tells the story of the trip to Iowa."

Tiara agreed. "My response, too! By the way, Mrs. Brownstone saw your article in the newspaper. She called me because we go to the same church. So, I would count on other people offering quilts or information, Gracie. You're going to get your answers."

The second quilt used a more subdued array of golds, browns, and blues in the north star pattern. Someone had fastened a note to each quilt with the owner's name. Gorgeous and understated, it was the work of an accomplished quilter.

Tiara waved a piece of paper at me. "I have interview notes with Mrs. Julia Brownstone. She's in her eighties and remembers her great-grandma talking about these quilts and her great-grandma's friendship with a lovely young woman named Lucy."

We sat down and read through her notes together. When Mrs. Brownstone was a girl, she attended a quilting club with her mama. Several of the women claimed one of the best quilters in Jubilee Junction had been a young Black woman named Lucy. Apparently, she came to town with two wounded soldiers during the Cival War, according to stories handed down by their grandmas. Then Mrs. Brownstone found out her great-grandmother had known Lucy and purchased these quilts.

"Could we capture her comments on audio, the way we did before?" I asked. "This is fabulous!"

"Yes, I wasn't thinking of it when we were talking. I was so excited about the quilts and finding information about Lucy."

Maybe I didn't have enough quilts for my new exhibit when we took the current one down. However, I had themes about traveling to freedom swirling in my brain.

"Thank you, Tiara. These are amazing. Thank you," I hugged her. "You don't know how badly I needed good news."

I couldn't wait to show them to Carl and David.

David met me at the museum later that afternoon, and I laid out the new quilts on my worktable. Before he could react, Carl entered my workroom and grinned as he saw the quilts. "This explains why you were so excited on the phone."

The two men put on cotton gloves and began examining the quilts.

"These are amazing. You need to send pictures to Robin," David commented.

"It's on my list for tomorrow," I assured him.

"The colors are still vibrant, and the stitching is strong," Carl noted. "By the way, my family thinks I'm going to take up quilting soon, because I sure talk about it a lot at home." He grinned again. "Wait until they see these two quilts."

I showed them the interview notes with information about Mrs. Brownstone. "Her mother stored them in her great-grandmother's old cedar chest. Her mother told her it was the sunlight that damaged the colors and stitches." I took pictures and promised to post them on the museum's Google Drive. "David's right. These quilts are amazing, and you have their provenance. Good job, Gracie. Tell Tiara thank you." He left my workroom and walked back upstairs, whistling.

I logged the two new quilts into my spreadsheet and took my own photos. We had eighteen verified quilts of ACW vintage, and permission to use them in an exhibit.

David helped me wrap each quilt with a sheet and then fold up Tiara's sheets, which I tucked into my messenger bag.

"Well, you're closer to having your exhibit," he said.

"Yes, I hope to get a few more quilts, but I'm feeling more confident we'll find them now. Thanks!"

"You know, Valentine's Day is coming up. I'm thinking we should celebrate." He kissed me, and I put my arms around him and kissed him back.

I picked up my purse and messenger bag and we headed for the door. As excited as I was by the recent additions, I felt frustrated by my growing list of questions about the red and green quilt. Had too much time passed? Would I ever get answers for Grandma Molly?

David and I found our favorite table in the back corner at Aunt Shirley's for supper. We ordered sandwiches and shared a side of sweet potato fries as we chatted about the quilts and his book proposal. After we finished eating, he reached across the table to hold my hand and smiled, those brown eyes looking deeply into mine. A quiver ran down my spine and I got a strange sensation of warmth spreading from my chest to—whoa! I sat up straight.

"What would you like to do for Valentine's Day?" he asked.

"Well, we enjoy eating dinner at Ruby's."

"Yes, Ruby's is one of our favorite places for dinner. But I had something else in mind."

"Like what?"

"I could make reservations at Rivertown's B and B. There's a restaurant next door, and it all overlooks the lovely Jubilee River."

A B&B? *Were we ready for this? Was I ready for this?* I had a million questions and a flood of mixed emotions—excitement, desire, and fear.

He saw my hesitation.

"Gracie, please think about it. Let's spend some time alone. We don't need to do anything you aren't comfortable doing."

This man was irresistible, and I melted.

"Yes, I'd like some time alone, too, David," I replied, and mentally inventoried my underwear drawer, thinking I needed to talk to Kathy or Shelly, or maybe Tiara. Suddenly, I realized that I'd pushed Steve away when we'd dated. I'd never believed in epiphanies before, but even though I'd loved Steve, I didn't want to get too close because then he'd control my life. Now, I didn't want to push David away. We had begun as friends, but somehow, along the way, we'd become a couple.

When I got home, I called Kathy. "I'm trying not to panic, but David wants to take me away to a B and B for Valentine's Day. What should I do?" Then, feeling guilty, I asked, "And how are you and the baby doing?"

Kathy burst out laughing. "Well, what an intriguing conversation starter. I think that's wonderful, Gracie. And yes, I'm fine, and the baby is doing well, thanks. Do you want to go away with David?"

"Yes, I'm excited—and nervous. I had a crazy thought earlier. I pushed Steve away because I didn't want to be intimate with him. But I don't want to push David away."

"Okay, let's talk about it. Have you told him you and Steve were never intimate?"

I gulped. "You're good at this. No. I haven't worked up the nerve to do it yet."

Kathy's voice was firm. "You need to talk to him, Gracie, before the trip. Take something sexy in case you decide to be intimate. But take precautions—like condoms. Then take something sweet and comfy in case you want to snuggle and relax. I have a couple of negligees and pajama sets that I think would fit you. You're welcome to stop by and see them."

"Yes, please. Thanks for the good advice."

If I were the person who did a happy dance, I might have done so.

Instead, I settled for therapeutic warm-up exercises, with Agatha weaving around underfoot. Then I saw myself in the mirror—happy, flushed, and in love.

Nineteen

Daniel and the Rustic Rose Quilt
Sarah

"I was the conductor of the Underground Railroad for eight years, and I can say what most conductors can't say; I never ran my train off the track, and I never lost a passenger."
~Harriet Tubman

On a road toward Charles Town, West Virginia
Wednesday, September 21, 1864

As we followed the teenager to his father's farm, I studied our surroundings. We'd tried to be careful, but a large wagon hitched up to four horses moves slowly and makes a certain amount of noise. Add two—no, three more horses, ten people, and two dogs, and I felt confident any stray Confederate straggler had indeed heard us coming and hid. Confederate patrols keeping an eye out for their stragglers would not have any fear of us. We'd passed several places where soldiers had camped, and we were thankful the Underground Railroad had protected us so far.

I thought again of my plan with Emily. How had we imagined we could travel in safety on our own? Thank goodness mother had encouraged me to ask Thomas to come along.

James had the wagon reins. Michael rode ahead on a horse to scout the area, and Rebecca, Lucy, and I walked with Thomas alongside the wagon, the dogs following.

Lucy tried to hide her concern, but Chloe had coughed off and on and now started wheezing. She and Bobby were riding, sitting next to the injured soldiers. Joseph rubbed her back and gave her a sip of water with some concoction designed for coughs that Rebecca had put together.

I glanced up and was startled to realize we'd reached the farm. It was late afternoon and getting chilly.

Michael was on the porch beside another man, who stepped down and greeted Peter. He looked us over, then asked Michael, "These are your friends?"

Michael nodded. "Yes, sir."

He turned toward the wagon and smiled. "Looks like you folks could use some help."

James replied, "Yes, sir. We'd love to rest for a while."

The man waved. "Welcome. Follow me."

He walked through a farmyard, back to a large barn like the one we saw earlier. We followed him and then stopped at the barn which was also adorned with a cross. He opened the doors, stepped inside, and lit a lantern.

Bobby stared at the cross and asked, "Are you a preacher?"

The man responded with a warm smile and kind eyes. "I have the honor of being a minister of the Gospel. Come in, friends."

James drove the wagon inside, and Michael followed on horseback with the dogs still walking beside him. Rebecca, Lucy, and I followed Thomas inside, and the man closed the barn doors behind us.

He assessed the group with a sharp eye, then smiled at the children. "My name is Brown. Reverend Brown. You folks seem tired. I imagine you'd like to have something to eat and rest." Then he saw the two injured men in the wagon and the little girl. Daniel with the quilt wrapped around him, wincing with pain, and Joseph with his swollen leg up on a pillow, trying not to groan. Little Chloe, still wrapped in a blanket, coughed and wheezed.

"You folks need a doctor," he said flatly.

I replied, "Yes, sir. We have two injured men, and the children fell overboard while crossing a stream earlier today. I fear they have caught a chill. Do you know a doctor who might help us?"

"Yes. I'll send for him." He nodded at Peter, and the boy left without saying a word.

We helped our injured comrades and the children to climb down from the wagon, and got them settled more comfortably in the barn. Rev. Brown drew Michael aside and the two men talked quietly together.

Moments later the barn door creaked open, and a grown woman accompanied by three younger women entered carrying food.

"This is my wife and daughters," Rev. Brown announced.

The older woman smiled at her husband, then urged us to eat.She didn't need to ask twice. We'd exhausted our supply of dry cornbread and were all hungry. We gathered around, ate, and thanked them profusely.

I fought tears as I watched the children eat. *They trusted us, the adults, to take care of them. How would we have survived on the road without these wonderful hosts?*

Rebecca and I carried plates of food and mugs of coffee to the two injured men.

One of the younger women brought a big kettle of hot water and reached in her apron for a canister of tea, a tea ball, and a spoon. Rebecca thanked her, put a mixture of herbs in the teapot, and added sugar and a pinch of one of her herbs—yarrow, from the looks of it. She had the children each drink a mug to help warm them up. She handed a mug to James and Thomas to do the same.

The youngest daughter brought a bowl of table scraps for the dogs and a bowl for their water. I filled the bowl with water and fed Duke and Scout the scraps. They rewarded me with several sloppy kisses before exploring the sights and smells of the barn.

The women showed us where we could go for the privy. They also pointed out an area with a curtain. This had a pump and a wash pan where we could freshen up, with lye soap and several towels folded on a shelf above. On the other side of the barn, a pump provided water for the horses.

Mrs. Brown pointed out the escape tunnel under a trapdoor and upward toward a place to hide in the haymow.

"Now rest," the older woman spoke. "You must all be exhausted. The doctor should be here soon."

I took her aside and thanked her again, my eyes filling with tears. "I don't know what we would have done without you. Thank you. God bless you," I managed. "I believe once we cross into West Virginia I'll breathe easier."

"But my dear, you are already in West Virginia." Mrs. Brown patted my shoulder. "You passed just south of Wheatland and are within a few miles of Charles Town."

I couldn't keep the tears from overflowing my eyes at the thought of being in free state, although I knew danger still lurked.

"I can't imagine what you've been through on your journey," Mrs. Brown added. "You're a courageous woman, and we're blessed to help you. God called us to do our part, you know. Now rest." The Brown family gathered what was left of the meal and left the barn.

Rebecca and Lucy took turns cleaning up the children's sticky hands and faces. Thomas took care of the horses while Michael and James joined Daniel and Joseph, who were settled on a pile of hay. The four Union soldiers talked quiety among themselves.

I spread out a blanket and sat down to consider our situation. Simon had wanted me to quit my teaching job when we got married. I loved teaching, and I loved children. I missed them both. But he'd wanted a suitable, beautiful wife. I realized now that he'd thought of me as weak. *What would Simon say if he could see me now?*

The barn doors opened, and Rev. Brown returned accompanied by a tall man wearing a Union uniform and carrying a small satchel. Rev. Brown introduced him as Dr. Richardson, an older gentleman with a kind face.

He headed straight for Daniel. Dr. Richardson removed the bandages to examine the wound. He checked for a fever, then examined the wounded shoulder. After gently checking Daniel's arm and shoulder for mobility, he turned to us. "Who has cared for this man?" he asked.

I stepped forward. "We've done our best, sir." I wasn't sure how he might treat Rebecca as a Black woman.

He asked again, "Who has cared for this man?"

Rebecca stepped forward. "Me, sir."

The doctor glanced at her. "Have you had any training?"

She replied, "No, but I helped the last two summers at Union field hospitals, and I paid attention. I watched them wrap up different wounds. I use traditional herbs for healing. So, I gave him white willow bark to chew on for the pain and packed yarrow into his wound to help stop the bleeding. Daniel was healing up real fine until he shot at a slave catcher chasing us, and that reopened the wound."

"What's your name, young woman?"

"Rebecca Stevens, sir."

The doctor beamed at her. "You've done an excellent job, Rebecca. He didn't break any bones. While he has a slightly elevated temperature, he's doing well. The wound doesn't smell bad and isn't red. You did an expert job of cleaning and wrapping the wound, and your natural products seem to have helped him. If an Army doctor saw him after this injury, they would have amputated the arm and given him lots of morphine. I'm going to examine the wound. Would you like to assist me?"

She stepped up. "Yes, Doctor, please."

Daniel mouthed, "Thank you," to Rebecca.

The doctor opened his bag and got to work, explaining things to Daniel and Rebecca as he worked. He asked for a small container of water and clean rags, which Thomas fetched. Dr. Richardson thanked him and then instructed Rebecca to hold a sponge with chloroform at the top of a cone over Daniel's nose and mouth. A short time later, the sedation worked.

The doctor rinsed his hands and wet a rag, then probed the wound, checking for fragments, talking to Rebecca the whole time. She asked questions, and he nodded, pleased, and answered them.

He turned to Rebecca. "Now then, what did you use? Yarrow leaves? Please fetch them. I'd like to observe your technique."

She smiled, and Thomas brought her the canvas bag with her herbs. She packed the yarrow leaves over the wound and wrapped it up with bandages.

Rebecca had asked for hot water and a teapot earlier. She rinsed her hands, poured a cup of something, then set it aside for later, when Daniel awakened.

The doctor regarded the teapot, and she explained that she'd used shredded white willow bark to make tea. He watched her with interest.

"Sarah, can you see he drinks that tea? It's bitter but will help with the pain," she asked.

The doctor rinsed his hands. The bloody bandages he'd removed lay near the bowl.

"Now then, do you have another patient?" He seemed more cheerful, and turned to Joseph, motioning Rebecca to follow him.

He examined Joseph's foot, ankle, and knee, skillfully probing. "I concur in part with Dr. Rebecca's diagnosis. You did indeed twist your ankle in the fall. But I fear the knee is a far more serious matter. You have torn up the ligaments and tendons in your knee. Not much we can do for it other than try to keep your leg elevated to alleviate the pain. It may heal some on its own, but it will take time, and even if it does you'll likely walk with a pronounced limp for the rest of your life. Until that time you'll need crutches to get around. Fortunately, I had a pair in my wagon. One thing I can say for sure is, you will not be able to march with the Army anymore. With that leg you would be more of a hindrance to our cause than a help."

The minister stood in the doorway and produced the crutches.

James and Michael helped Joseph to his feet and watched as Joseph tried the crutches. After a few tries, and with a little coaching from Dr. Richardson, he figured out the best way to position them. Scout and Duke found this entertaining as they walked beside him.

Twenty

The Doctor Checks Chloe
Sarah

"For no man who lives at all lives unto himself. He either helps or hinders all who are in anywise connected to him."
~Frederick Douglass,
The Life and Times of Frederick Douglass

Reverend Brown's Barn, West Virginia
Wednesday, September 21, 1864

The doctor turned to Chloe, who was sitting on her mother's lap and coughing from time to time. He listened to her chest, thumped her back, and held her hand, smiling at her.

"So, you and Bobby took a swim earlier?" he asked.

"Yes, we falled out of the wagon, and the water was cold. The dogs grabbed us. Mr. James lifted me up to Mama."

The doctor listened, nodding.

He turned to me and Lucy. "She inhaled a little water, and I suspect she caught cold. I'd put a poultice on her tonight. Her lungs sound good."

The doctor reached into his pocket for a hankie. A small peppermint candy fell out, and then a second one, both red and white. He glanced at the children. "Can you help pick those up, please? I expect you'd better keep them." His eyes were twinkling.

Bobby kneeled and retrieved the candy, handing one to Chloe.

"Thank you, Doctor," Bobby said. I watched the children enjoy their candy.

Joseph was still practicing using the crutches. He glanced at the doctor and minister and echoed, "Thank you," followed by a chorus of thank yous from the rest of us.

Michael pulled the doctor aside and asked quietly how much his fee was. Dr. Richardson waved him off. "You're doing God's work here, taking slaves to freedom," he declared as he packed up his bag. He performed a final check on Daniel, who was awake and drinking his tea. "I'm pleased to have met you all. Take care and godspeed. You're in expert hands with Dr. Rebecca."

We all stared at Rebecca, who stood a little taller and touched her head wrap. She wasn't used to praise, but her eyes were glowing.

The minister's wife approached through the barn door carrying a small basket. "I thought you might need to to dispose of the old soiled bandages. If you'll gather them up I'll take them out and burn them. And if you need more bandages, I've got an old sheet we can tear up."

"Yes, thank you," Rebecca answered. She grabbed her herb bag and talked with the minister's wife about what she'd need to make a poultice. Mrs. Brown listened and then left.

The doctor took Michael aside, and they talked for a moment in low tones. He scribbled a note and handed it to Michael, who folded it in half and tucked it into his pocket. They shook hands, and the Union Army doctor hurried off. He undoubtedly had many more sick and wounded patients to care for. I was amazed he took the time from his duties to help us.

Mrs. Brown returned and handed a basket of supplies to Rebecca who put together the poultice for the little girl. Chloe wasn't coughing as much by now and began yawning. She and Bobby lay down next to each other. Lucy sat down with them, told them a story, and tucked them in.

Rev. Brown remarked, "We'll be back with food in the morning, folks. Rest, now."

Hand in hand, Rev. and Mrs. Brown left the barn. The dogs followed them to the door and returned to me. Rebecca and I checked on Daniel and Joseph before covering them with the rustic rose quilt.

They thanked us. "Thanks, Miss Sarah," and "Thank you, Dr. Rebecca."

She and I nodded goodnight. As Rebecca joined the children and Lucy, she whispered, "Good night, Miss Sarah."

I found a spot, lay down on a pile of hay, and tried to get comfortable, wrapping both my shawl and blanket around me. Duke and Scout followed and lay down beside me. In the quiet of the evening, I wept for my sister and her baby. As if sensing my need for comfort, Scout scooted close and whimpered. I reached to pet him, and he put his muzzle in my face and gave me a slobbery lick.

I embraced him. "It's okay, Scout," I told him. "Good dog." He lay back down. I murmured a prayer for our safety, and I prayed for Mother. I wondered, *Will I ever see her again?*

Exhausted, I slept.

Twenty-one

The Journey Continues
Sarah

"Even when all is lost and your faith has weakened; life will still surprise you."

~Naide P Obiang

On the road toward Harper's Ferry, West Virginia
Thursday, September 22, 1864

The next morning, Bobby and Chloe came to check on me, the dogs right behind them. Scout barked twice.

"Is you awake?" Chloe demanded. "We eating breakfast."

I sat up. The children giggled—their job done. They ran back to the table with the dogs behind them. I used the privy, washed my hands, and walked to the table.

The soldiers had donned their uniforms this morning. I thought Michael was even more handsome than when he wore my dead husband's clothes. His uniform showed wear and tear from the battlefield, but it was cleaner than the first time we saw him.

Michael and James helped their injured brothers dress with some modifications. James cut a seam in Joseph's pants for his bandages, and Michael cut Daniel's shirt sleeve off.

We passed dishes around and chatted in good humor. Michael and I gazed at each other several times. He passed the butter to me, and his hand lingered on mine for a moment longer. Someone chuckled, and I realized they wanted the butter. I blushed and passed it on.

I heard Chloe whisper to Bobby, "Is that man her beau?"

Bobby shrugged. "I don't know. Maybe."

Lucy stepped in. "Now that's enough, children!"

For the rest of the meal, I avoided Michael's gaze. I told myself Michael was getting us to Baltimore and then most likely I'd never see him again. I drank a glass of water and pretended my hand wasn't trembling.

As we picked up the plates after the meal, Rebecca caught my eye. She came alongside me, gathering silverware as she did. "Miss Sarah, did the children upset you?"

I turned away, realizing I was on the verge of tears. "I'm all right," I lied. "A little tired."

She put the utensils down. "Miss Sarah, you've been through so much, losing Mr. Simon, then Miss Emily and her baby, meeting these soldiers, and rescuing Lucy and Chloe. If anybody's got a reason to be emotional, it's you. But I think it's something else. I think you and Mr. Michael like each other. Well, you have a right to be happy. Mr. Simon's gone, and he ain't coming back." Her stern expression rivaled that of any schoolteacher. Then her expression softened, and she picked up the silverware again and walked to the sink.

I took a breath. She was right, of course. I picked up the plates and carried them to the sink. We washed dishes, straightened up the area, and packed our gear in the wagon.

Rebecca tended to Daniel's wound and gave him some willow bark to chew before she checked on Joseph's leg. Lucy took the children to the privy and washed their hands. All the while, I sensed Michael watching me, smiling.

After breakfast, we loaded the wagon and refilled our jars of water. We thanked our hosts. Mrs. Brown gave us apples, cornbread, and cheese.

Michael and James asked Rev. Brown for the best route to Baltimore from here. He replied there was a strong Union presence at Harper's Ferry about eleven miles past Charles Town. They'd burned and rebuilt the bridge several times, but we should be able to cross using the pontoon bridge that was now in place. Once we were across the river, we shouldn't have any more problems with slave catchers.

The three men talked soberly for a few minutes. I only caught a few words—"not deserters... doctor gave us a note... we're in God's hands."

Rev. Brown shook their hands warmly, then gave us an envelope, which Michael handed to me. I put it in my bag.

"You'll be stopped in Harper's Ferry, and this note might help."

Michael nodded.

Then Rev. Brown suggested without explanation that Rebecca, Lucy, and I ride in the back with the children and injured soldiers. He said a quick prayer for our safety, then opened the barn doors and we got back on the road with James and Thomas riding our spare horses. Rev. Brown warned us that otherwise, any surplus horses were sure to be confiscated by the Union army.

We saw a sign for Harper's Ferry. As we approached we saw destroyed buildings. Michael told us the Baltimore & Ohio Railroad bridge had been blown up and rebuilt, as well as the bridge for wagons and foot traffic.

Several battles had taken place here, and the town had changed hands many times. The explanation for the mayhem lay in its location. Harper's Ferry lay at the junction of two rivers—the Potomac and Shenandoah. It was the gateway to the Shenandoah Valley and the crossroads of the region.

We came to a checkpoint outside of town, with half a dozen wagons ahead. A trio of Union soldiers examined us.

Michael and James had a quiet conversation with one of them. Michael showed him the note from the doctor. The second soldier studied the passengers in the wagon. The third walked around with a pencil and wrote something down on a piece of paper. He took a second glance at the two Black women and a black child in the wagon and a Black man on horseback.

Then an officer approached. My heart pounded, and I clasped my hands to hide their trembling. We'd debated about what to do—have the soldiers don their uniforms or stay in civilian garb? Michael decided last night that they'd best put on their uniforms if we were going through Union-controlled territory. But would the Army officials understand the situation? Would all four soldiers be arrested for deserting?

Michael nodded at me and asked for the note in my bag.

I found it and handed it over. Michael saluted, then handed the note to the officer returned his salute, then read the note. He pondered its contents for a moment then returned the note to Michael, who put it into his shirt pocket. I wondered what it said. I hadn't taken the time to read it.

The officer called one of the other soldiers over and commanded him to take us to the regimental surgeon's tent.

We followed, and Michael sat tall and proud in his Union uniform, but my heart was thumping.

We reached the tent, and the soldier entered, ordering us to wait. When he re-emerged, a tall man was at his side. I was relieved to see Dr. Richardson. Michael saluted, and nodded in recognition. He went back inside the tent, but returned a moment later with four envelopes and handed them to Michael. They spoke in hushed tones, then the doctor turned to the soldier and said, "Gather some food for these folks." Then he waved cheerfully at us. "Safe travels and God bless!" he said.

The soldier nodded, signaled to Michael to follow, and we did.

A few minutes later, he handed us several small canvas bags. Inside, we found hardtack and cheese, dried apples, and several cans of salted meat. I divided up the food among us and set the cans aside. We ate cheese and hardtack thankfully.

Michael handed the envelopes to me. "Sarah, please stow these where they will be safe."

"What is it?" I asked, taking the envelopes and putting them into my big bag.

"The doctor wrote up official medical discharge papers for Daniel and Robert, and he wrote a military passes for James and me attesting to our mission of seeing you to Baltimore before we return to our regiment," he replied with obvious relief.

As we proceeded forward we saw a large contingent of Union soldiers in town. Daniel leaned forward. "We heard that General Sheridan was coming here. Looks like he made it." Many more structures we passed were damaged, and the arsenal was in ruins.

We reached the second checkpoint and saw a most peculiar sight. I knew the railroad bridge had been destroyed several times. So had the regular bridge for foot traffic, horses, and wagons—or so I thought. What was that ahead?

Michael turned. "We're crossing on a pontoon bridge. They sink small boats filled with rocks as stays and lay down many pontoons to support the deck for traffic."

It resembled a crude boardwalk built on top of a series of boats— only moving up and down as the wagons passed.

I glanced at Lucy and Rebecca, whose skeptical expressions matched mine. We watched half a dozen men on horseback cross the bridge to the other side, following several wagons, leaving a gap between wagons. As the horses and wagons moved, the so-called bridge moved up and down with the water's movement.

Michael called over his shoulder, "This is safe, I promise you. We're next."

The children were excited to see the river, and I realized neither one had seen such a large body of water before our journey. Rebecca and Lucy kept a firm grip on them, holding the children on their laps, and I noticed neither child wanted to get too close to the sides of the wagon. Not far away the river flowed over large rocks and several downed trees toward the riverbank.

We had the most peculiar sensation of the water flowing underneath the pontoon bridge and the sense of moving up and down. The children watched the adults for our reactions. Bobby and Chloe were excited and a little afraid of the unfamiliar sensation. Rebecca, Lucy, and I focused on staying calm.

Daniel whispered to the children, "We're going to have a fine story to tell my folks!"

Joseph did his best to act calm and caught my eye, then nodded as I tried my best not to hold my breath until we reached the other side. Once we had, I exhaled and smiled at the children.

A soldier at the next checkpoint told Michael to follow the road thirteen miles to Jefferson, Maryland, and then another nine to Frederick, and he warned us that the terrain would became more challenging.

He was right. We went up an incline, with woods on the left and the river valley on the right. We climbed the hills more slowly, being careful. The road was rough in places, and the women and children all got out of the wagon and walked alongside. Thomas led one horse and James the other.

The road turned inland and away from the water. When we reached the outskirts of Jefferson, we stopped for a quick meal, dividing up our dwindling supplies, giving the dogs some water and our leftovers. Then, we got back on the road for the last leg of the day's journey, hopefully.

By the time we saw signs for Frederick, we were all weary. I chatted with Michael, who was driving the wagon. James was on horseback while Thomas walked with the dogs. The children had cuddled with Lucy and fallen fast asleep. The two patients snored. Only Rebecca was awake in the back.

We noticed the presence of more people on the road now, and a larger number of Union soldiers, which eased my mind considerably. Folks didn't seem quite as wary here. Michael waved at a young man herding some sheep, and called out to him.

"Hello, neighbor!"

"Hello, yourself," the young fellow replied with an easy grin.

"We're looking for lodging for the night," Michael called back.

The young man's gaze fell on our companions, and the grin on his face never faltered.

"I know a place," he declared. "Follow me." And without another word, he turned and walked down a side path. He let out a shrill whistle, and a dog I hadn't seen began chivvying the sheep ahead of him.

Michael and I exchanged a bemused look, then turned the wagon to follow.

An older gentleman stood on the porch of large farmhouse. The young man who served as our guide merely nodded at the man and continued on, as the dog herded the sheep into a pasture beyond the house.

The older gentleman called out, "Looks like you folks could do with a rest and a bit of food.

Michael replied, "Yes, sir. We'd like to rest and get some water for our horses."

The man gestured for us to follow him. Behing the house was a smaller structure with a cross on the front. He opened the doors, and we followed him inside.

"This is my father's church, but my younger brother, Timothy, and I help out as we can. I'm Timothy, by the way." He stretched out his hand, and Michael climbed down from the wagon and shook it. "You're safe here—you and your companions. The privies are out the side door and there is a pump behind the curtain with soap and towels where you can wash up if you'd like. There's another pump out back with a watering trough for your horses, and I'll have my brother bring feed for your horses too. My wife, Mary, is fixing supper, if you would care to join us."

Lucy gently shook the children awake and took them to the privy.

"I think we might be more comfortable out here, away from prying eyes, if you understand my meaning," Michael answered.

I thought of something and asked, "But perhaps if we might trouble your wife for some hot water to make tea?"

"Of course," Timothy responded. "I'll fetch some cornbread and that teapot. There are blankets in that large box in the corner," he pointed toward the back of the room. "I'll be back in a bit."

James, Michael, and Thomas worked together to care for the horses, using the pump in the back. Thomas got water and scraps for the dogs.

Rebecca changed Daniel's bandages, checked Joseph's knee and ankle, then led Lucy over to the box. "You and Chloe deserve your own blankets. Your quilt is too lovely to use on this trip." They found two blankets.

Lucy told her, "Thank you," and her eyes shone with tears.

Rebecca put her arm around Lucy. "You have friends now, Lucy, and we take care of each other."

Timothy returned a few minutes later with a big skillet filled with cornbread, and his younger brother, still grinning, carried a jar of molasses. A young woman I assumed to be Mary followed, carrying a big tea kettle. She put the kettle on the table and then reached into her apron for a tin box of loose tea, a spoon, and a tea ball. She nodded and left without a word.

Timothy set the skillet on the table and said, "Here you go. There are plates and utensils in the cupboard. We'll see you in the morning. Get some rest." Then the two brothers left, closing the barn door behind them.

Lucy sliced the cornbread up and placed each piece on a small plate. She put a spoon in the molasses as we gathered around the table. I poured water into tin cups for the children and the patients. Rebecca made her tea with the willow bark. I drank a cup of loose tea, savoring the warmth.

Thankful for the food and the hospitality of strangers, we ate our meal in near silence. Then Lucy and Thomas washed their hands and got the children comfortable on a bale of hay with their blankets.

Rebecca saw a curtain on one side of the room, hung there for privacy. "Lucy, please come with me. I have cream for the scars on your back." She was carrying her canvas bag.

Lucy followed her. I heard them whisper. A few minutes later, they walked out, smiling, and lay down near the children.

Thomas made his bed a respectful distance from Rebecca and Lucy. Michael and James lay down close to the wagon near Daniel and Joseph, and I lay down between the two groups.

I wrapped myself in my shawl and blanket against the chill of the night and closed my eyes, thinking of Simon. The dogs curled up in balls beside me and whined until I petted them. I whispered, "Goodbye, Simon. I loved you, but I need to let you go. Find peace."

Listening to the quiet breathing of the others, I fell asleep.

Friday, September 23, 1864

When dawn broke, the dogs barked and ran around in excitement. The children checked to see if I was awake. I grabbed them, and we rolled around giggling while the dogs barked.

The three women glanced at the curtained area in the back, which had a water pump, several towels, washcloths, and lye soap. We welcomed the opportunity to freshen up. I told Rebecca to go first, and I'd check on the patients.

Rebecca found a gentler soap in her bag of herbs and headed back, then came out serene, fresh, and beautiful, with her hair wrapped up in a beautiful kerchief. Next, Lucy and Chloe took their turn, and I was thankful for having clean clothes for all of them. We heard giggling. Lucy's face was shining with happiness when they emerged, and she was wearing one of my old dresses. Her daughter had a new dress, along with a sunbonnet.

While they were cleaning up, I evaluated the clothing I'd brought along at Rebecca's urging. When it was my turn, I picked out a pretty skirt and blouse and some fresh undergarments.

Rebecca saw me walk by with the dress over my arm and gave me an approving nod. "Good choice, Miss Sarah."

I was self-conscious when I emerged fifteen minutes later, feeling everybody staring at me. *What would Mother think? Is it too soon?*

Rebecca declared, "Miss Sarah, you've been wearing those black widow weeds for nearly three years. It's time to put them aside."

Thomas shook his head in agreement.

Bobby ran back to see me. "You're pretty, Miss Sarah, I mean Mama," and Chloe came over to feel my cotton dress. She smiled and held my hand.

Rebecca dug into the carpet bags and found clean clothes for Bobby, while Thomas did the same. He grinned at me. "I never took no trip before, but it's nice to have clean clothes." Then he took Bobby by the hand. Rebecca walked back with them, holding their clothes. The loving expressions that passed between them made my heart hurt.

As I walked to the table, Michael stood. "If I were wearing a hat,

I'd tip it to you. You're beautiful in that dress." The other soldiers nodded.

A knock on the barn door announced we had visitors. Timothy, his brother, an older couple, and the young lady walked in bearing pots, pitchers, and bowls. Timothy introduced us to his parents, the Reverend and Mrs. Taylor. We told them how good it felt to wash up, and his wife and mother grinned.

"I told them it would be a wonderful addition," Mrs. Taylor agreed.

We enjoyed a delicious breakfast of porridge, cornbread, butter, and molasses with coffee. Lucy jumped up to help serve, and they let her pass out the bowls. Then the children wanted to help, so they passed out spoons and knives and thick washcloths for napkins. Rev. Taylor poured glasses of water for the children and coffee for the adults.

Lucy regarded them in tears. "I never been served by white folks before. You folks are angels."

Mary nodded with a shy smile, "We're blessed to help."

As we got busy eating, Mrs. Taylor scooped the last of the oatmeal porridge into a bowl, set it on the floor, and told the dogs, "Here you go. You need to share." The dogs got to work eating and thanked her with a sloppy kiss when she bent down to pet them, and she laughed.

Thomas filled the dogs' bowl with water, and they had a good drink.

Mary took Lucy aside. "Someone donated a couple of small carpet bags. I wonder if you could use them?" She walked over by the barrel and returned with two small bags.

Lucy just stood there for a moment. Then, she replied, "Thank you!" She took them as Chloe ran over. "For us?"

Mary crouched down to reach eye level with the child. "Yes, dear, for you and your mama."

Lucy carried the two bags to the wagon and transferred things from the canvas bag to her new carpet bags.

Rebecca suggested, "I think we should put your quilt in a trunk," and Lucy agreed.

I transferred the slave catcher's purse to my reticule. If we needed more money for the boat and train, we would have it.

Michael and James finished eating, got up, and talked with our hosts. Rev. Tayler told them, "I'd encourage you to head east and turn onto the road to New Market about ten miles away for a rest. Then on to Lisbon, twelve miles away. You'll find help there. They can advise you about where to sell your wagon and horses before heading on to Baltimore."

Rebecca and Lucy gathered the dirty towels and brought them to our hosts and thanked them again. We filled up our jars with water.

Mary handed Rebecca a small basket filled with cornbread wrapped up in a towel, and another basket full of apples for our trip. "God bless and safe travels."

We felt refreshed and grateful for the kindness of strangers on the Underground Railroad. Everyone waved, and we settled in for another day of traveling through Maryland with our destination—Baltimore!

Twenty-two

Trouble down the Road
Sarah

There is no living thing that is not afraid when it faces danger.
The true courage is in facing danger when you are afraid.
~L. Frank Baum

On the road toward Baltimore, Maryland
Friday, September 23, 1864

It was a sunny day for a drive, and we fell into companionable conversation. It was Thomas's turn to drive the wagon, and Michael was on horseback, so James, Rebecca, and Lucy walked with the dogs.

Thomas and I chatted away. Michael rode ahead of us to check out the area and then returned. We passed through woods with mountains on either side. Daniel napped while the children skipped along and talked about everything they saw. Rebecca and Lucy talked about quilts as they walked, and James remained alert, bringing up the rear. Joseph also kept watch.

Thomas glanced over. "This is pretty country, isn't it?"

I agreed. "It's beautiful. I've studied these mountains all my life. I loved living in Boston and being closer to the ocean. But I've never been west of Virginia. It's hard to imagine how big our country is, even after checking maps. I can't wait to get on the train to Iowa."

"You reckon we gonna have enough money for all those tickets?"

"Don't worry. If we need more money, my best friend's father is a minister, and we're going to see them in Boston when we stop. He and his wife are abolitionists. Rebecca and I have been planning this trip with Emily for months now. Right now, we must have faith we'll reach Iowa."

Thomas agreed. "The good Lord got us this far. Rebecca is a wonderful woman, and we been praying." He sighed.

"I see you two making those lovey-dovey smiles at each other. Something tells me we better plan a wedding when we get to Iowa."

"If she'll have me."

I laughed. "Have you asked her?"

He shook his head. "I mean to ask her to marry me once we get out west, and I can set myself up in some business. A man wants to have his life in order before he asks a woman to marry him."

I nodded at his practical outlook. He was a good man. I was thankful again that Mother had urged me to bring him along.

So far, we hadn't run into any Confederate soldiers. We'd seen some abandoned packs earlier and evidence of a roadside camp, so we knew they had been along the road recently, and we tried to be cautious. I remembered the young man's warning earlier—it isn't safe here.

We reached New Market and stopped for a break, and Rebecca checked on the patients. I passed around the cornbread from our last stop, and we drank some water. Michael climbed up beside me to take his turn driving the wagon while James rode the horse on the lookout. Thomas, Rebecca, and Lucy walked with the dogs. The patients entertained the children by telling stories and pointing out features of the landscape they passed.

Michael glanced over. "It's going to be hard to say goodbye to you. We've done a good job of traveling together, haven't we?"

I was thinking the same thing. I would miss Michael.

The hours passed, the children and patients took naps, we changed drivers, and we ate the apples. James came back to say he'd seen a sign for Lisbon. Ten minutes later, we found another indication of what had guided us to the Underground Railroad before—a quilt over a chair by a window.

An older woman stepped out onto the porch. "Good afternoon, friends. Do you need help?" She studied our group.

Michael replied, "Yes, please, ma'am."

Her husband walked up from the farmyard. "I thought I heard someone. Come on back. My name is Reverend Walker."

Michael guided the wagon towards a large barn with a cross at the top. Rev. Walker opened the doors, and we followed him inside. James rode his horse inside and dismounted, then Rev. Walker shook hands with both Michael and James.

I tried to smooth my hair back with my hands. Then, I realized how foolish that was, after so many days on the road. Lucy whispered to me, and I asked the reverend if there was a necessary room for the children. He pointed toward an outhouse, and Lucy and Rebecca took the children to relieve themselves.

The men were discussing where to sell the wagon. The minister told us he knew people in Ellicott City, outside of Baltimore, now only thirty miles away. "I'd advise you folks to rest here, eat a good meal, and start out fresh in the morning."

He pointed to the trapdoor in the back, the tunnel for escape, and a place to hide in the hayloft. He pointed out two sources of water.

We were all weary. Michael and James glanced at me, and I nodded in assent. "Thank you for your kindness, Rev. Walker."

He gazed at me. "You folks are doing the Lord's work here."

Later, we enjoyed supper. The hosts, Rev. and Mrs. Walker, their daughter, and two young Black women, entered the barn with the food, and then joined us. We sat around a large table and ate as we talked.

"We've appreciated the kindness of several of the stops on the Underground Railroad," I commented. "You've all had these barns where we could pull the wagon inside, in case slave catchers were roaming the roads during the day."

Rev. Walker smiled. "In the early days, stops on the Underground Railroad around here were old barns, sheds, or cellars, all hidden places. A group of like-minded ministers decided we could do more. So, we built these big barns for our congregations to use on Sunday and included a few other amenities. Most of our guests arrive from the woods, but a few do come in a wagon."

He explained that the two young ladies—Hanna and

Phillis—were once runaway slaves. Mrs. Walker was teaching them to read and write, and the girls helped cook and care for the runaway slaves they sheltered. The girls enjoyed their work and chatted away with Rebecca and Lucy.

Michael and I sat by each other at supper. I was self-conscious because he kept smiling at me. Then it was time to clean up, and we needed to get the children to bed.

The family left, promising to bring breakfast in the morning.

Thomas and Lucy took charge of the children, washing sticky little hands and faces, then settling them down. Soon, the children fell asleep.

Rebecca and I checked on the patients while Michael, Thomas, and James took care of the horses. I watched them work together and reflected on the way we relied on each other, regardless of skin color.

Several big boxes of clothes were over against the wall. Rebecca rummaged through the boxes, searching for clothing for Bobby, Lucy, and Chloe, finding several things for each. Rebecca called Lucy over to see what she'd found. Lucy was more relaxed now. She opened her bag and folded up the things from Rebecca. Then she embraced her friend and thanked her.

Wrapping my shawl around my shoulders, I watched all the activity from where I sat with my blanket, weary from our journey but sad because I didn't want to say goodbye to Michael.

He sat beside me. "Thank you for all you've done."

"Thank you, Michael, but I see now we couldn't have made the trip without you and your friends. How would we have rescued Lucy and her daughter from those awful men?"

"Thomas could have done it alone, but it helps to have several men to scare off bullies like Mr. Hays and his assistant."

I shuddered. "What if they had attacked us? One gun against two doesn't sound like good odds. Emily and I were so proud of our plans, but now they seem inadequate. Thank God you found our barn."

Michael smiled tenderly. "God led us to your barn." He took my hand. "Are you nervous about the next stage of the journey? You'll be fine. Daniel's stronger and Joseph is moving around better. We'll send telegrams once we reach Baltimore, so your mother doesn't worry and alert my folks to expect you in a few days."

I stared at my hand in his and enjoyed the warmth and comfort of his hand. Then, I thought, *I cannot rely on this man. He's going away. That's what men do in wartime. I must be strong so that he doesn't worry about us.*

I caught an errant strand from my bun. "Yes, Mother will worry. I'd like to send a telegram to my friends in Boston, Abigail's parents. They'll help us if we need it."

"You'll like Jubilee Junction and Iowa." Michael stared at me with those lovely green eyes. "The people will like you as well." He paused. "I have a favor to ask."

I sat up straighter, wondering what he could want from me.

"Would you write to me and let me know how you're doing?"

"Certainly." I felt flustered. He took my hand again, and I flushed.

"It's going to be difficult to say goodbye, Sarah Elizabeth McDonald."

I blinked back tears, trying to keep my composure. He got up and moved away. Alone, I laid down and gave in to tears. The dogs padded over and whimpered until I gave them some attention, welcoming the distraction. I fell asleep grieving and feeling vulnerable.

I'd lost my husband after a single year of marriage filled with conflicting values and worldviews. Now, I'd found a man who listened to me and valued my opinion. But I'd say goodbye to him at the train station tomorrow, not knowing if he would survive the war to join me in Jubilee Junction.

Saturday, September 24, 1864

I woke up smelling something wonderful. Duke and Scout were nosing my hand with their muzzles.

The children stared down at me. "Is you awake?" asked Chloe.

"Get back, you two rascals—I'm going to sit up."

I saw they were serving breakfast. The children scampered back over to eat.

I washed up, sat down at the table, and watched as our group passed the food around like a family. People talked, ate, and helped with the children who were seated on either side of Thomas. Lucy, Rebecca, and I sat across from them, and Michael sat beside me. He glanced at me with a sweet expression, and I averted my eyes, because I didn't want to reveal my feelings for him.

Our host family came for the dishes and brought us a canvas bag of apples and hardtack for a snack on the road. We packed our belongings into the wagon.

Michael and James chatted with our host family, and Michael called me over. "We're talking about stopping outside Baltimore, where we can sell the wagon and four of the horses."

"Wonderful. Yes, I've wondered about that."

Rev. Walker suggested, "You should check into the train to Boston. It's faster."

"I didn't know if the railroads were safe."

"Earlier in the war, they were dangerous," he admitted. "But Union soldiers are guarding them now. They are quite safe," he assured me.

We loaded into the wagon, said our goodbyes, and departed for Baltimore with a new plan. Michael drove the wagon, with James on horseback. Thomas and Lucy walked, followed by the dogs. As we approached Baltimore, I finally began to relax.

A few miles later, Chloe began fussing in the back, and Rebecca leaned forward. "Can we have a rest break, please?"

We stopped, just as we had dozens of times before. The men walked off in one direction with Michael staying behind with the wagon and horses. The women walked off in a different direction.

I did my business and hurried back towards the wagon. Rebecca and Lucy lingered with Chloe, who told them her tummy hurt. Since she'd had several helpings of everything at breakfast, I wasn't surprised.

Suddenly, someone grabbed me around the waist from behind with one arm while the other held a large pistol, moving it back and forth in my field of vision. My feet dangled off the ground and my stomach churned from the stench of the man holding me captive—a ripe mix of tobacco, whiskey, and body odor. "Well, little Miss Do-gooder. Did ya miss me?" A low voice growled in my ear.

I couldn't move my arms, so I flailed, kicking my attacker as I tried to figure out who it was. The cool steel of the gun now pressed to my temple.

"Who are you?" I asked, repulsed by his stench.

"You killed my partner, Rufus Hays, but didn't you wonder where I went?" the man asked.

At that moment I realized—it was the slave catcher's partner.

Twenty-three

Rescue from Dougie and Back to Black
Sarah

*"We hope all danger may be overcome; but to conclude that
no danger may ever arise would itself be extremely dangerous."*
~Abraham Lincoln

On the road toward Baltimore, Maryland
Saturday, September 24, 1864

*T*he cold steel of the gun pressed to my temple.
I shut my eyes and prayed. The man was walking towards his horse
with me in his grasp.

I heard the dogs barking and some commotion—and my smelly
assailant flew through the air, releasing me from his grasp and
knocking me to the side. Only afterward did I understand that
Lucy and Rebecca had tackled him from behind.

"You let Miss Sarah go!" demanded Rebecca.

"Shame on you!" added Lucy.

His gun went flying, too.

Once the slave catcher was on the ground, Chloe and Bobby
ran over and kicked him.

"You a bad man!" Chloe recognized him.

"You tried to hurt my mama!" declared Bobby.

I observed all of this from my place on the ground, inelegantly
sprawled, as Lucy and Rebecca sat on his back, berating him. The
children ran around, chanting. "We caught the bad man."

Thomas and the dogs appeared, and Duke and Scout were

growling mere inches from my assailant's face. Thomas didn't call the dogs off, and his face reflected their hostility.

Michael and James each took an arm and helped me up from the ground. I tried to straighten my skirts, only to discover they were torn and soiled. We turned to see the man cowering on the ground, with two angry Black women sitting on his back. Two young children kicked his sides, while the circling dogs snarled, growled, and snapped at his face and throat.

James threw Thomas a rope from the wagon, and he tied up the prisoner. He then stood guard over the grunting bandit, giving him an occasional prod when his noise became wearisome.

Only then did the two women back off. Daniel and Joseph cheered them on from the wagon, trying not to laugh. Thomas bent down and praised the dogs, who licked his hand. He then took an aggressive stand next to the slave catcher, who alternated between swearing and pleading for mercy as he expected what appeared to be his imminent demise.

James made a point of aiming his rifle at the prisoner, and Michael turned to praise the dogs, while Rebecca wrapped her arms around me to comfort me. Lucy gathered the children into her arms, telling them what a good job they did.

"Thank you," I whispered to Rebecca, trying my hardest to breathe normally. I was shaken to my core. What would have happened if he'd reached his horse?

She replied, "I promised your mama I'd watch out for you, didn't I?"

I slumped in her arms for just a moment, weary to my bones. Then I straightened and whispered, "Thank you," again.

Michael turned to me. "Sarah, did he hurt you?"

"I'll be fine. My skirts tore, but I can change at the next stop." I spoke with as much dignity as I could muster. My back and knees hurt, and I wanted to burn the dress after having that disgusting man's arm around my waist. I tried to control my breathing to calm down.

James admitted, "I was going to help, but the ladies had it in hand. Then Thomas and the dogs arrived, and the children helped.

You were all fierce! Now what? What do we do with this scoundrel? We could shoot him and leave him here."

The unnamed scoundrel spoke up, "You all good Christian folks. You wouldn't shoot me in cold blood, now would ya?" The dogs sniffed him and barked.

James and Michael ignored him as they discussed his fate. James wanted to hang him from the nearest tree. Michael speculated it would be simpler to just slit his throat.

Daniel addressed the scoundrel, "So where were you when the three of us shot your partner after he fired at our wagon, with women and children on board? You were running away to save your skin. And what kind of man hunts down young mothers and their little girls? You are the lowest of the low."

The man shrugged. "My partner Rufus was sweet on that slave girl. I couldn't talk no sense into his thick head. He wanted to keep her for hisself and maybe sell the little girl. When he got shot, I turned around and headed home. Then I thought of all the money those slaves wuz worth and turned around again."

"So, what's your name?" demanded James.

"Beauregard Douglas Brown, or Dougie to my friends."

"That's quite the name. All right then, what shall we do with Dougie?" asked James.

Daniel called out, "I say we shoot him."

"If we're taking a vote, yes, shoot him," chimed in Joseph.

"I don't normally approve of violence, but in this case I'm willing to make an exception," I spoke up, and noticed Lucy and Rebecca comforting Chloe, crying because the slave catcher mentioned selling her. Both women glared at Dougie, who shrank back.

Michael took charge. "James, tie him to the back of the wagon, and we'll turn him over to our next host. Thomas, you can ride his horse and bring up the rear where you can keep an eye on him. And gag hm. I don't want to hear another word come out of his mouth."

Dougie spoke up, "Ain't you afraid I'm gonna tell on you folks, taking all these slaves somewhere? Maryland is still a slave state you know."

Michael retorted, "And will you also share the story of how two

Black women—two *free* women, mind you, *former* slaves—and two children tackled you after you grabbed a white woman, intending to kidnap her, and threatened to shoot her?"

Dougie shut up.

Michael reached out a hand to me and I climb aboard the wagon. We took off at a gentle pace. Dougie kept up. Duke and Scout walked with him, occasionally nipping at his heels. Rebecca, and Lucy walked behind him.

Twenty minutes later, he wasn't doing as well and faltered, then stopped. The children tried to encourage him, calling out, "Keep walking, Dougie."

Fortunately for Dougie, we were passing a big farmhouse. Behind it, I could see a large barn. We pulled over.

A large, bearded man was working in the front yard. He saw us stop, and he stared at Dougie, tied to the back of the wagon. He stepped toward us and called out, "Friends, do you need some help?"

Michael told him, "Yes, we do. This man, Beauregard Douglas Brown, or Dougie to his friends, attacked one of our women at gunpoint a ways back. Can you turn him over to the local authorities?"

Our host scowled at Dougie, who stared down. A second, younger man appeared behind him—a son, I presumed, because of their resemblence.

The older man said, "Howard, please get the sheriff."

The younger man snorted, "You mean Uncle Harvey?" and walked to the stable. A few minutes later, he appeared on horseback and rode off.

Michael and James got down and spoke quietly with the man who identified himself as a Methodist minister, Reverend Wright. Thomas tied Dougie to a hitching post in the side yard and James stood guard over him while the rest of us pulled into the barn.

Lucy escorted the children to the privy while I searched in my suitcase for another skirt. I found one and walked back to the curtained area and changed, wincing because my knees hurt. Rebecca saw my pained expression when I came back out and had me sit down. She lifted my skirts and examined my knees. I'd scraped them during the scuffle. She put some of her herbal ointment on them, and it helped.

"Thank you, Rebecca. We're so fortunate to have you with us."

She checked her bag of herbs. "I'll make a poultice for your knees later," she promised.

Thomas checked the saddlebags of Dougie's horse and discovered a stack of papers—notices of escaped slaves with their likenesses and the bounty for their return. Two of the images bore a striking resemblance to Lucy and Chloe. A sour look crossed his face, and he called to Michael and showed him his discovery.

"Burn those," Michael declared, the set of his mouth thin and hard.

Thomas nodded, set a match to the papers, then ground the ashes into the dirt under his boots. He returned to examine Dougie's horse and gave a low whistle. The slave catcher had been as vicious with his animal as he had been with enslaved human beings. He then led Dougie's obviously mistreated horse to the watering trough and groomed it, running his hands along its back and flank, checking for sores. His nostrils flared in anger. "A man that mistreats an animal is no better than an animal," he muttered, and the horse neighed in apparent agreement.

Mrs. Wright, followed by her two daughters, entered the barn with food and coffee. We thanked them and sat down and ate, making a plate for James and one for Dougie. Lucy and Rebecca took the food outside, and Lucy spoon-fed Dougie. I almost felt sorry for Dougie. Almost.

I wondered again if we would find welcome or hatred in Iowa. I'd lost my family in Virginia when Emily and her baby died. Simon had been dead for three years. Father was likely dead. I hoped Mother would make the trek to Iowa. But Thomas, Rebecca, and Lucy had become like siblings to me, and the children were like my own niece and nephew. What would I do if the people in Iowa treated them unkindly?

After a few minutes, Rebecca and Lucy returned and sat down to eat their own lunch, trying not to smirk.

Daniel asked, "So how is Dougie holding up?"

They reported he was alternating between swearing and begging.

Michael joined me as I ate. It was clear there was something on his mind.

"Out with it," I demanded. "You look like you've taken a bite out of a green persimmon."

A wry grin crossed his face, and he confessed, "I fear we may have a problem with Dougie."

I brushed crumbs from my skirt. "What kind of a problem?" I enquired.

"We confided our entire story regarding Dougie to Reverend Wright," Michael said. "He is a good man, and he sympathizes with our cause, but he warned me that his brother, the sheriff, is a stickler for the law. And the truth is, as things stand now, it's really our word against Dougie's about what happened on the road. Dougie could just as easily accuse us of murdering his partner, stealing his money, and assaulting him."

"That's absurd!" I declared. "The man is a slave catcher!"

"Which," Michael reminded me, "is not an illegal profession—and as Dougie mentioned, Maryland is still a slave state."

I suddenly feared the meal our hosts had so graciously provided was about to come back up.

"I told Rev. Wright about what happened with Rufus Hays and where to find his body, so he could relay it to the sheriff," Michael continued. "He said it sounded like a straightforward case of self-defense to him, but he did admit we've no proof that Rufus shot at us first. Rev. Wright said he thought he could convince his brother to hold Dougie for twenty-four hours, at least long enough for the sheriff to decide whether there is enough evidence to hold him longer."

I struggled not to wring my hands. "What are we to do?"

"We run," Michael said.

"Please forgive me, but I couldn't help but overhear," Mrs. Wright appeared seemingly from nowhere and sat down beside me. "I fear it is not just your Mr. Dougie that you must be concerned with. There are many in our state who sympathize with the Confederacy and would be only too happy to report runaway slaves and those who choose to help them so we need to find a safe way for you to travel West with your friends. I believe I can help, if you will allow me." She turned to Michael. "Corporal, if you will ready your wagon, Sarah and I have some preparations to make.

Bemused, Michael obeyed the feisty woman, and I followed her toward the back of the building where she opened a large closet which was well-concealed by a curtain that stretched halfway across the width of the room. "Rebecca, Lucy, will you come here please?" she called out, and my friends approached.

She studied the three of us women appraisingly, then opened the closet and pulled out three sets of black garments. She held one up in front of me and nodded. "Yes, she murmured, "this will do nicely." She handed a set of garments to each of us with the command to change quickly.

I asked, "What are these?"

"Habits," Mrs. Wright replied then gave a little clap. "Just imagine. Three faithful nuns escorting two poor, destitute orphans out west to their new families."

"But where in the world did you find nuns' habits?" I stammered.

"My dear," she giggled as if it were the world's greatest joke, "there is a reason this state is called *Mary*-land."

I looked ruefully at the garment and thought, *So much for giving up wearing black.*

One by one, Lucy, Rebecca, and I took our turns behind the curtain and emerged moments later as Sisters Sarah, Lucy, and Rebecca. Mrs. Wright completed our ensemble by slipping a crucifix around each of our necks and attaching a strand of small beads to our belts, which she called a chaplet.

I fingered the chaplet. *I thought I'd left my widow's garb behind me, but this is just as bad.*

Mrs. Wright examined each one of us, made a few adjustments, and then encouraged us. "Relax, my sisters. The hardest part of the journey is getting to Boston. You should feel safer there, but I'd stay in these habits until you reach your journey's end in Iowa. You never know who might be on the train."

Her plan made sense, but I wondered what Emily and Mother would say if they could see me now dressed as a nun.

We sat down with the curious children and the astonished men looked on. "We're going on a big adventure, and we're going to play make-believe," I told them in my best schoolmarm voice.

They were staring with curiosity at our habits. Bobby asked, "Do we get to wear costumes too?"

I thought fast, "We are going to make-believe that Rebecca, Lucy, and I are nuns, and you and Chloe are going to make-believe that you are little children. Won't that be fun?"

Chloe clapped her hands. "I like it!"

Bobby didn't seem as enthused. "So, what do I call you now? Mama? Miss Sarah?"

"You must call me *Sister* Sarah. And this is Sister Rebecca and Sister Lucy."

The children said, "All right."

Mrs. Wright gave us some pointers about our attire and how nuns would behave, including a couple of prayers we might say while fingering our beads. "You're perfect!" Then she whispered, "Good luck, and God bless you."

The Wright daughters handed us a basket with traveling food for the train trip. We thanked them again for all they had done to help us.

Rev. Wright told us, "Sister Sarah, you're doing God's work here. God bless you all!"

We loaded up, leaving Dougie's horse behind. Michael noted we didn't want to add horse thievery to the list of crimes Dougie might accuse us of.

The children waved and yelled, "Goodbye, Dougie!" and the dogs barked their farewell, but Dougie did not so much as wave.

As we headed down the road, I sat up front by Michael while James rode a horse alongside, and Thomas, Rebecca, and Lucy walked.

"We will pass a livery stable near the railroad station," Michael said to me. "The owner is Mrs. Wright's brother. She told me he'll buy your wagon and horses."

"What price do you think they will fetch??" I asked.

"The wagon should bring around sixty dollars and the horses at least a hundred and twenty-five each. All told between five and six hundred dollars. Your tickets won't cost near that much, so you'll end up with a nest egg to start your new life."

"Thank you, Michael. I wasn't worried."

But I had been worried, and he knew it.

Michael turned and gazed at me with those magical green eyes, and the butterflies fluttered in my stomach. I reminded myself he was leaving us at the train station.

I fingered the beads on my chaplet. *If only Emily and the baby were with us.* I shut my eyes, wondering how the funeral service had gone, and how Mother and the freed slaves fared. I fought back tears, wiping a stray drop that wriggled down my cheek.

I'm tired of tears, Lord, I prayed as I fingered a bead. *Please, help us get to the train station.*

Twenty-four

Farewell, Sister Sarah
Sarah

"A journey is best measured in friends, rather than miles."
~Tim Cahill

On the road toward Baltimore, Maryland
Saturday, September 24, 1864

We pulled into the livery station. The man who came out to greet us bore a striking resemblence to Mrs. Wright, our previous host. He asked, "Friends, do you need some help today?"

Michael replied, "Yes, sir. My friends are embarking on a long journey and will no longer have need of this wagon and four of the horses. They would like to sell them, but first we need to drop off our people and their luggage at the train station. They're catching the train for Boston."

The man nodded. "I'd best come with you. We can conclude our business there, then those of us who are remaining can return here."

We walked inside, where the man introduced himself as Paul Wilcox. Mr. Wilcox and Michael talked, and then I signed some papers. He chuckled as he took in my habit. "I have to assume you have met my sister and her husband, the Rev. and Mrs. Wright?" he asked as he counted out $600 and placed it in my hand.

"Why yes, we have—such a helpful, kind couple," I managed.

Mr. Wilcox chuckled, "Yes, indeed. Helpful and kind... *sister.*"

Michael snorted with laughter.

"Thank you." I put $550 into my reticule and handed Michael

$50. "You're going to need money for food and lodging to find your unit."

"I don't want your money."

Mr. Wilcox commented, "It's none of my business, but no good comes from arguing with women about money, especially nuns."

Michael relented. "I'll pay you back in Iowa."

Mr. Wilcox checked the clock. "We best get to the station with those trunks and buy your tickets, Sister Sarah."

We walked back to the wagon, and I climbed in back so Mr. Wilcox could sit next to Michael. He offered curt instructions to his assistant in the stable, then he directed us to the train station.

We soon arrived at our destination. The trains were large, smokey, and hissing steam. The children watched, fascinated but frightened by the crowds and noise. I realized they'd seen nothing like it in their young lives. As we got off the wagon, Lucy and Rebecca kept a firm grasp on Chloe and Bobby. The children stared at everything but stayed close to their mothers.

We each grabbed our small bags for the train trip. Rebecca tucked Bobby's rag doll and a few books into her bags, as well as the bag of herbs. I took a few pencils and a small tablet out of my suitcase and put them in my reticule on my wrist and grabbed my big bag. Joseph hobbled along on his crutches while Daniel walked next to the children, Lucy, and Rebecca. Thomas grabbed his bag and helped Rebecca carry hers. James carried two blankets, the red and green quilt, and two pillows for the trip. We'd packed the rest of our goods inside the trunks. The dogs followed along behind at Thomas' heels.

Michael and I stepped up and purchased the tickets to Boston, which only cost $1.50 each and $.50 for the children. We paid an additional fee for the three trunks, and several porters stepped up with a cart. First, they put tags on the trunks and gave me the tickets, which I tucked into the bag around my neck. Then they loaded up the trunks and took them to the baggage car.

As we walked towards the train to Boston, Michael and James followed us along with Mr. Wilcox. Mr. Wilcox pointed out our coach, and we stopped to bid farewell. James and Michael shook hands with each person and said goodbye. The dogs sat and wagged their tails, watching. Michael kissed my hand and told me he'd be praying for safe travels for us.

I replied, "I'll be praying for the same for you and James."

We hesitated and stared at each other, holding hands—not wanting to let go.

Daniel broke the spell. "Go on, man. Kiss her properly!"

James and Joseph encouraged Michael to kiss me as well.

Rebecca, Lucy, and Thomas all grinned. The children joined in, "Kiss her!" and jumped up and down.

I could feel myself blushing under all the nun garments.

Michael chuckled gently as he leaned in. "Sister Sarah, may I kiss you?" he whispered.

I nodded. He kissed me on the lips, and then I flung my arms around him and kissed him back heartily.

I whispered in his ear, "Stay safe and come back to me, Michael."

The people standing behind us chuckled, gasped, or made various comments.

Mr. Wilcox grinned. "Aye, the Lord works in mysterious ways!" He called one of the Black porters to his side, slipped him some cash, gestured to us, and smiled.

The porter came over. "Sisters, please come with me now and bring all your companions." He glanced down at the two hounds by my side, on their best behavior. I picked up my big bag, almost in a daze.

We boarded the train, and the porters escorted us to a private car with a dozen seats, a couple of benches, and a small washroom. We stowed our bags under the benches and glanced around. My heart was still thumping hard from Michael's embrace.

Thomas helped Rebecca get the two injured men settled and comfortable. The children stared out the windows. "Miss Sarah, um, I mean, Sister Sarah, you need to come over here."

They were staring at something outside. Scout barked once, looking out the window. Duke nuzzled my hand.

I glanced, and it was Michael, James, and Mr. Wilcox. They shouted something I could not understand, waving, and pointing toward their wrists. I waved back, not comprehending their meaning. The train was about to depart, when it dawned on me to look down at my wrist. That's when I realized what they were saying—my arm was bare! I'd somehow dropped my reticule with all my money.

A moment later the door to our compartment opened, and a porter handed me my reticule. "A soldier told me this bag belongs to you, Ma'am," he said.

Thanking the porter, I locked eyes with Michael, held my reticule up, and mouthed, "Thank you." I'd apparently dropped it when we kissed. I stayed there staring at him as the train pulled out of the station, and remained there until I could no longer see him.

When I turned, Daniel spoke in a reverent tone. "I feel better knowing that Michael is praying for all of us."

Thomas, Joseph, Lucy, and Rebecca chuckled. The children giggled, still at the window.

"He likes you, ma'am," Sister Lucy said.

Joseph snorted. "I think it's more than *like*. I never saw him kiss a nun before. But come to think of it, I'm not sure I've ever seen anyone kiss a nun before...at least not like *that* kiss."

The relief I felt at finally departing the station was etched on everyone else's faces.

Joseph spoke up. "We've made it this far, Miss Sarah. Thank you."

Daniel nodded, now sober. "You've taken good care of us."

"We've taken good care of each other, and thank the Lord for his protection and the folks who helped us on the Underground Railroad."

The porter told us the four hundred-mile journey to Boston would take about twelve hours, so we settled in for the trip. The sway of the railway car soon put the children to sleep. They cuddled up with sisters Rebecca and Lucy, Bobby clutching his toy, Chloe holding onto one of Bobby's hands, and a blanket over all of them. I realized how exhausted Rebecca and Lucy must be, walking so many miles, looking after the children and patients.

Thomas sat next to our patients, who fidgeted. No matter how hard we'd tried to make them comfortable, it was obvious they were both in pain.

I crossed the car to where Rebecca sat and pointed first at our patients and then at her bag. She nodded and drew some white willow bark out of her bag and handed it to me. I gave the medicine to each soldier with instructions to chew it slowly. They thanked me and obediently began chewing the bark, sighing.

Thomas and I made eye contact and smiled, but tears filled my eyes as I sensed relief and exhaustion. *How would I have done this without Thomas? Without Rebecca? Lucy and Chloe had provided companionship to Rebecca and Bobby.*

The dogs padded over, and Scout lay by the patients. Joseph reached down. "That's a good boy." Scout licked his hand. Duke patrolled the car, stopping at each person for a pat.

"You rest now, Miss Sarah. I can keep an eye out," Thomas told me and handed me the last blanket.

"Thank you, Thomas." I sat back down, thinking about all we'd done to get here. I rooted in my reticule for my pencil and notepad and made a list of what we needed to do in Boston. Then I wrapped my shawl around me and put the blanket over my knees. Duke sat at my feet.

My thoughts were in disarray. *Would I see Michael again? Would our nun's habits protect us? Could we get my new friends to freedom in Iowa?* My eyes shut and the pencil and notebook lay in my lap, as the rocking of the train lulled me to sleep.

I woke up when the porters brought our supper and something for the dogs. We watched the passing scenery and stared at each other in wonder.

Thomas asked the porter, "How fast we going?"

The porter shrugged. "It depends if we going straight or around curves or uphill. We average twenty to thirty miles an hour."

Thomas grinned. "It feels faster, somehow."

Traveling by wagon, with some of us walking, we'd covered 20 miles in a day. It seemed magical to cover that distance in an hour.

We entertained the children and ourselves by singing, telling stories, and playing silly guessing games. Then we settled down for the night, getting comfortable. Rebecca gave both patients some more white willow bark to chew and promised to get hot water for tea in the morning.

I sat up for a few minutes, staring out the windows with the dogs at my feet, feeling melancholy that each mile took me farther away from Michael. Scout circled the small train car, as if checking on each person. He settled down by the patients and Thomas. Duke whined, and I lay down, and he settled at my feet. The rhythm of the train put me to sleep before I could complete my nightly ritual of praying for Michael and James, and for Mother, and then I slept.

Sunday, September 25, 1864

The next morning, we woke up to the porters bringing in our breakfasts.

Bobby asked, "We there yet?"

The porter leaned down. "We're close. I'd say we're an hour out of Boston."

Chloe told him, "I slept all night on the train!"

The other porter grinned. "Good for you. I'm going to bed after working all night."

Rebecca checked on the patients, who fared better than expected, sleeping sitting up, sharing the red and green quilt.

Before we knew it, the train pulled into Boston, where we had a two-hour layover. Abigail and her parents were coming to meet us, while the rest of our group stayed onboard. The porters assured us they'd take the dogs off the train so they could take care of business and keep watch over them until we returned.

I got off the train to meet Abigail and her parents. Fresh grief at having to tell them about Emily and little George bubbled up. I hadn't warned them of my attire, so they almost walked by me when I stopped them, calling out Abigail's name. They turned, surprised.

Abigail burst out laughing and then covered it with a cough. She and I embraced, and she whispered, "I know you must have a great story with your nun's habit. I've missed you, Sarah."

My garb startled her parents, but they covered it well.

Rev. Saunders beamed as I explained. "Ingenious disguise, Sarah. We couldn't have done better."

Mrs. Saunders embraced me. "It's good to see you, Sarah. I'm so sorry for the loss of your husband, sister, and nephew. Perhaps Iowa will give you a second chance to find happiness."

I invited them to come on board and meet my new family. I introduced everybody, and Rev. Saunders shook everyone's hands, even the children, who giggled. Mrs. Saunders carried a large bag, sat, and started chatting.

Rev. Saunders asked if I had enough money for our tickets to Iowa, which reminded me I needed to buy those tickets. We left the train car together. I assured him I had enough money from the sale of my big wagon and horses. But, when we arrived at the ticket window, Rev. Saunders stepped forward and bought them, saying he was my uncle. The tickets cost $30 a person, and half price for the children, so the total was $210, an astonishing amount of money.

We stepped away with me clutching the tickets, in tears at his kindness. Rev. Saunders regarded me with pride. "Sarah, you've done an extraordinary thing rescuing these folks. Let me help you. I am your uncle, after all." Then he added, "Sister Sarah, I mean," and tipped his hat at me.

"I wouldn't have done it without meeting Abigail—and you and Mrs. Saunders. I just wish Emily and her baby were here. It was her plan, after all." My eyes filled with tears of gratitude and sorrow. *Will I ever understand why my sister had to die—and her poor little boy? Why, Lord?*

I put the tickets into my reticule and retrieved my handkerchief.

He comforted me with an arm around my shoulder. "I wish Emily and her baby were here, too. God only knows why it happened, but Emily would be proud of you. We certainly are. You've become our second daughter, Sarah."

I wiped my tears as Rev. Saunders gently guided me back to the train.

When we entered the train car, Chloe was sitting on Mrs. Saunders' lap and telling her about getting the bad guy, with lots of dramatic gestures. Bobby helped to tell the story. The rest of the adults contributed bits and pieces of information.

Abigail glanced up. "It sounds like your trip to Baltimore has been an interesting one."

I sighed and sat down beside Abigail. "Thank the Lord for the help of those Underground Railroad friends. And thank God for our four soldiers and Thomas. Emily and I thought we would be fine on the road with Rebecca and Bobby and her baby."

Daniel glanced up. "You and Doctor Rebecca helped us, too. And without Dr. Rebecca, I might have lost my arm."

Joseph agreed. "And now we're headed home, because of you, Miss Sarah."

Rev. Saunders examined us thoughtfully. "I think the good Lord brought all of you together to help each other. You shouldn't have problems for the rest of your trip. The porters will look out for you and your companions."

He glanced down at the dogs and patted them. "We'll pray for you. Sarah, please send a telegram when you get to Iowa?"

"I won't forget."

His wife spoke up, "I'm happy you rescued Lucy and her daughter from the slave catchers. But please stay on the train until you're safe in Jubilee Junction—and stay together. Don't mingle with passengers from other cars because they could be Confederate sympathizers." I agreed, and the rest of the group nodded.

Abigail and I sat next to each other, chatting quietly, holding hands. I promised to write to her as soon as we got settled.

Before they left, Rev. Saunders asked us to hold hands and pray in a big circle, standing near the soldiers. He shook everyone's hand, and his wife and Abigail embraced all the women and the children. The dogs wanted attention as well. So, the minister stroked Duke's ears and rubbed Scout's muzzle, and the dogs rewarded him with a few licks.

I thanked Rev. and Mrs. Saunders for their help, trying to keep the tears at bay. *If I were their second daughter, they were my second parents. Would I see them again?*

Twenty-five

Romance and Discoveries
Gracie

*"Doubt thou that the sun is fire, Doubt that the sun does move,
doubt truth to be a liar, but never doubt that I love."*
~William Shakespeare, Hamlet.

February 2013

David and I talked a few days before our trip over takeout from Aunt Shirley's. After our meal of burgers, salad, for me and fries for David, we moved to my couch. I told him I was still a virgin, and he repeated what he'd told me earlier. "I just want to spend time with you, Gracie."

Then, I told him what happened to me when I attended Iowa State during my junior year, my first year away from Jubilee Junction. I struggled with tears as I told him how two students attacked me during a football game's halftime; how we had walked around talking to people and they took me to an isolated place where they assaulted me. My brother came looking for me with a friend and brought a campus security guard with them.

David's warm brown and gold-flecked eyes reflected tenderness and love. He put his arms around me and pulled me close. "I'm not surprised Mark came looking for you. I'm proud of you for fighting back, but two on one is no fair fight."

Fortunately, I had a box of Kleenex nearby. I wiped my tears and explained, "I tried to forget about it and move on. But when

Dad had his heart attack, I came back to help with the newspaper and felt safer here. Steve thought the next step for his political career was to get married. I knew if I was intimate with Steve, he would control my life. So, I pushed him away, telling myself that I was a good Christian girl. But I didn't want to marry him. I was afraid of his anger, and when he hurt me, I realized I could never trust him again. But I was too ashamed to tell anyone what he'd done to me—what I let him do to me. So, I hid the injury and he almost got away with it."

We were sitting on my couch, and I'd started crying and shaking, remembering Steve hurting me. I'd just turned down his proposal and tried to leave the restaurant with his younger sister. Steve jumped up and grabbed my wrist and wouldn't let me leave. Finally, his parents intervened, made him let go of me, and apologized. However, there was a bright red ring around my wrist, and it hurt all the way to my heart.

David wrapped his arms around me, let me cry, and wrapped us up in the blanket I kept on the back of the couch. We sat like that for half an hour until I felt calmer. I felt lighter and freer for having told David my secret.

David and I looked forward to having a wonderful weekend at the B & B, and I was so glad I'd talked to Kathy. I borrowed one of her negligees and a cute pajama set and packed an overnight bag. I took Agatha to Mark and Kathy's so she could play with Felix.

Kathy hugged me and handed me a small paper bag. I peeked inside and blushed. "Have fun, Gracie—but be safe."

Then David picked me up, and we were off for the short drive. It was a crisp Friday evening, and we were both excited, chatting and admiring the scenery in the snowy February weather.

We checked into the B & B and glanced around our suite. Our room included an electric fireplace, a big TV, a couch, a kitchenette, and a small table with two chairs near the windows overlooking the river and woods. It was private and romantic.

David and I enjoyed a delicious seafood meal at the adjacent restaurant. We talked about the semester while we enjoyed salads, crusty rolls, grilled salmon, green beans with almonds, and roasted yams. He and I avoided mention of the red and green quilt that had held our attention during the past two months.

Afterward, we took a box of cheesecake back to our room. It was a chilly walk, with the frosty air coming off the river, and I was thankful our B & B was next door. David's hand felt warm on mine. We were beaming at each other as we entered our room.

David turned on the gas fireplace, while I unwrapped the cheesecake and checked the kitchenette for forks. We relaxed on the loveseat and ate our cheesecake while watching the snow fall.

The suite also featured an inviting king bed. I shivered, thinking about what might happen there later.

But David surprised me. "I'm falling in love with you, Gracie. I'm attracted to you, but after what you've been through, I don't want to rush into a physical relationship. Let's sit and talk, kiss a little, and watch a movie. The only rule—no quilts or crazy aunts."

I brushed my teeth and put on one of Kathy's pretty PJs and got into bed. Then it was David's turn. He went into the bathroom and emerged wearing flannel PJ pants and a T-shirt. He looked at me tenderly, aimed the TV toward the bed, propped up the pillows behind us, and found a romantic comedy movie.

I lay in his arms and felt safe. We began talking and soon clicked the movie off. At some point, he nuzzled my neck and told me he loved me, and I told him I loved him back. We drifted off to sleep. The next thing I knew, someone was kissing me awake around eight the next morning. I sighed, thinking I was dreaming.

"The B and B stops serving breakfast at ten, and I didn't know how long you need to get ready."

I realized he'd just gotten out of the shower because his hair was wet.

"Thanks, David. No problem." I grabbed my overnight bag and headed for the bathroom. A half-hour later, I was ready.

After breakfast, we strolled down the street to a couple of shops, including an antique store and a used bookstore with a coffee shop. We enjoyed browsing the antique store, chuckling at a display of antique kitchen utensils, but spent more time in the bookstore. I bought a couple of books, and so did David, including a compilation of Civil War combat experiences.

Then, we took a drive, winding around the river, admiring the view, watching eagles feeding on fish, and staring at a huge eagle's nest in a massive tree along the road. Instead of going out for lunch, we picked up some sandwiches, fruit, and iced tea and coffee, which we ate at the bistro table back in our room. We watched the scenery outside—bare trees and large rocks near the frozen falls, overlaid with a layer of snow and ice.

We spent the next portion of the day sitting side by side on the loveseat, reading one of our new books. We changed our clothes and drove to the local movie theater to see *Lincoln*, with Daniel Day-Lewis in the title role and Sally Fields as Mary Lincoln. It transported us back in time to 1865 and the American Civil War. I shut my eyes during most of the battle scenes and clutched David's arm and buried my head on his shoulder when they showed the stack of amputated limbs.

Afterward, the restaurant next door delivered lasagna, salad, breadsticks, and two slices of chocolate cake for dessert. David and I drank some sparkling water instead of wine. "Wine just makes me sleepy," I had confessed. We ate the meal at the bistro table, gazing out at the frozen river and waterfalls. We were in our own world.

David and I talked about the movie, the cast, and the portrayal of Lincoln and Thaddeus Stevens.

"I enjoyed the movie, but the opening scene isn't accurate with Black soldiers reciting the Gettysburg address. But that's Hollywood for you. It was an incredible speech. No doubt every newspaper ran it in the next edition. The movie doesn't give enough credit to abolitionists like Thaddeus Stevens for getting the thirteenth amendment passed. Maybe it gives too much credit to Lincoln." David told me.

I agreed. "Still, they told an interesting story, and the casting was brilliant. I loved Sally Fields as Mary Todd Lincoln."

"Yes, and Daniel Day-Lewis did an amazing job as Lincoln and so did Tommy Lee Jones as Thaddeus Stevens, as a radical committed to racial equality. Politics is messy, and politicians have always had to compromise to accomplish great things. But the movie made me think about *what might have been. . ."* His voice trailed off for a moment.

He continued, "Just think about how different our country might be today if Lincoln had lived. The movie focused on his accomplishment of abolishing slavery, which became his legacy. Imagine if Lincoln had survived, and we'd never had President Andrew Johnson. He looked down on both Native Americans and former slaves and broke the promise of a mule and forty acres. What he did to the Native Americans was even crueler, of course, driving them off their ancestral lands.

"Frederick Douglass said Abraham Lincoln was the first President who rose above the prejudice of his times because he was both the white man's and the Black man's president. Many historians think Lincoln would have supported suffrage. They think he would have done much more to educate those freed slaves and prepare them to support themselves and their families."

David glanced at me. "Sorry, Gracie. I didn't mean to go into professor mode and lecture."

"It's okay. I enjoyed it. It sounds like you've thought about this scenario."

"Yes, and so has every other historian for the past 150 years. Do you realize that there are 15,000 books about the 16th president? The movie we just saw is based on just a few chapters of Doris Kearns Goodman's massive book, *Team of Rivals*. Many are biographies, but some of them are fiction and alternative history."

"Like the one about Lincoln as a vampire slayer?" I asked, "He finds out a vampire killed his beloved mother, and pledges vengeance—not that I had time to read it, of course."

David grinned, "Yes, I suppose so."

Sunday morning, we checked out and drove home to attack student papers, plan lectures, grade tests, and get ready for the new week. His goodbye kiss stayed on my lips long after he left.

Early March

My column asking for help in locating more ACW-era quilts

worked, and the interview on Tiara's radio show helped as well. We got another half dozen quilts, some interesting old letters, photos, and parts of a Union soldier's uniform. However, nothing answered my questions about who'd made the red and green quilt.

Then, Aunt Violet called me one day, excited over a recent discovery. She wouldn't say what she'd found, which intrigued me even more. David wouldn't finish classes until after five, so I texted him and drove over alone.

When I arrived, Aunt Violet, usually so composed and cheery, was buzzing with excitement. She ushered me in, Beatrix not far behind. I shrugged off my jacket and hugged her.

We walked into her living room, and I stared at the dining room table, covered with several layers of documents and sticky notes. An open banker's box sat on the floor by the coffee table. A box of file folders, labels, sticky notes, and a couple of oversized three-ring notebooks filled the dining room table.

She'd opened a package of protective plastic sheets and had a half dozen sheets with documents on the coffee table. A coffee mug full of markers, highlighters, and pens sat in the middle. My aunt was a very tidy person, and I'd never seen such organized chaos at her house, not even in the middle of moving.

My face must have shown my emotions. Aunt Violet shrugged and told me, "Pardon the mess, Gracie. I feel like I'm playing amateur detective, sorting through piles of documents to help you. Your mother ran me to the store for supplies. I'm trying to organize things, so I'm labeling everything." She glanced down at the coffee table, picked up a piece of paper already placed into a plastic sheet, and handed it to me.

It was a note. I laid it down and took a photo with my phone.

"Dear Uncle Peter and Aunt Lillian,
Daniel & Joseph are on the train, headed home.
Please help Sarah, her son, and her friends.
They gave us shelter after the battle.
Rebecca cared for Daniel's wound.
She also tended to Joseph's injured ankle and knee.

Thomas helped take down a slave catcher.
I commend Sarah for her courage, keeping a promise to take them to freedom.
She has a kind heart & suffered a great loss.
Yrs. Truly,
Michael."

I glanced up, "Uncle Peter and Aunt Lillian—Nelson? Wow! The date got smeared. Looks like sometime in September 1864. Good job! Now we know Sarah—whoever she was—was with a group of people, including our boys from Jubilee."

Aunt Violet nodded.

"Sarah suffered 'a great loss.' What does he mean?" I stared at it again. "Wait a second—Rebecca—is she RS? Could she be our quilter? But what does it mean, Sarah was taking them to freedom?" I tried to fit the puzzle pieces together.

Aunt Violet stared at me like I was a student, and she was the teacher. "Think, Gracie. Who needed freedom in 1864?"

I thought my eyebrows would fall off my face. "Sarah was helping a group of slaves escape from Virginia?" I asked, incredulous. My heart was thumping. I couldn't wait to tell David—and Carl.

"Can I borrow this letter?" I asked.

She smiled. "Sure. I put my address label at the bottom of the plastic sheet. Make copies and skim it in, or whatever you do with the computer."

I held it and said, "Skim? Oh, you mean scan! Yes, we will scan this letter."

I hugged her. "Thanks, Aunt Violet. This is an incredible find. Love you!"

I pondered which man to contact first—David or Carl? David would still be in his committee meeting, poor thing. I was closest to the museum, so I drove there. I walked in to find David and Carl discussing whatever was on the computer screen in front of them.

"Hi, guys! I have something to show you!" as I waved the plastic sheet.

"Hi, Gracie," David glanced up. "The committee meeting was

short, so I figured if your Aunt Violet found something valuable, you would bring it here."

I opened and closed my mouth, still clutching the document. Was I that predictable?

Carl reached out an eager hand. "Let's see what you have."

I handed it over. He stared at the letter and handed it to David for a full thirty seconds before taking it back and almost racing to the printer/scanner/copier.

I asked David. "Isn't it amazing?"

He complained. "Who knows? Carl snatched it away."

So, I showed him the pictures I'd taken on my iPhone, and David read it. "Well, he names almost everyone on the journey. Very interesting."

I glanced at him and agreed. "There are layers of truth here."

"What?"

I repeated what Aunt Violet asked, "Who needed freedom in 1864?"

He blinked. "Oh, my gosh. Free Blacks came to Jubilee Junction before the end of the war?"

David stared at me, and I knew I had to call Tiara.

The squeals on the phone were mutual. Tiara was packing up at the college, talking to Shelly, getting ready for her night class. When my ears recovered, I asked, "Want me to send you a picture?"

Tiara agreed. "Sure thing, I'll show it to Shelly. But then I'm on my way, so don't you go anywhere, okay?"

I glanced at David. "I think she's excited."

Carl returned from the copier and sat down. "This is a genuine treasure, Gracie. And it came from your Aunt Violet? "

David was grinning by now, reading his own copy of the letter.

"I love her, but Aunt Violet's gone nuts. I've never seen this side of her before. She was digging into one of those bank boxes and had folders, papers, and two cartons of plastic sheet protectors strewn all over her tables. She told me she's digging for treasures for me."

"Well, she struck gold," Carl and David agreed.

Tiara made record time and walked in, out of breath, about ten minutes later. She hugged me, then David, and Carl, who warmed up and hugged her back.

"Now, show me this document. I couldn't read and drive," she demanded.

I handed it to her and watched her facial expression change. "This verifies it. Free Blacks arrived in Jubilee Junction before the end of the Civil War." she asked. "I need to sit down. Grandma was right!"

"This is big," Tiara gazed around with tears in her eyes.

I nodded, David nodded, and Carl agreed.

"We don't have all our answers, but it looks like Rebecca could have made the quilt," I pointed out.

"This is getting exciting, and it came from your Aunt Violet's boxes?" Tiara asked.

"Yes." I sighed. "She's digging for treasures. Yes, we all want to go over and help her sort."

Carl made a copy of the letter for Tiara, who stared at it, her eyes shining with tears.

David turned to us. "How about something to eat?"

Tiara, David, and I headed for Aunt Shirley's, but before we left, we handed the original to Carl, which he then filed. Carl's phone rang, and he stepped away to answer it.

Tiara glanced at me, and I knew we were both thinking about our grandmothers and wanting to know more about their stories—their legacies.

Twenty-six

Train Trip to Iowa
Sarah

"The mystic chords of memory, stretching from every battle-field, and patriot grave, to every living heart and hearth-stone, all over this broad land, will yet swell the chorus of the Union, when again touched, as surely they will be, by the better angels of our nature."
~President Abraham Lincoln

Leaving Boston, Massachusetts, heading West
Sunday, September 25, 1864

Abigail embraced me before she got off the train. "Sarah, the hardest part of your journey must surely be over. Please write when you get to Jubilee Junction," she told me.

I embraced her. "Thanks, Abigail. Yes, I hope you're right. It's been good to see you and your folks again. I will write to you."

And then we were on our way to Iowa.

I saw Chloe playing with a beautiful rag doll with a calico dress and dark hair and skin. She clutched it. "Miss Abigail gave me a doll. I named her Miss Abby."

"Miss Abby?" I asked.

"Coz Miss Abigail made it for me." She hugged her doll.

Bobby had a new picture book from Miss Abigail.

Rebecca came to sit by me.

"Your friends treated us so kindly. I see why you love them."

"Rev. Saunders said he was my uncle and bought our tickets. Here, I'd worried we wouldn't have enough money for them."

"You gave up everything to bring us to safety," Rebecca told me. "None of us had money for tickets, so it was all on you. I was happy when Thomas found the slaver's bag of gold coins. It will help you in Iowa."

"You, Thomas, Lucy, Chloe, and Bobby are my family now, so the money will help us all. I'm going to divide it up."

Rebecca and I talked about our expectations of Iowa. "I've been thinking about what life will be like in Iowa, not being a slave," she said. "I don't remember being anyplace else than Evaline Plantation."

"Mama Cee certainly treated you like a daughter and taught you all about herbs and how to help sick and injured people," I responded.

"Yes, I love her and Papa Joe. I don't know if the people in Iowa will accept us, freed slaves."

"It's the frontier, and a chance to begin again. And you're not alone. Joseph, Daniel, and I won't let people mistreat you, and they have families who are going to welcome us," I told her. I hoped I was right.

We settled in, checked on the children, and took care of our patients. Daniel and Robert were happy to be headed for home, but both were still in a lot of pain. Rebecca gave each some willow bark to chew.

Our porters, Moses and Jacob, brought us lunch. As we ate, we observed the changing landscape outside and talked about the states we were traveling through, starting with Massachusetts and its state capital, Boston. I knew Boston was a bustling city with a waterfront and many shops, taverns, and factories. The porters assured us that there were several Union ships anchored there in the harbor. Soldiers were guarding the railroad station and harbor.

As we left the city, we saw small towns with houses, churches, and shops. The train rolled past fields, small villages, and farms. From what we could see, there were no signs of the ravages of war here, but we saw older men and more women and children tending to animals, crops, and fields.

We stopped at the train station in Albany, New York. Moses took the dogs out for a short walk, checked on us and brought us supper.

We passed through New York state with its small towns, farms, and rural spaces. At some point, we crossed into Pennsylvania.

Monday morning, I woke up and stretched. The bench was hard, but I was thankful to have a place to lie down at night. The patients were still sleeping, and so was Thomas. Bobby curled up next to Rebecca and Lucy. Even the dogs were still asleep. But there was no sign of Chloe.

Where is Chloe? I glanced around, then stood up so I wouldn't wake up the patients. No reason to alarm anyone else until I knew for sure she was missing. Walking back to the washroom, my heart was now beating harder. I examined the train car and didn't see her anywhere. But I saw something to make my heart rate go up even more. Her cherished doll, Miss Abby, lay on the floor a few feet from the door to the next car. What happened while we all slept?

I walked over to the door connecting us to the next train car and peeked through the window. I didn't see our porters. Normally, one was walking up and down the aisles, keeping a watchful eye on us. I wondered if a small child could open the door. I hoped no one had come in and taken her while we all slept. *If only Michael was here—he would know what to do. He would take charge.* But he wasn't here. I was, and it was up to me.

I took a big breath, put on a stern, pious face, and reminded myself I was wearing a nun's habit and opened the door. A middle-aged man got out of his seat and approached me, smiling. "Can I help you, sister?"

Something about his oily grin made me cringe inside.

Fingering the individual prayer beads on my chaplet, I murmured. "No, thank you. I'm just stretching my legs while I say my morning prayers." I glanced around the train car as walked a few steps forward.

There she was—Chloe was curled up in a nearby seat, asleep. I started for her, and the passenger followed. I bent low and gently shook her leg to wake her up. Then, I told her, "Chloe, dear child. It's Sister Sarah. You wandered off. Let's go back to our car."

Chloe sat up sleepily. "Sister Sarah," she yawned as I picked her up, and her little arms wrapped around my neck. Then she stiffened and whispered in my ear, "The bad man is here, Sister Sarah."

Shocked, I turned to go, but an older white woman blocked my way.

"Charles, I didn't know they were letting those people on this train," she snarled. The man, Charles, I assumed, studied me.

I whispered to Chloe, "Dougie? Where is he?" she whispered back. "He's sitting over there, Miss Sarah. Dougie's looking at us."

I turned to the woman and regarded her sternly. "By those people, do you mean nuns–or little Black children?" I demanded. "Have a care how you answer, madam, for God is listening, and so is this child. The Bible tells us we are all his children, and the Kingdom of Heaven belongs to little children like Chloe."

The woman appeared flustered, then her eyes narrowed, and she seemed poised to say more when Jacob, one of our porters, rushed up. "Is there a problem, Sister Sarah?"

I held Chloe tightly. "This good woman seems offended that you allow . . . *nuns* . . . on this train. Can you escort us to our train car, please?"

The woman sighed and moved aside, her cheeks reddening, but her husband was nowhere to be seen. I hung onto Chloe, who was trembling. Surely, she was mistaken. We left Dougie behind with the sheriff. *I can't look. I must look. What if she's right?*

Jacob nodded. "Sorry, Sister. Let's get this child back to bed."

He opened the door for us and, once inside, I put her down, feeling lightheaded with relief. "Chloe, please don't leave this car again," I told her as Scout and Duke came over to us, whining.

I turned to the porter. "When I woke up, she was gone. So, I went to look for her."

I stepped back to the window and looked carefully, then ducked.

Dougie was on the train, and he was talking to the man and woman who had taken Chloe. From their animated gestures, I could guess the topic of conversation.

Everyone was awake now. Lucy kneeled before her daughter and asked, "Chloe, where did you go? Why did you leave?"

Chloe was close to tears. "I'm sorry, Mama. You were sleeping when I waked up. I wanted a drink of water. The man came to the window and waved. He opened the door and said I could go into the other car and he held my hand. He got me a drink of water and then I got sleepy again."

"The man? What man?" I asked, pacing. "The bad man?"

Bobby came over with her beloved doll and handed it to her. Then he sat down beside her to comfort her.

Chloe hugged Miss Abby. She put her thumb in her mouth and cuddled up to her mother. "The man you talked to, Miss Sarah. The bad man was sitting in the back side of the car. He talked to the other man and laughed and said he would be back."

I made eye contact with Jacob. We got up and checked the door's window. The couple had vanished, and so had Dougie. Had she imagined him? No, I'd seen Dougie, too.

Jacob considered the matter. "I'll report this incident to the conductor. One of us was monitoring the door to your car but was called away. We'll be more vigilant. I'll be back with breakfast." He left the car, shaking his head with concern.

Thomas came up to me. "Is she alright?" He asked.

Her mother got her a drink of water and sat back down on the bench next to Bobby, and they cuddled under the blanket, with the dogs settling down beside them. Lucy looked up, "She's alright."

Rebecca came up and embraced me. "You got Chloe back, and she's fine. We're all mighty proud of you. Sit down now. The porters should be here with breakfast soon."

I sank down on the bench. I took a big breath. "We aren't fine, Rebecca. Chloe saw Dougie on the train, and so did I just now. He was talking to the man and woman who lured Chloe into the next train car."

"Dougie?" Lucy was terrified. "He's here for the two of us, isn't he?"

Rebecca whispered. "He's really on the train?" She sat down and exhaled.

I nodded. "I can't imagine how he got on the train, but that's not important now. We need a plan."

Rebecca said, "A plan? We need a miracle."

Thomas regarded us, appearing resolved. "We need to take turns keeping watch. If Dougie's on the train, he will come for us, so we need to be ready."

The soldiers nodded in agreement.

Thomas turned to me. "I'm sorry, Miss Sarah. I should have put a gun to that man's head when we had him tied up." He clenched his fist, remembering.

Thomas helped the soldiers one at a time to the washroom. We each took our turn, waiting for breakfast.

Moses and Jacob came rolling a cart with breakfast. One of them took Thomas and me aside, back by the soldiers. The couple claimed the little girl opened the door on her own. They gave her some water and had her lie down and covered her up. The couple denied any interaction with a man named Dougie and got off at the next train station. But the porters hadn't believed their story.

I described Dougie, and the porters hadn't seen him. However, there had been some thefts of food, clothing, and blankets from the supply car.

Jacob promised that they'd report this incident to the conductor and the porters would increase their security at our door. Thomas and the soldiers pledged to be more careful.

Daniel admitted, "I think we let our guard down, thinking we'd made it to safety. I'm sorry. We'll be more vigilant."

Joseph agreed.

Moses assured us, "We all be watching. Now don't you let your breakfast get cold." They poured tea and coffee.

The group gathered by the porters. Lucy and Rebecca brought food to the injured soldiers. The children brought their bowls of oatmeal porridge and sat on the floor, talking to Daniel and Joseph.

I gazed at the porters. "Thank you."

The rest of Monday passed as we took turns watching the door and the children. We admired the changing scenery outside and marveled at the size of our country as we traveled through Pennsylvania.

The group tried to come up with a plan. The soldiers had surrendered their rifles, but the porters promised to see if they could return at least one weapon to defend ourselves. We were determined to stick together and guard Lucy and Chloe as best we could.

The train stopped in several large cities along the way. We stayed on the train, still vigilant, but we hadn't seen Dougie again. Our porters took turns taking the dogs out for a walk. They smiled and spoke kindly to the children, who seemed to perk up, seeing adult Black faces. I wondered what it would be like to be the other in a world of white skin.

On the train headed West
   Tuesday, September 27, 1864

Tuesday passed as we took turns watching the door and the children. We admired the changing scenery outside and marveled at the size of our country as we entered Ohio and later Indiana.

My heart ached for Bobby, caught between two worlds through no fault of his own. Rebecca made it clear to me that while she loved her son dearly, she wanted to give him his best chance at building life in the new world of Iowa—with me as his mother.

I protested things would change after the war, but Rebecca smiled sadly and shook her head. "Folks don't change easily," she declared. "I suspect it's going to take more than a war to change people's hearts."

I nodded, and with that, we agreed I would become Bobby's mother. We would not speak of it again until we reached Iowa.

We watched the changing scenery out the window, cared for our patients, and entertained the children. Sometimes Bobby and Chloe would sit with me to cuddle, talk, or ask for a story. I'd scribble notes to myself about our journey and what we needed to do once we reached our destination.

Overnight, we crossed into Illinois. Wednesday morning, we stopped in Chicago while we were eating breakfast. We looked with interest at the city we could see from the train station, but we stayed on board.

Later that afternoon, we crossed the Mississippi River and entered Iowa. We were officially in what we deemed The West. Daniel and Joseph talked to us about what we'd see—woods, ponds, small towns, and farms that were not much different from back home in Virginia. They told the children about the animals in Iowa—the buffalo, deer and elk, black bears, and mountain cats, and of course, the farm animals like cattle, sheep, and chickens.

The soldiers sensed my mixed emotions and encouraged me several times. "You're going to be fine, Sarah. Our families will take care of all of you."

Crossing into Iowa felt at once exhilarating and calming. There had been no further sign of Dougie on the train. Moses and Jacob opined he had gotten off at an earlier stop. They didn't suggest that maybe, just maybe, Chloe had imagined his presence. I knew she had not imagined it, nor had I.

There was only one stop left before we arrived at our destination, Jubilee Junction, Iowa—our new home.

Home? I pondered the word. With all we'd been through, would I ever truly feel at home anywhere ever again?

The train chugged to a fitful stop. Moses and Jacob entered our car with a cheery greeting, leashed Duke and Scout, and led the dogs off the train for one last break. Joseph and Daniel also declared their need to use the washroom, and Thomas helped Daniel hobble toward the facilities while Joseph followed close behind with his crutches.

Shortly after that, the door to our car opened, and a porter pushed a cart into our car. I thought it odd that he didn't close the door behind him, as had been their custom. He pushed his cart past me without so much as a greeting, stopping only at the washroom door. He wedged the cart up against the door and then turned to face me.

I realized then that it was Dougie wearing a porter's uniform. I stepped back and screamed for Rebecca to take Bobby and find our porters. She was halfway to the door when Dougie pulled a revolver from his belt and pointed it at me.

Dougie said, "Don't get in my way, Miss Do-gooder. I'm taking back what's mine and your friend over there had better sit back down." He turned to grab Lucy and Chloe.

Something snapped inside me. I rushed at him and pummeled his back with my fists. "Keep your hands off them." Lucy screamed, too, and fought back. Dougie raised the gun, turned around, and knocked me to the ground. "I told you to stay out this!" he growled.

I tried to sit up, dizzy, and touched my forehead because I felt something running down my face. I was bleeding.

He grabbed Chloe and held the gun to her throat and gestured again for Rebecca and Bobby to sit down. They did.

Chloe tried to kick Dougie, but he held her tightly and looked at Lucy, who cried, "Give me my baby!"

Dougie pointed the revolver at Lucy. "You're coming with us. I can get a handsome price for two runaway slaves. And now that Rufus is dead, I don't have to share the reward." He cast a leering grin at me and added, "I suppose I have you to thank for that."

Lucy stood still as if her feet were frozen to the floor. Dougie pushed the barrel of his revolver against Chloe's temple and growled, "I ain't gonna tell you again. Get over here, now!"

Lucy seemed resigned to her fate and shuffled to him, quietly sobbing. "Oh, Lord Jesus, help us!"

From the floor, I seethed between clinched teeth, "You're not going anywhere with Lucy and Chloe."

"Who's going to stop me?" he asked, "Where's your dogs, Sister Sarah? Your men? Your guns?"

Then I realized he'd been watching us and knew our routine, so he knew just when to come. I felt helpless.

The men banged on the door of the washroom where they were trapped, shouting threats, but the door didn't budge.

"Dougie, if you hurt anyone, you'll regret it. We will hunt you down," declared Daniel.

"Coward. Too afraid to face us—" Joseph yelled.

Thomas sounded like the voice of reason. "Let them go, Dougie, and you can walk away."

Dougie snorted. "No, thank you. We'll be going now."

Chloe began sobbing, and Dougie shoved her toward Lucy. "Shut her up!" he demanded as Lucy gathered Chloe into her arms. The slave catcher grabbed the collar of Lucy's blouse and forced her in front of him as he moved toward the open door. He cocked his revolver and pointed first at me, then back at Lucy. "You all been a great deal of trouble, but the reward for returning these two runaways should make up for it."

I shot Rebecca a pleading look, and she shook her head in despair.

Bobby began wailing, "Don't take them, Dougie!"

Just as Dougie stepped onto the platform between the train cars, I heard a familiar noise. The sounds of paws running on the ground. Duke and Scout both leaped upon him—Duke tearing at his leg while Scout bit deep into the arm that held Lucy. Dougie screamed, whether in pain or anger, I couldn't say. But he released his hold on Lucy and Chloe and struggled to point his revolver at the dogs.

Lucy and Chloe scrambled away from Dougie. Rebecca grabbed them both by their arms and helped them back inside our car.

A shot rang out, and the dogs shuffled back.

Dougie stood still for a moment, shock registering on his face, and then he fell face first from the platform onto the ground

I stood, shaking now, wondering what had happened. Rebecca embraced Lucy while Bobby comforted Chloe.

Duke and Scout trotted into the car and whined and sniffed until I gave them both a tentative scratch behind the ears. Stunned, it was all I could do to pet the dogs, my hands were shaking so bad.

Our two faithful porters stepped into view. Moses held a smoking pistol and kept it trained on Dougie. Jacob helped me to a chair. "It's alright Sister Sarah. You all done real good. You're safe now."

Rebecca rushed over to me, a wet rag in one hand and her jar of ointment in the other. She tenderly treated m.y wound while I sat trying to process what had happened.

Lucy and Chloe gathered around me while Rebecca was finishing up. Bobby sat on my other side and he patted my arm with his small hands. "I'm glad Dougie is dead."

"You saved us, Moses," Lucy said between sobs. "How can we ever thank you?"

Moses tipped his head. "It seemed divine providence. We got permission to bring one pistol for protection. It worked."

Chloe hugged my knees. "I'm sorry the bad man hurt you," she said. Duke and Scout trotted around the car, seeming to check on each person.

The men were still banging on the washroom door, demanding to know what was happening. Jacob hurried to remove the cart blocking the door and the men burst out.

"What happened?" Thomas demanded.

"A clear case of self-defense," Moses declared, still holding the weapon. "We saw the whole thing. We was walking back from taking Miss Sarah's hounds for a walk. That man hit her with the gun, threatened Lucy and Chloe and was going to kidnap them. Then he pointed the weapon at Rebecca and Bobby. The hounds didn't like that much, and they ran and attacked him."

Then Joseph held out his hand. "Looks like my pistol." Moses handed him the gun. "Good thing you got it just in time."

"That man just needed killin'," said Jacob. "He wasn't gonna stop."

The train was delayed in it's departure while the local sheriff was called to the scene. After taking statements from all the witnesses, he agreed it was self-defense and declared we were free to go, but to hold ourselves ready to testify in case there was a further inquest. But he also noted that there was a wanted poster with a face that strongly resembled Dougie's tacked on the wall in his office. "If memory serves, there was a $500 reward, dead or alive," he said. "So let me know how to reach you in Jubilee Junction."

The train approached Jubilee Junction, and we got excited because our second chance was about to begin. I nervously fingered my chaplet, realizing I took comfort in praying with the beads. Mrs. Wright had shown us how to make the sign of the cross and say, "O God, come to my assistance. O Lord, make haste to help me." I repeated this ritual a dozen times a day.

Rebecca looked at me. "How's your head feeling? You look better."

My head still ached, but not as much. "I'll be alright. Thanks for your nursing skills yet again," I told her.

Joseph studied us. "You'll love Jubilee Junction. It's a friendly, small town. We're near a river and the railroad, with farm fields, woods, and small farming villages nearby. You can fish, you can pick berries, and you can go for a horseback ride. Our uncles and grandfather have a big farm, and our families are going to love you because you helped us."

Daniel glanced at me. "Besides, who doesn't like nuns? Especially one my big brother seems to be sweet on, right?" He grinned, and the children giggled.

We pulled into the train station and gathered our things. Thomas and Joseph folded up the red and green quilt and offered it to Rebecca, who demurred. "I think it's your quilt now, Daniel."

The children stared out the window and saw people waving, so they waved back.

Daniel peered out and exclaimed, "It's our mothers!" The dogs got excited, too, standing up and wagging their tails.

Our two porters came to help us and shook every hand. Lucy and Chloe embraced both, and they smiled down at the children.

I said, "Thank you for everything. Can't I give you a tip?"

Moses patted my arm. "Rev. Saunders took care of it—don't you worry none."

I took a long last look at them. "You kept us safe from Boston to Jubilee Junction. We'll never forget you."

Moses nodded and smiled. "We all got our jobs to do, Sister Sarah."

Jacob shook our hands. "Good luck, and God bless you all."

We descended the steps of the train, excited to have finally arrived. Thomas helped Joseph down the steps and handed him his crutches, and Daniel carried the quilt. The three men headed to the luggage car with several porters to get the trunks. The dogs stayed with the children.

I faced Michael's mother, Mrs. O'Connor, who smiled tenderly and opened her arms. "How can we ever thank you for all you did for our boys? You must be Sarah, or should I call you *Sister* Sarah?"

Mrs. O'Connor saw the bloodstain on my habit. "Are you alright?"

"Yes. It's a long story. We'll explain everything later, but right now, we're just happy to be here, thank you," I told her.

She embraced me and glanced around to include everyone else. "Welcome to Jubilee Junction!"

Twenty-seven

When it Rains, it Pours
Gracie

"There is no better high than discovery."

~*E. O. Wilson*

Early March, 2013

*W*e walked toward Aunt Shirley's, but Tiara and I kept staring at each other laughing and saying, "Can you believe it?"

David humored us for about two minutes. "Can you two settle down? We're going to a respectable local eating establishment. I can't afford to get kicked out of Aunt Shirley's because I'll starve. Otherwise, we're going to have to get takeout."

Takeout? That gave me an idea. I called Aunt Violet. "Have you eaten supper yet? Can I treat you to take out from Aunt Shirley's?"

"No, I've been too busy. If you're going, how about getting me the taco salad?"

"Sure. We'll be there soon." I got off the phone and grinned. I called my parents, and invited them to join us too.

We ended up taking salads and sandwiches to Aunt Violet's. Those of us under-forty sat on the floor and kindly gave the couch and recliner to our elders. Tiara joined us on the floor, muttering she was barely over forty.

Aunt Violet covered the papers on the coffee table and the dining room table with sheets, even though no one was sitting near there. "I love you all, but don't drizzle on my precious family papers," she warned us.

I tried to resist the urge to do a *Lord of the Rings* Gollum impression, and kept a straight face, although David picked up on it, too. He mouthed, *My precious!*

David and Tiara told Aunt Violet how important the letter was, and she beamed. We let my parents read the photocopy.

"Peter and Mrs. Nelson?" Dad glanced up. "Holy smokes! The Nelson family was one of the three town founders and an ancestor on your mother's side. Michael is an ancestor on my side. This letter is an endorsement for the folks bringing back the two injured soldiers."

Then Dad paused. "In those days, a Black person needed something like this to settle in Iowa." He looked uncomfortable and apologetic.

David exhaled. "Iowa's laws made it difficult for free Blacks to settle here. They needed to post a $500 bond and present a certificate of freedom. Emily and Sarah had their family lawyer draw up the freedom papers for Rebecca and Bobby. Since they were under the sponsorship of the Nelsons and O'Connors, no one would ask them for money."

"Don't forget, they also liberated five slaves! Sarah brought two women, two children, and one Black man from Virginia. Girl, Sarah was another badass ancestor," Tiara reminded us.

Dad jumped in. "I agree. I'd like to hear the story behind it all. How did Sarah and her band of slaves meet a group of Union soldiers? I want to know more."

Mom turned to Aunt Violet. "You're doing a good job here, Aunt Violet. But it looks like you've made it through only part of the first box, and you've got three more boxes to go through. Can we help you? Could we divide up the work and take these boxes to the newspaper or the museum? You're finding wonderful stuff, so I imagine we'd find more treasures."

Aunt Violet admitted, "Yes, it was fun at first, but I'm sort of tired out, and I've made quite a mess."

Mom nodded. "Well, let's finish eating and figure out our strategy."

Her aunt agreed, relieved, and dug into her taco salad.

I made eye contact with Mom and mouthed, *Thank you.*

Tiara whispered, "Girl, your mama should get a job as a hostage negotiator. She's another badass woman in your family."

After supper, we collected the materials and loaded them into the back of Dad's SUV and followed him to *The Jubilee Times* office. Aunt Violet joined us to supervise.

We ended up spreading the contents out on four long tables. We promised to show Aunt Violet anything we found relating to the quilt. Later, we'd decide how to archive materials, giving her copies of the things she wanted to see. We also welcomed Aunt Violet to help us. As I studied the four tables, one for each box, I wondered if we would find more answers about Sarah, Rebecca, and Michael.

Which soldier came home with his bloodstain on the red and green quilt? I mused.

Mom got four spiral notebooks and four pens and set one of each on the tables. She explained we should make a list of the contents of the boxes. Then, we'd put things into the plastic protective sheets and label them.

David, Tiara, and I each grabbed a box. Mom took the box that was left. Dad needed to work on several articles for the newspaper and left us to work while Aunt Violet sat nearby at Mom's table and watched.

We sorted, listed, labeled, and put things into the plastic sheets. Mom found some stacking trays for each table, reserving the top tray for the "treasures about the quilt, the soldiers, or Sarah."

We worked for about two hours, finding fascinating old photos, letters, and legal documents, but no one had found anything worthy of their top tray.

We called it a night.

David drove us back to the museum where Tiara and I got into our cars and drove home. My parents took Aunt Violet home and later called to report she felt relieved to get our help.

The next morning, a Saturday, my phone rang. It was my Great-Aunt Trina, my Grandma Molly's younger sister-in-law.

"Hi, Aunt Trina. What's up?"

"Gracie? Your mama called and told me you and your new

boyfriend are investigating the old Civil War Quilt. I have something you need. Can you stop over?" she asked.

"Sure, is now a good time?" I asked. David had just arrived. We were going to plan our Spring Break activities

We drove to Aunt Trina's new apartment at the Prairie View Senior Living Community, where Aunt Violet lived.

Aunt Trina met us at the door. "Gracie, come in. You must be David."

"Yes, this is Dr. David McNeil. We work together at the community college." I added, "And yes, we're also dating."

David grinned. "Nice to meet you."

Aunt Trina held out a large yellow mailing envelope, battered and discolored, showing its age. "I have a confession. Want to sit?"

I stared at the envelope, feeling shaky. Was that the envelope we'd searched for?

We sat down in her cozy living room.

She took a big breath. "Many years ago, we had a big fuss about this envelope. It was safety-pinned to the red and green quilt, but it wasn't until we were clearing out Grandma's house that we knew about it. Our Great-Aunt Tressie was determined to destroy it, based on overhearing a snippet of conversation many years before. I didn't know if your Grandma Molly would stand up to her, so I helped by taking the envelope before our aunt could take it."

We sat, listening to her story. "So, Grandma Molly doesn't know you took it?" I asked, stunned.

"No," she replied, "I guess I need to tell her, don't I?" She resembled a naughty child more than the elderly adult she was, even if everyone still called her the *baby* sister.

David leaned forward. "Did you open it? What's in the envelope?" He captured her with his serious demeanor.

Aunt Trina was eager to help. "Yes, I did. You know, I worked in my husband's law office for many years. So, I was very careful, wore gloves, and made photocopies of it all. There are legal documents inside, declaring three slaves free. And a letter from a woman named Sarah describing her journey to bring the slaves to freedom to fulfill a promise made to her dying sister, Emily."

I was still processing all this information when she added, "Another letter was from Michael O'Connor. He and his brother Daniel left for the war with James and Joseph Nelson. He describes their encounter with Sarah and the slaves when the four soldiers got separated from their unit after a battle in Virginia. She found them in her barn and gave them food and drink. Joseph was injured, and so was Michael's younger brother, Daniel, so she and a young, enslaved woman treated their wounds. The soldiers escorted her group to Baltimore so they and the injured boys could take the train to Iowa."

"Michael O'Connor? That name is familiar. Isn't he my great-great-great-grandfather?" I remembered his grave in the family cemetery.

"Yes, my dear, you're right. My great-great-grandfather was Michael O'Connor." Aunt Trina handed over the yellow envelope.

Three slaves? I glanced at David and my aunt. "I thought it was five slaves. Is this a different story?"

"Three former slaves," David reminded me. "Iowa would be a good place to start over. It was the frontier, after all."

I nodded my head. Then something clicked. "Can we see the photocopies? I don't want to handle the originals. Can you read me the names of the freed slaves?"

She handed me a folder, and I opened it up to see a stack of photocopies.

I divided the stack in half and gave part to David. Flipping through, I saw the names of Rebecca Stevens, Thomas Philips, and Bobby Phillips.

"This is very interesting. Thank you, Aunt Trina," I gave her a kiss on her cheek, and she whispered, "He's very handsome. I think my granddaughter would call him a hottie."

Either David read lips, or he had excellent hearing because he grinned again. I sighed. My *hot boyfriend* had won over yet another one of my elderly aunts.

Then something else occurred to me. "Aunt Trina, I'm confused now. *Who* pinned the envelope to the quilt?"

"I presume Great-Great-Grandma Beth—or maybe Sarah. The safety pin was old and rusted. I removed it," she replied earnestly.

"Why didn't Grandma Mary open the envelope? I mean, her answers were all answered with the contents."

Aunt Trina glanced up, surprised. "Her answers?"

I sighed. "This is the problem with secrets, Aunt Trina. You never saw Grandma Mary's note wrapped inside the quilt?"

"What note? What did it say?"

I brought it up on my iPhone and read the note. "She claims to not know who made the red and green quilt. We should reward kindness. She wants her daughters to find out who made the quilt, and it's her dying wish."

Aunt Trina's mouth opened and closed in surprise. I sat down beside her, regretting my sharp tone.

David told her, "What's done can't be undone. Apparently, *no one* had opened the envelope before you took it."

She looked down. "I thought I did something good when I took the envelope forty years ago. I didn't know Molly was so upset. She never talked about it with me. Our great-aunt was obsessed with destroying the quilt and envelope. She said our family legacy was at stake."

"So, your great-grandma's sister was the one raving on?" I asked.

Aunt Trina regarded us. "Yes. Great-Aunt Tressie. I'm so sorry. In moving in here, things got jumbled. I've been searching for this pesky envelope for weeks and weeks. But since I didn't want to tell the family I took it; I couldn't ask for help."

"It's okay. We've got it now. But please call Grandma Molly." I tried to sound firm as I stood up. "She's been worried for forty years!"

David stood as well. "You did the right thing, ma'am, showing it to us."

Aunt Trina smiled at him. "Oh, please call me Trina! I'm too young for ma'am."

David replied, "Well, then—Trina. Good job!"

I gave her a long hug and whispered, "I love you, don't worry," and we left, as I clutched the precious envelope.

As I fastened my seat belt, I exhaled. "I swear. All the older women in my family are crazy. Wow! Forty years! My grandma worried about that envelope for forty years, and her sister-in-law had it all that time."

"Why is there a crazy aunt in every generation trying to protect the secrets?" David asked.

I nodded. "Alright. Let's review. Rebecca gives the rustic rose quilt to Daniel O'Connor at the end of the journey to Iowa. My fourth Great-Grandma, Beth O'Connor—or her daughter-in-law Sarah—puts the documents into a large legal envelope and pins it to Rebecca's quilt. It's passed from one generation to the next. Grandma Mary finds it but decides not to open the envelope. She wraps a note inside the quilt, never having the nerve to undo the safety pin. Grandma Molly takes it home after Grandma Mary's death. She doesn't open the envelope either. After hearing her great aunt threaten to burn the envelope, Trina steals it from her sister-in-law Molly's house forty years ago. She doesn't realize that she's leaving Molly the note wrapped up in the quilt."

"Well, at least it isn't sixty-four years, right?" he asked, referring to my twin aunts on Mom's side. They had a falling out and didn't talk about it for sixty-four years.

I sighed, "Yes. Oh, and thanks for being sweet to her."

He grinned. "Hey, she called me a hottie."

We made eye contact and hooted.

"David, you *are* a hottie. It was just funny hearing my seventy-five-year-old Aunt Trina use the word."

We headed to the museum with the folder in hand, encouraged, because we were holding a puzzle piece. Carl was there to meet us.

He regarded the battered old legal envelope and its documents with genuine interest.

David and I sat at a worktable with Carl and passed the copies of the documents back and forth as the originals were too fragile to handle.

Carl sat back and beamed at us. "You've solved one puzzle. The initials on the quilt for RS—RS must be Rebecca Stevens, the freed slave. The papers mention she was a gifted healer/nurse, quilter, and seamstress. So where was she from?" The writing had faded.

Carl glanced again at the photocopies. "We'll scan the originals.

Then we can sharpen the images and recapture what has faded…"
He used a full-page magnifier to scrutinize the legal documents.

I stood up and peered over his shoulder and shrieked, "Evaline!
It was on her freedom papers. What's the legal term?"

"Oh, you mean manumission papers, I think."

I nodded. "Yes, that's right. It's stitched into the hem of the quilt,
along with her initials. Is it a town?"

Carl shrugged.

"Carl, can you read off the list of battles? I have an interactive
ACW map I'm going to bring up." David sat down at the computer.

As Carl read the list, they stopped to examine each place, to see
if it matched the list of battles the 24th fought.

They worked their way through almost a dozen places when
David stopped. "I found it! Evaline is not a town. It's a plantation
on the outskirts of Winchester, Virginia."

"Thank you!" I hugged David.

"It's been a long day. Think we should check out Aunt Shirley's
specials?"

"I thought you'd never ask. Let's go."

"Carl? Want to go along? My treat?"

"No, you're not leaving until I make photocopies of these documents. I'll safeguard them here, and you can have copies of them."

Carl moved to the copy machine and made three copies of each
document.

"Okay, we can wait a few more minutes." I sat down, searching
my purse for a mint or some gum. I'd eaten yogurt hours ago. We'd
gotten a few answers, but we didn't have the entire story yet.

Twenty-eight

Welcome to Jubilee Junction
Sarah

"I love her, and that's the beginning and end of everything."
~F. Scott Fitzgerald

Joseph's mother, Mrs. Nelson, greeted Rebecca and Lucy. "Which one of you is Doctor Rebecca?

I put my arm around Rebecca. "This is Rebecca, and yes, the Army doctor called her *Doctor* Rebecca."

Mrs. Nelson welcomed her. "Michael wrote you took good care of the boys with herbs. You saved Daniel's arm and took good care of my Joseph's ankle and knee. My husband wants to talk to you. Come here, my dear."

Rebecca beamed. "Thank you, ma'am."

Mrs. Nelson now regarded the children. "And who do we have here?"

The children giggled, and the dogs sat, tails wagging, tongues lolling.

Bobby said, "I'm Bobby, and this is Chloe."

Chloe told her, "The three ladies are wearing costumes. Bobby and I are wearing disguises, too. We're pretending to be a boy and a girl! Miss Sarah said so."

Bobby shifted to big-brother mode. "It's *Sister* Sarah, and she's going to be my second mama."

Mrs. O'Connor listened to this and exchanged an amused glance with me, Mrs. Nelson, and the others. "I wondered if you two were wearing disguises. Good job, children!"

Then Rebecca turned to Lucy to introduce her. "This is Lucy. Michael and James rescued her and her daughter, Chloe, from a pair of nasty slave catchers. You can be proud of your boys, ma'am."

"Oh my. Welcome, Lucy. I'm so happy they rescued you."

I added, "And the young man who accompanied your sons to get our trunks is Thomas. He has been invaluable to us on this arduous journey. I don't know what we would have done without him. Without everyone, really, all working together."

Mrs. Nelson knelt and embraced the children. "Welcome to Jubilee Junction, children." Then she asked, "What are your dogs' names?"

"Scout and Duke," Bobby answered. Hearing their names, the dogs sat beside him, and both mothers petted them and said hello.

The men returned with a porter pushing the trunks on a cart. Joseph clumped along on his crutches while Thomas helped Daniel, who was trying to keep up.

Mrs. Nelson told us she was taking Joseph, Thomas, Lucy, and Chloe with her, and Mrs. O'Connor would take Daniel, Rebecca, Bobby, and me with her, as well as the hounds. Rebecca and Thomas gazed at each other.

Mrs. O'Connor noticed, and said, "You'll all see each other tomorrow for supper. We've planned a homecoming meal for the two households."

The porter loaded the trunks onto Mrs. O'Connor's large wagon, much like the one we used on our journey to Baltimore.

I apologized to Mrs. O'Connor for having so much luggage, and she shushed me. "You left your home to bring our boys back home and your friends here to safety. We have room for these things. Don't worry."

Before they left, we made sure Thomas, Lucy, and Chloe had their carpet bags. We visited the telegraph operator before we left the station and sent telegrams to Michael, Mother, and the Saunders to let them know of our safe arrival. Then we headed back to Mrs. O'Connor's house.

Daniel sat upfront chatting with his mother. He peeked over his shoulder, pointing out landmarks in town. Bobby sat between me and Rebecca, holding hands with both of us. The dogs ran alongside us, glad to get some exercise. We rode past the blacksmith shop, the livery stable, and the lumberyard.

Jubilee Junction was a growing frontier town, with a saloon/hotel, a general store, a butcher shop, bakery, the Jubilee Cafe, and a lawyer and doctor's offices downtown. Mrs. O'Connor took us by the big Methodist church and the Catholic church. Jubilee Junction was the county seat, so we drove by the building used for trials and a jail. Mrs. O'Connor noted the county planned to build a courthouse.

We drove through another half dozen streets lined with houses, modest cottages, and cabins. A few people waved and called out hello to Mrs. O'Connor, and she waved back.

Then we arrived at the O'Connor house, a sprawling two-story house with a wraparound porch on a large corner lot. There was a big shed in the back, gardens, and a nice yard with several mature oak trees.

I whispered, "It's going to be all right. We're here!" I turned away so they wouldn't see the tears on my cheek. "Emily, we made it," I whispered to my sister.

Our hosts put the three of us into a large bedroom with a single bed on one side of the room, as well as a double bed with a trundle bed underneath on the opposite side. I didn't want to separate Bobby from Rebecca. We put the carpet bags in our bedroom and admired the view of a flower garden outside the window. Beyond it sprawled a large vegetable garden.

Rebecca gazed out and pointed, "Coneflowers and yarrow!"

Daniel put us at ease. He and his mother gave us a tour of the house, a homey, comfortable one. A parlor, a large kitchen, a dining room, a small office/library, a washroom, and one bedroom filled the main floor. Four bedrooms filled the second floor, each with a fireplace. Each bedroom had a stand with a big bowl and pitcher for washing up and a chamber pot. Kerosene lamps helped illuminate the home as dusk came.

Downstairs, Mrs. O'Connor showed Bobby a box of toys that once belonged to her children. He showed her the bag of children's books from my house, and he sat down to explore the new things.

Rebecca and I carried my trunks upstairs to our room and put them in the corner. The smaller one held books, portraits, personal possessions, and some clothing. The larger ones held clothing, quilts, blankets, and the things Rebecca had gathered. These trunks held all that remained of my former life.

The dogs explored the backyard while we settled in, but Mrs. O'Connor assured me they could come inside and sleep upstairs with us.

Mr. O'Connor came home for supper and welcomed us. Then he became emotional when he saw Daniel and embraced him. Dr. Peter promised to visit the next day and check on Daniel to see how his injury was healing. Mr. O'Connor thanked Rebecca for her excellent care.

He thanked me also, and I told him we couldn't have made the trip without the soldiers. He assured me he'd do all he could to help my friends. Then he and Daniel sat down to talk in the parlor.

Rebecca and I helped Mrs. O'Connor with supper. Bobby followed us around, and she asked him to help set the table, placing a napkin and silverware at each place.

She served a beef stew with what she called Irish potatoes, a special kind producing larger spuds than usual, with some weighing three or more pounds per tuber. Daniel's parents expressed curiosity about the Underground Railroad and the people who helped us. I told them we couldn't have made it to Baltimore without their help.

After the meal we helped Mrs. O'Connor clear the table and do the dishes. She told us it was wonderful to have women in the house again, since both of her girls had married.

Bobby walked around the house with Daniel, staring at everything. "Let's go read a book," Daniel suggested, and he led Bobby into the small library. Bobby gazed around in delight. They settled down to read out loud from *The Swiss Family Robinson*.

Mr. O'Connor read the newspaper in the parlor but kept putting the paper down to listen to them. He walked into the kitchen and told us Bobby was a remarkable young boy.

I exchanged a questioning look with Rebecca, who nodded back at me. I drew a deep breath and once again considered the enormity of our decision, then said, "Mr. O'Connor, may Rebecca and I speak to you of a matter of utmost importance?"

He raised a questioning eyebrow, but showed no other indication of surprise. "It sounds as if we should discuss this in the parlor since the boys are in the library."

Rebecca and I followed him into the parlor and disclosed our desire for me to formally adopt Bobby as my son. Mr. O'Connor asked Rebecca if this was truly her wish. "Once it is done, there is no turning back," he added gravely.

"Miss Sarah can give my son a life I never could," she replied bravely, although a single tear trickled down her cheek.

"Very well," Mr. O'Connor said. "I shall draw up the adoption papers tomorrorw."

Later, Rebecca and I got Bobby ready for bed. We read one of his books aloud until he fell asleep clutching his rag doll, happy to have arrived in Iowa. When we were alone, he called us "my two mamas."

Rebecca and I talked afterward. We were thankful to be out of the wagon—and train car—and sleeping on actual beds with pillows, sheets, and blankets.

She thanked me for having the courage to leave everything behind and make the journey. "Emily's looking down on us with her little boy," she declared. "She would be so proud of you. You kept your promise to her—and to us."

I thanked Rebecca for saving my life from Dougie, and we broke down into giggles. It would have been difficult to take him too seriously if it hadn't been for the terrifying reality of the gun pressed to my temple.

We talked about Michael, the war, and if he would survive and return to Jubilee Junction.

"He loves you, Miss Sarah. He'll do all he can to survive."

"Oh, Rebecca, after all we've been through, you can stop calling me Miss. Just Sarah, all right? Yes, I want him to survive. I love him, too." Then, I added, "Speaking of love, Thomas wants to get settled, and then he'll propose, so be ready. He's a hard worker."

"He's a good man. I love him. He's watched over Bobby and me for years. I hope he doesn't wait too long."

Over the following weeks, we settled into our new lives in Jubilee Junction. Daniel and Joseph were right: we loved Midwestern village life! It was the frontier, and wagonloads of people passed through town every week, moving west, still exploring this vast land. But I'd found a home, a family, and a second chance at life.

We realized it would be a challenge for the community to adapt to seeing freed slaves, as it would be a challenge for the freed slaves to navigate the community. Mr. O'Connor told us there had only been about a thousand Blacks in Iowa at the start of the war. Now, Blacks were coming to work in the coal mines, building railroad tracks, and serving as porters. Others were passing through to go west with the promise of free land or north to Canada.

On the first Sunday, Rev. Luke Carlson was preaching in town, both families marched into church with their guests. We'd dressed in our Sunday best.

Rev. Carlson welcomed us and asked that we sit up front, along with Daniel and Joseph. Then he called us all to come forward. Joseph stood beside Thomas and whispered something to him, and Thomas stood taller.

Daniel stood on the other side, next to Lucy, and he whispered something to her, making her smile. The minister put us at ease and summarized our story without identifying Bobby's mother. Bobby stood between me and Rebecca, with Lucy holding hands with Chloe, who was shy and staring down, sucking on her finger.

At the end of his comments, the pastor turned to us with a smile. "Well, I understand you ladies arrived in Jubilee Junction disguised as Sisters Sarah, Rebecca, and Lucy. I commend you all for your courage. You helped bring our boys, Daniel and Joseph, home. You're all going to be fine additions to Jubilee Junction. Welcome!" And he invited the audience to welcome us as well.

The congregation stood, clapped, and called out, "Welcome!" Our host families stood up, approached the altar, and embraced us all in front of God and the congregation. When two of the founding families embrace you in public, it's a commendation. And when the third founding family—Charles and Eva Carlson—joined them, it's even better.

The kindness of our hosts was immense. Michael's father did the legal paperwork to change Thomas's last name to Thomas Settler. Then, Thomas began an apprenticeship with Philip Nelson, who was a blacksmith. Thomas loved horses, and they loved him. They stood patiently as he checked their feet for problems. Though they didn't like it, they were quiet as he checked their shoes or made new ones. A competent blacksmith, Thomas could fix a broken wagon hitch or reinstall a wagon rim. Philip would later ask him to become his partner.

As I predicted, Thomas proposed to Rebecca a few months later, and Rev. Carlson performed the ceremony in the sanctuary of the Methodist church. Lucy enjoyed helping make her dress—a lovely white satin gown with a fitted bodice trimmed with lace on the skirt, sleeves, and neckline. Lucy and I served as her bridesmaids, with Joseph and Daniel as the groomsmen for Thomas.

Thomas and Rebecca moved into the loft above Peter Nelson's office for six months while building their small house. Friends and family members helped with the construction or donated furniture, and by the time they'd moved in, they'd become part of the community.

Rebecca worked with Peter Nelson, an herbal doctor, who used plants to heal people. She and Peter explored the woods, and they compared notes, learning from each other. Having examined Daniel's shoulder and seen how well it had healed, with yarrow packed into the wound, Peter praised Rebecca's treatment. They grew an herb garden and created teas, creams, and tinctures for their patients for a variety of ailments. Rebecca was eager to learn from him as well.

Peter taught Rebecca what he'd learned from the local tribes of Native Americans. She told him what happened to Emily, how she'd torn during childbirth and bled to death, and that the baby had suffocated during the arduous labor. They created an oil made from lavender and oils that midwives used to prevent tearing during childbirth, and another from Shepherd's Purse to stop postpartum hemorrhaging.

Other soldiers who returned from the war with injuries were

not as fortunate as Daniel and Joseph in receiving competent care. Those suffering from crude amputations endured terrible pain. Overwhelmed Army doctors gave them morphine, which, while effective, carried the risk of addiction. Now that they were home, they were still in pain, needing morphine. Peter and Rebecca tried natural products to care for their wounds, but with limited success. They discovered caring for these injured soldiers presented dilemmas.

Mr. O'Connor drew up the adoption papers, and we appeared before the Jubilee County Judge, The Right Honorable Robert Carlson, and Bobby became my son. Beforehand, Rebecca, Thomas, and I sat down with him to explain it all, aided by Mr. and Mrs. O'Connor.

He surprised us. "I know. My arm matches Miss Sarah's arm. I'm going to have two mamas. We talked about it before." Months had passed since that conversation in my kitchen back in Virginia, and it seemed long ago, somehow, but this young boy remembered.

As part of the adoption, we changed his name to Samuel James McDonald. Bobby had turned seven by now, and observed, "I think we have enough Michaels already, don't we?" Mr. and Mrs. O'Connor chuckled.

Bobby liked the name Samuel from having met Rev. Samuel Saunders. He liked the name James from knowing James Nelson. However, he apologized. "Sorry, Daniel. I only need two names." Daniel nodded.

The months passed, and we found happiness in our new home. Having the O'Connor and Nelson families sponsor us made the difference for most of the townspeople. I wrote letters to Michael every week and told him how well we were settling into Jubilee Junction. I prayed for his safe return as I had prayed for the town to accept my new family.

Twenty-nine

Settling into Jubilee Junction
Sarah

"In giving freedom to the slave, we assure freedom to the free—honorable alike in what we give, and what we preserve. We shall nobly save, or meanly lose, the last best hope of earth. Other means may succeed; this could not fail. The way is plain, peaceful, generous, just—a way which, if followed, the world will forever applaud, and God must forever bless."

~Abraham Lincoln

Mother—Harriet Douglas—arrived on the train in March 1865. We found a house for her and helped furnish it. Samuel and I moved into it with her and brought Duke and Scout. Mother told me she'd signed over her house to Peter and Susanna. They'd taken in half a dozen former slaves and planted a large garden. Peter took care of horses and was learning to be a blacksmith.

Mother wanted to start a new life out West. Father had died in the war, and though she was heartbroken, she was determined not to sit in her house in Virginia and mourn. We seldom talked about Emily's death or her baby, because then Mother would be in tears. She treated Samuel like her grandson, and he loved her.

I taught at the Jubilee Junction schoolhouse, and both Chloe and Samuel attended school, along with 18 other children. Most of these students lacked formal schooling, so we worked on the basics of reading, writing, and math. They made substantial progress in the first few months.

Lucy and Chloe stayed on with the Nelsons and used an extra

bedroom for her work as a seamstress. People brought her clothing to mend or asked her to make clothing. Several nights a week, I spent time with her, teaching her how to read, write, and do arithmetic so Lucy could run her business. Chloe and Samuel sat at the kitchen table and read books. Mrs. Nelson often brought biscuits or cornbread for the children. She adored Chloe's precociousness.

I corresponded with Michael all this time and enjoyed each new letter, whether it was a couple of brief paragraphs or several pages. I prayed for the end of the war.

In the meantime, Rev. Saunders and his wife Cassandra moved West. We didn't have a regular minister. Rev. Carlson was a circuit preacher, traveling across eastern and central Iowa. All those communities needed him. So, when I told them about Rev. Saunders, the church board wrote him a letter and offered him the pastorate, which he accepted. Two months later, we welcomed them at the Jubilee Junction train depot. Abigail moved west with her parents, and I enjoyed having her so close.

We found a house for them near the church and helped them get settled. Mother and Mrs. Saunders became good friends and enjoyed the company of Mrs. Nelson, Mrs. Carlson, and Mrs. O'Connor. Together, the group of ladies began working to create a town library.

They decided Abigail would be our first librarian. They got to work collecting books, and Daniel built some bookshelves. I thought of all my father's books left behind and sent money for Mama Cee to box them up and send them. They arrived several months later.

Then, one day, the telegraph agent at the Jubilee Junction Depot came running down Main Street past the school, the general store, the law office, and the doctor's office. He yelled, "It's over! The war is over!"

He ran into *The Jubilee Times* with the telegram in his hand. That week's edition ran with big headlines. "War Ends! April 9th, 1865, Robert E. Lee surrendered the last major Confederate army to Ulysses S. Grant at the Appomattox Courthouse."

When I heard the news, I wept. I'd opened our windows to let air into the schoolhouse, so we all heard him yell as he ran past us.

I got my composure back and told the children to continue with their lessons, but tears continued to flow from my eyes.

Samuel and Chloe both came up and embraced me. Soon the other children joined them, and we had a group hug. Many children were in tears as well, since all of them had family members who had gone to war—fathers, uncles, big brothers, and cousins.

Abigail came rushing into the classroom and joined us, her face shining with tears.

Soon, our church bells were ringing.

When we quieted down, we talked about the war for a few minutes. A handful of free Blacks now lived in the area, but Chloe was the only Black child the students knew. Chloe was now five, and her resilience gave me hope.

The children sat around me in a circle with Chloe and Samuel sitting next to me. I wouldn't have asked Chloe to talk about what it was like to be a slave. I didn't have to ask her. She stood up, and Samuel stood up with her.

"My mama has scars on her back from being whipped because a bad man said she wasn't working fast enough," Chloe told them. "He scared me. We went to bed hungry, and I saw people get branded with hot irons. I didn't like being a slave."

"Mama and I ran away, and then some bad slave catcher men chased us and almost caught us, but the soldiers rescued us. Samuel and I became friends."

The students listened intently. Samuel stood beside her and then jumped into the story. "Then one of the slave catchers came back and grabbed my mama, so Miss Lucy and Aunt Rebecca knocked him down! And Chloe and I helped, and so did Thomas and the dogs."

Chloe added, "His name was Dougie, and he smelled terrible!"

The other children looked skeptical and glanced at me, while Abigail struggled with her composure.

"It's all true," I assured them. "Slavery is wrong and now it's against the law. Fortunately, there are still good people in the world, and they helped us on the Underground Railroad in Virginia and Maryland."

Then, I wiped my eyes and faced the class. "Thank you, Samuel, and Chloe. We've enjoyed a big hug and heard stories about slavery. Let's go back to our lessons."

The day we'd been praying for arrived when a group of us met at the Jubilee Junction's train depot to welcome home some of our returning soldiers, including Michael and James and another dozen young men.

When Michael stepped off the train, I saw him before he saw me. I let his mother embrace him first, and then she turned to me. "It's your turn, Sarah."

His eyes lit up, and I stepped into his arms. Michael embraced me like he didn't want to let go. Neither did I. He kissed my cheek. I sighed, and he kissed me on the lips. Then I heard a chuckle behind us.

James mused out loud, "I wish I had a beautiful schoolteacher to greet me!" I laughed, turned around, and greeted him, holding both his hands and remarking on how glad we were to have him home.

Daniel and Joseph were there, too, of course, to welcome home their brothers.

We fixed a feast—ham and gravy, yams, cornbread with honey, and strawberry-rhubarb pie. Afterward, we sat talking and gave them a chance to tell us what they had experienced in the last months of the war. Michael said that it had been difficult. They'd lost too many soldiers, and they were glad to be home. James nodded soberly.

We didn't press them for details. Unfortunately, half a dozen boys from Jubilee Junction didn't come home. Four soldiers came home with serious injuries, missing arms, or missing a leg, hobbling on crutches.

We didn't know then that they also came home with lice, digestive problems because of their terrible diet, and some had contracted syphilis. Dr. Nelson and Rebecca kept busy and ordered every family to burn their soldiers' clothing and had them scrub themselves to get rid of the lice.

Out of the 1,000 men in the Iowa regiment, the death toll was appalling. Three officers died of disease and nine died in battle.

One hundred and nineteen enlisted men died—or fell, mortally wounded, in battle. Two hundred twelve enlisted men died of disease or calamity.

Many men suffered chronic pain from amputations, and too many of them became addicted to dangerous drugs like opium and morphine. It would be thirty years later, in 1897, before the Bayer company used salicylic acid to create the wonder drug, aspirin. Rebecca's willow bark contained natural salicylic acid, explaining why it had helped her patients with fever and pain.

Michael O'Connor came home with the rank of corporal. He began working with his father in the law office. Lawyers didn't have to attend law school in those days. Instead, they could *read* the law with an established lawyer.

His father liked to quote Abraham Lincoln's advice for young lawyers. "Begin with *Blackstone's Commentaries*, and after reading it carefully through, say twice, take up *Chitty's Pleadings*, *Greenleaf's Evidence*, and *Story's Equity Jurisprudence* in succession. Work, work, work, is the main thing." So, Michael studied with his father.

Michael and I courted for three months before he proposed. We were at a family dinner, having just finished the meal. Michael got down on one knee and presented me with a lovely antique ring. "Sarah, will you marry me?"

I nodded, unable to speak because of the tears.

He slipped the ring on my finger, and everyone cheered. I said, "I would have said *Yes!* the moment you got off the train!" And he kissed me.

We planned a simple wedding. Rebecca and Lucy made my wedding dress. We married in early October 1865. Abigail, Rebecca, and Lucy were my bridesmaids, while James, Daniel, and Joseph were Michael's groomsmen.

Samuel was excited Michael was going to be his father, and Mr. and Mrs. O'Connor would be his grandparents. He'd already told Rev. and Mrs. Saunders he was adopting them, so they would be his grandparents, too. He'd heard Rev. Saunders call me his second daughter, and they responded graciously.

Chloe wanted grandparents of her own. Mr. and Mrs. Nelson

told her they would be her grandparents, and she was happy again. Mother lamented that she didn't have any granddaughters, so maybe Chloe could adopt her, too. She became Grandma Harriet.

For someone who felt alone just a few months earlier, I now had a family. With my beloved Michael, our child Samuel, Mother, my in-laws, my siblings Thomas, Rebecca, and Lucy, niece Chloe, and my second parents, the Saunders, close by. Best of all, Abigail and I spent hours talking and catching up as we unpacked and set up the house for her and her parents. She became my other sister.

At several community gatherings, I saw James talking to Abigail, and asked Michael, "They would be a good pair, don't you agree?" He agreed.

We gave them time to get to know each other, inviting them to several gatherings at our home. Abigail confided to me James walked her home from a band concert in the town square. He took her for a Sunday ride in his buggy with his mother as a chaperone.

I saw Mother and her group of friends watching, too. It was plain there would be another wedding in Jubilee Junction soon.

Not everyone in Jubilee was friendly to our new friends, however. I was shopping with Rebecca one day at the General store, and realized I'd forgotten something, and walked to another part of the store to get it. When I returned, an irate clerk was asking Rebecca why she was in the store because *her kind* wasn't welcome there.

Rebecca stared down in shame, gripping her basket filled with goods. I positioned myself between her and the young man, and informed him she was with me. Also, she was a free woman, and he should get used to waiting on her—or we would drive five miles to another shop, and he would lose all my business.

I took the basket from her hand, put it on the counter, and declared, "I don't think my husband, Michael O'Connor, will be happy when I tell him what happened. And when he talks to the Carlson and Nelson families, I don't think they'll be happy either. You owe my friend an apology or we leave now."

The clerk paled. I knew the shop was owned by the Carlsons.

He gulped, "I'm so sorry, Miss—?"

She glanced up, made eye contact, and spoke firmly, "Mrs. Settler."

He gulped. "No need for any unpleasantness, Mrs. Settler. I apologize." He rang us up, and we paid the bill and left.

I talked to Michael's parents about what to do, and Mr. O'Connor's face seemed troubled. "Some may find it harder to accept your friends, but let's give them time to show they're good people."

In the meantime, Peter Nelson walked around town with Rebecca as his assistant, and his patients saw Rebecca at his office. Daniel and Joseph talked about their experience of being injured during the battle of Winchester, and how Rebecca had taken care of them.

Another day, a man entered Philip's blacksmith shop, saw Thomas, and called him *boy*. Thomas was working on mending a wagon hitch while his partner was out back fixing a wagon. The man asked, "Where is Philip? Who can help me?"

Thomas glanced up and spoke calmly, "Philip's out back fixing a hitch. I'm here, and my name is Thomas. What do you need?"

The man seemed startled, but explained what he needed, and Thomas helped him fix the broken piece.

The man apologized when he paid. "I heard a slave was working here."

Thomas replied, "I'm not a slave anymore. I'm a free man."

"Yes, and you did a good job. I'll be back."

One evening, after Samuel was in bed, Michael and I sat at our kitchen table, talking about all we'd experienced in the past year. So much death and destruction, cruelty, and injustice. But there were still good people in the world, like those ministers and their families who'd helped us on the Underground Railroad. How would we have gotten to Baltimore without their help? And of course, his family, the Nelsons, and the Carlsons had shown us kindness and acceptance.

I felt the need to give back and do what I could to make a difference after receiving so much help. I told him I was determined to work for equal rights for all people, Black and white. He nodded in assent and took my hand.

Thirty

Samuel Marries Maggie, 1881
Sarah

"You live life looking forward, you understand life looking backward."

~Soren Kierkegaard

As part of her town history project, Abigail asked me to reflect on my life since moving to Jubilee Junction.

Michael and I have had a wonderful life. We watched Samuel grow up and become a big brother to our other four children. He attended law school at the University of Iowa and graduated with honors. Samuel was taller than his father had been, and he stared down at Michael and Thomas with amusement, while Rebecca and I tried to keep him in pants long enough.

Mother has always been fond of him. "The boy's a gentle giant."

Samuel flirted with Mary Margaret "Maggie" O'Connor at several parties and community gatherings. She was a beautiful young woman and flirted back. Rebecca and I talked, of course, and worried. We talked about the situation with Michael and Thomas, who thought we were worried about nothing.

Michael pointed out, "He's a handsome man, and I see a few young ladies smiling at him. Who knows what will happen?"

Thomas agreed.

Rebecca and I disagreed. "I see him stare at Miss Maggie the way you used to stare at Sarah," Rebecca told him. "He's made his choice, mark my word."

I agreed.

"He's about to turn twenty-four. He wants to settle down and start practicing law."

Several weeks passed, and then Samuel sat us down and told us he was going to propose to Maggie. He'd asked Grandma Harriet for a family ring. Michael and I gazed at each other. "Have you told Rebecca and Thomas yet?"

"No, Mama Sarah, but I'm on my way." He kissed me and shook his father's hand.

The four parents talked then and discussed what to do but couldn't decide. In the meantime, Samuel proposed, and Maggie accepted. She was in love and excited about starting her life with him. Her parents began planning the wedding. Grandma Harriet produced a beautiful family ring—a delicate silver filigree with a small diamond.

We sat down with Samuel and encouraged him to tell Maggie the entire story about his two mothers. Only a handful of people knew he was Rebecca's son when we came to Jubilee Junction—almost eighteen years ago. He listened and agreed.

To the town, Samuel was my son, and when Michael and I married, Michael became his father. Mrs. O'Connor and Mrs. Nelson were our champions and helped us to build new lives. The town saw him as a white boy—now a white man. Of course, his father had been white. His birth mother, Rebecca, was a lighter-skinned Black, so he'd been born a light-skinned slave who could pass for white. Maggie should know the truth before they married.

Mrs. Nelson and Peter were visiting grandchildren in Colorado. But Mrs. and Mr. O'Connor were in town, and we decided we needed them there, too.

So, we visited Maggie and her parents, Rose and Eli, Michael's younger cousin. He'd gone to war the year after Michael and Daniel. Eli and Rose seemed surprised to see Samuel with his Aunt Rebecca and Uncle Thomas, but welcomed us all into their large parlor.

My handsome son fell to his knees in front of Maggie. He'd already asked her to marry him the previous week, and now realized he couldn't do so without telling her the truth about his parentage.

"Maggie, I must tell you something. My birth mother is not Sarah, but Rebecca, who worried about me. Sarah adopted me at age seven and raised me as her own. I love them both as my mothers. When Sarah married Michael O'Connor, he became my adoptive father, and he and Thomas have both been fathers to me."

Then he told her about the circumstances of his birth, and explained Emily and Sarah's plan to free the slaves, Emily's death, meeting the four soldiers, and their journey to Iowa.

"Michael and James put us on a train to Iowa. Peter and Mrs. Nelson and your grandparents, Mr. and Mrs. O'Connor, took us in, with gratitude for our help in caring for Daniel and Joseph. My birth mother, Rebecca, knew all about herbs and used them to help with Joseph and Daniel's pain."

As our son talked, Rebecca and I watched Maggie's face.

She listened to Samuel's story.

"None of this makes a difference to me, Samuel. I love you. Your mothers have both shown great courage."

She reached out for his hand, and he took hers into his.

But her parents' faces showed their shock and outrage.

Her mother stuttered, "I'd no idea! I cannot believe you would deceive us in this manner."

Her father put his arm around her shoulder. "Dearest, I do not believe anyone attempted to deceive us. Please calm down." But his face looked troubled.

I stepped forward then with a folder of papers. "Here is the document declaring his freedom, the adoption papers, and the document showing his name change. I intended to fulfill the promise to my sister, who watched this boy grow up, and wondered about his future as a young light-skinned boy whose mother was Black. I never wanted to deceive anyone and debated telling you a thousand times. Michael's parents promised to keep our secret about Bobby and consider me his mother. When Samuel began courting your daughter, Rebecca and I debated about what to do."

Maggie dismissed her parents' concerns. "I love you, Samuel! None of this makes any difference to me. I want to marry you, and I admire Sarah and Rebecca both!" She was trembling with emotion and on the verge of tears.

A knock on the front door interrupted us. Eli walked back with the O'Connor grandparents.

Mr. O'Connor shook hands with Samuel, asking him about law school. Samuel leaned down so Grandma could embrace him. "Samuel, you're such a handsome young man. Your two mothers have done well," and she nodded toward both of us.

Maggie's mother sputtered, "You knew?"

Maggie's father tried to calm her.

Mrs. O'Connor glanced around the room. "Your father and I were grateful for the compassion of these two women, who cared for our son, Daniel. The doctor in Maryland checked the wound. He told them the Army doctors would have amputated the arm. The herbs Rebecca applied prevented infection and allowed the wound to heal."

"Bobby looked like any other white boy, but Bobby was Rebecca's son, and she worried about his future. So, she asked Sarah to adopt him. Your father and I are glad that we took them in. They were all hard workers, but more than that, they became trusted members of the family. Thomas and Rebecca soon married and set up housekeeping on the north side of town, near the school. Sarah's mother, Harriet, moved to Iowa and invited Sarah and Samuel to move in with her. Later, Sarah married Michael. Our family continued to grow. We agreed to keep the secret and were thankful to have Daniel home."

Maggie's mother was still scandalized. Her father paced. "This is a lot to take in. I need to think about this."

Maggie implored her parents. "None of this matters to me. I want to marry Samuel. I love him."

Samuel gazed at her father and mother. "I know it's shocking, but I've grown up with two wise mothers, and they urged me to come talk to you. We will leave the folder with you and give you time to think. We want your blessing."

Maggie's father nodded. "Thank you, Samuel."

Her mother's face revealed her greater level of turmoil. "Yes, we need to think."

Samuel stood and shook Eli's hand.

Rebecca and I embraced Mrs. O'Connor, and she embraced

Thomas, too. Then Mrs. O'Connor embraced Samuel and her grand-daughter. "It's going to be alright, children."

Mr. O'Connor shook hands all around and then sat down as if he meant to stay. His calm, pleasant demeanor contrasted with that of Maggie's parents.

A tearful Maggie clung to Samuel, who held her close.

Then we left, Samuel walking head and shoulders taller than his four parents.

Several of the aunts and uncles gathered to discuss the dilemma. I heard all about it from a younger aunt. Eli and Rose withdrew to consider the matter. Maggie's younger sister ran to a relative's house, and soon the house was full of family members.

A younger aunt studied the room. "Samuel can provide for her. He's a handsome young man, and he'll do well in the family's law practice."

"But do you want one of those people in your family tree?" Aunt Tressie's voice was sharp.

A shocked silence met her remark.

Maggie burst into tears. "What do you mean, *those people*, Aunt Tressie? We're talking about Samuel. You've known him almost all of his life. How is he any different today than he was last week?" She fled to her bedroom.

Mrs. O'Connor agreed. "He's a fine young man. I've known him for most of his life, and I come to know his mothers, too. I believe we would be fortunate to have him in our family tree, but I'm not sure about some of you!" Then she left to comfort her granddaughter.

Mr. O'Connor scanned the room without saying a word and followed his wife as the room fell silent. Aunt Tressie appeared ashamed and stared down at the floor.

The next day, Maggie's parents asked Rev. Saunders to come over, along with all four of Samuel's parents.

Rev. Saunders addressed the group. "Samuel's a fine young man. And he's one of God's children. I remember going to the train station in Boston with Cassandra and Abigail to see Sarah and her companions. Bobby looked like any other little white boy, but Sarah had told me his story. I saw the bond between Rebecca and Sarah. Going west meant that Bobby could live a life and have opportunities he would not have otherwise." He nodded at me.

I declared, "Rebecca is one of my two dearest friends. She was my sister's companion and knew Emily well. We spent time together before the trip west, caring for Emily during her miscarriage and then her subsequent pregnancy. Rebecca trusted me to raise Samuel, and we shared a unique bond as his two mamas. I'm not colorblind, and neither is she, but Rebecca's my sister. We couldn't have cared for your uncle Daniel without her skills and knowledge."

Rebecca chimed in, "I agree with Sarah. Emily suggested she adopt Bobby, but after she died and we set off with Sarah, I realized I could trust her with my child. I love Sarah and Michael. They've given our son a wonderful upbringing."

Michael and I sat on the fine horsehair sofa, holding hands. He leaned forward. "I love Samuel. He's my son. He's grown into an exceptional young man. Anyone can see Samuel and Maggie love one another. Let them marry with your blessings."

Thomas leaned forward. "Tell the truth or keep it a secret, but they belong together."

Eli and Rose regarded each other. She nodded.

Eli cleared his throat. "Rose, go get your daughter, please. It's time to finish planning the wedding."

Michael stood and walked over to shake Eli's hand. Then he and Thomas shook hands. All three men laughed. Both fathers embraced Samuel, while Rebecca and I embraced. She and I were both crying tears of joy. Our son was getting married.

Rev. Saunders wiped his eyes and then embraced Samuel, smiling.

Two months later, the four of us watched with pride as our son, Samuel James McDonald, married his sweetheart, Maggie. Rebecca made Maggie's wedding dress with the help of her friend Lucy.

At the wedding reception, Michael's Uncle Harrison, editor of *The Jubilee Times*, commented it would make a great story for the newspaper. "Imagine the headline, *The wedding happened after a shocking revelation by the groom.* It's a shame I can't publish it."

Thirty-one

Intruder at the Museum
Gracie

"The sacrifice our ancestors gave yesterday Gave us today and our tomorrow."

~Stephen Joseph Kuta

Spring Break, March 18–22, 2013

$\mathcal{M}$onday evening, I got a call from the Jubilee Junction Police. I was sitting at my desk, having just closed the lid on my laptop and laid down my clipboard. Agatha was playing with a toy mouse on the floor.

It was the first full day of Spring Break, and I'd spent it cleaning my house, grading, and grocery shopping. I still had work to do at the museum, but I felt pleased that I'd checked off so many other things from my to do list.

"Hello, is this Gracie O'Connor?"

"Yes, it is," I replied, alert.

"This is Lt. Carlson. Can you come to the Jubilee County Museum to see some video footage? There's been an attempted break-in."

"A break-in at the museum? Is anyone hurt? Anything damaged?"

"No, it happened after hours. We'll explain when you get here."

I put on my sneakers and jacket, then grabbed my purse and keys. Ten minutes later I arrived at the museum and saw a police car out front, along with Carl's car. I hurried inside.

I glanced at the quilt exhibit, but everything seemed in order. I saw someone in Carl's office and headed there.

"Hi, Gracie. Thanks for coming down." Carl wore a troubled expression on his face.

A handsome young officer turned to me. "Miss O'Connor? I'm Lt. Carlson. We need your help."

I saw them watching the computer monitor for the security cameras, which we'd gotten with a grant earlier in the year.

Carl took a breath. "A teenager found a place to hide until after we closed. He didn't realize we had motion-activated cameras. The camera shows him going into a storage closet and peeking out before closing. We check the museum's rooms but not closets. Then the cleaners showed up a few minutes after we closed. He peeked out, saw them, and shut the door."

I watched Carl play the surveillance tape, thankful we had a tech-savvy board member who researched the security system and helped get the funding.

Carl continued, "An hour later, the cleaners left. As soon as he opened the door, the security cameras activated. You can see his face here. Then, when he moved toward the quilt exhibit, the motion-activated alarm sounded. He panicked and ran for the exit."

I stared at the face and squinted. "Can you make his face bigger?" But I had a sudden sinking sensation.

Lt. Carlson stepped in and helped Carl adjust the image.

I let out an enormous sigh. "I know the young man. He's a second cousin—Lance Sullivan—my Great-Aunt Catharine's grandson and a senior in high school."

"Thanks, Miss O'Connor."

Carl stared at me. "I'm sorry, Gracie. Any idea why Lance would hide in the museum or what he might have been after?"

I sighed again. "I'm not sure. Lance's grandmother called me really upset a few days ago. She didn't want me to add the rustic rose quilt to the next exhibit and kept saying it would destroy our family's legacy. I can't imagine she would put him up to this, though."

Carl took off his glasses and rubbed his face. "Not everyone appreciates history the way we do. Sometimes families have secrets they don't want to be exposed. We need to figure out the rest of the puzzle pieces."

The young police officer studied us, skeptical. "You think this incident is about a quilt?" he asked, holding his pen and pad.

"Not just any quilt. This is a Civil War-era quilt made by a young Black woman—a freed slave. She came to Jubilee Junction in 1864, accompanied by two Union soldiers, Daniel O'Connor and Joseph Nelson. We're still uncovering some family history. I don't understand why my great-aunt was so angry about Rebecca's quilt."

Lt. Carlson jotted down a few details in a small notebook. He glanced up, "Joseph Nelson, huh? Thanks for your help. We'll take it from here." He left.

I turned to Carl. "I think I need to go see my Great-Aunt Catharine."

He nodded. "Take David, please, or your parents."

As we walked out of the museum, he set the alarm.

"Get some sleep, Gracie. See you tomorrow," Carl told me, watching me get in my car before he headed for his vehicle.

I didn't bother my parents, wanting them to get a good night's sleep. But I called David, who offered to come over. I declined, but we talked for half an hour, catching up on things. Before he hung up, he told me, "I love you, Gracie."

I felt loved as I climbed into bed. But I was unsettled by the day's events. An hour later, I still tossed and turned. Why was my great-aunt upset? Why did Lance hide in the museum after hours? Every scenario seemed too outlandish to be true. Agatha gave up and retreated to her cat bed.

Tuesday

In the morning, I headed to the newspaper where I told my parents about what had happened at the museum the night before.

"I need to see Great-Aunt Catharine," I sighed

Dad suggested, "Let me call her, then let's all go over."

I glanced around the office. "Dad, do you have an alarm system? If not, you need to get one. What Lance wanted to do in the museum after hours makes me nervous."

Dad nodded. "I've talked to a friend about it and will check on it again. Let me go call Aunt Catharine."

He headed to his office.

Mom sighed. "I remember how cute Lance was when he was a baby. He's grown up too fast. I can't believe he's a senior in high school. This situation makes no sense. Why would Lance hide in the museum?"

Dad returned with a fiery expression in his eyes. He had his car keys. "Let's lock up. Delores is coming later to staff the reception desk, and she's got keys."

We drove to Aunt Catharine's house, a big Victorian with turrets and a rounded tower with several fancy attic windows. Dad straightened his shoulders and rang the bell.

Her daughter Victoria opened the door, and we could see she'd been crying. Mom stepped forward and gave her a hug. "Oh, Vikki, what's going on?"

"Come in, Becky and Matthew. Hello Gracie. Things aren't going well," she told us tearfully. "Lance is trying to tell mother what he was doing at the museum. Aaron's off on a business trip." Aaron was her husband and traveled for his job with a local AG business.

We walked into the house and towards the noise in my great-aunt's large living room. I'd been to several family gatherings here and admired the large windows, built-in window seats, and fireplace, but we were walking into a family fracas.

Glancing at Mom, I resisted the urge to back out of the room. She nodded at me.

"I heard you talking to Gracie about some stupid red and green quilt and letter. So, I wanted to find it and get rid of it. I thought you'd be happy," Lance told his Grandma Catharine in a belligerent tone.

She shrank back in her recliner as her grandson leaned over her.

Dad walked up to Lance, tapping him on the shoulder. "Lance? Hey, buddy, let's sit down and talk, and give your grandma some space, okay?"

Lance turned to him with tears on his face. "I don't get it, Uncle

Matthew. Why is she mad at me? If I'd just gotten the quilt, she'd be happy now, right?"

Vikki suggested, "Why don't we all sit down? Mama, do you want a glass of water?"

Mom gestured for me to sit on the sofa. Dad remained standing with an arm around Lance's shoulder.

Great-Aunt Catharine shook her head, a Kleenex to her nose. "This is a disgrace. The Jubilee Junction police brought my grandson in for questioning about an attempted break-in at the museum. What would your grandfather say?"

Lance stepped away from Dad, folded his arms, and stood straight. His voice was defiant. "Grandpa would say it's better to do something than boss people around. I heard you talking to Gracie about the quilt."

Great-Aunt Catharine flinched. "You don't understand, Lance. I'm trying to protect the family legacy."

"What do you mean, Grandma? Why do you care about the family legacy more than your family?"

My great-aunt seemed to shrink into the chair.

Dad cleared his throat. "Aunt Catharine, can you tell us why you were so upset? What legacy do you mean? We represent two of the founding families of the town, and we have a proud history. You've nothing to worry about."

She turned to me. "What have you learned about Sarah and Michael?"

Caught off-guard, I hesitated. "They rescued two slaves—a mother and her daughter—and drove a big farm wagon with four soldiers, two of them injured, plus three other freed slaves. A slave named Rebecca helped care for the soldiers. People on the Underground Railroad helped them reach Baltimore, where they boarded the train to Boston, and then on to Iowa. We have four boxes from Aunt Violet, so we may find more information."

Great-Aunt Catharine stared at me. "And what about Rebecca? What have you learned about her?"

I glanced at her in confusion. "Rebecca made lovely quilts and used herbs to treat the soldiers' wounds."

She glanced at me more intently, her blue-gray eyes flashing. "Whose son was Bobby?"

"Sarah's son, of course. What do you mean?" I asked.

"Sarah adopted Bobby when they reached Jubilee Junction. They changed his name to Samuel James McDonald, after his adopted mother," she replied.

Dad recognized the name. "Wasn't he the frontier lawyer who fought for civil rights in the 1880s? He and his wife fought for women's right to vote?"

His aunt stared at him coldly. "Yes, he married Mary Margaret O'Connor in 1881. He became part of this family. But who was his mother, Matthew? I'll tell you. His mother was the slave, Rebecca, and he was the product of a distasteful, illicit relationship with the master of the plantation. I understand she was only fourteen or fifteen when she became pregnant with his child. Samuel was one of those light-skinned people who passed for white."

I stood up, suddenly furious. "Relationship? Don't be ridiculous. The plantation owner must have raped her—at fourteen or fifteen she was under the age of consent, even if they didn't think slaves had any say in the matter. So, what—Rebecca had a child who Sarah adopted? I don't get it. How does that destroy our family legacy?"

Lance jumped up. "You're saying one of my ancestors was a Black man?" He ran out of the room. The front door slammed, and we all stared at Great-Aunt Catharine.

She shut her eyes and slumped in the chair.

My parents were stunned, and Vikki sat down.

The doorbell rang, and I left to answer it. "I think it's David."

I opened the door and David glanced at me, startled. "What's going on? A teenage boy came rushing out and almost knocked me down."

I sighed. "Welcome to a dysfunctional family gathering. We discovered Sarah adopted Bobby, and he was Rebecca's son, a light-skinned slave—passing for white. Lance didn't take the news well."

"Okay, I suppose that explains the hasty exit." David took my hand. "How are you handling things?"

I shrugged, close to tears. "Lance said he was at the museum to find the quilt for his grandmother."

We walked into the living room. Dad was kneeling by his aunt.

Dad asked, "So how do you know this?"

Great-Aunt Catharine gazed downward. "I found a letter from my great-grandfather, tucked inside an old family Bible. Michael Sr. wrote a letter to his son to document that he had drawn up the adoption papers for Bobby, as well as handling the name change to Samuel James McDonald. The paperwork listed Rebecca as his birth mother, Sarah as the adoptive mother, and the father as Mr. George Phillips, the owner of the plantation." She touched an embroidered hankie to her moist eyes and took a moment to compose herself.

She continued, "My sisters told me you were searching for papers about the family in the 1860s. I got down my boxes of family papers and found the Bible a few days ago." She pointed to two boxes on her dining room table. "Please take them. Perhaps they will help you, but I hope you will reconsider showing the quilt in your exhibit and exposing our family to shame."

My parents glanced at each other.

Dad stood up. "I'll see if I can find Lance. I'm sorry you're upset, Aunt Catharine, but we can't change the past." He left the room, acknowledging David with a nod.

I whispered a few details to David. Mom took Vikki into the kitchen to make tea. Great-Aunt Catharine sat, hands in her lap.

I hesitated and then walked over. "Aunt Catharine? I'm sorry," and hugged her. She cried as I held one of her hands and noticed her firm grip.

"What have I done? Have I driven Lance away?" she asked.

I tried to figure out a graceful way to introduce David.

He came over to kneel beside her. "Hello. I'm David MacNeill, and I'm dating Gracie. You discovered some shocking information about your family. Lance overheard you talking to Gracie and jumped to the conclusion he needed to find the quilt for you. Remember, he's a teenager, and they're impulsive creatures. He'll be back." She gave in to his charm, clutching his hand.

Vikki arrived with a teapot and a stack of cups on a tray. Mom carried the second tray with milk, sugar, lemons, and a package of thin lemon cookies. Vikki poured the tea into cups, and we joined her around the dining room table. We engaged Aunt Catharine in some casual conversation, and the tension eased.

David flashed me a smile, and my heart responded. *I love this man, and he loves me.* As I sipped my tea, I tried to process all this information. Samuel grew up as the adopted son of Sarah, who married Michael. But his biological mother was Rebecca? How had we overlooked that fact? Samuel married into my family. What would Grandma Molly say when I told her about Samuel's biological mother? I worried about Lance, but I couldn't wait to sort through Great-Aunt Catharine's boxes and find that Bible. What else might we learn about Sarah, Michael, Samuel, and Rebecca?

Thirty-two

Breaking News at The Jubilee Times
Gracie

"There is nothing more frightful than ignorance in action."
~Johann Wolfgang von Goethe

Spring Break, March 18–22, 2013

The next day, I was still trying to absorb everything we had learned about Sarah, Michael, Samuel, and Maggie. Dad tried to find Lance, but he'd taken his mother's car. Vikki stayed at her mother's house to wait for him to return. We had tea and tried to calm Great-Aunt Catharine's fears.

Then we walked out to the kitchen, where mom and Vikki were talking. Lt. Carlson brought Lance in for questioning and let him go with a warning, since there was no damage. Carl decided not to press charges, but emphasized if he'd found him disturbing the exhibit, it would be a different matter.

We left Great-Aunt Catharine's house around nine p.m., and Lance still hadn't come back. Vikki planned to spend the night with her mom, so my parents ran her home for a few things. David and I stayed and chatted with Great-Aunt Catharine. I took the two boxes from her house home with me, figuring we already had our hands full with Aunt Violet's boxes at *The Jubilee Times* office.

David and I had arranged for a few hours together the following day. We enjoyed a leisurely breakfast at Aunt Shirley's then picked up Agatha and drove out to visit Kathy and Mark for a few hours.

Seeing the two cats together was always fun. They got along well if each got the same number of treats.

Kathy was doing well, getting bored with bed rest and up for some company.

We gave them an update on our progress on the red and green quilt and the hubbub created by Lance at the museum.

Mark shook his head. "What a stupid thing to do. He's a smart kid. What's going on?"

David tried to defend him. "I think he's a decent kid, just confused. He flipped out at the news that one of his ancestors was a light-skinned Black person who passed for white after being adopted by a white relative of the family."

Mark sat back in his chair and exhaled. "Well, there's that. How would anyone react? I guess it would be a bit much to expect a teenager to think like an adult."

Kathy sighed. "Your Great-Aunt Catharine can be intense, but I can't even imagine the scene you walked into, Gracie."

"I wanted to run back to the car," I confessed.

Mark and David did a pizza run, and I put together a salad. We ate in their big bedroom, at a small table with four chairs that Mark and David had moved in weeks before. Kathy wasn't supposed to do stairs.

Wednesday evening Dad stopped at *The Jubilee Times* office to get something he'd left behind when he saw the door was ajar, and its window broken. He called the police from his cell phone and waited for Lt. Carlson to arrive. They entered the office together to find Lance and two of his friends ransacking the workroom, where we'd been sorting the boxes from Aunt Violet.

The teens froze when Dad and Lt. Carlson walked in, but the floor was already covered with documents and folders from the boxes the boys had dumped out. Lance later told us he and his friends were searching for the quilt. When they saw the boxes, they got curious, and thought they'd search for information about slaves in town after the war.

Mom called to let me know.

When I arrived, Mark was working to secure the front door and cleaning up the broken glass.

I asked, "Is Dad okay?"

Mark grimaced. "This isn't good for his blood pressure. I did some sleuthing online and found Lance and his buddies posted to a white supremacist Facebook page. I printed out their posts for Lt. Carlson and sent the police the links in an email. Lance and his friends are in custody. The police took the boys to the Jubilee County Jail. High school suspended them while the investigation continues. They have a court date coming up—Uncle Joey's their lawyer. Dad, Carl, and Charlotte are putting their heads together to come up with an alternative to them sitting in jail, because I don't think the three families have money for bail," Mark explained. "If they're fortunate, the court will release them on their own recognizance."

I walked upstairs and saw my cousin Allie and Aunt Delores cleaning up the mess in the workroom. I wanted to cry. All our careful sorting was now a jumble of papers, photos, and folders dumped on the floor. The boys had discarded some papers and the trash can was overflowing. Aunt Violet would be heartbroken. I was.

Mom came out of her office to give me a hug. "I know, dear, it's a mess."

Kneeling on the floor, I began putting files and papers back on the four tables in some sense of order. After working for a few minutes, I realized more documents remained on the floor than were on the tables.

"What was he thinking?" I asked no one in particular.

Allie gazed at me. "He's young—just eighteen—and trying to find his identity. Apparently, they found he'd been posting to white supremacy chat rooms."

I shook my head. "Hasn't he heard the stories about our relatives fighting on the Union side?"

Aunt Delores came over and hugged me. "I know you're frustrated. I don't pretend to understand teenagers, and Lance is at that age where you want to slap him—and his two friends—silly." Her grin reminded me of why I loved her so much.

"Need help?" David arrived. Mark had filled him in downstairs.

About forty-five minutes later, we restored some order to the room. We searched the trash can and found four documents torn up, but Allie sat down with tape and put them back together.

"You can scan them in, Gracie," she assured me.

Then Dad walked in, his face grim.

Mom approached him. "How did things go at the police station?"

He sighed. "There's enough evidence to charge them with breaking and entering, and vandalism because the surveillance cameras across the street caught them throwing a brick at the window and breaking in. Then Lt. Carlson and I arrived to find them ransacking the workroom. Lance overheard his grandma complaining about an old red and green quilt and an envelope, and he wanted to find them. He also overheard her talking rather sternly to Gracie, and that upset him. Apparently, he, Andy and Tyler met some young men in a local white supremacist group calling themselves Proud White Boys. Of course, Lance didn't want his friends to know his ancestors were sympathizers to abolition and helped a group of free slaves come to Jubilee Junction. Or that one of his ancestors was a freed slave, a light-skinned man whose mother was Black."

Aunt Delores and Allie stared at us.

"Wow," Allie got out.

"Yes, it's on the O'Connor side." I exhaled. "Maybe we should sit down for a quick update."

David and I summed up what we'd discovered so far, with my parents' interjecting information about Dad's side of the family and Great-Aunt Catharine.

Aunt Delores told us, "I can't wait to tell your Uncle Rich. He used to think family history was boring—well, until last year, of course, with the California quilt."

Allie went for the broom and dustpan. Married to my cousin R. J., she was a wonderful addition to our family with her cheery personality.

We finished cleaning up and left just as Uncle Rich and R. J. arrived to put a board over the broken glass and install a security camera.

David followed me back to my house. We sat on the couch with his arms around me, holding me close.

"I feel guilty, like this mess is my fault. If we weren't investigating the rustic rose quilt, Lance wouldn't be in jail. I'm worried about him and his Grandma Catharine."

"This isn't your fault. Lance did something criminal and there will be consequences. Your aunt is upset, but she'll get over it, I hope. The important thing is your family history was supposed to be shared down the generations."

"Yes, thanks for the reminder. I've just never seen my aunt like this before."

Then I glanced over at the two boxes on my coffee table, wondering if Lance had seen something in those boxes at his grandma's house.

David saw me and grinned. "It's still early. Let's see what else we find."

I took a box to the coffee table, and David put his box on the dining room table. We were methodical, using pencils and spiral notebooks to document what we found. David and I worked away, removing the contents of the boxes and making a list.

Then David called me over. "Gracie, check this out!" He'd found some old photos, file folders, and underneath, a treasure.

David pointed to an object in the box and lifted it with his pencil. It was an old-fashioned purse, the colors now faded, fringed on the bottom, with a fancy braided cord for a handle and a simple clasp.

I dug in my messenger bag for some cotton gloves and picked up the bag. Setting it down, I took a series of pictures with my iPhone. I found the following in the purse:

A lovely piece of old costume jewelry, a long, beaded thing I didn't recognize.

- An antique comb.
- A dainty old handkerchief.
- A small pencil and a notepad faded with age.

I opened the notebook and saw Sarah McDonald's name written inside.

David leaned closer. "This is Sarah's purse!"

I took pictures of the purse and the notebook. Then I called Mom and asked her to stop over if it wasn't too late. She arrived a few minutes later with Aunt Delores.

I pointed to the boxes. Still wearing my cotton gloves, I gently picked up the purse.

Aunt Delores and Mom came over and stood behind me.

"What a lovely old-fashioned purse—what did they call those?" Mom asked.

"It's called a reticule, and it's worn on the wrist. It's big enough to hold a few things. Think fanny pack in the 1860s."

When Aunt Delores saw the objects that had been inside the purse, her eyebrows raised. "That's a chaplet. It is a string of thirty-three prayer beads and hangs from a nun's belt. What would Sarah be doing with a nun's prayer beads?"

I glanced at my aunt with respect. "How do you know that?"

"I know stuff. My best friend in high school was Catholic, and one of her great aunts was a nun, real old school, you know—the long black habit—and she wore a chaplet on her belt."

I knew I should let Carl, Charlotte, and Tiara know we'd found some items, so I sent them the pictures and texted,

```
Big developments.
C'mon over, if it isn't too late.
```

It was only eight p.m.

David scanned the contents of the other box. "Gracie? I see a piece of paper in the family Bible." He'd picked up my other pair of gloves and was grinning.

Opening the Bible, I carefully removed the letter. I'd brought a carton of the page protectors from Aunt Violet's house and placed the letter into the plastic page protector once I'd unfolded it. Slowly, I read it out loud.

My dear son Michael,

All is well here. We're taking care of your friends, and they're remarkable people.

As you requested, I helped Thomas file papers to change his name from Thomas Phillips to Thomas Settler, a fitting name. His loyalty to Sarah, Rebecca, and Bobby is clear, and he's also protective

of Lucy and Chloe. Thomas works hard as an apprentice and is especially gentle with horses needing new shoes.

Rebecca, Thomas, and Sarah came to the law office to do the paperwork for the adoption. They brought the young boy, and I asked him if he understood what was happening. Bobby told me his arm matched Sarah's and his mama wanted him to be safe, so Sarah was now his second mama.

We did his name change as well, and Samuel James McDonald walked out of my office with his two mamas. While they were there, I asked Rebecca if she wanted to do the paperwork for a name change, and she glanced over at Thomas. So, I believe they have other plans to change her name.

We did the paperwork for Lucy and her daughter, Chloe, to change their last names to Settler, because Thomas said he saw them as his sister and niece now. Your father filed all of the appropriate legal documents, making them all official.

Came before me in the City of Jubilee Junction the above-named Sarah E. McDonald , et al, & acknowledged the foregoing instruments of writing to be their proper act and deed for the purposes there-in mentioned, Witness my hand & seal at Jubilee Junction September 30, 1864.

Michael O'Connor (Seal)

Sarah told us the story of you and James rescuing Lucy and Chloe from the two slave catchers. We're proud of you two. She also told us why they arrived with the three women dressed as nuns. The idea came from a minister's wife on the Underground Railroad, hoping it would ensure safe passage. Sarah, Rebecca, Lucy, and Thomas took good care of your brother and Joseph on the train trip home, and we are eternally grateful to them.

Look after yourself and James.

Your father, Michael O'Connor, Sr.

I tried to absorb the information from the letter when David grabbed a plastic sheet protector, placed both the newspaper clippings from the *Jubilee Times* and the wedding announcements inside, and then handed them to me. Faded with age, they were still readable. First was Michael and Sarah O'Connor.

"Michael O'Connor, Junior, marries Sarah Elizabeth McDonald. October 5, 1865"
"Michael Junior O'Connor, son of Elizabeth and Michael O'Connor, Senior, married Sarah Elizabeth McDonald, daughter of Harriet and Sergeant John Douglas, in a candlelight ceremony performed by Rev. Samuel Saunders, Jubilee Junction Community Church on October 5, 1865."

Then, the wedding announcement for Samuel James McDonald Marries Mary Margaret O'Connor—complete with a lovely picture of a handsome young groom, Samuel, and a beautiful bride, Maggie. Mom and Aunt Delores came over and stood behind me to see it.

"June 15, 1881, Jubilee Junction, the wedding of Samuel James McDonald and Maggie O'Connor." (Headline)
"Samuel James McDonald, son of Sarah and Michael O'Connor, married Mary Margaret O'Connor, daughter of Luke and Mary O'Connor, in a candlelight ceremony performed by Rev. Samuel Saunders, Jubilee Junction Community Church on June 8, 1881."

"I found a scrap of this clipping in Aunt Violet's box, but it didn't mention the bride!" I told them.

Aunt Delores pointed at Michael O'Connor's letter. "Sarah and the other two women wore nun's habits on the train to Iowa. That explains the chaplet in Sarah's purse. I'd like to use it to say my prayers."

"Who knew your Great-Aunt Catharine's boxes would fill in so many of the missing details?" David examined the old Bible. "This is a treasure, Gracie, with many family names, birth and death dates. It belonged to Michael, Junior."

We searched the boxes, waiting for Dad to arrive. We now knew why Sarah carried a nun's chaplet in her purse. The letter affirmed many other details. We'd gotten closer to understanding what happened almost 150 years ago. What else might we learn?

Thirty-three

Charlotte's Discovery
and Great-Aunt Catharine's Rebuke
Gracie

"Discovery should come as an adventure rather than as the result of a logical process of thought."

~*Theobald Smith*

Spring Break, March 18–22, 2013

I'd gone home for lunch and was on my way out the door when Charlotte called. I'd asked Carl to send her the information we found. She surprised me.

"Gracie, I found some papers you're going to want to see. We have a folder of Sarah's letters and papers in our special collections, and it got mislaid."

"I'm on my way."

Before I could grab my keys and purse to drive to the library, however, I got another phone call. It was my grandfather's older sister, Catharine. We had never been close. I only saw her at the occasional family gathering. Now she sounded agitated.

"Gracie, this is your Great-Aunt Catharine. My baby sister, Trina, called me to confess she'd taken the envelope from the red and green quilt forty years ago and hid it away. Then she gave it to you. You cannot display the slave's quilt in your exhibit and talk about its origins. You would destroy our family's legacy."

"Great Aunt Catharine," I began—

She shouted over me.

"Take the slave's quilt out of the exhibit, or I'm talking to your father. Do you understand?"

"But——-

She interrupted me again.

"No buts. Burn the quilt and envelope or hide them away." Then she hung up.

I took a breath and called Grandma. "Grandma Molly, I got an irate earful from Great-Aunt Catharine about the quilt and the envelope Aunt Trina took. What's going on?"

Grandma Molly's voice was weary. "I'm so sorry. It started a few days ago. Trina called me to confess about taking the yellow envelope. She was crying and trying to explain. I was astonished, of course. I didn't know she had the envelope, and she didn't know someone had tucked a note inside the quilt until she talked to you. What a mess!"

Grandma continued. "Trina confessed to her big sister, too, which turned out to be a mistake. Ever since then, the two of them have been arguing and crying and calling me and Dorrie, the middle sister, and their children, and getting the whole family worked up. Your grandfather told his big sister to stop fussing. He won't be happy she's calling you now."

"I don't understand why she was going on about our family's legacy being destroyed. But it shocked me when she ordered me to take the slave's quilt out of the exhibit. I didn't think my family was racist, and now I'm sort of embarrassed," I confessed.

Grandma exhaled. "Well, I hope you and David can figure that out. She kept repeating herself about destroying the family legacy. She was almost hysterical. I couldn't get her to explain herself."

Recognizing my grandma's distress, I tried to lighten the mood and asked, "I hope the family legacy isn't having a crazy aunt in every generation?"

Grandma Molly's voice sounded exasperated. "Well, I'm wondering about it myself, Gracie. I'm so sorry."

"Grandma, I'm sorry too. But don't worry, we'll figure something out," I told her and ended the call because I needed to get to the library. Next, I called Carl to explain I'd stopped home for a quick lunch and planned to be at the museum by one.

Finally, I called David, and he promised to come to the museum after his class got out at three.

I arrived at the Jubilee Junction Public Library and walked straight to the front desk where Charlotte was sitting with a gleam in her eyes.

"How much do you appreciate me?" she asked, holding up a three-ring notebook, slightly out of reach.

"I really appreciate you," I assured her and reached for it.

Charlotte smiled. "Those are the copies—two. One for you and one for Carl. I know about his secret drawer." She reached into a drawer and brought out a second notebook.

"Thank you. I'm astonished."

"So, want to see the real thing?"

I nodded and sat down in a chair by the desk. Charlotte put on gloves and handed me a pair as well. Then she placed a series of documents encased in plastic on the desk.

I picked them up, and my heart skipped a beat. I was holding a letter from Sarah to her mother, another to her friend Abigail, and another to Michael. My heart was thumping.

When I found my voice, I asked, "And you found these in Special Collections?"

Charlotte nodded. "Yes, your ancestor Sarah left several documents for us. The first librarian, an Abigail,"—she checked her notes—"Nelson was her friend. Abigail married James Nelson."

"My James Nelson?" I asked. "I mean, Joseph's big brother?"

"The war veteran who escorted the group to Baltimore with his friend Michael O'Connor, yes."

I exhaled. "How many letters did you find?" I asked.

She checked her notes. "I found twenty-five items—letters and other documents, but I'll keep searching for more. Hearing about your Aunt Violet's boxes got me thinking. We have a storeroom in the basement with two long tables piled with boxes filled with materials from past exhibits. That's where I found these."

Thinking of my Aunt Violet's boxes, I sighed. "Thank you, Charlotte. Have you read through all of them?"

She sighed, too. "Not yet. I'm looking forward to reading them all. I made a copy for myself. We'll scan them in, of course. Then I need to finish sorting things in the storeroom."

"Good job, Charlotte. Abigail would be proud of you." I handed her the documents and peeled off the gloves. "I'll let you know if I find anything juicy." I stood up. "Now I better get to the museum. Thanks!"

As I walked to my car, I felt like I'd just mistaken David's double shot of expresso for my iced tea. I was full of adrenaline. This was our big break; I was sure of it.

At the museum, Carl met me at the door with an expectant expression. "Well?" he asked.

I grinned and handed him his notebook. "One for you and one for me. She may have more in some boxes set aside years ago. And yes, she'll scan them in and share those with us."

We walked to the workroom, where I sat down and opened my notebook, filled with several dozen documents in protective plastic sheets.

Carl chose another large table. "I'm going to spread mine out over here."

I removed the plastic sheets from the notebook, grabbed a notepad, and made an inventory. I picked them up and skimmed each one, making note of the contents.

I was so absorbed I didn't hear David come into the workroom. He sat down. "Anything good?" He gave me a quick kiss.

I grinned. "More gold." I slid a couple of documents his way.

September 23, 1864

Dear Sarah,

We are well here and praying for your travels west. The battle raged on, not far away. The Union Army beat Early's smaller force on Sept. 19th. Then, the Union officer sent his men out to seize or destroy livestock and provisions. The soldiers burned barns, mills, factories, and railroads. They wanted to deprive the Confederates of supplies, but it also caused turmoil and deprived our citizens of their food and income.

The Union army focused on the big houses, the plantations, and didn't burn down the barn on your old property. We got the animals away from Evaline and sheltered them here in your barn. The army burned the barn and fields at Evaline, but no one ransacked the big house. They moved on to the next place.

We had a brief funeral service for Emily and her baby and buried them together, as she wished. I wouldn't have gotten through the service without my new friends. Many of our neighbors have fled the area. So, the minister, several old friends, and our group accompanied Emily's body to the churchyard and buried her and the baby there.

Then we returned to your house, and I climbed into your bed and tried to sleep. I was tired from weeping. Mama Cee brought me tea and patted my back.

I had Peter and Papa Joe go over to Evaline and check on the big house. The women will go over and look at what more we might bring here, of clothing and personal possessions.

Susanna, Mama Cee, and I are busy with the garden, harvesting, and canning. Your neighbors left their house, and we saw their apple trees were full of apples, so we picked them. Stragglers from the armies will enjoy them as well.

There is no word from your father. We await news of your arrival in Iowa.

Love,
Mother

1865
Dear Sarah,

It grieves me to inform you that your father died in battle several months ago. I only now received notification. He served with honor and died a hero.

But, after living with our new friends for the past few months, I see what you were trying to tell me. I am ashamed of my previous beliefs that slavery could be justified if you were humane to people. The buying and selling of a person now seems as outlandish a notion as anything I can imagine. To think your father died to keep slavery in place makes me grieve more. I miss you, Rebecca, and Bobby. I intend to sell what

I can, deed my house to Peter and Susanna, and come to Iowa. When I have my tickets, I will write again.
Your loving Mother

The set included half a dozen more letters from her lawyer regarding the estate of George Phillips, the former master of Evaline, and Bobby's father. Sarah arranged for the estate to be transferred to Bobby, who changed his name to Samuel James McDonald when he arrived in Iowa and Sarah adopted him. The lawyer arranged for the Quakers to set up a school for freed slaves in the old plantation house.

David glanced up. "We owe Charlotte dinner. This is a treasure trove." He took another document off the pile and held it so we could both read it.

My palms seemed sweaty. We knew more about Sarah and her friends now. But who made the rustic rose quilt? Would we ever find all our answers?

Thirty-four

Day in Court
and Second Chances
Gracie

"People do make mistakes, and I think they should be punished. But they should be forgiven and given the opportunity for a second chance. We are human beings."

~David Millar

March, 2013

Judge George Nelson presided over the hearing for the charges against Lance and his friends, Tyler and Andy. David and I were at the courthouse to support Lance, who was understandably nervous.

The three teens had spent two nights in the county jail. It was a sobering experience. The jailer separated the three boys, and Tyler's cell mate was an older man who sat on his cot and muttered things under his breath. Lance and Andy shared a cell, but worried about their friend. None of them knew until the hearing that the museum and *The Jubilee Times* decided not to press charges, with two conditions.

The County Attorney, Ruth Egger, presented the deal she'd struck with the defendants' lawyers. First, Lance, Tyler, and Andy must read five books on race, including the topics of slavery, the holocaust, white supremacy, and racism. Next, they would discuss them with Charlotte and Tiara at the library and with Carl, Uncle Vern, and David at the museum.

Second, they must give up their laptops when done with homework and give parents their cell phones for three months. They could not post to any white Supremacists' social media pages, and a reformed hacker would monitor their online activity for a year.

The County Attorney and Defense Attorney presented the case to the judge. He withdrew to his chambers to deliberate.

While the judge was deliberating in his chambers, a carload of five young men pulled up outside. They walked up the courthouse steps, but deputies stopped them at the door. The gang demanded to see Lance, so three deputies and the court security guard escorted him out of the courtroom to the top step. David and I were curious, so we peeked out the door to see what was going on.

"Hey man, we're here to bust you out of jail," one of them bragged, and turned away. Their spokesperson, Billy, was a scrawny older teen whose patchy beard didn't cover his acne. He was holding a baseball bat and trying to channel a tough guy. I noticed a teen behind him holding his iPhone up to take a video of the encounter.

"Look, guys, we aren't going to jail. We have a deal if the judge agrees. Don't mess it up," Lance told him. "Billy, please go home."

"What kind of deal?"

"We have to read some books and talk to some people, and the judge will drop the charges, but we can't post to your website ever again."

"Another example of the oppression of White males." Billy glanced at the three deputies with a sneer and then turned to smile for the video, shaking the bat in a menacing way.

One of the three deputies guarding Lance was Black, and another was Hispanic. They stared at the young man taking the video, obviously puzzled.

The Black deputy, Jerome Johnson, glanced at his Hispanic partner, Tony Martinez. "So, we're the bad guys in this scenario?"

Tony shrugged. "I guess."

Another teen unfurled a small Confederate flag he's been holding, again posing for the iPhone video.

The third guard, a white deputy named Jim Nelson, turned to them. "I have been feeling oppressed by you two lately."

The courthouse guard coughed to cover his smirk, but maintained his professional stance.

Someone nearby laughed.

Then the fourth teen held up a small cross, planted it in the grass near the steps and whipped out his lighter.

Billy whirled around to see who laughed.

The young man taking the video stopped and glanced at the deputies. The teen with the lighter hesitated.

"Are they making fun of us?" Billy asked.

Lance stared back, uncomfortable. "Billy, forget about me and my friends. Nobody's oppressing us. We just want to get our lives back on track."

The fifth teen adjusted his jean jacket, exposing a handgun tucked in his waistband. He didn't look old enough to get a permit to have a gun. What was going on?

Deputy Martinez was standing closest to the teen. He grabbed the young man's arm. "Have a permit for that gun?"

He whipped out his handcuffs while the teen clung to the handgun. Just as the deputy grabbed for his wrist, the young man jerked his hand back and shot himself in the thigh and collapsed, screaming in pain.

The deputies went into action. The security guard called for an ambulance. Deputy Martinez bent down, retrieved the gun, and slipped it into an evidence bag. Deputy Johnson knelt and grabbed the young man's hoodie and tied it around the wound, pressing down to stop the bleeding. He checked the young man's vitals and assured him help was on the way.

The teen taking the video uttered a string of curses. The other three boys scrambled down the steps, bumping into each other, dropping the flag and lighter. As they retreated, the young man lying on the ground stared at them. "You're leaving me here?"

Billy glanced back. "Sorry, dude."

Deputy Nelson whipped out his notebook, recorded the plates of the car, make, and model. "Want to tell me your name, and your friends' names?" Then, he took pictures of the teens and the car with his smartphone.

The wounded teen swallowed, glanced at Lance, and hesitated before giving his name. "D. J. Jones."

Lance sighed. He recited the other young men's names, all from a nearby town.

A crowd was gathering now outside the courthouse. Hearing the shot, several bystanders came and helped, or watched, including us.

"Forget those losers, D. J." Lance told him. "Do you want to hang out with them?" Deputy Nelson escorted him down to his friend.

"Guess not. What's going to happen now?" D. J. asked. He was in pain and trying not to cry.

Deputy Martinez told him, "You're going to the hospital, and one of us will stay with you. We'll call your parents. Then we'll figure out the next step."

The ambulance arrived, they loaded D. J. into it, and Deputy Martinez rode along.

By now, a dozen people had gathered, including a young woman wearing a Jubilee County Sheriff's Office uniform. She marked off the courthouse steps with yellow crime scene tape helped by another young woman in civilian clothes. The second woman stooped to examine the courthouse steps, where a few drops of blood had fallen onto the concrete. She took a series of photos and then collected the blood. I watched her, fascinated, wanting to ask her a question. But the courthouse guard opened the double courthouse doors, so David and I followed them back inside.

Deputies Johnson and Nelson escorted Lance back inside. Deputy Johnson thanked Lance for his help in identifying the other young men.

Lance apologized, "I'm sorry, sir. They seemed cooler on Facebook. I never imagined they would show up like this, with guns and crosses, trying to shoot a video."

Deputy Nelson studied him. "It's time to hear from the judge."

Tyler and Andy were already in place. Lance sat down hurriedly.

The bailiff stood. "All rise. Jubilee County Court is now in session. The Honorable George Nelson presiding."

We stood. The judge entered the courtroom, studied the three young men, and glanced past them towards those of us standing behind them.

"Be seated."

The judge asked Lance, Tyler, and Andy to stand up and face the court.

They stood, along with their lawyers.

The judge consulted his paperwork. "Tyler Thomas, Andrew Jensen, and Lance Carter, I've considered the generous offer of *The Jubilee Times* and the Jubilee County Museum to drop all charges against you, on the condition you fulfill certain tasks. I'm going to add a provision. I need to get periodic reports of whether you are following their recommendations for reading specific books, talking to people with expertise, and doing the community service assigned to you."

He continued, "This court cannot emphasize how lucky you are to not have gotten further involved with White nationalists or White supremacists. I have personal knowledge of Lance's family tree, and your ancestors fought in the Civil War on the Union side, with great bravery, alongside some of my ancestors. Therefore, this court declares you guilty, but with a deferred sentence based on satisfactory completion of the assigned tasks. You're all young, and your future is ahead of you. I encourage you not to jeopardize it. I'm releasing you into the custody of your parents after you meet with Carl Patten, director of the Jubilee County Museum."

He turned to the clerk, nodding. "Before you leave, your lawyers have copies of the court agreement. You need to sign and date it. Good luck."

Lance turned to his lawyer, who handed him the papers and a pen. He signed and received his copy of the court's decision and stipulations. Then Lance glanced behind him and saw us and tried to smile. He mouthed, "Thank you."

He turned to Tyler and Andy. "I'm sorry."

Carl stepped up to greet the three boys.

Carl told the three boys, "I'm Carl Patten, the Museum Director. We've reserved a conference room. Let's have a chat, and then you can go home."

Deputy Johnson led us to a large conference room. Everyone sat down, the deputy standing in the back. Carl introduced Charlotte Lewis-Garcia, the Reference Librarian at Jubilee Junction Library.

Charlotte opened her messenger bag and took out a series of documents. She passed them around to the three boys. "Your judgment states you must complete a certain number of tasks and left it up to us to determine the curriculum. Here is the list of books we're going to read. You can check out the books at the library or buy them. We'll meet as a group to discuss the books."

Carl added, "You'll also attend a series of talks at the museum. We've lined up a World War Two veteran to talk about the holocaust and Hitler's master plan. We've scheduled other speakers who will talk about the reality of racism and the rise of white nationalism. The schedule is on the last page of Mrs. Lewis-Garcia's handout. Questions?"

Lance raised his hand. "Not a question, but an apology. This whole mess is my fault, and I'm sorry, so I want to take responsibility for it. My friends and I got done with our homework one night and were texting back and forth. Andy saw a Facebook video complaining about immigrants, and we responded to it. The next day, I overheard Grandma talking to Gracie about some old red and green quilt, and she was harsh." He took a breath.

"I told Tyler and Andy about it. Then, Andy introduced us to his cousin D. J., who just got involved in a new group called PWB, for Proud White Boys. They wanted to make sure white men got jobs, which sounded okay. I mentioned the Civil War quilt to Billy and told him that maybe a slave made it, and he wanted us to break into the museum and find the quilt as our entrance test. When we couldn't find it, we headed to the newspaper office to search for it because we knew the O'Connor family was involved. We were wrong to break into *The Jubilee Times* office—we sort of got caught up in this chase to find the quilt. Then, we began having second thoughts when Billy started talking about getting guns and going after Blacks and Native Americans. I guess I'm saying we're all sorry for being stupid."

Tyler and Andy both nodded.

Tyler sat up straighter. "Yes, sitting in jail gave me time to think. I'm sorry. We got sucked into a video on a Facebook page."

Andy swallowed. "And I'm sorry for getting us involved with the Proud White Boys and Billy. He's the loser. Billy wanted the video to make him look like a big man. I hope D. J. is all right."

Carl studied the boys. "Thanks, Lance, Tyler, and Andy. We're off to a good start."

Deputy Johnson, standing in the back, spoke up. "Tony sent me a text. They removed the bullet from D. J.'s thigh, and he's in recovery."

Andy exhaled, and Charlotte and I exchanged a glance. I hoped the boys were sincere. We knew from Sarah's letters that Jubilee Junction had dealt with hate and fear in its history. We didn't need more, especially from a White supremacist group operating out of Jubilee County.

Thirty-five

The Forgotten Cemetery
Gracie

"And always, I tell my children the secret about my son Samuel and his two mothers. I want them to remember the lessons Michael and I have learned. People, regardless of color, can be good, bad, cruel, or kind. It is the heart, not the skin color, that counts."

~Sarah O'Connor

March 2013

As we examined the documents we'd found one afternoon, David asked, "Where's the notebook of letters Charlotte gave you? Did we read all the letters? I remember seeing something about the cemeteries."

I grabbed my thick three-ring notebook, full of plastic sheets and documents. Flipping through the artifacts, I found the document David meant, and stared at it again. How had we overlooked it?

History of the Carlson Cemetery, 1868
I love Jubilee Junction, but it isn't a utopia, and we've faced some challenges along the way. Last year, we lost several townspeople, including an older Black woman named Fanny Baker. By this time, we had a thriving Black church with Rev. Louis Johnson as the pastor.
When the family tried to buy a plot for Fanny, they discovered they couldn't bury her in the Founders cemetery, because the man

who donated the land stipulated that they would bury only Whites. The man who owned the land had died without changing his mind. The three founding families were angry and frustrated that the matter had never come up.

Rev. Johnson contacted Michael O'Connor Sr., who checked his own plot deed and discovered a racial covenant clause. He promised Rev. Johnson he'd find a solution.

The founders—Charles Carlson, Peter Nelson, and Michael O'Connor—met with the mayor, Henry Carlson, to discuss the matter. Charles owned a small plot of ground that he'd donate to the town with the assurance that anyone, of any race, could be buried there. He estimated the plot would hold about three dozen graves.

Michael did the paperwork, and the Carlson Pioneer Cemetery came into existence and, at last, Fanny had a proper burial. The field had a line of trees providing shade for visitors. Michael and I bought our plots there because we refused to be buried in an all-white cemetery. Rebecca and Thomas bought plots close to ours, and so did Lucy and Louis, and Samuel and Maggie. My mother proclaimed her desire to be buried there, as well as James and Abigail.

We drove out there one Saturday afternoon with a bunch of wildflowers for Fanny. It was a lovely place, with the sounds of nature all around. Birds, insects, and small animals explored the field, with half a dozen trees providing shade. Rebecca and Thomas came with us, and we walked around the small area.

We put the flowers on Fanny's grave, marked by a wooden cross. Michael suggested, "Let's get Fanny a nice stone, as the first person buried here."

So, we did just that.

Fanny Baker
1800–1868

Our journey to Baltimore forever forged a bond between us. Rebecca, Lucy, Thomas, Chloe, and Bobby became my new family. When I married Michael and became an O'Connor, my two families became one.

Rebecca, Lucy, and I wore those nuns' habits on the train, and to this day, when I pray, I use my chaplet to count my blessings.

And always, I tell my children the 'secret' about my son Samuel and his two mothers. I want them to remember the lessons Michael and I have learned. People, regardless of color, can be good, bad, cruel, or kind. It's the heart, not the skin color, that counts.

One of those blessings was my friendship with Abigail, who married James Nelson, Michael's best friend. They have three girls and two boys. She became Jubilee Junction's first librarian. She and I decided Jubilee Junction's history needed to be preserved. So, we mean to collect letters and documents and place copies in the Jubilee Junction library. I hope someday my descendants will read them and better understand their town's history—their families' legacy.
Sarah McDonald O'Connor

Thirty-six

Death Threats
and the Proud White Boys
Gracie

"Not everything that is faced can be changed, but nothing can be changed until it is faced."

~James Baldwin

March 2013

I was working my way through the notebook with Sarah's letters, scribbling notes, when my cell phone rang.

Dad's voice sounded grim. "There was a burning cross in front of the newspaper office this morning, along with a letter with death threats about you. Some group calling themselves the Proud White Boys are upset because of the exhibit coming up with Rebecca's quilt. Lt. Carlson is here and wants to talk to you. Ben thinks it's the group who came to the courthouse to speak with Lance. Lance already gave us their names, and the police are searching for them. Okay, here's Lt. Carlson."

The police officer's voice was no nonsense. "Miss O'Connor, is your boyfriend with you? Please put this call on speakerphone."

I did, and David leaned forward. "I'm here."

Lt. Carlson replied, "Good, David. The note was quite nasty and explicit. Gracie, we don't want you to be alone until we take these perps into custody. David, please help her pack and get out of there. Take Gracie to your house or go with her to a hotel. I don't want her left alone, and I don't want her to stay at her house."

My father interjected, "Her mother and I spend so much time at the newspaper office, and they've already broken in here. I don't think she will be safe at our house, either, since everyone knows where we live."

David exhaled. "Message received. I'll take care of Gracie. I won't leave her alone. We'll pack up and leave for my apartment within an hour. I will send you both a text with my address. Lt. Carlson and Mr. O'Connor, I'm on it. We'll be in touch."

"Thank you, David. Gracie, stay safe and let the police sort this out." Dad sounded tired. "We love you."

After saying goodbye to my father, I examined my little house. I'd always felt safe here. I tried to process such an outlandish thing. A death threat because of Rebecca's quilt? Against me?

David nudged me. "Pack a bag. How can I help? Do you have a cat carrier for the beast?"

Agatha meowed.

"Yes, in the front coat closet." I fought tears.

I scurried around, grabbing several sets of clothes, shoes, pajamas and robe, makeup, and toiletries in an overnight bag. I packed papers to grade, my planner, a clipboard, laptop and iPad with its charger, and put them all into my messenger bag. I grabbed a six-pack of Diet Dr Pepper and put several yogurts and a bag of Dove chocolates into a bag.

David located the cat carrier and sweet-talked Agatha into it with a minimum of fussing. He grabbed a box out of the garage and put her bowls, food, and a couple of toys into it. He returned for the litter box.

I locked the door and followed David to his Toyota RAV4 within forty-five minutes of Dad's call. We loaded up and headed for David's apartment. Before starting the car, he grabbed my hand.

"I know you're freaked out, Gracie, but we're going to stick together. Think of it as an adventure. You know, like our favorite movie, *North by Northwest*, but without the train."

As we drove down the street in my very safe neighborhood, I added, "And maybe without the death threats?" I sent a brief text to Mark and Kathy, letting them know I would be at David's apartment and his address. Next, I sent a quick text to Mr. Harrison, my neighbor, to let him know I wouldn't be at home, explained why, and then asked him to be on alert.

Agatha yowled her displeasure in the back seat. She hated the cat carrier and thought the vet's office was our destination.

I sat up. "What about the museum? My exhibit?"

David turned the corner. "Let the police worry about the museum. I'm sure they've spoken to Carl, and the museum has an alarm system."

I texted Carl and Charlotte, letting them know I would be with David, and asked them to be careful.

A few minutes later, David pulled into a parking lot and then his assigned slot at the Prairie Meadows Apartments. It was a new two-story building with a view of the Jubilee River and a wooded area. I grabbed my bags while David managed the beast and her box.

We walked into David's one-bedroom apartment with an open floor plan for the kitchen, dining room, and living room. His desk, the dining room table, and two bookcases took up most of the dining room, but he had arranged everything neatly.

Agatha peered out of her carrier mewing, so David opened the latch to let her explore the place while we settled in and unpacked. He found a place for her bowls of water and food and then went back out to the car for her litter box.

I sat down on the couch, watching Agatha, still trying to process the absurdity of anyone wanting to hurt me over the rustic rose quilt. David put the litter box down and then sat beside me.

"We'll be okay. I'll change the sheets, and you can have my bed. My couch makes out into a bed." David put an arm around me.

"I can take the couch. I don't want to be a bother."

He hugged me and got up to get the sheets.

I stood up. "It's easier with two."

David and I compared our class schedules. We decided I'd go to his morning classes except one held at the same time as mine. Then he would go to one of my classes, and we'd share office hours.

Campus security patrolled the hallway outside my classroom and his office.

The museum installed motion sensing security cameras on the front and back doors, as well as in the reception area. Two nights after I left my house for David's apartment, several teens planted a burning cross in front of the museum and took video. Two others lurked by the back door of the museum as the cleaning crew's supervisor, Terence, brought out the trash. He noticed both boys wore gray hooded sweatshirts pulled up over their heads, had backpacks slung over their shoulders, and one carried a brick in his hand.

Terence yelled, "Hey!" and they spooked like a couple of deer, dropping the brick and a backpack, and running away. But he called it in, and the camera got a couple of excellent pictures. Lt. Carlson logged the pictures and decided not to worry us. They didn't seem dangerous, but the two teens were on his list, and whatever was in the backpack became evidence.

We had a terse call with Lt. Carlson the next day. The group posted their video of the two burning crosses on their social media. He described the incident with the boys outside the back of the museum. There was a crude pipe bomb in the backpack and a letter threatening future attacks. So, two boys were in jail, but we needed to be careful while they found the rest of the gang.

The sheriff assigned one of his deputies to patrol the museum when it was open, and I appreciated having him walk around the building. David picked me up after work, and someone else drove me to the museum.

Then Carl received a video in his email. It included images of the burning crosses and repeated much of the common white supremacy dogma. It referred to the red and green quilt and ordered us not to display it. A slave had made it, so it must be substandard quality, adding colorful profanity with horrific grammar and spelling. It threatened me with physical violence as well.

Carl called Lt. Carlson, who came for the note. Then, he coordinated with the Jubilee County sheriff, arranging for a drive-by of the museum and newspaper several times a day. I didn't find out about the videos or note until later, either.

When I finally did, I had the strangest notion that somewhere, someone was distributing copies of a poster with my face on it.

David and I ate dinner one night with my parents at Aunt Shirley's.

Aunt Shirley came over to say hello and check on me. "Did they catch those punks yet?"

I shook my head "no" as she brought me a fresh blueberry muffin, crusty around the edges, soft and moist to the center.

She hugged Mom and sent one of her daughters over to get our order. I glanced at my parents and then at David.

"This town isn't very good at keeping secrets, is it?" I asked, fighting tears.

Mom leaned forward. "Gracie, there's safety in numbers. If people know and they see something suspicious, they'll speak up."

Dad nodded and so did David, who reached for my hand.

They outnumbered me. I tore off a chunk and nibbled the muffin, savoring the sweet crumbly crust despite myself.

My parents and David made small talk as we ate.

Later, David and I sat at his dining room table to grade. After an hour, I got up to stretch and made some hot green tea for us.

Agatha prowled around David's apartment, hopping on a dining room chair, then jumping down, weaving under our feet, and over to the front door.

He gazed at me. "I think she misses your house. But I enjoy having you here."

I liked it here, too, because I felt safe.

Several days later, David's cell phone rang one evening at 9:30 p.m. as we worked at his dining room table, and he glanced at me when he answered it. He murmured into the phone for a few minutes and then regarded me. "They found a boy in your backyard. His buddy was a couple of blocks away. They got them, Gracie."

I glanced at him. "What is it?" I asked. "What aren't you telling me?"

He hesitated. "The boy in your backyard carried a backpack with a handgun, ropes, duct tape, and granola bars. He told the police he wanted to take you to the next meeting of his white supremacist group."

I studied David's face. "I understand what the rope and duct tape are about, and I hope the gun was unloaded and intended for waving at me. What's with the granola bars? Are they for me, the hostage, or the bad boys?" I took a big breath. "It's over?"

The tears came then, and David held me. We moved to the couch, which was already folded out for the night, and took off our shoes. He covered us up with a comforter and we lay back against the pillows, my head on his chest and I cried while he held me and murmured sweet things until we fell asleep. At some point, Agatha jumped up and snuggled down beside David, the little traitor.

Gracie's Secret Comes Out
Gracie

"Clouds and darkness surround us, yet heaven is just, and the day of triumph will surely come, when justice and truth will be vindicated. Our wrongs will be made right, and we will once more taste the blessings of freedom."

~Mary Todd Lincoln

Late March, 2013

We woke up about six-thirty when David's alarm sounded. He made coffee while I showered and dressed, and then he ran me home to get my car. Agatha yowled in her despised carrier. David slowed down as he turned the corner onto my street. "What's going on here?"

A police car was in my driveway, and a sheriff's car parked out front. As we drove up, we saw a man in a gray hoodie being escorted out of the backyard by two deputies while Lt. Carlson spoke to my next-door neighbor, Mr. Harrison.

They put the young man in the back of the sheriff's car. Then Lt. Carlson waved at us. and David rolled down his window.

"That young man is the webmaster for the Proud White Boys website and Facebook page Lance stumbled across. They split off from another group and didn't have much of a following.Cut off the head and the snake dies. You should be fine now."

"So, what did this young man have in his backpack? Girl Scout cookies and handcuffs?" I joked.

Then I saw the serious expression on Lt. Carlson's face and stopped.

"It's a nasty prank." He hesitated. "You drop Mentos in a two-liter Diet Coke bottle. It explodes and sends a geyser of pop shooting up. The young man confessed to wanting to draw you outside so he could kidnap you. He was carrying an assault rifle, an AR-15, but I'm not sure he knew how to use it. He thought it made him appear more threatening. Your neighbor saw him prowling around and called it in. We got here before he could do anything. Stay here. I'll be back."

He walked to the squad car and talked to the young deputy.

I tried to process this information. "So, it's a messy science experiment?"

David shrugged. "I've seen the videos on YouTube. If you didn't know what it was, it could be alarming."

Agatha meowed in her cat carrier, and I joked, "Why not unleash Agatha on the geek?"

David exhaled, watching things unfold as the law enforcement people talked.

The sheriff's deputies waved at us and left, taking the prisoner to be booked into the county jail.

Lt. Carlson did a walkthrough of my home and then gave us the okay. We got out of the car, grabbing my overnight bag and Agatha's carrier, and entered the house.

"We'll be in touch, Gracie. By the way, your cousin Lance has been a big help." He nodded shook David's hand. "Thanks, David."

We filled Agatha's food and water bowls and set some of her favorite cat toys out in the living room. The litter box returned to its place in the pantry. She meowed and followed us. I shut the doors to both bedrooms and the bathroom, part of my normal morning routine, and she seemed to relax.

I grabbed a Diet Dr Pepper out of the fridge, a yogurt, and a granola bar, put them in my bag, and picked up my purse. "See you tonight, Agatha."

We walked out to the garage, and David opened my car door and kissed me. "I'll follow you to college."

Once in the office, Shelly and Tiara hugged me.

"What a nightmare. I'm so glad they caught these guys," Shelly told me. "But it's so disturbing to think of people burning crosses in Jubilee Junction." Then she studied me. "Have you seen the videos yet?"

I didn't know what she was talking about. I took a big breath. Tiara clicked on YouTube, and there they were. I watched two short videos of young men filming their friends putting a crude wooden cross into the ground, dumping lighter fluid over it, and then lighting a match. The first cross was placed in front of the entrance to the pioneer cemetery, while the second one was at the edge of town by the big sign welcoming people to Jubilee Junction. As the flames ignited, they made a hand gesture and shouted, "Proud White Boys!"

I sat down, shaken, and disgusted. Tiara stopped the video and touched my shoulder. "I'm sorry. I thought you should see it for yourself before someone asks you about it."

Shelly gazed at me, thoughtful. "Think it opened some eyes, Gracie? Aren't we known as Iowa Nice? These hate groups have always been here, but they used to hide. Now, they're out in the open. And they're on social media, recruiting young white males wanting to blame others for their path in life."

I hadn't told my students about the death threats, but several of them came up to me at the end of class and asked if I was okay. While I assured them things were fine, the truth was I still felt wary. Campus security walked by my office and classrooms once or twice a day.

That afternoon, my neighbor came over to talk to me. David had just arrived. Mr. Harrison was the one who called the police about the suspicious young man lurking around my back door.

"That kid acted like he was some dangerous criminal, wearing baggy jeans, a hoodie, and a baseball cap." He declared, "If I were twenty years younger, I'd show him what we did to those punks in Vietnam. He didn't know how to carry that darn rifle, either. I called nine-one-one as soon as I saw him heading for your backyard. I sat down at the kitchen table with a cup of coffee, reporting his actions to the dispatcher. They arrived, and it was over. It disappointed me they didn't let him finish his thing with the Mentos, but it makes a big mess." He seemed wistful.

David nodded. "I've always wanted to do that," he admitted. "Have you seen it on YouTube?"

I sighed and handed him my laptop, and the two men watched in fascination as the pop bottle erupted in a geyser of foam and pop.

Other neighbors stopped over and asked how things were going and expressed concern. They knew my family, after all.

My parents gave me a big hug when I walked into *The Jubilee Times* the next day.

Dad glanced up from his laptop. "I'm writing an editorial about White supremacy taking hold of bored young white men searching the internet for excitement. From what I'm reading, these men live in Iowa's small towns and big cities alike. I've been talking to Lance. He was a big help to the police, and we're proud of him."

Mom warned, "Your Uncle Joey is going to meet with us in a couple of days to prepare for court. He's collecting witness statements, and so are the police for the county attorney."

I hadn't thought about going to court or getting up to testify against the White supremacist group. The panic began. Not only did my butterflies have a dance party, but I fought the urge to run away and hide.

Dad peered at me. "It's going to be alright, Gracie. Carl and I must testify because we got the threatening notes and videos, and so do you and David—and Lance and his three buddies. But you're the star witness because you were the target, the intended victim. What's wrong?"

As soon as Dad uttered the word "victim," I started sobbing, sank down on a chair in the reception area, and my messenger bag and purse spilled onto the floor. "I hate that word—I don't want to be a victim, and I don't want to make a statement to the police. I don't want to go to court. But at least this time, I didn't get roughed up by two drunk college boys."

Mom sat down beside me. "Gracie, what do you mean, *this time*?"

She glanced at Dad, who came over and knelt on the other side of me.

"Do you need to tell us something?" he asked.

Then, it came out—the sexual assault at college, seven years earlier, during a football game halftime. A group of Mark's friends left to get food at the concession stands. I'd wandered off with two guys I thought of as his friends, who saw a friend tailgating. We walked around and joked and laughed, but they drank several beers, and I hated beer, so I got bored.

I was ready to go back to the game, but the two boys had walked me to an isolated area by a chain-link fence. Suddenly, one boy held me by my arms to restrain me from behind, while the other boy touched me, said disgusting things, unzipped my jeans, and ripped my t-shirt and bra to fondle my breasts—and then Mark and a friend were there with campus security and rescued me. They came searching for me when we didn't come back from halftime.

Mom knelt and put her arms around me while Dad paced in frustration.

Dad stopped pacing. "Thank God Mark came looking for you."

"Yes, but I didn't want to testify in court because I didn't want to be seen as a victim—an object of pity. Also, I didn't want you and Mom to worry about me, away at college my first semester," I confessed. "But I'm sorry I kept it secret. Mark and Kathy were wonderful. They took me to the police station. I can still see Mark's friend and the campus cop backing those boys up into the fence."

"Of course, we aren't upset with you. Don't be ridiculous. You did nothing wrong. I understand why you didn't want to go to court. But you're essential to this case, and you have your whole family supporting you," Dad told me.

"I'm sorry it happened," Mom added. "I wish the police had charged them with assault, but I understand. Did you see a counselor?"

"Yes, half a dozen times."

"Did Steve know?"

"No, I didn't want him to think I was an idiot. But I told David, and he was wonderful."

Mom studied me thoughtfully. "I think you should see someone again. We need you to be strong in court. The last few weeks have been stressful and would traumatize anyone, but you're still dealing with the attack."

I got out my planner, and there was Charlene Carter's business card from Kathy, paperclipped to the inside cover.

"I'll call her tomorrow," I promised.

Dad stared at me until I dialed Charlene's office. The after-hours service took my information and promised to have her office contact me for an appointment in the morning.

I put my phone away and stared at my parents. "Thanks. I'm sorry I didn't tell you before."

Mom replied, "We should learn the lesson from your Grandma Grace—secrets create problems in families. Your father and I sensed something was troubling you, but Mark kept your secret, and so did Kathy. Now that we know about the attack, we can help you as a family. You did nothing wrong. But you've kept this secret buried for seven years, and it's bubbling up. You need to talk with a counselor."

I nodded, drained, but knew mom was right. All afternoon I'd been fighting panic after seeing the video of the burning crosses. I was angry, but I was also afraid. It was unnerving to know that someone wishes you harm. But she was right—I couldn't fall apart in court because I couldn't let these young men do this to anyone else. I needed professional help.

Thirty-eight

Digging for Gold
Gracie

"A discovery is said to be an accident meeting a prepared mind."
~Albert Szent-Gyorgyi

Late March, 2013

On Saturday, I picked up Aunt Violet. We headed for *The Jubilee Times* office where we got to work. She took Tiara's box and a short time later, I heard her say, "Gracie! Come here!"

I put the pen down from listing documents and rushed to her.

Aunt Violet smiled modestly, then handed me something—it was a small, old-fashioned diary. She had opened it to a handful of entries for September 1864. I knew I would read the whole diary and scan it in.

Lillian (Lily) Nelson, 1864

Saturday, September 24, 1864. Received a telegram from Michael and James saying Daniel and Joseph were injured in battle near Winchester, Virginia. They're coming home on the train from Boston with new friends. Beth O'Connor got the same telegram. We're worried about our boys but thankful they're coming home.

Tuesday, September 27, 1864. Beth and I met the group at the depot. Daniel appears to be healing up. Joseph used crutches and his leg was swollen. Sarah is a beautiful young lady with a handsome young son. She promised her sister Emily to take the slaves to freedom. Beth invited Sarah, her son, and Rebecca to stay with her and Daniel. I took Joseph, Thomas, Lucy, and her daughter home with us. So thankful both boys are safe now.

Wednesday, September 28, 1864. We had a big dinner at the O'Connor's home. The group told us all about their trip, and how they met in Sarah's barn. We're proud of James and Michael for taking care of their brothers and helping Sarah.

Thursday, September 29, 1864. Rebecca wrapped Daniel in her lovely red and green quilt to keep him warm on the long wagon ride and used herbs to treat his injuries. Peter wants her to work with him. Sarah is a devoted mother and a widow. She's also a schoolteacher, and we need one.

October 5, 1864. Michael and James are back with their unit. The Regiment listed them as missing after the battle at Winchester. Rebecca and Lucy started a new quilt about their journey here, and it's lovely. Daniel's wound is healing up, and Peter thinks he will regain full use of his arm. I believe God led our boys to Sarah's barn in Virginia. I love them all and see a deep friendship between the three women.

There were more entries. I beamed at Aunt Violet. "You did it again! Gold!"

I walked out to my parents' offices. "Please come back to the workroom."

Then, I called Carl and Tiara. I told them what we found and made photocopies of the fragile entries. Five minutes later, my parents walked in. "What's this?" Dad asked.

Aunt Violet reported, "My old family papers. I was digging through my box and found a diary. We're finding clues to the mystery quilt."

Mom came over. "How wonderful!" She hugged us both.

I filled them in, highlighting what we'd learned from Aunt Trina. I passed around photocopies.

Carl walked in and saw the boxes on the tables, and grinned. "I knew you'd find more." He stared at the latest find, the diary. "We should scan this whole diary in, I think." I saw then he had a messenger bag. He set it down and took out a document holder and a dozen plastic sheet protectors.

Tiara arrived a few minutes later. She saw the diary had come from her box. "I gave up too quickly."

She and I read through a few of the diary entries. "This proves it. We had free Blacks here in 1864. This must be what Grandma was talking about."

"Yes, but let's get everything pulled together, okay? I want to tell my Grandma Molly a story, not bits and pieces. So, for now, let's keep all of this to ourselves until we've tied up the loose ends."

She nodded, "Sure, Gracie. That makes sense."

I sent David a text. He'd gone to visit his family, and I debated bothering him, but I knew he'd want to know.

He sent a text back.

```
I can't leave town without you and Aunt
Violet finding more treasures? ☺
I'll see you tonight. ♥
```

Tiara glanced at me. "You're so cute when you read his texts." Then she turned to Aunt Violet. "I'm here now, so let's keep digging."

So, we reshuffled, and she took over David's box. We had gotten about a third of each box cataloged. Dad decided we needed to have a place to display our treasures, so we found a card table and placed the diary on it.

Tiara shrieked, "Come over here, Gracie!" She'd found a scrapbook full of newspaper entries from 1865. We gathered around to examine it, and Carl took the diary and scrapbook for safekeeping. He would make copies for us.

We continued to dig for another hour, finding many interesting things, but nothing specific to Michael and Sarah and the group of free Blacks in the 1860s. Tiara and I decided it was time to stop for now.

Mom came out from the business office. "I called a couple of my Carlson cousins, and they're searching for things as well. You've done a great job, girls."

Tiara and I headed over to Aunt Shirley's Cafe for lunch. It felt like a good day for a slice of lemon pie. Aunt Shirley featured a different type of pie every day of the week, so maybe any day was a good day for dessert at her restaurant.

We relaxed over our sandwiches and chatted.

"This is exciting, Gracie. I never thought history could be so much fun," Tiara told me.

I grinned. "Yes, I know. We searched for answers for so long, and now, we're getting a better idea day by day about what happened almost a hundred and fifty years ago. Now we know Rebecca made the red and green quilt and why it had a bloodstain on it, and how it ended up in poor Grandma Mary's possession. And none of it was supposed to be a secret at all."

Tiara agreed. "I've been keeping my mother updated on the whole saga, and she's thrilled. She grew up in Jubilee Junction and left after graduation. But she loved her grandma and her great-grandma and their stories."

Aunt Shirley set two slices of her famous *mile high lemon chiffon pie* on the table and sat down. "You girls are grinning over here, and I think you've had a breakthrough in your research. Am I right?"

I glanced at the pie, held slightly out of reach. We gave Aunt Shirley a quick update, and she winked and slid over slices of what Grandma Grace had always said was her favorite pie. According to Aunt Shirley, the recipe was some old family secret.

I focused on grading papers when I got home. After an hour, Agatha jumped onto the desk and put her butt on the paper I was reading. I grabbed her, and we played for a few minutes. Then I got a couple of her cat toys out and tried to interest her in them. After another hour of grading, I was ready for a break. I stood up, stretched, and walked out to the kitchen to make chamomile tea.

The doorbell rang. Agatha and I both perked up and headed to the door.

David came in and gave me a hug and kiss and then knelt and paid attention to Agatha. When he stood back up, he asked, "So, what did you find today?"

I finished making the tea as we chatted. I carried two cups to the coffee table, and we sipped tea while I told David about the diary and the newspaper clippings. As he listened, I realized he enjoyed the work we were doing, as did I.

We sat on the couch talking, with his arm around my shoulder, while Agatha complained. He glanced at me and then at her, "C'mon up, Agatha." He patted his lap, and she jumped up and settled down. *Great. Now I'm sharing my boyfriend with my cat?* Then she nuzzled him and me, and I realized she might have given me her blessing.

Thirty-nine

Building Family Trees
And Searching for Graves
Gracie

"I have a dream that my four little children will one day live in a nation where they will not be judged by the color of their skin but by the content of their character."
~Martin Luther King Jr

Early April, 2013

Charlotte, David, and I spent several hours searching for information on genealogy websites to discover the descendants of Rebecca and Thomas Settler, Michael and Sarah O'Connor, James and Abigail Nelson, Lucy and Rev. Louis Goodman, and Samuel and Margaret McDonald. We built a series of family trees using census data, then added the birth and death records from the Jubilee courthouse. We added information from the archives at the Methodist church in Jubilee Junction and Michael's family Bible. But as we worked, I questioned my memories of the old family cemetery—what we called the Founders Cemetery—despite its name on the gate, Jubilee Acres. Where were these people buried? I didn't remember seeing any of their graves in the big cemetery on a hilltop overlooking the valley.

Cornfields were across the road, some still belonging to my relatives, and a row of a dozen ancient oak trees marked its location.

I called my parents, Aunt Violet, Uncle Vern and Aunt Maggie, and Grandma Molly. Carl grabbed the keys to his van, and David,

Tiara, and Charlotte came along. My family met us at the Founders Cemetery, about two miles from the family farms.

We walked through the family cemetery, using the homemade map that Great-Grandma Ginny had copied from her mother—and which my mother had updated. We located Michael O'Connor, Senior, and his wife, Elizabeth, in a plot with a marble obelisk marked by clasped hands and a dove. Another marble obelisk marked the resting place of Peter Nelson and Lillian, his wife. Their marker featured The Rod of Asclepius and an angel. Uncle Vern and Aunt Maggie walked just a few steps away and found the obelisk and marker for Charles and Eva Carlson. The three founders were all buried here. A crew from the township cared for the cemetery with regular mowing and maintenance, and one of my aunts was a trustee.

Aunt Violet and Uncle Vern glanced at each other.

"Should we look at the old Carlson Pioneer Cemetery?" Vern asked.

"What's that?" I asked, confused.

David was kneeling, taking photos, and scribbling notes in his pocket notebook. He stared up at Vern.

"It's a tiny cemetery near here," Aunt Violet explained. "I haven't been there in years. It's next to a field, and the lane gets muddy and rutted after winter and needs smoothing out to be safe."

"I wonder if it's even passable," Vern wondered. "We might need to chop down weeds and brush at the entrance and smooth out the road. But it isn't far, so let's go see."

Aunt Maggie and Grandma Molly glanced at each other.

Grandma Molly nodded. "Oh my goodness, we haven't been to it in years either. The last time we visited the lane was a muddy mess because some cows had gotten out of the pasture."

Mom folded up her map, put it away, and we got back into our cars. We followed Vern a short distance, turning into a narrow lane. Then we saw a faded sign—Carlson Cemetery—obscured by the trees and brush on either side of the entrance. The rough entrance resembled a hundred others that farmers used to enter their fields.

We drove down a short dirt lane, jerking between the ruts and through potholes before stopping. We parked and walked the rest of the way through weeds and ruts. Dad gave Aunt Violet one arm, and David offered her an arm, while Uncle Vern helped Aunt Maggie, and I took her other arm. Everyone else held on to each other to navigate the rough terrain. Mom and Carl helped Grandma Mollie.

Just ahead, we saw an old metal fence around a tiny cemetery. Mature evergreens lined the east and west sides, with a farm field to the west and a wooded area of silver maples trees on the south. The trees blocked out much of the sun, adding to the solitude of the place. As we approached, we found an older gate with a latch.

David exhaled beside me. "How long has it been since you visited here?"

I gazed around, bewildered. "I don't even remember this place."

Uncle Vern opened the gate. "I'm ashamed to admit I can't remember the last time we were here. The field next to us belonged to my Great-Grandpa Carlson, so I guess his ancestors donated the land. A group of Carlson and Nelson cousins and uncles came to do some maintenance on the road, repair a couple of fallen tombstones, and fill in some rough spots back in the late 1940s, and again once or twice a decade. But I don't think I've been here since the late 1980s. I'd have to check with my son Paul, because I remember him coming here with some cousins to do the same thing at least twice. I thought those township folks took care of it now."

Aunt Violet spoke up. "This lane was always a muddy mess. Tractors used it to get to the field next door. Mama was determined to decorate the graves, but after she passed, we focused on the big cemetery."

Grandma Molly agreed. "We came here several times, Matthew, but you were a little boy."

Mom looked around, studying the small cemetery. "We came here several times in my childhood, but I'd forgotten it was here."

Dad walked back to the car for his camera and returned. "We need to check in with the township trustees—this place has been forgotten. They need to bring in some gravel to fill in the potholes, and maybe some drainage tile."

Charlotte glanced at me, and I asked, "I wonder where we can find a few young men to do some mowing, weeding, and such?"

Charlotte grinned.

We opened the old metal gate and entered. David saw the GAR markers for the Union Army and headed for those graves. Sure enough, we found graves of veterans of the ACW.

He got out his notebook and iPhone. The Grand Army of the Republic's emblem was a bronze-colored star with GAR, 1861–1865.

David glanced up from kneeling. "I'm wishing I'd grabbed a bucket and rags or tools to weed this morning."

The cemetery needed mowing, weeding, and the stones themselves were dirty and hard to read. A marble headstone in the back corner was leaning over. All we could see was "Fa" and moss covered up the rest.

A large granite headstone nearby read "Mother," but the last name and dates were unreadable. Several other headstones needed repair, were cracked, or tilted over, whether from vandalism or the ground settling.

We scattered among the gravestones and obelisks. I didn't stop to count, but guessed there were at least thirty graves.

My parents located what they thought was Michael and Sarah O'Connor's obelisk, near what might be the granite tombstone of Rebecca and Thomas Settler, but the only letters visible were 'T Set.' Mom dug in her purse for the package of wet wipes she always carried.

Aunt Violet, Aunt Maggie, and Uncle Vern gathered around Michael and Sarah's monument, brushing away dirt, pulling a few weeds, and trying to read the inscription, including several symbols—a dove in flight, clasped hands. A bronze marker bore his GAR symbol.

"Yes, it's Michael and Sarah," Uncle Vern reported after Maggie used a wet wipe to clean her hands.

After clearing some weeds, Grandma Molly and Carl called, "Here's Samuel and Maggie!"

Soon after, Charlotte and Carl found Lucy and her husband,

again pulling a few weeds. "Remember, Chloe married a minister and moved to Colorado," I reminded people.

David and I found James and Abigail Nelson's stones not far away—after pulling a few weeds and brushing away moss and dirt and using wet wipes for our hands.

Everyone with a smartphone took pictures of the various tombstones while Dad used his big Nikon. David made notes in his small notebook between taking pictures. Tiara and I scribbled notes in a small notebook from my purse. We discussed who to call first regarding our discovery of Sarah bringing five freed slaves to Jubilee Junction late in 1864.

Carl and Charlotte were excited to have stumbled onto something so historic. Almost all the graves had birth dates in the early 1800s, and deaths ranged from the late 1800s to the early 1900s. Several people buried here had been born in 1795. The last burial here was in 1905.

David snapped more pictures, scribbled in his notebook, and walked around the ACW veterans' graves. We'd only identified half of the people buried here. We had work to do.

Uncle Vern remarked, "I thought Michael Junior was in the big cemetery."

Aunt Violet agreed, "Yes, me too. But now we know it's his parents buried in the Founders' cemetery."

Mom asked, "So, why aren't these folks buried in the big one too?"

We all jumped to the same conclusion. Tiara's face responded, and she slumped.

I walked over to stand beside her. "Please don't tell me they discriminated against Rebecca, Thomas, Lucy, and her husband for being Black."

Carl considered the situation. "Many cemeteries allowed only white people to be buried there. As late as 1947, the Cedar Falls' Greenwood Cemetery plot deeds limited burials to those of the Caucasian race. But why would the rest of these folks be here? We see both Black and white people buried here."

Charlotte studied the cemetery. "Everyone who came to Iowa with Joseph and Daniel is here, except for Joseph, Daniel, and Chloe?"

"Yes, good point," David looked around. "I don't know what happened 150 years ago. But I see friends and family buried here. Michael and Sarah are close to Rebecca and Thomas. Samuel and Maggie are nearby, and Lucy and Louis aren't far away. Abigail and James are close, too. I don't see segregation."

Tiara and I both exhaled, relieved.

Carl spoke up. "I will contact the township trustees and find out what happened. Why did this old cemetery get so little maintenance? Then, I'd like to come back with safe cleaning materials, rubbing materials, and make an inventory of these graves. But we need to weed and cut the grass. You said you thought Lance and his friends might be available?"

Charlotte grinned. "Yes, I think we can guarantee it. What better way to learn about Jubilee County's history?"

David suggested, "I'd like to bring some of my history students here once it's cleaned up. There's a lot of history here."

Dad jotted a note. "We need to adopt this place and make it easier—and safer—to visit. Carl, I'd like to know what happened as well, so let's keep in contact."

Carl added, "We need to get permission from the cemetery owners or trustees before doing any cleaning or repair. Cleaning can damage some stones, but it doesn't seem like this place has been getting regular attention. There are several stones that need repair and they're all covered in dirt, mold, and moss."

Grandma Molly observed, "We need a bench or two outside the fence so people can sit and rest—and visit."

Aunt Maggie added, "Maybe one or two benches inside, in the shade."

Mom and Aunt Violet walked around, and Aunt Violet told her stories about our ancestors buried here. David followed, scribbling furiously.

I remarked, "I've got an idea for a series of articles, Dad."

Dad nodded, still taking pictures.

Uncle Vern reached out and touched Michael and Sarah's stone. "We have work to do."

When it was time to leave, people paired up to help our seniors.

The rest of us held onto each other, walking through the ruts. Fortunately, it was a dry day.

We got into our vehicles, waved, and backed out onto the road, driving off with ideas about restoring the small cemetery—and reclaiming part of our legacy.

Later, Charlotte and I picked up our ancestry work and compared notes. "So, Michael and Sarah are my multiple great-grandparents. In ancestry terms, she's my 3rd Great-Grandma. They had two sons and two daughters. Two children traveled west, but two stayed here. Their grandson Andrew served as the Editor of *The Jubilee Times* and married Emma Nelson. She's my great-grandmother." I glanced up from my laptop and stretched.

"What are you finding about Lucy and Chloe?" I asked Charlotte, working on her own computer.

We were sitting at her desk. The library was quiet today because school was still in session. Several women browsed the new fiction display not far away.

"We already knew that Lucy married a pastor, and they started the AME church here in Jubilee. Her daughter, Chloe Settler, attended Normal school in Jubilee Junction to become a schoolteacher." Charlotte replied. "As a Black woman, it would have been difficult to attend a university, but with the three founding families underwriting the Normal school, she had their support."

She scrolled down the screen. "Chloe decided she wanted to be a lawyer, so she read the law with Michael Junior and his father. Then, she married a young evangelical preacher, Jeremiah Carter, and they worked for universal suffrage. They had three sons and three daughters."

"Here's the part I wanted to show you—Chloe, Maggie, Sarah, Rebecca, and Lucy marched in an early suffragist parade. Sarah, Maggie, Lucy, and Rebecca and their husbands were in the gallery when the 19th Amendment passed the Iowa Legislature. Chloe and Jeremiah moved to Granby, Colorado, where they continued their ministry and advocacy. They worked with many others to pass a referendum on women's suffrage, which passed Nov. 7, 1893. They left instructions to be buried in the cemetery at their mountain top church."

I glanced at Charlotte. I'd been taking notes but put them down, still angry that the Founders Cemetery didn't allow Blacks to be buried in it.

Charlotte saw my face. "I checked the records, Gracie. They didn't outlaw racial covenants until Congress passed the Fair Housing Act of 1968—about a hundred years too late for our freed slaves coming west."

She showed me what she'd found so far for Lucy's family tree using ancestry.com. I saw a name and said, "I have to call Tiara."

"What was your great-grandma's name again?" I asked her.

"Sally Johnson. Why?"

"Can you come to the library? I'd like to show you something."

When Tiara arrived, I handed her the printout of our latest version of Lucy's family tree. She smiled before breaking down into tears. Lucy's great-granddaughter was Ruby, whose granddaughter Sally was Tiara's grandma.

Later, I sat down with David, Charlotte, Tiara, and Carl to draft my statement for Grandma Molly and the other members of the O'Connor family. "So, one of my ancestors was born a light-skinned slave who passed into white society after being adopted by Sarah." I paused. "Can I say the word *slave*, or should I use *enslaved person*?" I asked.

Tiara shrugged. "You're talking about the past, and I don't see why you can't say *freed slave* or *former slave* in your exhibit materials."

I sorted through the collection of documents from Sarah, finding one of her statements that said it all.

"Part of your legacy is that my adopted son Bobby—Rebecca's son—was born a light-skinned slave after the owner of the plantation raped her. Bobby grew up loving two mothers, one Black and one white. Rebecca and I became the best of friends, having forged a bond through our travels and the death of my beloved sister, Emily. Rebecca thought I was going to save her and her child. The truth is more complicated. Bobby, Rebecca, and Thomas

became my new family. They saved me."
I glanced around the table: we'd found our story, our legacy.

Forty

Setting up The Exhibit
and A Surprise
Gracie

"Your story is the greatest legacy that you will leave to your friends. It's the longest-lasting legacy you will leave to your heirs."

~Steve Saint

April, 2013

I knew how to organize my ACW quilt exhibit now. It will be a story of the friendship between Rebecca, Sarah, and Lucy, transcending race and social class. I would use Lucy and Rebecca's "Journey Quilt" as the focal point, and its symbolic story of the journey to freedom from Virginia to Iowa. We had twenty-six quilts. And yes, we included the rustic rose quilt, what my family had dubbed the red and green quilt.

It helped me to keep busy. The police had arrested three more men and the county attorney was building her case against the five young men now in custody.

I began seeing Charlene twice a week for counseling. Kathy had been right. Her friend Charlene was skilled at suggesting exercises for decreasing my anxiety about going to court and being triggered by the word "victim." Kathy and Mark sat in on one session as we explored the incident at Iowa State seven years ago. David sat in on another, and my parents also joined us for one session. Charlene helped me understand I'd tried to ignore the trauma from that encounter, and in doing so, created more anxiety and stress. As I worked with her, I began to heal and let go of my shame, anger, and anxiety.

I recruited my friends and family to help us organize the new quilt exhibit, along with our regular museum volunteers. We spent an afternoon rearranging the quilts into chronological order. We placed all the quilts with Lucy, RS, and Rebecca & Lucy stitched on the border before and after the magnificent quilt that told the story of coming to Iowa.

Tiara contacted students, and they volunteered to help capture audio clips with their phones or tablets. We created short audio clips describing each quilt, telling stories of the families, and focusing on the three women central to our story—Sarah, Rebecca, and Lucy. We asked my aunts and Grandma Molly to read snippets of Mrs. Nelson's diary entries, Sarah's letters, and some of the era's poetry, and we recorded them. David, Deputy Johnson, and Carl read excerpts from letters home from Michael, Daniel, Joseph, and James. Dad searched his archives and found a yellowed issue of *The Jubilee Times*, with an interview with Thomas at the end of the Civil War. We located half a dozen descendants of Rebecca, Lucy, and Thomas. We asked them to talk about the quilts, including Tiara, her pastor, and several members from her church.

Finally, we added brief video clips with some historical context with a timeline, facts about slavery, the war, and Iowa's role. I found the statistics I needed on the Iowa PBS website. "By 1865, over 76,534 Iowa men served in the Union army. In relation to its population, Iowa sent more soldiers to the conflict than any other state. Of those, 13,169 died. More Iowa soldiers died from diseases than died in combat."

I discovered a Black man by the name of Alexander Clark, who lived in Muscatine, recruited an all-Black unit that became the U. S. 60th and fought for the Union.

Jubilee Junction's train depot was one of the last stops going west when the war began. The demand for coal at Iowa's coal mines provided good wages and drew Black miners to towns like Buxton, now a ghost town. By 1890, Iowa had over ten thousand Black citizens. Blacks became an integral part of the Iowa culture and economy, even if the state's white citizens didn't always acknowledge their contributions. As the railroad expanded west, they recruited Blacks to build the tracks, work in the rail yard, and serve as porters.

The initial signage for the exhibit seemed drab. "Our Civil War Legacy: Quilts, 1860–1865." We needed a visual element.

Tiara recorded a video, an introduction to the exhibit.

"Sarah promised her sister to take three slaves to freedom— Rebecca, Bobby, and Thomas. Four Union soldiers joined them, two of them injured. Along the way, they rescued a mother and daughter, Lucy and Chloe. Their story is one of friendship, second chances, and overcoming prejudice, fear, and grief. Above all else, it's a story about keeping promises, cherishing friends, and preserving legacies. The exhibit celebrates the work of women in Jubilee Junction during and after the Civil War."

We discussed several options for incorporating an American Civil War ambiance into the exhibit. Carl and David suggested a clever idea to create visuals for the exhibit. They recruited a group of photography students and their teacher, Art Callahan. We found Civil War-era costumes from another museum, a costume shop, and the community theater wardrobe department. The college drama department got involved as well, with costumes, hair, and makeup. Several of my family members sewed dresses or did alterations for the rest of the costumes.

The poster for the exhibit would feature a picture of Sarah, Rebecca, and Lucy standing in profile. We'd use the photos on the walls, promotional materials, and presentation. Tiara and one of her students volunteered to portray Rebecca and Lucy while I took on the role of Sarah. Next, we found some Union uniforms, which required us to recruit some guys: Carl, David, Mark, and my cousins James and RJ filled the bill. We asked Jerome Johnson, the deputy assigned to the museum, to portray Thomas. The college drama teacher found a young boy to play Bobby, and a young Black girl to play Chloe.

We spent a Saturday morning taking pictures at the college by the old barn where students once cared for cows and sheep—it was now used for storage. Uncle Vern and Mark brought in an old farm wagon, hitched it up to four horses, and parked it outside. Several people donated vintage trunks, so the photographer took lots of shots of us sitting in the wagon and standing by the wagon.

Aunt Delores volunteered Uncle Rich and one of his friends to be the slave catchers, so we found costumes for them as well. We posed for the photographer with Uncle Rich holding a toy gun to my head, then both of us getting tackled by Rebecca and Lucy, which wasn't much fun for Uncle Rich or me, but the pictures had an authentic appearance.

Aunt Delores rushed over to check on me after we got tackled. "Gracie, are you okay?" she asked, helping me up.

Uncle Rich was still on the ground. "Hello? I'm down here."

Aunt Delores put her hands on her hips with a theatrical flourish. "Nobody likes nasty slave catchers. Right, kids? Stay in character, dear. Gracie needs to be presentable for the next picture." She brushed me off, moved me away from the photographer, and grinned.

The two children sat on Uncle Rich, pretending to pummel his back as Tiara and her student, Keke, berated the slave catcher, all the while trying not to laugh.

Everyone was having a good time, and the photographer assured me he was getting some wonderful photos for the display.

The old barn wasn't far away from the Founder's House. We gathered there for lunch and enjoyed pizza and pop, which the college provided.

The room was full of people—college students, faculty and staff, museum volunteers, community members, family, and friends. Shelly and a few other teachers helped set up and serve the food. We'd pulled together for the photoshoot, and I couldn't wait to see the pictures and order some oversized posters for the exhibit. We'd also post some videos on the college's YouTube channel.

After lunch, I thought we'd start cleaning up when I realized something else was going on. David's parents walked in with his sister and the children. My family joined them.

Before I could ask what was going on, David, in his Union soldier uniform, dropped to his knees, and proposed to me, handing me a small ring box.

I opened it to find a beautiful antique white gold ring, with a European-cut diamond and filigree on the band.

David gazed at me with those brown eyes, gold flecks dancing. "Gracie, will you marry me?"

"Yes, yes!" My heart pounded with joy.

David slipped the ring on my finger, and it fit.

He kissed me then, and yes, they took pictures.

Daisy and Jack ran over and hugged me, which was challenging in that big hoop skirt.

"You gonna be our Aunt Gracie now?" Jack asked, while David grinned and picked up Daisy, who hugged him and giggled.

"Yes, I am!" I replied.

Daisy clapped.

"Yea!" cheered Jack.

David set Daisy down to hug his mother, who then hugged me. "Welcome to the family!" David's father patted my shoulder, grinning.

My family walked over for hugs and handshakes. Then we introduced them to David's family. Harry started talking to Dad, while Ruth and Aunt Delores chatted away.

Mark stood nearby using an iPad to do FaceTime for Kathy and Mom.

"I want to say hi to Mom and Kathy, please?" Mark showed me Kathy sitting up in bed, with Felix lying beside her. Mom smiled as she held up her iPad, but she had a Kleenex in her hand.

Kathy beamed. "Let me see your ring and dress," so I held out my hand toward the screen. Then I twirled around.

She laughed. "Your ring and dress are gorgeous. Congratulations."

Mom's eyes danced. "We saw the whole thing! It was beautiful!"

Then David approached from behind and grabbed me around the waist. "Hi, Becky. How are you doing today, Kathy?"

She shifted position. "I wish I could be with you, but I don't think any of your dresses would fit me. Little *whosis* here is getting more active. But I feel good. Becky's babysitting, so Mark can be there. Congratulations!"

Shelly and Tiara walked up, wanting to see the ring and congratulate me. I hugged each one and twirled again for them while David chatted with Mark and Kathy.

Shelly and Tiara both greeted Kathy.

Shelly said, "I'm so happy for Gracie and David! Wish you could be here, Kathy."

Tiara agreed, "Girl, your baby bump is popping there, but you look good. Yes, Gracie and David belong together!"

Kathy asked, "Was she really as surprised as it looked?"

I answered for them. "Yes, I was blown away. But you know what? It was perfect. David turned the occasion into the most romantic proposal ever!"

Forty-one

Twins & Moving News
Gracie

"To be pregnant is to be vitally alive, thoroughly woman, and distressingly inhabited. Soul and spirit are stretched—along with body—making pregnancy a time of transition, growth, and profound beginnings."

~Anne Christian Buchanan

April, 2013

Mark and Kathy had big news a few days later, after her doctor ordered a sonogram that revealed she was carrying twins. This explained why she was so tired and getting so big. Twins ran in the family, and we were all excited, but there were practical concerns. How would they handle twins in their farmhouse?

Vern, Maggie, Violet, and Vera had a hasty phone call that included my parents. They decided that Mark and Kathy and their brood should move into Aunt Violet's house. After all, it had five bedrooms, and had sat empty for the past nine months. Mark could still manage the farm since they were only a mile apart.

Mark and Kathy's current farmhouse had a spacious kitchen and a large living/dining room, but only two bedrooms. "It's a good starter home for a new couple," Mom explained to David and me. "But it's much too small for a family with twins."

Kathy's parents welcomed the news, and her mother made plans to take early retirement and come help with the twins. Her father would also take a leave of absence, so they'd have some help with the babies.

We planned to recruit family members to collect boxes and tubs, pack up Mark and Kathy's possessions, and get them moved. Aunt Violet, Aunt Maggie, and Uncle Vern rejoiced, because a new generation was moving into the home that had long been the heart of our family gatherings.

When I visited her, Aunt Violet's eyes twinkled. "Didn't I tell you, Gracie, that my old house wouldn't be empty much longer?"

On the Saturday after the big news, I visited Kathy, taking Agatha along to visit Felix. I showed off my ring and shared our crazy idea.

"I want you, Shelly, and Tiara to stand up with me at a wedding this fall. But we think we might do it backward. We're going to take the honeymoon this summer, and then enjoy the big wedding. Carl and Shelly are going with us to the Jubilee County Courthouse, and Judge Nelson will marry us at the end of the semester. We'll have both of our parents, Uncle Rich and Aunt Delores, Aunt Violet, Aunt Maggie, and Uncle Vern, plus my grandparents and Shelly. We'll use FaceTime to include you and Mark."

Kathy regarded me with an amazed expression. "You're the planner, the checklist maker, and the procrastinator with big decisions, and you're just up and getting married? I'm amazed."

"Yes, I know. But when you find the right person, why wait? David and I are going on a road trip, retracing my 3rd Great-Grandfather Michael's route, and visiting Civil War battlefields along the way. Uncle Rich is loaning us one of his RVs as a wedding present."

"Also, we're going to help you move because David and I are moving into your farmhouse later this summer. We need a place big enough for two teachers, with all our computers and books. David's packing up now and giving his notice at the end of the month for his apartment. His lease is up. We'll squeeze into my place for a few weeks."

I stared around her bedroom, and she laughed. "Want to measure? You'll have room for your makeup and jewelry table and bench, and we have an enormous closet. They remodeled in the

1990s and combined two smaller bedrooms into this master suite. You'll need to go furniture shopping, though. We have a king-sized bed, and there's plenty of room for our dressers. You have what? A double bed? You want a nice new bed, Gracie, but people in our big families are bound to have a table or chair or couch to give you if you need it."

I grabbed my small spiral notebook out of my purse and took notes.

"One of you can use the guest room for an office," she pointed out. "The kitchen has a place in the corner where I have a small desk and bookcase for my cookbooks and a few textbooks. I've sat there to grade papers and check email on my iPad, but it isn't ideal. There's a better option, the walk-up attic room. It's good-sized up there and has two windows. Take a peek at it while you're here."

I walked out to the hallway, opened the door, and walked upstairs to find a room with a hardwood floor and finished walls. One of Vera's children had a bedroom up here years ago, because I saw a large closet in a corner, with a simple built-in desk, bookcases, and two dormer windows. I estimated it was fifteen-by-twenty at least. We'd slap a little paint on the walls, and it would make an excellent home office. I couldn't wait to show it to David and took a few pictures with my phone.

I popped back in to see Kathy. "Yes! Great space for a home office."

She sighed. "I kept thinking I could use it for a craft room or something, but between teaching, speech contests, committees, grading, the garden, and family, I never found the time. It's a cute house. You'll love it here."

Forty-two

Preparing for the Trial
Gracie

"The administration of justice is the firmest pillar of government."

~George Washington

April, 2013

Uncle Joey called us to his office in April. We sat around the large conference table, staring at each other. Carl, my parents, David and me, Terence—the supervisor of the cleaning crew who saw the two men in gray sweatshirts—and my neighbor, Mr. Harrison. Lt. Carlson was present as both a witness and police officer, and Deputy Johnson joined us, as did Lance, with his three friends.

Several assistants gave us each a folder with several documents.

Uncle Joey glanced around the room with a serious expression on his face. "First, I want to give you an idea about what to expect in the following months. I'd normally prepare you for the court case by explaining what's going to happen and collecting witness statements. However, these crimes fall under the category of hate crimes, and the defendants are members of a small white supremacist group, the Proud White Boys. The county attorney's office prosecutes local crimes. When you have a hate crime, the FBI gets called in to help local law enforcement investigate the case."

He clicked on his remote, and a list of events appeared on the screen across the room. "Let's examine a timeline of events:

Lance stumbled onto a White supremacy website through a Facebook video in late February. He and his two friends posted to the Facebook page over the next six weeks. The group's leader, Billy Flett, was part of the Proud White Boys of Iowa, but had a falling out with the leader and left. He thought he'd start his own group in Jubilee County."

Lance interrupted to apologize, but Deputy Johnson pointed out how much Lance had helped the police with details about the group, their Facebook page, and website.

Uncle Joey continued, "The local leader—Billy. Members included Jake, Tom, D. J., and Ryan. Frank was the webmaster and kept the Facebook page. Lance said he and his friends were told that they needed to break into the newspaper for their entry to the group. A gang of five young men came to break Lance out of jail, carrying baseball bats and a couple of handguns. Frank waited in the car with a loaded long gun. It was a publicity stunt, with one man using his iPhone to capture the encounter on video. They planned to post it to social media to attract the attention of the larger group and gain respect. D. J. showed a loaded handgun on the courthouse steps, shot himself by accident, and ended up at the hospital by ambulance for treatment before being taken into custody."

Now D. J. interrupted and apologized for having the gun. "Billy wanted publicity from the stunt at the courthouse. They weren't trying to free Lance and his friends. Billy wanted the state leaders of the Proud White Boys to see what he was doing, now that he had his own group."

Lt. Carlson commented that Billy himself had confessed to the stunt.

Uncle Joey continued: "Lance and his two friends and D. J. turned state's witness against the other five men (Billy, Jake, Tom, Ryan, and Frank). A search of the five young men's homes uncovered a trove of weapons, ammo, survival gear, and bomb-making materials, along with instructions about constructing bombs from the Anarchist's Cookbook. Members' laptops were full of hate sites, chatter between members of various groups, and Billy's had a list of local targets."

He looked down at his notes. "Billy was trying to impress his old friends and get their attention. They were searching for something to use, and Lance's comments about the red and green quilt and its origins provided them with what they needed. On the morning the group gathered at the Jubilee Courthouse, Billy wrote a group text. *Bring a bat, gun, or knife. We're gonna mess them up and free our three friends.* Then he assigned one of them to take a video that they could post on social media."

Uncle Joey then turned to us. "Next, my assistants will take you aside for your witness statements or depositions, which we'll submit to the county attorney to enter the official court record."

As we sat listening, the butterflies were dancing around, and I was wishing I had Sarah's prayer beads. I clutched my small clipboard and cross body bag with my phone, Kleenex, and pen, my hands feeling sweaty.

David held my other hand and whispered, "It's going to be alright, Gracie."

"Tell them what you saw—what happened," Dad told me as he and Mom left, and she nodded reassuringly.

When it was our turn to go give our statements, David nodded, and I began doing one of my breathing exercises to calm the anxiety.

He followed one legal assistant and lawyer, and I followed another.

I sat down and retrieved my clipboard with a tablet, almost filled with my testimony, because I didn't want to leave out any information.

When we were done, I felt drained. The young lawyer nodded. "Good job, Ms. O'Connor."

Several weeks passed, and we heard nothing, which was both understandable and nerve-wracking. I tried to prepare myself to get up on the stand and stare at the five young men I saw at the Courthouse.

I continued the counseling sessions with Charlene, which helped my anxiety. In the meantime, I kept busy with my classes and the exhibit. The Sheriff continued to patrol the Museum. People at the Jubilee Café speculated they might move the trial to Cedar Rapids or Dubuque.

Then, at the end of April, we got a phone call to meet at Uncle Joey's office. Ruth Egger, the Jubilee County Attorney, Lt. Carlson, and Uncle Joey greeted us. They asked us to sit around the big table.

Two FBI agents were there as well, from the Omaha, Nebraska Field Office. One stood up front while the other agent stood in back, feet apart and eyes focused.

Jubilee County Attorney Ruth Egger introduced Agent Carter, who read a simple statement. "Thank you for your cooperation. Five defendants have pleaded guilty to lower charges, and four witnesses offered to testify against the others. The case is closed."

They thanked us for our help.

I stared at Uncle Joey. "That's it? It just goes away?"

I felt shaky. David put his arm around me.

Uncle Joey shrugged, conflicted. Clearly, he knew more, but couldn't tell us.

Agent Carter thawed a fraction. "It's good news, people. It means you don't have to rearrange your lives around a trial, and we turned four young men against the others. We think we can use them to get to the larger group of white supremacists in your state."

Then, the law enforcement people shook hands. The FBI agents left with a nod. County Attorney Egger smiled and shook our hands, thanking us for our help.

Once they left, we took a collective breath. David held my hand and squeezed it several times.

Uncle Joey addressed us. "This is good, folks. We have the five Proud White Boys in custody. D. J. was a new member, and they were trying to recruit Lance and his two friends, but those four young men were helpful. Fortunately, the FBI has resolved the case."

Uncle Joey looked down to check the paperwork in front of him and then pretended to be surprised when he saw we were still there. "So, why are you all still here? Don't you have classes to attend, or teach, and a newspaper to put out? David and Gracie, I hear you're planning a wedding."

We got up, started talking, and made our way towards the door.

I hugged Uncle Joey. "Thank you, Uncle Joey. I got my life back—we all got our lives back."

David agreed, and they shook hands.

Mom hugged me and Dad shook David's hand, thanking him for taking such good care of me.

In the following weeks, Lance and his friends focused on their high school classes, hoping to graduate with decent grades. D. J. lived in a nearby town, and they kept in touch, still wary of contact from other members of the Proud White Boys.

The Jubilee Times covered the court case. The Jubilee County Sheriff released video footage of the cross burnings to the press. Several news outlets around Iowa ran them as a way of talking about racism, hate groups, and white supremacy in Iowa.

In the meantime, we began hearing stories about someone driving a Ford F-150 decorated with a Confederate flag across the hood and hate symbols littering the rest of the vehicle. Several reliable witnesses reported it to the authorities, but so far there was nothing the police or sheriff could do, since it was his first amendment right to drive around.

My neighbors stopped over to check on me when David and I returned from the meeting with Uncle Joey. Mr. Harrison had conflicted emotions about the case being closed so quickly. Since he lived next door, he'd watched the young man approach the back door and fumble with his backpack before bringing out the Mentos and a 2-liter bottle of Coke. I realized he was bored and a little lonely since his wife passed. I saw him peeking out his window, watching the parade of neighbors stopping by to check in with me.

He knocked on the door after another neighbor brought a coffee cake, which perked me up. David found my coffee maker while I grabbed my sun tea pot in the fridge.

"You okay, Gracie?" Mr. Harrison asked, checking out the coffeecake in my hands.

I invited him in and cut generous pieces for him, David, and myself. David made coffee and poured a cup for Mr. Harrison, who brightened up. We sat at my kitchen table.

I drank tea and saw how skillfully David asked questions as we sipped tea and coffee. Mr. Harrison began telling stories about going to Vietnam as an 18-year-old with a group of boys from

Jubilee Junction. His stories were harrowing, and David proved to be a good listener and interviewer. I'd known Mr. Harrison and his wife all my life, but never heard him talk as much.

An hour passed. We'd had a second piece of coffee cake, and Mr. Harrison glanced up at the clock, surprised. "I better go. Thanks for the cake and coffee."

"Thanks for coming to check on me," I told him and gave him a hug and another piece of coffeecake for later.

David stood, shook his hand, and asked if Mr. Harrison would ever come to the college and talk about his war experiences to one of his history classes.

"Oh, I don't know if I'd have much to say that isn't in your history books," Mr. Harrison remarked, despite having talked for the past hour about what he'd experienced.

David responded, "It's one thing to read about it. To these students, hearing about it makes it much more real. Your eyewitness testimony was important in Gracie's case, you know. You were also an eyewitness to what happened in Vietnam."

Mr. Harrison promised to think about it.

On Saturday, David and I drove over to Mark and Kathy's house and started planning our move. David was hanging out more at my house, still in protective boyfriend mode, and I didn't mind. He was packing things up, and I went to help him that afternoon. We made several trips with both cars and began stacking boxes in my guest room and garage.

Agatha and I were soon back in our daily routines; however, I avoided using the back door, thinking about that Diet Coke and Mentos pop bomb. Sure, it was a prank. But one done to get me out of the house to kidnap me. I didn't want to dwell on it, but I wasn't comfortable using that door when alone. I looked forward to marrying David and moving to the farmhouse.

Forty-three

Work on the Carlson Cemetery
Gracie

"We come, not to mourn our soldiers, but to praise them."
~*Francis Walker*

May, 2013

May was a busy month, with grading and finals at college. David and I talked on the phone and saw each other daily. When we both turned in grades, we celebrated with pizza at his apartment, watched a movie, and snuggled on his couch.

Carl and David recruited students and community volunteers to go out to the Carlson Cemetery. There was work to do between cleaning and repairing the gravestones, pulling weeds, and mowing grass. Workers installed two benches right inside the gates with another one outside. A county crew took care of the drainage issues, got rid of the ruts, and laid a layer of gravel. They also cleared the brush that hid the entrance. Dad got photos for the newspaper.

Lance and his three friends helped with the work and, as they learned more about his family history, took special care of the Civil War veterans' graves.

David overheard Lance point them out. "Do you see the small military marker with GAR? It's Michael O'Connor's grave. He's a distant grandfather and an Civil War Veteran. He made rank before the war ended—he was a corporal, I think. Over here is Samuel McDonald. He was a prominent lawyer. He's in my family tree, too."

A local sign company provided us with a metal sign fastened to the fence, listing some of the notable people in the cemetery and its origins. They also provided a better sign to mark the entrance of the driveway.

I told Tiara, David, and Carl that I saw a future exhibit for the museum—a series of photos of the cemetery blown up to poster size, with audio and video clips about those people, and they agreed.

I glanced at Tiara. "Maybe your students could do speeches about these people, and then we could turn them into YouTube videos?"

She beamed. "You read my mind, Gracie. This is a wonderful opportunity to learn about the history of Iowa's early settlers, Black and white alike."

We attended Lance's high school graduation with the rest of the family. He and his three friends had put in their time at the library, discussed the five books, and helped clean up and restore the old cemetery. Uncle Vern talked with them about World War Two and the holocaust. Tiara talked about racism and the Civil Rights movement; Carl discussed Iowa's contributions to the Civil War ; and David talked about the rise of Neo-Nazi movements and their use of the internet.

Charlotte met with them and talked about the racism she experienced as a mixed-race child, half Meskawkie, half White. Her mother, Chenoa, was from the local Meskawkie tribe and attended the University of Iowa on a scholarship. She met and married her white college boyfriend after graduation, so Charlotte and her sister and brother were some of the few mixed-race kids in her school. Then Charlotte married a Hispanic man she met at college, and they had two children, so she was raising mixed-race children of her own.

The four boys also visited with Lt. Carlson and the Sheriff's Department about the rise of white supremacy gangs and violence. It had all made a difference. They no longer wanted anything to do with Billie's group, or White supremacy.

Lance enrolled at Jubilee Junction Community College for the fall semester. He wanted to go to either Drake University or

Iowa State once he decided about a career. He was considering law enforcement using his computer science skills, specializing in forensics, to track down cybercriminals. Tyler and Andy still hung out with Lance, as did D. J., Andy's cousin. D. J. was healing up and thankful to be away from Billy. The three boys were all going to JJCC with Lance in the fall.

Soon enough it was time to put up the new exhibit, following the map I'd created. We had the signage printed at the newspaper's new print shop, and the photographs printed by the photography department at college. I arranged the photos between the quilts and added enlarged snippets of Sarah's letters and Mrs. Nelson's diary. Once the exhibit was up, we gathered the audio files the students had done and organized them.

The museum set the opening for the new exhibit for Monday, May 20th.

Mark and Vern brought in several horses and the wagon again, and we got permission to use the costumes for the opening. They parked it outside, and those of us in costumes posed for photos with people, with student photographers from the college helping us. The students kept track of people and their email addresses, and promised to send photos to people, and then they could order prints.

Shelly and I recruited students to help us with the computer stations, and we planned a simple reception, with Aunt Shirley providing cookies and scones, and the new coffee shop donating coffee and tea.

The museum's parking lot was full, and so was the nearby bank's parking lot on the day of the American Civil War Quilt Exhibit's opening. We got another flurry of social media buzz for the town with Facebook and Twitter. *The Jubilee Times* ran a series of articles about the quilts, and the remarkable women who created them, Black and white alike. People admired the oversized photographs of the group of travelers who arrived in Jubilee Junction in 1864. The photographer was right—he'd taken a lot of great photos of us posing with the big farm wagon.

Lucy and Rebecca's set of signed quilts fascinated visitors who wanted to know more about the Underground Railroad in Iowa.

So the Jubilee County Museum gift shop added books, and we created bookmarks, postcards, and a calendar. Students from the college helped to design those products and earned college credit, as teachers saw an opportunity to get involved.

People visited Jubilee Junction from around the county. We now had a small gift shop inside *The Jubilee Times* and print shop services at the reception desk. Tourists enjoyed the daily specials and pie and coffee at Aunt Shirley's Jubilee Cafe and the new coffee shop down the street. Both places also had a few postcards and gifts near the cash register.

We'd worked hard, and our reward was to see Lance doing so well, the Carlson cemetery restored, and the new exhibit in place.

Now, it was time to tell my family the story of the rustic rose quilt.

Forty-four

Sharing the Family Legacy
Gracie

"There is no doubt that it is around the family and the home that all the greatest virtues… are created, strengthened and maintained."

~Winston Churchill

Late May, 2013

*O*nce the exhibit was up, we planned two family meetings. First, Grandma Molly and Grandpa Patrick invited his sisters to their house. David and I asked Carl and Charlotte to join us, as well as Tiara, my parents, and Aunt Violet, since she'd found several of the treasures.

The family gathered in Grandma's large living room, munching on an assortment of cookies and drinking tea or coffee. David and I hooked up a small Epson projector to my laptop and pointed it at a white sheet that we hung on the wall.

I took a big breath, stood up, and encouraged everyone to go around the room doing introductions. Great-Aunt Catharine seemed suspicious. Grandma Molly was eager to get the story told. Great-Aunt Trina flirted with David while Great-Aunt Dorrie seemed interested in our other guests.

"Thank you all for coming today. Earlier this year, Grandma Molly gave us a task—to find out who made the red and green quilt and to unravel the mysterious note wrapped up in the quilt about rewarding the kindness of strangers. During the past five months, we've enlisted the help of several people who are here today: Carl, my boss at the museum; Charlotte, librarian; David, my fiancé and fellow researcher; Aunt Violet, who had family papers; and Tiara, my friend and colleague at the college."

I turned on my laptop.

"We made several startling discoveries." I showed a series of pictures on the screen.

"This is our 3rd great-grandfather, Michael O'Connor, who joined the Union Army—the 24th Regiment, Iowa—during the American Civil War with his brother and their two best friends."

"This is the woman he married, Sarah McDonald, and her son, Bobby, who later became known as Samuel. And these are her friends Thomas and Rebecca, freed slaves, who all came from a plantation named Evaline in Winchester, Virginia."

Great-Aunt Catharine spoke up, interrupting me. "It's disgraceful to dig into our family history. Pretty soon, the whole town will know we're related to a young Black man."

I glanced at her. "That's right. We're gathering the three families and telling them all about our legacy. But we have some surprises."

Great-Aunt Catharine protested, but her brother Patrick moved to sit beside her. "That's enough, Catharine. Let Gracie talk."

"First, my friend Tiara is a descendant of Lucy, the young woman Michael and James rescued from two slave catchers. Lucy's Journey Quilt is the star of the show in our exhibit.

"I can't tell you how wonderful it is to think of our ancestors, Lucy, Rebecca, and Sarah, being friends, and 150 years later, Tiara and I being friends."

Catharine seemed startled and stared at Tiara, who grinned at her and waved.

Grandpa Patrick spoke up. "Catharine, no more fussing. I admit I was a grump about the old red and green quilt, and I apologize. Molly, you were right to hang onto it and ask Gracie and David to investigate its origins. I'm sorry you're upset, Catharine, but our family history is priceless." He gestured for me to continue. "Give Gracie a chance to explain."

I nodded. "Thanks, Grandpa. Great-Aunt Trina took the yellow envelope with the three slaves' freedom papers forty-some years ago when one of her aunts threatened to burn it. Apparently, Grandma Mary was afraid to open the envelope because of gossip she'd overheard, so the legal envelope remained in place for several generations, pinned to an old quilt passed down from grandma to granddaughter."

Then I gestured around the room. "This has been a team effort. Great-Aunt Violet found diaries from Lilly Nelson and Sarah McDonald O'Connor. Charlotte located letters from Sarah in the library archives. Trina saved the envelope and gave it to me. Carl and David discovered the list of battles Grandfather Michael fought in and located Evaline. Great-Aunt Catharine came across the family Bible with lots of genealogy information, and a letter from Mr. O'Connor to his son. David found Sarah's purse with her prayer beads. Finally, we rediscovered the old Carlson Pioneer Cemetery, where many of these folks were buried near each other. It had been forgotten and needed work."

Great-Aunt Trina added, "I want to apologize to all of you for taking that darn envelope. I was afraid Aunt Tressie was going to destroy it."

Grandma Molly told her, "I'm not upset. Who knows? She might have taken it if you hadn't. It worked out in the end."

Great-Aunt Dorrie spoke up, "If we're worried about being related to one little boy, Catharine, this family is in big trouble. I'm not ashamed. Are you, anyone?" She surveyed the room. Her sister sighed and stared down.

Dad stepped over to his Aunt Trina and hugged her. "You helped us unravel this story, so thank you for taking good care of those old family papers."

Great-Aunt Catharine thought about it. "Well, at least you didn't find any bank robbers or embezzlers. Then we'd have a scandal."

Dad turned to Great-Aunt Catharine and hugged her.

Great-Aunt Dorrie walked over to Tiara and told her, "Welcome to the extended family!"

Tiara smiled as they shook hands and then hugged.

Grandma Molly dabbed her eyes with a Kleenex. "Gracie, you

and David, Carl, Charlotte, and Tiara have done a wonderful job. It's an amazing story. Thank you all."

I replied, "Thanks, everyone. I wanted you to hear the story before the big meeting, because I didn't want you to be shocked."

We put an invitation on the front page of *The Jubilee Times* to spread the word about the Carlson-O'Connor-Nelson reunion, to be held at the community college in the large meeting room. We needed a big place, since we'd found connections with all three families in the Carlson cemetery.

Charlotte and I knew we weren't done with the family trees, with the possibility of cousins back in Virginia. But just as a quilter puts the last stitch into a quilt block and stops to admire it, it was time to tell as much of the story as we could.

People came from surrounding towns, farms, and cities across the area. It was a midwestern style potluck, with lots of Jell-O, cold potato salad, pickled beets, and more than enough to eat and drink. Vern and Mark donated a pig which Uncle Rich and his friends roasted until it was tender. They pulled off the juicy meat and piled it on toasted sourdough buns. Bottles of BBQ sauce ranged from mild to hot. The coleslaws were creamy or made with vinegar.

After we ate, David, Carl, Charlotte, and I presented what we'd found. We told the story of the four soldiers—two Nelson and two O'Connor brothers—escorting Sarah and the freed slaves to Baltimore, and on to freedom in Iowa. We talked about the rustic rose quilt being handed down through the generations, the controversy over the yellow envelope, and Great-Aunt Trina's misguided attempt to save it from being burned. We passed out copies of the family trees. We asked the crowd to add names and send us an update at the email on the handout.

When we finished, we took a dozen questions, and then people clapped in applause and shouted out, "Thank you!"

David and I watched as relatives waved across the room, walked around, talked, hugged, compared notes, laughed, and scribbled down phone numbers and email addresses. We saw Lance and his friends in a corner talking to Lt. Carlson and Judge Nelson and a couple of other law enforcement officers.

As David, Carl, Charlotte, and I watched the crowd, we realized there were a dozen Black relatives, and another dozen Hispanic relatives. Charlotte recognized a couple of Meskwaki folks from the settlement. We turned to each other and grinned.

David shook his head. "Poor Great-Aunt Catharine was worried about the damage done to your family's legacy by one light-skinned Black boy. We may not have done away with racism and fear a hundred and fifty years later, but your extended family has made peace another way."

People surrounded Carl, asking questions about the museum, the new exhibit, and how to volunteer. They saw how much fun we had dressing up in vintage clothing, and wondered if we could repeat it for Jubilee Days, our annual celebration of the town's founding. They asked if they could help or dress up themselves. Carl grinned and took names and phone numbers in his notebook.

Charlotte stood by smiling as library patrons came up to praise her work and asked if she needed volunteers. Others wanted help to trace their own family trees and didn't realize the library had such helpful resources. She held a clipboard and pen and filled a page with names—and then another.

Extended family members gathered around us and congratulated us on our engagement. Others had visited the museum and enjoyed the exhibit and thanked us for helping them rediscover their family stories. If anyone wondered when we planned to get married, they were too well-mannered to inquire.

I smiled, feeling content, and reading their minds, because I would have married him on the spot. We stood close together, his arm around my waist, watching people reconnecting.

I hoped Sarah, Rebecca, and Lucy would be proud.

Forty-five

Wedding Planning Without a Dress
Gracie

"Whatever our souls are made of, his and mine are the same."
~Emily Bronte

June, 2013

I'd checked everything off my to-do list—the exhibit, cemetery, small family meeting, big family meeting—and now it was time to talk about getting married.

Mom and I discussed what to wear at the courthouse for our simple ceremony. David had a nice dark suit, of course. After searching my closet, I panicked. Nothing I had was suitable. She and I spent an hour tearing apart my closet back home, and then checking the closet in the guestroom. Jean dresses, old prom dresses, a couple of dated fancy dresses for parties in college.

She frowned. "We got married in the seventies. I wore a sundress, and your dad wore jeans. We didn't want the fuss of a big wedding, but I feel bad now that I don't have a dress for you to wear."

The next afternoon, Shelly and I made a hasty trip to the bridal shop downtown, where I tried on five or six dresses and rejected each one. They were too elaborate, too pricey, would take too long to alter, or just not my style.

We even visited a consignment store to see if they had any used wedding dresses. They had a couple of prom dresses, but nothing suitable.

"Shelly, I should have looked for a dress weeks ago, right after the proposal. What was I thinking?" I told her, in tears, in the dressing room.

"You were taking care of everything else on your list. Don't worry. We'll find a dress," she assured me.

Later that afternoon, I told David I couldn't marry him after all and burst into tears. He held me close. "Gracie, I'd wear jeans and a T-shirt to marry you. I'd wear swim trunks to marry you. I'd wear my pjs to marry you. Don't worry."

I told Mom I didn't want to wear a jean skirt or jumper for my courthouse wedding and all the wedding dresses at the bridal shop were not my style.

"Mom, I'm tired of shopping, and I don't know what to do!" I told her, on the verge of hysteria.

"What about that southern dress you wore for the photographs? Could you wear that dress again and have David wear his Union uniform?" Mom asked.

"The dress worked for the exhibit photos, but it wasn't comfortable, especially with the hoops. I don't want a *Gone with the Wind* wedding," I argued. "It's enough that my engagement photos are in Civil War costumes. What am I going to do? Should we postpone the wedding?"

"Let me see what I can do, okay?" she said sympathetically. Mom made a few phone calls, and within twenty-four hours, I had a dozen wedding dresses, ranging from vintage to almost new. A cousin offered to help me do any alterations.

Shelly and Tiara joined me at Mom's house, where she'd hung the wedding dresses on a rolling coat rack in the guest room—my old bedroom. Mom used her iPad to FaceTime Kathy so she could share her opinion.

Our relatives had loaned us a group of beautiful dresses, all in my size.

Shelly looked at them and said, "Gracie, there are three short dresses here. You said you wanted something short and simple for the courthouse. These could work."

Tiara nodded and grabbed those dresses for me to try on.

I gazed over at the long dresses hanging on the rack because I'd seen a couple I really liked. My butterflies calmed down. Maybe it would be okay, thanks to my mom and my extended family.

"Can I look at the other dresses when we come back from our trip?" I asked Mom.

"Sure. I'll check."

Mom brought in an old folding room divider so that I could change dresses with a measure of privacy. I tried the three shorter dresses on and twirled. Shelly and Tiara helped with the zipping and buttoning and getting the lovely gowns back on hangars.

We checked out the first dress in my old bedroom's full-length mirror—it was a simple satin shift with a lace overlay that fell below the knees. It had a dropped waist, a scoop neck, and short sleeves.

Shelly said, "It's a flapper dress!"

Tiara said, "I love it!"

I glanced at Mom. "Whose dress was this?"

Mom thought, "I'll have to ask your grandma. I should have asked her over."

She called and put it on speakerphone, "Molly, whose dress was the satin shift with lace overlay? I think it's from the 1920s."

Grandma Molly asked, "Does it fit? I'm driving over to see. Grandma Mary wore it—she's the woman who wrote the note wrapped up in the quilt."

I twirled for the camera because I liked how it felt and looked, and so did Tiara and Kathy.

Next, I tried on one from the 1940s, so cute I expected to hear the Andrews Sisters jump out of my closet and belt out the "Bugle Boy" song. It was a white satin suit with big shoulders, three buttons, a fitted waist, and a skirt that flared.

Shelly really liked it, but I felt torn. It was super cute.

"Whose dress is this one?" I wondered.

Mom thought, "Maybe Violet?"

I tried on the last one, from the 1960s, also short. It made me think of Twiggy, the super skinny fashion model my mother had admired. The hem had fringe on it. I twirled and giggled. "Who wore this one, mom?"

Mom squinted, trying to remember. "I should have invited

Delores." She dug out her cell phone and called. Aunt Delores was on her way.

While we waited, Shelly and Tiara held up the rest of the other dresses, one by one, so Kathy could see them.

Kathy agreed. "I think you're right, Gracie. A shorter dress works well for the ceremony at the courthouse. But you have some lovely gowns here for the big wedding in August."

The doorbell rang, and Mom answered it and came back with Aunt Delores and Grandma Molly.

Aunt Delores came in. "What fun!" She sat on the guest bed and examined the rolling clothing rack with interest. "Not a bad haul for twenty-four hours."

Grandma Molly's eyes sparkled, and she sat on the bed. "Let's see our choices."

I was still wearing the dress I'd dubbed the Twiggy dress. They both liked it. Then I tried on the 1920s dress.

Aunt Delores sighed. "Oh, to be young again—and be beautiful in something as simple and elegant as that dress. I like it. Can't you see the wedding guests dressed up like flappers with those cute little headbands and hats?"

Then she picked up the 1960s dress. "I should hate you, Gracie, because my dress fits you better than it ever fit me."

Mom apologized. "Yes! Now I remember. Don't be silly. You were a beautiful bride, Delores. I was trying to remember. I didn't have time to make a list of every dress and name, but I'm going to do that now." She grabbed a clipboard from the desk nearby. Yes, I'd inherited my love of clipboards from Mom.

Grandma Molly smiled and cried, which is a normal grand-mother's behavior, but startling in someone as normally composed as my grandma.

"You're beautiful, Gracie. It's a lovely dress." She fumbled for a Kleenex in her purse. "I kept Grandma Mary's dress in our cedar closet all these years, and now I know why."

Kathy chimed in. "That's my favorite, too. What did you think, ladies? Gracie, turn around."

I did a slow twirl.

Shelly agreed. "I like it the best, too."

Mom nodded.

Tiara agreed. "It's classy, and I have the perfect earrings—you can have them. They're long, dangly—I think they're called chandeliers. You're beautiful, Gracie."

Shelly chimed in, "Yes, and you need sheer hose and some cream-colored Mary Janes or simple flats. We need to find a lace headband with rhinestones on it or make one."

I gazed around. "Yes, I like your ideas. Thank you. This is my favorite." I twirled one more time, my eyes closed, enjoying the sensation of the satin against my bare legs.

"What's wrong with me? I'm getting married, but I'm also thinking of how fun it would be to do a display of wedding gowns over the generations."

Shelly nodded. "That would be fun."

I stepped out of the dress behind the privacy of the folding room divider and handed it to Shelly and slipped back into my t-shirt and denim skirt. Then I crossed the room and kissed my grandma. "Thanks, Grandma Molly. It's perfect."

Suddenly, it hit me. I could marry David—I had a dress! Irrationally, I began sobbing. I sat on the bed, trying to explain myself to Mom, Aunt Delores, and Grandma Molly, while they just patted me on my shoulder and murmured sweet things.

Shelly went to get me a glass of water. Tiara found Kleenex and said, "Gracie, it's okay, really. It's normal. Getting your dress is a big deal, and you were worried about it. Most brides suffer from pre-wedding jitters."

Twenty minutes later, I had blown my nose, downed a glass of water, and felt better. I washed my hands, grabbed my purse, and found my clipboard. I thought out loud, "So I have my ring and my dress. Cousin Alice is putting together a simple bridal bouquet, and Aunt Shirley is making a small cake." I glanced around.

"We're all set for the courthouse. What else could we need for August?" I joked.

Apparently, wedding planning was serious stuff, because the facial expressions of my family and friends ranged from astonishment to laughter. Then Kathy, Shelly, and Tiara laughed, while Grandma Molly tried to be more dignified.

Aunt Delores snorted and watched Mom. "Wait for it," she warned me.

"Gracie, we have to find a venue, firm up your wedding party, gather guest lists, do invitations, arrange bridal showers, sign up for gift registries, hire a photographer, and get flowers and decorations." My normally unflappable mother stopped and took a breath while her face reflected her agitation.

Kathy jumped in. "It's okay, Becky. Gracie's kidding, right? She knows we need to plan for the big wedding in the fall. For now, pick a date, find an officiant and a place like your church for the service, and a venue for the reception."

Everyone else agreed, nodding.

"Oh, sure. I was joking." I grabbed my clipboard and scribbled all those items down to talk to David about later.

Tiara mused, "When I got married, you bought a copy of *Bride's Magazine*, and it had all these checklists. But a friend got married two years ago and used a wedding planning website."

Aunt Delores nodded. "Allie and R. J. used one of those. Good idea."

Kathy told me, "I'll send you a text with some links." Soon, my phone pinged with a text message.

My eyes widened as I opened the link to the Knot website, and I stared at the list of details. I thought curriculum planning was intricate, but this was daunting. My face must have revealed my panic.

Shelly pointed out we had four months at least, and everyone would pitch in and help, as was my family's style. "Gracie, just think of how your family moved your Aunt Violet. You folks work together, and you have friends. It's going to be okay."

Tiara hugged me. "You got this, girl, and David will help, too."

Mom thought out loud. "I still have the Excel spreadsheet with the guest list from Kathy and Mark's wedding. It will give us a start. Ask David to give me his mother's email and phone number, and we will get the groom's guest list. Once you know the date, I can talk to the pastor. He'll do a few sessions of counseling. We'll check around at venues for the reception. The girls and I'll come up with a list, okay?"

Grandma Molly was excited. "I can help."

Aunt Delores agreed. "Count me in, too."

The next day, David and I sat down with our wedding planners—our moms, Grandma, Shelly, Tiara, and Kathy on the iPad—at Mom's house. Delores held down the fort at *The Jubilee Times* office but sent several texts with advice. David's mother, Ruth, drove over and brought a list of the addresses of relatives and friends to invite. Mom printed the checklists, we split up the phone calls, and we made progress. We booked our church for the wedding in late August and talked to our pastor to set up half a dozen premarital counseling sessions.

Our mothers worked on combining the guest list.

We set up a gift registry at a local store and online.

I announced, "I'd like Shelly as my matron of honor, and Kathy and Tiara as my bridesmaids. I'd love Jack and Daisy to be the ring bearer and flower girl."

David added, "I'll ask my younger brother Alex, your brother Mark, and Cornell, an old friend from Chicago, to stand up with me."

We picked a photographer, a baker, and a florist, including two cousins. We would visit all of them in person later.

I took David's mother up to Mom's guest room and tried on the 1920s wedding dress for her. Ruth got teary, hugged me, and told me she loved it.

By the day's end, I'd filled up several To-Do sheets and taken six pages of notes. I hoped our late August wedding date would give us the time to paint the attic room, find furniture, get moved into the farmhouse, and settle in for the new semester.

David held me close before he left my house that night. "We have a busy summer ahead, Gracie. I can't wait to marry you twice."

Forty-six

The Wedding
Gracie & David

"The family—that dear octopus from whose tentacles we never quite escape, nor, in our inmost hearts, ever quite wish to."
~Dodie Smith

Wedding Day, 2013

Tiara and Shelly helped me get ready at my mother's house. I felt sleek and pretty in Grandma Mary's wedding dress, with cute cream-colored Mary Jane shoes, those long dangling earrings from Tiara, and a lace headband that Shelly made to control my curls. It was worth it all to see David's face when I walked in.

"You're beautiful, Gracie!"

We walked into the courthouse with our parents, aunts, uncles, grandparents, and a few friends. A cousin took the photos, while another made my bouquet. Shelly wore a turquoise sundress under a cute jacket. Carl cleaned up nicely in a navy suit with narrow lapels.

Judge Nelson scanned his crowded courtroom and smiled. "I haven't seen a friendly crowd like this for some time. Let's begin."

It was a heartfelt ceremony. When the Judge said, "You may kiss your bride," and we kissed, I knew my life was going to change.

David whispered, "I love you, Gracie! We're going to have a lot of adventures together."

"I love you, David. I can't wait!"

My grandparents hosted the reception at their house. Aunt

Shirley's café provided small sandwiches, salads, and sides. The cake was beautiful and quite delicious with a chocolate layer and a vanilla layer. We cut the cake, fed each a few forkfuls of a slice, and posed for photos.

Daisy and Jack clamored for cake, too. David glanced at me with a mischievous grin. I giggled as he cut small pieces and put a couple in my hand. Daisy and Jack nibbled at the pieces of cake from our hands. Everyone else laughed, too.

Then Aunt Delores bustled over. "Go wash your hands, you two. We want to see you smooch. You can't make noise with plastic cups!"

We obeyed and David smooched me on cue for cameras half a dozen times. Then, we stood watching as people ate, and he nuzzled my neck, sending a frisson of pleasure down my body.

"How long do we need to stay?" he whispered, and I sighed.

We walked around and chatted with everyone and thanked them for coming.

Aunt Violet, Aunt Maggie, and Uncle Vern smiled as they hugged us. They'd been visiting with David's father. R. J. and Allie chatted with David's sister Joanna and brother-in-law Jared as they watched Jack and Daisy play.

I whispered to David, "See? Our families are getting along."

A few minutes later, our mothers came over to us, hugged us, and Mom told us, "You've been social. Now go home and start the honeymoon! We'll help you pack up the RV around eleven in the morning, okay? We'll meet you at the airport."

Aunt Delores handed us a small cooler with cake, leftover sandwiches, and sides for later, with some leftovers and cake for Mark and Kathy.

Grandma Molly stood at the door and gave us a hug. "You're so beautiful, Gracie!" She dabbed her eyes while Grandpa Patrick shook David's hand.

"Allergies acting up, Molly?" My grandparents smiled tenderly at each other, and he put his arm around her. I got teary-eyed, too, remembering the tension between them earlier in the year.

We got into David's car, glanced at each other, and kissed. We stopped by the house to refrigerate our leftovers. David picked up

Agatha, put her into the cat carrier, and grabbed the box of her cat toys, dishes, and food we'd packed. He returned to get the litter box and bag of litter.

I didn't change clothes because I wanted Kathy to see grandma's wedding dress in person. Agatha meowed like she knew something was going on. I told her, "Fun with Felix" over and over, and she settled down.

I admired my ring, my dress, and most of all, my handsome groom. As we drove, I stared at his profile and sighed. "We're married," I told him.

David grinned. "Yes, we are, and tomorrow we're setting out on our RV honeymoon."

"Are you more excited about marrying me or driving that RV?" I demanded, half amused.

"I'll answer that question when we get home," he told me. "But, yes, I'm looking forward to our road trip honeymoon."

Once we arrived at Mark and Kathy's house and were inside, he released the beast, who found Felix.

Mark and Kathy welcomed the leftover food and cake.

Then I twirled for them, and Kathy admired the dress.

"It's lovely," she declared. "You're beautiful, Gracie."

The longer I wore Grandma Mary's lovely dress, the more I wanted to know about her. She'd been just another ancient grandmother in the photo album when I was growing up. Wearing her dress made me curious about her as a young woman, and now I had questions about her. I was thankful that Grandma Molly had taken such good care of Mary's dress, had it dry cleaned, and stored it in her cedar closet.

Kathy and I chatted about the RV and our upcoming trip. The men walked back into the room.

I remembered the family tree Charlotte and I had worked on so diligently.

"Mark and I are the seventh generation of our family in Jubilee Junction."

"Your twins will be the eighth," I reminded them, thinking *someday we'll trace David's family tree as well.*

Then we drove home. I went into the bedroom, realizing *it's our bedroom now!* I took off Grandma Mary's dress with David's help, hung it up carefully in its protective bag, and put on a sexy new nightie and matching robe. David undressed and put on a short robe.

We toasted with glasses of sparkling grape juice to a vacation from quilts and crazy aunts. Then we kissed each other passionately on the couch until David whispered, "Should we pick this up in the bedroom?"

All the waiting was worth it.

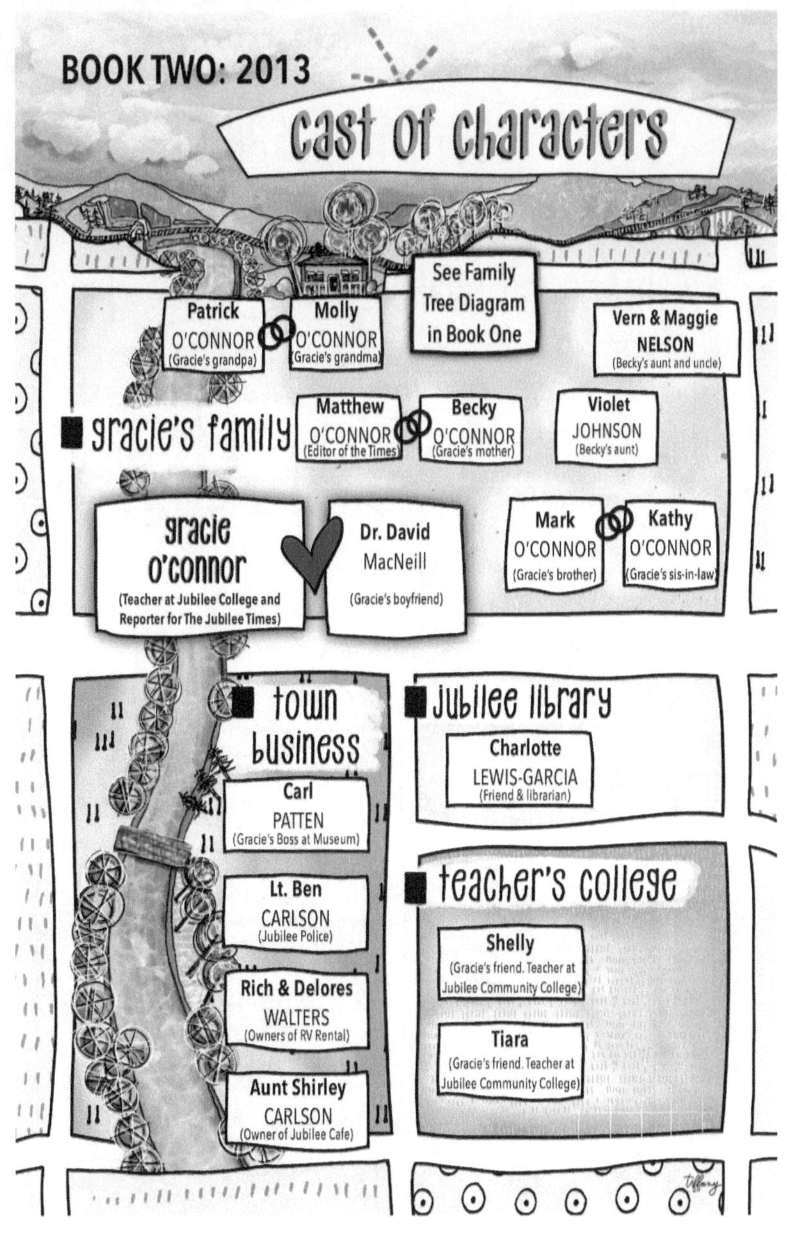
BOOK TWO: 2013
cast of characters
Patrick O'CONNOR (Gracie's grandpa)
Molly O'CONNOR (Gracie's grandma)
See Family Tree Diagram in Book One
Vern & Maggie NELSON (Becky's aunt and uncle)
gracie's family
Matthew O'CONNOR (Editor of the Times)
Becky O'CONNOR (Gracie's mother)
Violet JOHNSON (Becky's aunt)
gracie o'connor (Teacher at Jubilee College and Reporter for The Jubilee Times)
Dr. David MacNeill (Gracie's boyfriend)
Mark O'CONNOR (Gracie's brother)
Kathy O'CONNOR (Gracie's sis-in-law)
town business
Jubilee library
Charlotte LEWIS-GARCIA (Friend & librarian)
Carl PATTEN (Gracie's Boss at Museum)
Lt. Ben CARLSON (Jubilee Police)
teacher's college
Rich & Delores WALTERS (Owners of RV Rental)
Shelly (Gracie's friend. Teacher at Jubilee Community College)
Tiara (Gracie's friend. Teacher at Jubilee Community College)
Aunt Shirley CARLSON (Owner of Jubilee Cafe)

BOOK TWO: 1864

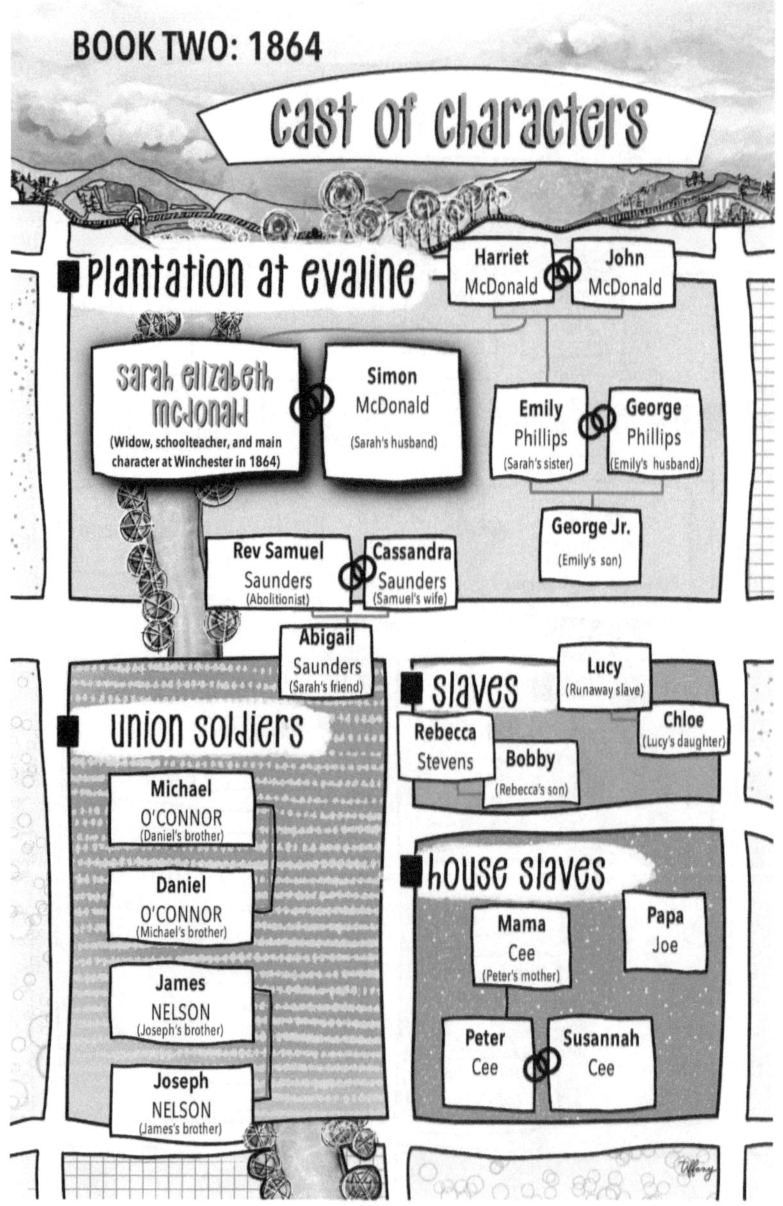

Acknowledgements

No one writes a novel without some encouragement and feedback along the way!

Our friends Steve and Hope Wells visited us maybe fifteen years ago, and she and I dug out my family's quilts one afternoon. We laid them out on my dining room table and took pictures. Hope helped me label them with their pattern, and when we came to the red and green quilt, she got excited. She encouraged me to take it to the Grout Museum in Waterloo and get its date verified. I did just that, and yes, it was an American Civil War-era quilt.

Fifteen years later, Hope agreed to create a dozen quilted hot mitts for me to give away at my book gigs. Thanks, Hope!

Special thanks to my friend and mentor Barbara Lounsberry for reading and critiquing an early draft and encouraging me to think a little bigger and bolder! Barbara and I have worked together for twenty years to promote Iowa author Ruth Suckow, celebrated by *Smart Set* editor H. L. Mencken as "unquestionably the most remarkable woman . . . writing stories in the republic." So, I enjoyed creating a young literature teacher whose grandmother met Suckow, bought all her books, and grew up reading her short stories and novels.

Many thanks to Beth Lyman, my lifelong best friend and beta reader for the entire series. She read many drafts and gave me feedback. Her encouragement kept me going. She believed I would get my stories published—and maybe the Hallmark Channel would make them into movies. Thanks, Beth. She dreamed I made it to the *Today Show* to talk about my series, and she helped tote my books around!

Thanks also to other mentors from the Cedar Falls Christian Writers Conference like Shelly Beach, who gave me feedback and helped me polish the draft. She's the founder of the workshop and has helped dozens of writers publish their books. Thanks also go to Lee Carver, who edited an earlier draft and gave me feedback.

Special thanks to my other writing mentor, Gail Kittleson, who continues to inspire me and give me a push when I'm stuck! We share a love of Iowa history, writing historical fiction about strong women, and sharing our faith in our stories. It was Gail who read a draft of my first novel, gave me some invaluable advice, and said, "Oh, my publisher would like this novel!" Turns out, he did.

Thank you to Mike Parker, Wordcrafts Press, for his master class on writing and publishing a novel over the past two years. Thanks for all your timely counsel on the process, feedback, and the incredible job of formatting my book.

Thank you to Mike Dargan for his expertise with the ACW battlefields, artifacts, weapons, and farm machinery. He tolerates me getting caught up in my novel, keeps me laughing through the bumps in the road in life, and fixes a mean bowl of oatmeal or scrambled eggs when we don't want to cook.

This series would not have been possible without the careful work of my mother, Charlotte, who documented our family's genealogy and history and preserved the quilts handed down to her. There's a lot of my mother in Grandma Grace. When Charlotte died almost twenty-five years ago, her little sister, my Aunt Jeanne, became my second mama and cheerleader. I based a character on Aunt Jeanne's personality, faith, and kindness—Gracie's Great-Aunt Violet. Aunt Jeanne was pleased to hear that Aunt Violet was still contributing to the storyline in Book Two, and I assured her that Aunt Violet was a vital presence through Book Five. I put a copy of the first book, *The Gift*, in Aunt Jeanne's hands a week before she passed away at 98, and she lives on in Aunt Violet. I miss her phone calls. "How are my kids?"

~Cherie Dargan

and now a Sneak Peek at:

The Promise

"The Middle West is open to the eye. There is no pretense about it."
~Iowa writer Ruth Suckow

$\mathcal{S}$aturday morning, I woke up to David kissing my neck and cheek, his arms wrapped around me. "Good morning, Gracie, or should I say Mrs. MacNeill?"

Savoring his embrace, I countered, "I better be Mrs. MacNeill if you're in my bed."

Eventually we got up, dressed, had some coffee and tea, toast and yogurt, and finished packing up. David shut the front door and waved goodbye to Mr. Harrison, our neighbor next door. Then we drove to the Jubilee Junction airport, where Uncle Rich kept six RVs for his rental business.

Our parents were already there, along with Shelly and Tiara, who were hanging around the back of the RV, giggling like teenagers. We started unloading our car with help from both mothers and Aunt Delores, so soon we had half a dozen people inside the RV finding places to stow our things. Our fathers were around the side with Uncle Rich, looking at the features of the RV and talking about gas versus diesel. They'd already found a place for the small folding table and chairs.

I ran back to David's car for my messenger bag with my iPad, chargers, and notebook. David had his laptop in his bag, already safely placed in the bedroom. I put them on the bench of the dinette and did a quick inventory.

David's car was empty. I hoped we had everything we needed.

Outside, Uncle Rich and David were chatting about something, and David came up to the door and gestured, so I stepped outside.

"Gracie, what do you think about taking two bikes along? Your Uncle Rich has a couple right here," David asked, pointing to two bikes by the RV.

"Sure. It gives us another option to explore the campgrounds and battlefields." I looked around, "Thank you!"

Rich and my dad strapped them onto the rear of the vehicle, where a bike rack was attached to the bumper. Dad handed me two helmets and two small bags that fit on the bike racks. David stowed them away in an outside storage bin.

"Consider them a little wedding gift, and thank your mom, Aunt Delores, and Ruth, David's mother. They came up with the idea."

"Thanks!" I gave them all a hug.

I noticed Tiara and Shelly adjusting something and stepped closer.

"Your uncle wouldn't let us use balloons, glitter, or shaving cream," Shelly explained, and Tiara shrugged. "No tin cans, either!"

They'd printed out "Just Married!" in giant letters, added streamers to the rungs of the ladder, and fastened the poster board to the rear of the RV.

I hugged Tiara and Shelly. "It's perfect. Thanks for not saying *honk for honeymooners.*"

Tiara grinned. "We thought of it! Have fun, Gracie!"

Shelly smiled. "We want to hear all about it!"

We promised to keep them informed of our progress and left copies of our itinerary with Uncle Rich and both parents. We'd be back in three weeks. I hugged Uncle Rich and David shook his hand again, thanking him for the loan of the RV.

A car drove up, and Uncle Joey got out with my grandparents. Grandma Molly said, "I told Patrick we had to hug you one more time before you left on your honeymoon. Joey had just stopped by and offered to drive us."

Uncle Joey shrugged. "I can assure you I didn't speed." He grinned at his mother.

She hugged us both, and Grandpa put an envelope into David's hands. "Something for the road trip."

Grandpa said, "How about a prayer for safe travels?" He held out his hands, and everybody held hands while he led us in prayer.

"Father God, watch over Gracie and David. Protect them from all danger. May they have wonderful weather and roads, make wonderful memories, and grow closer together. We ask these things in Jesus' name. Amen." There was a respectful moment of silence.

Then people were talking, laughing, and hugging us.

Aunt Delores grinned. "Go on, you two. Get this honeymoon on the road."

Uncle Rich gave David a couple of last-minute reminders, but I was hugging my parents. We got in, buckled up and everyone waved and yelled goodbye. David honked as we pulled away. He glanced at me and smiled. "We're off!"

I waved until they were out of sight.

"Wow. That was an amazing send off, wasn't it?" I asked.

He nodded. "Yes, it was. I like the way our families are getting along so far. Don't you?"

"Yes, our moms bonded over the wedding dresses. I think our dads bonded over the RV! It's fun being up so high. This big window is amazing. You can see so much more. I feel like a trucker, don't you?"

David laughed. "Not really, but I'm going to have fun driving this RV. I used to think only retired people drove these things, but RVs are cool now."

He'd enjoyed the practice drive and looked forward to driving the RV across the country. We'd planned the trip together and mapped out each day, choosing some of the historic sites on my grandfather's journey during the Civil War when he was a soldier fighting in the Union Army. Then we'd added some stops for us, so I knew we were going to do a lot of driving. However, Uncle Rich sat upfront with David on our practice drive. So, this was my first experience looking out the enormous front window and enjoying the comfortable ride.

My chair swiveled to the rear, as did the driver's seat. A small round table was between us, perfect for morning coffee when stationary. Now, I was using it to glance at our day-by-day agenda, with printouts marked up in David's precise handwriting and organized in a large three-ring binder. David had tucked a couple of Civil War battlefield guides and instructions on the RV in the notebook. Then he printed off our reservations and organized them in a series of pockets for each day.

We chatted, listened to music and news, and the miles flew by. Two hours later, we pulled over to a big rest stop so David could get up, walk around, and stretch his legs. I pulled out a few sandwiches and sides provided by our mothers, and we ate a quick lunch. Then we checked our route and got ready to get going again.

We saw the sign for Illinois, looked at each other, and smiled, because our real journey had begun. Eventually, we'd take the highway south to St. Louis. We meant to trace the route taken by my 3rd Great-Grandfather Michael's 24th regiment, starting in Helena, Arkansas.

We crossed into Missouri. A few hours later, we reached our first stop overnight, at a campground outside St. Louis. After checking in at the office, we found our spot. We reviewed Uncle Rich's checklist to get hooked up to the park's utilities. First, we connected the water and electricity. Next, while my hubby connected the gray/black water outlet, I went inside the RV and connected to the Wi-Fi using our VPN. Finally, David used the corner jack stands to level the RV and provide some stability. Uncle Rich warned us of what could happen otherwise.

David smiled, and we high-fived as I checked off an item on Uncle Rich's checklist. "Well, with two masters' degrees and a doctorate between us, we should be able to operate this rig," he joked.

He grabbed the step for the entrance and a grass mat so that we could clean our shoes before entering the RV.

Finally, we placed bright yellow chocks in front of the rear wheels and leveled the RV by sliding out the stabilizers under the slide outs in our bedroom and dining room to provide more support.

David grabbed two of our folding camp chairs out of the exterior storage bay, and we sat down to watch the neighborhood.

"Look at the size of that RV." I pointed to a nearby behemoth fifth wheel with multiple slides.

"Yes, I'd love a tour!"

My phone rang. I was just about to text mom we'd arrived and turn it off.

"Hello? Gracie here."

"Hi, Gracie. It's Angela, your cousin. I'm Vikki's older sister, remember?"

"Yes, Angela, I remember you."

"I saw your wedding pictures on Facebook. Congrats! I loved your wedding dress. Mother told me it was from our Great-Great-Grandma Mary, from the 1920s. I have something to give you from Grandma Mary, and I don't feel comfortable shipping it to you, so could I bring it to you? I talked to your mother, and it sounds like you're going right by me—I live in St. Louis, Missouri. She gave me your phone number. I hope that's okay."

"Well, sure. What is it? You sound kind of mysterious."

"It's an old quilt from the World War One-era, and I know you collect quilts. Grandma Mary made this quilt while her fiancé was in France, serving in the Great War. Mother gave me an antique hope chest from Grandma Mary some years back, and I thought it was empty. When I cleaned it, I found a false bottom. So, I lifted it up and discovered a bundle of letters, linens, and the quilt underneath. Since you're interested in family stories and antique quilts, I thought you'd like to see them and take the quilt with you."

I'd put my phone on speakerphone, and David and I exchanged looks.

"We're at the KOA St. Louis RV Park on Jefferson."

"Oh, I know the place. Let me come to you. What kind of RV do you have, and where are you parked?"

I told her, and she replied she would arrive in forty minutes.

David glanced at me and grinned.

We set up three chairs outside, pushed the button for the awning, retrieved the outdoor table, and stretched our legs. David got us each a cold bottle of water from the cooler, and we sat on our new camp chairs and surveyed the campground, each other, and our loaned RV.

I sighed. "Well, at least we got out of Iowa before we encountered our next quilt mystery—but why hide something in a hope chest?"

David gazed at me. "A hope chest with a false bottom? You have a lot of imaginative people in your family, Gracie. I wonder what sort of mystery you've gotten us into this time?"

*T*he "red and green quilt" is one of my prized possessions, representing my mother's side of the family. It's an example of the rustic rose pattern. I'm thankful for the generations of strong women on my mother's side. I'm especially thankful for Charlotte's Great-Grandma Diana Lewis, who made the rustic rose quilt in the 1860s. Diana and Samuel came to Tama County, Iowa

The "Red and Green" Rustic Rose Quilt

as pioneers, and settled near Garwin. Then their little boy died. Later, they adopted a baby boy, the son of a grieving and impoverished French woman whose husband had died. They named him Frank and later adopted his sister, Jane.

Diana made the rustic rose quilt for Frank, her adopted son. My Great-Grandma Eva, who married Frank in 1894, handed the quilt down to her daughter-in-law, Nellie Lewis Egger. Nellie handed it down to her daughter—and my mother—Charlotte

My daughter, Mikki McGrath, walking toward the pioneer cemetery.

Lewis Patten. Then it came to me, with a scrap of paper with a note, in Grandma Eva's handwriting, confirming Great-Grandma Diana Lewis created the quilt.

Cherie by the obelisk for Diana and Sam Lewis, her pioneer ancestors.

About twenty years ago, I took the rustic rose quilt to the Grout Museum of History and Science in Waterloo after seeing a photo of their display of Civil War era red and green quilts in the Waterloo Courier. Robin, the expert there, examined the dyes, examined the quilt, and grandma's note and said, "You have provenance, or the history of the quilt in your family." She verified its age based on the dyes.

The quilt is now one hundred sixty-three years old. It's a link to the ACW and a reminder that my family came to rural Tama County, Iowa in the 1850s. It inspired me to tell this fictional story, thinking, "What if?"

Another part of my family's legacy is that several members fought in the ACW, including twenty-year-old Robert Filloon. He was Grandma Nellie's grandfather, who served with the 24th Iowa Regiment. He was the inspiration for Michael O'Connor's character, and it is his regiment's battles that David and Gracie follow on their honeymoon.

Finally, some of our ancestors are buried in a pioneer cemetery, just down the road from what

The author, Cherie Lynn (two or three years old) with Great-Grandma Eva.

was Nellie's farm in rural Tama County. The people buried there include the woman who made the red and green quilt, Diana Lewis, and her husband James Lewis.

The poem "Snowfall" was written by my Aunt Jeanne Lewis Egger, who is the inspiration for Aunt Violet.

Great-Grandma Eva married Frank Lewis in 1894 when she was just 17. It was his mother, Dianna, who made the red and green quilt around 1860. Eva died in 1969 but made quite an impression on me. I was twelve when she died. She called me her little baby doll. She was the most affectionate grandma, and I take after her in several ways.

Notes

Historians record over 9,000 men died or were injured during The Third Battle of Winchester. The Union Army moved on, leaving those killed to be buried and the injured to be cared for by others.

About the Author

$\mathcal{A}$fter nearly 30 years in education, and 20 years teaching writing, literature, and educational technology courses at Hawkeye Community College, Cherie took early retirement in 2016. She joined the Cedar Falls Authors Festival planning committee, celebrating the five best-selling writers with ties to Cedar Falls—Bess Streeter Aldrich, Ruth Suckow, James Hearst, Robert Waller, and Nancy Price. They hosted 60 programs during 2017-2018. She also became its webmaster.

She wrote two chapters for collections of academic essays: one about Iowa writer Ruth Suckow and the other about the literary history of Cedar Falls, Iowa. During Covid, Cherie finished the first in her series of novels called *Grandmother's Treasures, The Gift* and drafted four more books. WordCrafts Press published *The Gift* in October 2022 and *The Legacy, Book Two*, in 2023. She's at work revising the third book, *The Promise*.

Cherie became President of the League of Women Voters of Black Hawk-Bremer Counties in 2017, advocating for voting rights for all, organizing voter registration events, and writing letters to the editor. But one of her favorite titles is "mom" to her four children (Mikki, Sean, Jon, and Anna) and "grandma" to grandsons Corbin and Mason, 10 and 13, and granddaughter Nora, 1. Cherie and her grandson are working on a children's book together called *Your Grandma's Grandma*, about their family stories. Cherie is married to retired librarian Mike Dargan, who serves as her tech support, fact checker, and cheerleader.

Connect with Cherie online at:
Substack: https://cheriedargan.substack.com/
Facebook: https://www.facebook.com/CherieDarganAuthor/
https://www.cheriedargan.com